THE MAN WHO LIVED
AT THE RITZ

THE MAN
WHO LIVED
AT THE RITZ

a novel by

A. E. HOTCHNER

G. P. PUTNAM'S SONS   NEW YORK

Library of Congress Cataloging in Publication Data

Hotchner, A. E.
    The man who lived at the Ritz.

    I. Title
PS3558.08M3 1981   813'.54   81-10600
ISBN 0-399-12651-1   AACR2

Printed in the United States of America

For my friend, Paul

Then I realized I had been murdered.
They looked for me in cafés, cemeteries and churches,
    but they did not find me.
They never found me?
No. They never found me.
                                        —*Federico García Lorca*

Part One

YESTERDAY

A way of life only lasts
As long as life itself.

1 ⸻⸻⸻⸻⸻⸻⸻⸻⸻⸻⸻⸻⸻

Philip Weber met Hermann Goering for the first time in the small elevator on the Vendôme side of the Ritz. A few moments before, Philip had entered the Ritz through the Vendôme revolving doors, which were flanked by two armed sentries. In the lobby, immediately to the left of the doors, Philip had paused for inspection in front of what formerly had been a small writing room, but was now the gun repository for German officers. The *Kommandantur* of the Ritz had forbidden guns on the premises, so the officers, on entering, were required to unstrap their sidearms and hand them to an orderly who placed them in name-bearing pigeonholes.

Although many months had passed since the Germans had occupied Paris and taken over the Ritz, as a civilian American Philip still felt self-conscious entering the lobby of the hotel where he had lived for twelve years. Unlike their use of other Paris hotels, which they had taken over completely, the German High Command had occupied only half of the Ritz, the Vendôme side, and allowed civilians to stay in the other half which fronted on the narrow Rue Cambon. But Philip had a special room, number 515 on the garden side, a room on the top floor under the mansard, originally intended to accommodate the traveling companions of the wealthy and the titled who occupied the suites below. The two rooms next to his were occupied by Charles Ritz, the sole progeny of the founder of the hotel.

Since Philip's room was not deemed suitable for officers of the High Command, he was allowed to retain it and to use the Vendôme entrance. As Philip made his way across the lobby toward the elevator, self-conscious as always among the throng of German uniforms, he was intercepted by the concierge, who informed him that there was a message for him from Mademoiselle Chanel: she had returned to the hotel but was in a different room, and would he please come to see her as soon as possible.

Philip and the concierge smiled at each other, both happy that

Mademoiselle Chanel, who had fled the Ritz shortly before the Germans appeared, was back among them.

It was then that Philip had stepped into the small elevator, pressed the button for the fifth floor and waited for the doors, always slow to respond, to close. But before they did, a tall, elegant officer approached the elevator and in authoritative German ordered Philip to leave; before Philip could react, a huge form blocked the doorway, and Hermann Goering entered.

"That's all right," Goering said in German. "We can all ride together." As Goering stepped in, Philip could feel the elevator lower under his bulk. The aide followed him, pressed the third-floor button and glared impatiently at the passive doors.

Philip was so unnerved by the awesome presence of the Reichsmarschall of the Third Reich, second in command to Hitler, a figure familiar to him from the newsreels, that he had difficulty drawing breath. But he did breathe well enough to be aware of the heavy odor that clung to Goering—a mixture of rich cologne, Havana cigars and cognac. Goering was taller and even more massive than he appeared to be in the newsreels. The small, cramped interior of the elevator doubtless contributed to the impact of his size. Philip was also struck by the luminous, waxy color of Goering's skin and by his unexpected handsomeness. Also, the black-and-white newsreels had not prepared Philip for the striking, cobalt-blue color of Goering's eyes, the color enhanced by his pale skin. He was wearing a fawn-colored uniform, magnificently tailored to his bulging body. On his chest was a single gold-enameled decoration. His boots glistened like fresh-polished brass, and Philip was struck by the smallness of Goering's feet and by his hands which were also very small, and delicate; his nails were lacquered and had been manicured with infinite care.

Goering and Philip were face to face. Goering did not take his eyes off him, and Philip did not know where to look.

"May I say, sir," Goering finally said, "that I admire the suit you are wearing." He was soft-spoken, his voice not at all that of the Goering who gave speeches in the newsreels. "Is that not a beautifully tailored suit, Karl?"

"Yes, Your Excellency," Karl said, giving Philip a quick, uninterested look.

"The workmanship on the lapels," Goering said. "Only the French . . ."

The doors began to close.

"May I inquire where it was tailored?"

"At Lanvin," Philip said, and, wanting to be deferential, he added, "sir."

The elevator started to rise in its slow fashion.

"Where is this place?" Goering asked.

"It's an establishment on the Rue du Faubourg-Saint-Honoré. The tailoring department is on the second floor."

"Make a note of that, Karl."

"Yes, Excellency."

The elevator stopped and the doors opened. Karl smartly stepped outside and held his hand on the doors for Goering.

"You're not French, are you?" Goering asked.

"No, sir. I'm an American."

"You speak German very well."

"Thank you."

Goering left and the elevator rose a notch.

When Philip got to his room, he went over to the radiator, which was lukewarm, and sat on it. He had been working in Man Ray's unheated studio for several hours, and the damp cold had penetrated his bones. Philip's room was small, simply furnished and uncluttered except for his desk, which was piled high with disorganized papers. The room had none of the rich elegance associated with the Ritz. As Philip sat on the radiator, thawing from the chill and the unexpected confrontation in the elevator, he leaned his head against the wall and listened to the hum of Charles Ritz's toy train as it whizzed along its tracks. Charles had two rooms, one in which he lived, the other completely occupied by his model railway. Philip sometimes visited Charley to watch the trains as he maneuvered them through their maze of complicated tracks and switches. And sometimes, while the train was running, Philip would help Charley tie trout flies, at which Charley was an expert. His train, and trout fishing, were really the only things that interested Charley. He was forty-nine years old and he had been working on his railroad for forty-two of those years. His father, César, who founded the hotel and gave it his name, was long dead, but his mother was very much alive and she ran the hotel with an imperious thoroughness that kept the large staff in constant fear of her. It suited her that Charles, who had never married nor ever had a girl friend (that his mother knew about), did not attempt to involve himself in the affairs of the hotel.

Philip turned on the faucet in the basin and was pleased to feel the hot water as it washed away some of the paint on his hands.

There was no hot water or heat in Paris except in those hotels occupied by the Germans, and in the restaurants and whore-houses which they frequented. There was plenty of coal in France but no way to get it to Paris. Most of the freight cars had been conscripted for Germany, there was no gasoline for the trucks, and all the barges which used to carry coal down the Seine had been consigned to German waterways. This absence of transportation had also seriously impaired the availability of food, wine and other goods essential to Parisian life. Farmers fifty kilometers from Paris were feeding their milk to the pigs.

Philip put on a clean shirt, rubbed some Schiaparelli cologne on his hands to mask the odor of the paint, and felt happy that he was going to see Gabrielle. Almost everyone else called her "Coco," but it had taken him a long time to overcome calling her Mademoiselle Chanel, and when he finally did, at her insistence, "Gabrielle" was as far as familiarity would take him. Besides, she seemed more a Gabrielle to him than a Coco.

She was his most reliable friend. There were periods of time, weeks might go by, when he would not see her at all, but when he did see her, he was always warmed and uplifted by her spirit and inventiveness. When Philip had first arrived in Paris, Gabrielle was living in a suite overlooking her shop on the Rue Cambon, and it was she who had the patience to criticize his attempts to speak French, and help him perfect it.

In those days, she often took him, as her guest, to play tennis at the Racing Club in the Bois. Gabrielle was a passionate player who loved to win at tennis as she did at everything else she undertook, and when she discovered that Philip had played on his college tennis team, he was immediately enlisted as her partner in all mixed-doubles events. There were rules limiting the number of times a member could entertain a particular guest, but Gabrielle worked out a rather unique provisional member-ship for Philip that required no dues or assessments but permit-ted him to use the courts as if a member.

It was while playing tennis at the Racing, away from the bilingual haven of the Ritz, that Philip was forced to converse in French and thereby happily discovered that he had a quick aptitude for vocabulary and accent. Within six months of his arrival in Paris, he was speaking fluent French, and six months after that, with Gabrielle as his taskmistress, he was speaking it grammatically. His accomplishment filled him with pride, but Gabrielle was always realistic about such things.

"My dear Phi*lip,*" she said, accenting the second syllable to conform with the French, Philippe, "the ability to speak foreign languages well is a gift that has been lavished on every maître d' in Paris."

When Hermann Goering stepped out of the elevator, there was an orderly waiting for him with a report on the day's blitzkrieg of England. One thousand aircraft, six hundred of them fighters to protect the bombers from the R.A.F.'s Spitfires, had struck at British ports and airfields with results that looked impressive, but Goering frowned when he saw the number of German aircraft shot down in the attacks. He was annoyed that the Spitfires were not only outdueling his Stukas but even getting the best of the twin-engine and, most incomprehensibly, the single-engine Messerschmitts on which he had been counting to clear the skies of opposition. He would have to do something about those annoying Spitfires.

When he entered the salon of his four-room suite, however, his annoyance over the Spitfires gave way to the anticipated pleasure of learning what new art treasures were available for his collections. As a matter of fact, Goering cared much more about art acquisition than about Wehrmacht gains and losses. He was obsessed with getting his hands on certain masterpieces. Nazi superiority in number of aircraft made it a foregone conclusion that despite the heroics of British airmen, England would sooner or later be subjugated. It was simply a matter of absorbing lesser loss to inflict greater loss, a principle that had worked to perfection in all the countries that had been bowled over by the Nazi war machine.

But the skirmish being fought over acquiring the world's greatest paintings and sculpture was much less of a sure thing. Goering's chief antagonists in this grim combat were Goebbels, Hitler, and Alfred Rosenberg, who was in charge of the task force that was collecting the art from museums and private collectors, especially Jews. Goering was the best-informed of the lot, and the only one who actually participated in the art scene. But the others, especially Hitler, had knowledgeable representatives and competent spies with the E.R.R. (*Einsatzstab Reichsleiter Rosenberg für die Besetzten Gebiete*—Reichleader Rosenberg's Task Force for Occupied Territories) which was the designation for Rosenberg's unit. Goering had a special passion for paintings of nudes, particularly those of Venus, and his favorite painters were Cranach, whose Venuses had little pot-bellies, and Rubens, whose nudes had the roundness and flesh rolls that he admired.

Waiting for Goering in the salon, which was furnished in Empire antiques and Napoleonic accessories, was Baron Kurt von Behr, the chief of the E.R.R. office, his assistant, Fräulein Ilse Pütz, Dr. Bruno Lohse, an art historian who held the rank of lance corporal in the Luftwaffe, Fräulein Gisela Linberger, manager of Goering's own Paris art office, and Dr. Hermann Bunjes, director of the Paris branch of the German Art Histor-ical Institute. Goering went the rounds, shaking hands; then, establishing himself in a high-backed upholstered chair with the light from the Vendôme windows at his back, he asked, with anticipated pleasure, "Do we have the Rubens?"

His valet, Robert Kropp, poured him a glass of champagne but offered none to anyone else. Kropp also placed a plate of biscuits on the table beside Goering's chair.

"Well?" Goering inquired when no one answered. "What about the Rubens?" He was referring to Rubens' *Diana at the Bath* which had originally been painted for Cardinal Richelieu and which was one of the prize nudes in the confiscated Roths-child collection. The E.R.R.'s first official act, after setting up in Paris, had been to sequester the thirty-eight thousand homes owned by Jews and appropriate the contents. This resulted in an accumulation of well over twenty thousand works of art that had to be inventoried and appraised, and there was no way to know just what masterpieces might arrive at the E.R.R. headquarters in the Jeu de Paume on any given day.

Baron von Behr, a baleful look on his face, cleared his throat and spoke. "Your Excellency, there have been certain complica-tions about the Rubens."

Goering put down his champagne glass and stared at him, awaiting further explanation.

"The Rubens had been definitely committed to you—"

"I affixed a tag myself," Dr. Bunjes interjected.

"But when I went to collect it this morning," Fräulein Linberger said, "to place it in the exhibit we are arranging for you, it was not there."

"What happened to it?" Goering demanded.

"There is a suspicion," the Baron said, "that it was spotted by one of Dr. Goebbels' spies and the tag changed."

Goering's face tensed and he precipitously rose from his chair, knocking the glass of champagne to the carpet. "That's outrageous! Thieving like that! I want to know who did it."

"Yes, Excellency."

"And I want that Rubens intercepted. Does Goebbels have a shipment ready to go?"

"His private train is due in tomorrow," Fräulein Pütz reported.

"Then all his stuff must be at the warehouse, ready to be trucked to the Gare Saint-Lazare. You get down there tonight and find that Rubens!"

"There are armed sentries," Dr. Bunjes said.

"Well, show up with a couple of crates and say you have to add them to the shipment. That will get you inside. Do I have to think of everything? You know how important that Rubens is to me. Why didn't you tag it in the name of the Führer— Goebbels would never have touched that—and then have it delivered to my train and put on board?"

"But, Your Excellency, we would have had to run the risk that the Hitler representative might come across it," the Baron said. "They have become very active, and the Führer shares your enthusiasm for the Dianas."

"I want to see that Diana tomorrow when I go to the Jeu de Paume," he said. "That's all."

The art people left very quickly. Goering went into the master bedroom and collapsed on the brass-postered bed. Kropp began to undress him, as he always did; Goering did not like to dress or undress himself. He was wet with perspiration. He reached his hand into a crystal bowl on his bedside table and extracted three white tablets which he put into his mouth and began to chew.

When he was naked on the bed, Kropp sponged him all over, dried him carefully, anointed his body from head to foot with 4711 cologne, and then powdered him lightly with a large puff. After that, Kropp took from the closet a white silk garment, shaped like a night dress with puffed sleeves, and helped Goering get into it. He put a pair of satin slippers on Goering's feet. On the bedside table he placed a snifter well filled with a rare cognac. Not a word passed between them.

His eyes closed, Goering was considering who in his art group had betrayed him. His thoughts centered on Baron von Behr, whom he was beginning to dislike. He was too communicative with that swine Rosenberg, too handsome (Goering had an innate distrust of good-looking men), an ignoramus about art, a self-proclaimed lady-killer, much too social and party-going to suit Goering, who was not, and, worst of all, he was married to that dreadful Englishwoman with the large lower jaw who enjoyed the suffering he inflicted upon her. Goering equally disliked von Behr's assistant, Fräulein Pütz, because she had the kind of sanctimonious air about her that could only be a cover for a black heart.

Goering reached his chubby fingers into the crystal bowl and withdrew two more of the white tablets, which he popped into his mouth. As he chewed, he thought about his dead first wife, Karin, as he did every evening about this time. He wished he were at Karinhall so that he could visit her shrine. It always soothed him to talk to her.

"Robert!" he called. "I won't be going down to the restaurant for dinner. Phone Albert Speer, who's staying at the Crillon, and present my regrets. He was to be my guest. And then phone Field Marshal Milch at the Bristol. Perhaps they can dine together—do Speer and Milch get along? At any rate, I'll be dining up here alone. Order me caviar and a saddle of mutton. No dessert. And a bottle of Château Latour-Lafitte, '29."

"Will you be taking cheese, Reichsmarschall?"

"No, it puts on weight. I promised Professor Kahle. Lay out my green silk evening gown. And bring me my emerald ring. They better not foul up the Boucher shepherds—I'm telling you, Kropp, anything happens to those Bouchers and I'll eliminate the whole lot of them. If information is leaked and the Führer finds out about those . . ." Goering was referring to a pair of Boucher erotica originally painted for Madame de Pompadour's boudoir by order of Louis XV, depicting shepherds and shepherdesses in antic delight. The ribald interplay between the two sexes was precisely the subject matter that Hitler coveted for his own collection.

"On second thought," Goering said, "I'll have *profiteroles* for dessert—whipped cream, not ice cream. But no chocolate sauce. Now run the water good and hot." He took two final tablets and put the crystal cover back on the bowl.

"Put in a call to Frau Goering. She's at her mother's in Munich."

When the smell of the heated bath oil permeated the room, Goering stood up, drained the cognac in his glass, shed his gown onto the floor, and, naked, headed toward the bathroom.

The white tablets were morphine.

*   *   *

Baron von Behr's staff car was waiting at the Ritz entrance. He sat alone in the back of the car; Fräulein Pütz sat up front next to the driver. Not a word was spoken during the journey to the Hôtel Commodore on the Boulevard Haussmann, where the E.R.R. art offices were located. The Baron felt traitorous whenever he met with Goering, because as head of the E.R.R. his primary allegiance was supposed to be to his boss, Alfred Rosenberg. But Rosenberg rarely came to Paris and it was to the Baron's advantage to maintain a favorable posture with Goering, who was well above Rosenberg in the Nazi hierarchy.

As they turned onto the Boulevard Haussmann, Fräulein Pütz turned and looked at the Baron. He nodded to her and she looked away. When they got off the elevator on the fourth floor of the Commodore, the Baron went into the E.R.R. office, but Fräulein Pütz continued on down the corridor, to the farthest door. She opened the door with a key that she took from her bag, and disappeared.

The room she had entered was the salon of a corner suite which the Baron had commandeered. His regular residence was a confiscated apartment near the Arc de Triomphe on the Avenue Victor Hugo. This Commodore suite was intended solely for his private use. On the walls of the salon were a large Gauguin, a Renoir, a Picabia and two small Picassos, all of which the Baron had been ordered to destroy, as it was the official party position that all art beginning with Impressionism was degenerate.

Fräulein Pütz proceeded directly to the bedroom, where she turned on a small table lamp and began to undress. The room was completely hung in black silk, even the ceiling, where the black silk was gathered at the center and bloomed to the ornate cornices. There was a thick white rug on the floor. On the wall above the bed, which was outsize and round, was Teniers' *Adam and Eve in Paradise,* which had never found its way onto the inventory of the art confiscated from Jews.

As she undressed, Fräulein Pütz hung her clothes neatly in the armoire. When she was naked, she critically inspected her body in the full-length mirror inside the door of the armoire. She pushed at her full breasts, fluffing them as one might fluff a pillow. She closed the armoire and went into the bathroom, where she used the bidet; afterward, she took a bottle of Chanel cologne from a drawer in the dressing table and saturated her body briskly, especially under her arms and along her crotch.

She returned to the bedroom and selected a record from a

repository beside the record player—the overture to Wagner's *Das Liebesverbot.* She opened a drawer in the night table, which was filled with masks, and chose a bright-red one with lace at top and bottom, which she slipped on her face. On top of the night table was a metal warming device with an empty glass on top of it. Fräulein Pütz took a bottle of schnapps from underneath the table and half filled the glass. Then she lit the squat candle that was underneath the glass.

She stripped back the heavy brocaded black silk coverlet on the bed; underneath were black sheets of the finest silk. She removed a jar of Nivea cream from another drawer in the night table and got into bed with it. She dipped her fingers in the soft, succulent cream and began to spread it all over her inner thighs, her stomach and her vagina, enjoying the sensuous feel of it.

She heard the door open and close, and as she continued to rub in the cream she followed the sounds the Baron was making as he prepared himself in the dressing room on the other side of the bathroom. She put away the jar and activated the music. The opening strains of *Das Liebesverbot* filled the room as the Baron entered from the bathroom. He was naked except for a rhinestone-studded belt which circled his waist, and a mask which was covered with the fur of some animal. He turned on a wall switch, and the room was suffused in a red glow which ignited the black silk.

He jumped upon the bed and knelt between Fräulein Pütz's legs. He picked up the glass of warm schnapps and began to sip it. Fräulein Pütz did not have an outstanding body, but she had large, firm pink-nippled breasts which were particularly pleasing to the Baron, whose English wife had arrested breasts with hairy nipples. Fräulein Pütz also had heavy, powerful legs which, when they gripped around him, dug into his rib cage with mounting pressure, causing him intense pain which he relished.

As the Baron sipped the warm schnapps, Fräulein Pütz took him in her Nivea-creamed hands and fondled him. He rubbed a hand all over the creamed area of her body and he became physically aroused by the greasy feel of her, and emotionally warmed by the Wagnerian music, which he adored. When the music began its crescendo, the Baron roughly pushed Fräulein Pütz's hands away, drained the glass, and savagely thrust himself into her. His eyes, peering through his mask, were on Adam and Eve in Paradise. Her legs had never hurt him more. Locked in their masked, writhing embrace, they were two exaggerated characters in a Wagnerian opera.

The telephone rang, the sound rending the Baron's ecstasy. It was his secretary. His ears were clogged with his passion, and her voice came to him from the end of a long tunnel. Dr. Goebbels had unexpectedly arrived from Berlin, the secretary said, and wanted to see him immediately. Something about a Rembrandt taken from the Jew, Rothschild, that had been promised to Goebbels by Rosenberg. The secretary said that Dr. Goebbels sounded furious.

2

Mademoiselle Chanel was fussing with her steamer trunks in the corridor outside her room when Philip came upon her. She greeted him with a cry of delight, bussed him on both cheeks, and then, leaning back as she held him, looked at him intently.

"Let me examine you, Philip—thin, sad-eyed . . ."

"That's because of missing you, Gabrielle."

"You're still at your painting."

"How did you know?"

"That rotten Schiaparelli cologne couldn't disguise anything."

"I've run out of yours, and your shop is closed."

"I will have to open it. I hear that the Germans are confiscating all the closed establishments, are they?"

"Yes. They choose someone to put in charge and take them over."

"Well, they spared me my trunks—look, they haven't even opened them."

"That's because your name is on them in large letters. Chanel No. 5 is very big in Germany. But they took your lovely room."

"I don't care, really. Seven years in the same room is long enough. I've never been dependent on where I live. What is it, anyway? A place I create. This room is smaller, but come look . . ." She led him inside.

"My Coromandel screens can make any room. It's not so bad—what do you think?" In addition to strategic placement of the magnificent screens, she had supplemented the Ritz furnishings with her own antique brass bed, two Mapple wardrobes, and several pieces of Louis XVI furniture. She had also hung some of her own paintings—an early Picasso, courtesy of the struggling artist, a Masson forest, a self-portrait of Vuillard; above her dressing table was a dazzling Russian icon, and over her bed an ornate Byzantine cross.

Philip nodded his approval. "You've made it in your image—it's you, Gabrielle."

[24]

She was pleased to hear that. Although she was old enough to be Philip's mother, there was nothing motherly about her; the relation between them was brother and sister. She was small, thin, graceful and sensuous, and although her round face was showing its age around her eyes, the dark vibrancy of her eyes and the vivacity of her facial expressions maintained the impression of youth. She was wearing the simple black suit with white-trimmed neck and sleeves which had endeared her to women the world over.

"You must tell me what happened to you after you left the hotel—how far did you go?" Philip asked.

"Oh, my Philip, what an unbelievable turn of events it was, truly a nightmare! I think we need a glass of Piper to ease the pain of remembering." On a small gateleg table there was a bottle of Piper-Heidsieck nestled in the ice of a silver cooler.

"Oh, my!" she exclaimed after her first sip. She held up the glass, looked at the champagne admiringly and then, quickly draining off the remainder of the glass, held it out for a refill. "My first bubbly since I left here—can you imagine?"

Gabrielle had fled Paris by automobile two days before the Germans marched in. She and a woman friend had taken to the road without a set destination, only seeking a way to elude the German conquerors. Gabrielle had urged Philip to join them, but as a neutral American he felt he was much better off in the secure bastion of the Ritz. Also, the prospect of unplanned travel made a coward out of Philip. He was only thirty-eight years old, but he was set in his ways. In his twelve years at the Ritz he had left Paris only twice, and both times, although only on trips that took him a few hours away, he had regretted the excursions.

Gabrielle had headed due south, she told Philip, but the roads were choked with what seemed like half the population of France, and the autos, trucks, wagons, carts, bicycles, motorcycles, and masses of foot travelers made it virtually impossible to go forward or to return to Paris. The enthusiasm for escape had expired by the time they had inched their way into Vichy, anxiously watching the last of their gasoline evaporate. There were no hotel rooms, no gasoline, no food in the restaurants, and what few food shops were open had little or nothing on their shelves.

"It was then and there that I realized that being a refugee did not become me. I suffered too much privation early on. Hardship can give you nothing but calluses—and, in the case of ideals, disillusionment.

"We were desperate to get out of there, but at first it seemed hopeless. However, I long ago learned that to overcome great trouble one must go to the highest authority. So I went to the office of a Vichy prefect of police, and I sent in a little note attached to a bottle of No. 5. Two minutes later the prefect himself was bowing my way into his chamber. It was from him I learned that life in Paris was unperturbed—he even telephoned the Ritz on his military line and confirmed that I could have an accommodation. And, most importantly, he allowed me to fill the tank of the car from the police pump—all for a bottle of No. 5 and the ego boost of recounting to his wife and confederates how he had rescued the great Chanel.

"But getting back to Paris was a nightmare—that is why tonight we must dine very well. But not here in the hotel. One of our old haunts. Are some of our old places open?"

"Yes, but they don't serve the same. They can't. Les Halles is barren. Farmers have no fuel, and besides, the curfew doesn't allow them on the road until six-thirty, so it's afternoon by the time the few do arrive who have the fuel to get there."

"Well, I'm sure we'll eat all right. I have a friend arriving in Paris and I want you to meet her. Tell me about conditions here in the hotel." In the absence of her maid, who had fled Paris on her own and not returned, Gabrielle was now taking her clothes from suitcases and placing them neatly on hangers and in drawers.

"As you doubtless know, the big-shot Germans have all of the Vendôme side and exclusive use of the main dining room. The rear dining room is for lesser officers and the Cambon civilians, who always keep a row of empty tables between the Germans and themselves. But would you believe there is now a table-d'hôte dinner for sixty francs?"

"My God."

"And a bowl of whipped cream is put on every table at the start of each meal. The Germans put whipped cream on everything."

"What about breakfast—do they serve as usual?"

"Not really—the German coffee is good, not the ersatz stuff that most people must drink now, but there are no croissants at all, and brioches are served only on Thursday, Friday, Saturday and Sunday."

"Well, good coffee and coal—we really can't complain. Can one get around?"

"Very difficult. No taxis or buses, in fact no gas for any cars except those of the Boche—you don't hear a single horn from morning till night. You can use the Métro when it runs, but service is highly erratic. But there are *vélotaxis* and sometimes a horse and carriage outside the Cambon door and on the Rue de Rivoli."

"I have to meet Lili at the Scribe—why don't we dine around nine at La Pompe d'Or?"

"You'd better make it eight-thirty. There's an eleven-o'clock curfew for non-Germans."

"Eleven o'clock! We must work on getting special papers. Don't you know someone?"

"I met Hermann Goering in the elevator just now—he complimented my suit."

"Is he fat?"

"Well . . . imposing. He's a strange . . . presence."

"How do you mean?"

"He paints his fingernails."

Gabrielle laughed. "That makes him strange?"

"I thought he was rather imposing—the face of a baby and the body of a warrior."

"Well, if you ask me, they're all bullies, enormous bullies, Goering and all the rest."

"More than bullies with the Jews."

"Oh, the Jews—yes, that's something else."

"Anyway, until you can find a way to get us special passes, we'd better meet no later than eight-thirty."

"Promise me you won't fall in love with Lili."

"Who's Lili?"

"I told you I was bringing a friend. All men fall in love with Lili. You must restrain yourself. Put your emotions on ice. Promise me? She may be staying here if I can get her a room. You don't want to suffer through another Helga, do you?"

"I wasn't in love with Helga. It was her disappearing, that's all."

"Well, when it comes to disappearing, Lili could give lessons to Houdini. Just do me a favor and don't fall in love. I have enough problems as is."

3

The charade for Dr. Goebbels was carried out to perfection. Although Baron von Behr had little knowledge about the art over which he presided, he was an expert on the politics of survival and advancement in the Third Reich, an expertise that had landed him his enviable job despite his lack of qualifications.

Goebbels did not have a permanent suite at the Ritz as Goering did, for his visits to Paris were infrequent, but the *Kommandantur* of the hotel had nevertheless provided him with a sumptuous suite, which was where he received von Behr. While the men sat, facing each other on chairs at opposite sides of the Empire desk, Fräulein Pütz stood erectly in back of the Baron's chair, a manila file tightly grasped in her left hand. She was uncomfortable because there had not been time to wash off the cream she had smeared on her body. Under the heavy wool of her uniform, her itching skin adhered to her clothes.

"I can assure you, Dr. Goebbels," the Baron was saying, "that the Rembrandt was allocated to your disposition."

"It was not for my personal acquisition, you understand," Goebbels said, "but for the national collection. But we have just completed an inventory, and it is not among the pieces received in the last shipment."

"Fräulein Pütz has the file which clearly shows a receipt for the crated picture when it was turned over to your train dispatcher in the last shipment." The Baron put his hand up, without turning his head, and Fräulein Pütz smartly put the file in his grasp. He removed a sheet of paper and placed it on the table in front of Goebbels. "Rembrandt, *Man with a Turban*" was circled in red, but Goebbels did not look at it.

"The crate arrived with the shipment," Goebbels said, in a flat, deadly voice, "but it was empty."

"That is shocking—the first we hear of it. All the paintings were stored at the Gare Saint-Lazare under constant guard."

"Were there other paintings besides mine?"

"Yes, there was a shipment of art taken from the Jews, assigned to Reichsmarschall Goering."

"All in the same place?"

"Yes."

"Perhaps I should have a talk with the Reichsmarschall."

"Perhaps. Would you like me to be present?"

"No, I think I will have a private talk. It's about time."

As was his custom, Philip went into the Little Bar to have a cocktail. The Little Bar was presided over by a short, compact, energetic barman named Bertin whose quick eyes behind thick lenses missed nothing that transpired in the small wood-paneled room. Bertin's domain consisted of six tables, banquettes along two walls, a stand-up bar that could, at most, accommodate three clients, and two grooms who waited on the tables, kept them supplied with potato chips freshly made in the kitchen, and ran errands at the flick of Bertin's finger.

Before the Occupation, Philip had patronized the main bar on the other side of the Cambon entrance, which was run by Georges, who was the barman. Georges was a smiling man of obsequious power who was able to provide favored clients with virtually anything their hearts desired that was available in Paris, animate or inanimate. The main bar always bustled with English and Americans, and Philip especially enjoyed listening to the gossip of those who had just debarked from the big transatlantic liners at Le Havre. They were people of money and power and culture, and their talk was a bridge for him with the States.

Now the Occupation had turned Philip away from Georges' bar because not only were there no English and only a trickle of uninteresting Americans, but the German officers all congregated there, leaving the Little Bar relatively empty. Philip also benefited from Bertin's practice of charging him for only one drink although he constantly refilled his martini glass with leftovers from each new batch of martinis which he mixed. Philip often talked fishing with Bertin, who cared about little else. On those occasions when Ernest Hemingway was at the Ritz, he often joined their discussions, his knowledge dominant. Despite the fact that Philip had had no actual fishing experience, his reading had given him a certain basic knowledge and enthusiasm for the sport.

On this particular evening, Bertin did not talk fishing. There was a heavyset man at the bar, one foot up on the rail, drinking cognac, who was talking to Bertin nonstop in stentorian French with a heavy Teutonic accent. All the tables were filled. Sitting alone on a corner banquette was an attractive woman, expensively dressed, who had been drinking all afternoon. Her lipstick was slightly off center. As Philip looked around the room, waiting for his martini, the woman's eyes sought his and her faint smile was one of invitation. In all his years at the Ritz, Philip had avoided any alliances with transient women in the hotel. He knew that Madame Ritz had her spies everywhere and that she rigorously objected to the presence of an unregistered woman in the room of a male guest. Nothing mattered to Philip as much as his room at the Ritz, and it was not in his nature to take any risk that might jeopardize his tenancy.

One of the grooms approached Philip and in a low voice confided to him that the lady at the corner table wondered if he were the gentleman she had met the previous winter at Saint-Moritz.

"Tell her no," Philip said. "Tell her I've never been to Saint-Moritz."

Although he had not planned to leave so early, Philip signed his check and departed, carefully averting his eyes from the woman on the banquette. As he was leaving, he almost collided with Colonel Hans Stuppelmayer, *Kommandant* of the Ritz, who was just entering the bar. Philip mumbled his apologies and stepped aside in deference to the colonel, who adjusted his monocle and ignored him.

Colonel Stuppelmayer, a veteran officer of the Sipo-SD, was responsible for the security of the Ritz as a bastion for the illustrious leaders of the Third Reich who stayed there. It was he who issued the edict forbidding sidearms in the hotel, although he himself carried a small Luger in a discreet inner pocket.

Prior to his assignment at the Ritz, Colonel Stuppelmayer had headed Section IV of the Sipo-SD, which was the branch of the Gestapo concerned with the protection of important visitors. Most of the Gestapo agents on his staff were vicious Parisian gangsters whom Stuppelmayer had recruited with the understanding that as their remuneration they could have control of the highly lucrative black market in food and fuel which had quickly entrenched itself in Paris. Stuppelmayer had installed these gangsters in a Gestapo branch which he set up in an apartment on fashionable Avenue Henri-Martin; working with these hoods, he converted the apartment into a torture chamber where secrets could be extracted from suspected members of the Resistance. Some of the methods which Stuppelmayer devised were even more barbarous and heinous than the torture devices then in vogue in Berlin.

Stuppelmayer's boss, Reinhard Heydrich, was so pleased with the results of Stuppelmayer's operation that he put him in charge of the Ritz; Stuppelmayer appropriated a suite on the garden side, where he and his French mistress lived luxuriously. As part of the deal with the gangsters who operated the black market, Stuppelmayer received a regular weekly payment in cash, a considerable sum of money that enabled him to live in fine style.

Stuppelmayer ruled the Ritz with a steel fist that struck fear into the employees. As one of his first acts, he had recruited key personnel as informers, and although a few of his choices had not cooperated—among them Bertin and Georges, the bar chiefs, and the two concierges, Henri Bretonne and Pierre Duvay—he nevertheless was able to establish a network of spies among the employees. At the executive level, he had recruited the assistant manager, Albert de Chabert; in the dining room he had the waiter, Ferdinand Bouchère; in the kitchen, a pastry chef, Jean Delocque; and an assistant housekeeper, Madame Hélène Félix.

Albert de Chabert became an informer because he was intensely ambitious and he hoped that, after years of playing second fiddle to the director of the Ritz, the Nazis might install him, as they had installed Pierre Laval in Vichy, as the new director of the Ritz.

The waiter, Ferdinand Bouchère, had become a Stuppelmayer informer because his wife was Jewish and his cooperation was the price of her safety; Stuppelmayer had assured him that his wife would not be dispatched to a concentration camp in Germany with the other Paris Jews as long as Bouchère did his job properly.

Jean Delocque, the pastry chef, turned informer purely and simply to indulge his greed for the bonus money which Stuppelmayer promised all of them.

Madame Félix was cooperative because she was an Alsatian and the Germans were her heroes.

These four reported to Colonel Stuppelmayer anything which happened in the hotel which they regarded as the least bit suspicious, whether it was the behavior of employees or guests, civilian or military.

Stuppelmayer himself made unexpected appearances throughout the hotel, and he established an elaborate search system for arriving and departing employees. Even tradesmen and their cargoes were searched. All phone calls in and out of the offices of employees were monitored, as were calls to and from the bars, the valet service, the barbershop and the dining rooms. Very little escaped Stuppelmayer's scrutiny. Any transgression met swift retribution. When a waiter in the main dining room had the misfortune of spilling a little hot lobster bisque on the sleeve of General Gustav Heineman, Stuppelmayer had the offending waiter hustled out of the dining room and into the kitchen, where Stuppelmayer himself took a kettle of boiling water off the stove and drenched the waiter's arms with it.

The Rue Cambon was deserted. Philip walked to the adjoining service entrance, where, just inside the door, he stored his bicycle. He slipped a pants clip around his right ankle and started to bicycle down the Rue Cambon toward the Place de la Concorde.

There was very little motor traffic, not even in the usually frenetic Concorde. An occasional German truck or staff car, but that was all. The bicycles, their bells tinkling, their little magnesium lights fireflies in the gathering dusk, only heightened the deserted quality of the evening.

When he got to the Seine, Philip dismounted and propped his bike against a tree. He put his arms on the stone balustrade and peered down at the dark, rippled water. The *quai* below was deserted. Even the traditional fishermen of the Seine had disappeared as a result of a German mandate that required a written permit to fish.

He felt a wash of emptiness, of sadness. The uncomfortable half hour in the Ritz bar had affected him. Face the reality, he told himself, that all the parameters of your life have changed for the worse. The Ritz was no longer the Ritz; Paris was no longer Paris. Most of the people he enjoyed seeing were gone, and those who remained, struggling to cope with the German presence, were no longer themselves.

Painting in Man Ray's studio without Man being there, without the energizing ions of his talent and personality in the air, was an empty chore. Philip had been cheered by Gabrielle's return, but, alas, like everyone else, she was now primarily absorbed with survival and diminished by compromise. But Philip marveled at how superior to him she was in self-esteem. Of course, he mused, Gabrielle is much older than I—fifty-six, although she looks and acts forty, and I'm just thirty-eight—so there is time, if I am a late bloomer. But down deep in his heart Philip felt no assurance that this was the case.

That is not to say that Philip had not made several efforts to establish some kind of work life for himself, but there were not many ways that an American could support himself in Paris. Work permits were virtually impossible to obtain, and even if Philip had succeeded in getting a permit, he really had no skills or work experience to offer to French employers, who harbored traditional prejudices against Americans.

Philip had been in awe of the expatriate writers he had met, and he had, during an extended period, tried his hand at writing, but he finally had to face the fact that he did not have the talent for it. During one of Hemingway's sojourns at the Ritz, as a favor to Charley he had read some of the material Philip had been writing. Over drinks in the bar, Hemingway, in his direct fashion, had given Philip his verdict: "The stuff's okay, Phil, but it falls somewhere in between the letter writers and the pros— you're a bat, not bird nor animal. You haven't a feel for the right punches. You only throw jabs when the openings are there for hooks and uppercuts. Do you box?"

Philip smiled in memory of the two of them sparring for a moment in the bar, open-handed, Hemingway testing Philip's moves. "Too bad you can't feint and flick jabs like that on the written page," Hemingway observed as he returned to his table and motioned to Bertin to refill their glasses. "You've got a classy little head fake."

Thinking about Hemingway reminded Philip that he had not received a letter from him for several months. It was always a joyful event when a letter arrived bearing Cuban stamps and the San Francisco de Paula return address, or Spanish stamps on letters from Madrid and Barcelona, or United States stamps on the letters from Sun Valley and Key West. There was an immediacy, a personal thrust to Hemingway's letters that did not exist in his published writing. The letters were written out of a need to communicate with someone outside the turmoil of his personal events, as a man imprisoned might send word to someone safely outside the walls.

Philip wondered where Hemingway was, how the fall of his beloved France had affected him. Philip knew it would be a long time before he would see him again, and, realizing that, he felt a stab of emptiness. Hemingway was the man Philip would have liked to be, but he didn't have the courage or imagination or talent.

The German voice, in very bad French, came from directly behind him: "You there, frog, remove your behind so these ladies can pass."

Philip straightened and turned around. A German captain, monocled left eye, a tart on each arm, was standing on the walk which Philip and his bicycle had been partially obstructing. The tarts giggled at him. Philip nodded deferentially and grasped the handlebars of his bike. In perfect German he said, "I apologize, Captain, and especially to you ladies." He mounted his bicycle and pedaled away. He felt a satisfaction at having surprised the captain with his perfect German. He had Helga to thank for that.

Although she had come from Cologne, she spoke with the pure accent of the north, not the provincial dialect of Cologne. And it wasn't only German that Helga had taught him. It was a consuming mystery to him the way she had disappeared without warning, without leaving a trace, never to be heard from again.

4

It was just now turning night, and as darkness fell Philip rode more cautiously. One of the first edicts of the Occupation had been to put Paris on Berlin time, which was two hours earlier, thereby forcing Parisians to start the day in pitch-black darkness; dawn did not arrive until nine or ten o'clock, its arrival always unexpected, some grotesque stage business from the Grand Guignol.

The Germans' enforcement of the blackout was so severe that Philip had difficulty finding his way to the restaurant to meet Gabrielle. There was no light whatsoever on the streets and pavements; if a German patrol detected a slight seam of light between blackout curtains, the patrol often fired a warning shot through the curtain, angled upward toward the ceiling. But Philip had learned to recognize streets by their pavements and their slopes, and of course it was always possible to call out for street identification if someone was heard passing on foot.

Mademoiselle Chanel, incorrigibly unpunctual, had not yet arrived when Philip entered and presented himself, with a warm handshake, to the proprietor of La Pompe d'Or, Monsieur Laquelle. The restaurant was crowded, mostly with German officers, but Monsieur Laquelle immediately seated Philip at a choice table in an alcove, on which there were settings for three. Philip ordered a bottle of Kronenbourg, an Alsatian beer.

How many times, at how many restaurants, had he waited for Gabrielle, knowing she would be late, but punctuality was so ingrained in him that he could never bring himself to delay his own arrival. He listened to some of the German talk around him, which was primarily about women whom the officers had met and had had adventures with. Very few of the Germans had women with them.

Monsieur Laquelle placed a small dish of *moules ravigote* in front of Philip. "To flavor your drink, Monsieur Weber." He pronounced "Weber" with a *v,* in conformity with the pronunciation of "Rue Weber," since the *w* sound does not exist in French. Some of the alienation from Paris that Philip had felt earlier was alleviated.

Gabrielle was being led to the table by Monsieur Laquelle. Philip marveled at how young and vibrant she looked, and although the diners whom she passed did not know who she was, they arrested their conversations, knives and forks suspended, to watch her as regally, smilingly, she approached Philip's table. What remained of Philip's gloom rose off him and he returned her smile. She wore a small hat perched forward on her head, one of her simple suits in mottled brown with a gaily colored silk scarf knotted around her neck. Philip rose and they kissed, and only then did he see the woman who had been following Gabrielle.

Gabrielle introduced them: Philip Weber, Countess Lili von Jorosjc, but just call her Lili. Philip found himself incapable of uttering a word of greeting. Lili smiled at him and offered her hand. Gabrielle had warned him, but no warning was sufficient preparation for the woman who now confronted him. He touched her hand, which she had offered in a manner to be kissed, but he was too off balance to react properly.

"Now, Philip, it will be easier to dine if you seat yourself," Gabrielle said. "I gave you fair warning about Lili, didn't I?"

But not warning enough, Philip thought. Lili was an exquisitely proportioned petite woman, not over five feet tall, hair shoulder length, blond to the roots, almond-green eyes, with a slight scar at the tip of her left eyebrow, tiny, flat ears, high, full breasts, long neck decorated with a three-strand pearl choker, a slight cleft in her chin which was dominated by a full lower lip, a rose glow to her skin, her body a sensuous invitation. On her left wrist she wore an antique ruby bracelet, and on the middle finger of her right hand was the gold head of a lioness whose face was encrusted with emeralds.

"What language should we speak?" Gabrielle asked. "What do you prefer, Lili? Philip is at home in French, English or German."

"Then let Philip choose," Lili said; her voice was soft and, Philip thought, as sensuous as her body.

"Is English all right?" Philip asked, his own voice sounding strange in his ears.

"Lili speaks English so well that when she was in New York no one took her to be a foreigner."

"I like to be considered a native of wherever I am."

"How many languages do you speak?" Philip asked.

"Oh, eleven, I guess, not counting Switzer-Deutsch, which is too ugly to be counted a language."

"But are you Polish—von Jorosjc?"

"No, that is an acquired name."

"Lili is the most mysterious woman I know," Gabrielle said. "I never know where she's been or where she's going. We met at a costume ball in Constantinople. She was a swan."

"I will tell you where I came from this time," Lili said, her English as impeccable as Gabrielle had predicted. "From San Remo to Paris, it took six days. Imagine, six days! The first three days there was nothing to eat but oysters—Belon, thank God— and the last three days nothing but pastry. You can't imagine what the war has done. I look forward to tonight's dinner, I assure you."

As if on cue, Monsieur Laquelle approached the table with a bottle of white wine. "The Montrachet which Mademoiselle Chanel favors," he said as he poured a sample into her glass, although, by proper standards, the first taste should have gone to Philip.

"Ah!" Gabrielle exclaimed, "home again."

As he poured the wine, Monsieur Laquelle explained that his restaurant could not be as it was. Les Halles did not function, and only vegetables, rabbit and some bony fish were in supply. Not even flowers for the table, since most of the growers had switched to vegetables. The caviar which Mademoiselle Chanel favored with her Montrachet was no more. "You cannot believe all the things that have ceased to exist," he said. "Tonight we are serving a rabbit ragout, but I have managed a small supply of veal which will be hidden beneath the sauce for this table only— and the Germans will be none the wiser. Ah, the Boche—all they ask for is schnitzel, sauerbraten and potato pancakes. Try to come on Thursday—I have been promised some lamb by a herder I know who has a gasogene truck equipped to burn charcoal."

Gabrielle requested a Pernod, which made Monsieur Laquelle look even sadder. "Alas, the *Kommandantur* of Paris has decreed no hard liquor on Monday, Wednesday and Saturday, only beer and wine, but beyond that, my dear Mademoiselle Chanel, Pernod is totally forbidden now. The First World War took away absinthe, and now this war kills off Pernod."

"I used to enjoy watching the white drips melt the sugar cube," Gabrielle said wistfully. "Whoever said 'War is hell' had it right."

"The consolation," Monsieur Laquelle said, "is that champagne is in ample supply."

Gabrielle laughed. "Your saying champagne made me think of the time Sam Goldwyn brought me to Hollywood—the Mont-Saint-Michel of tit and tail—to create costumes for one of his films. He came to see me at my hotel when I arrived. I offered him a glass of champagne. 'No, thanks,' he said, 'I don't like mixed drinks.'"

Lili laughed, a musical laugh, small white teeth exposed, tremulous pink tongue; Philip had never heard more beautiful laughter. He tried to turn his eyes away from her, but he couldn't. Gabrielle had never seen Philip like this before, and she found it very amusing.

"How old is she?" Gabrielle asked Philip. "She refuses to tell me her age."

"I—I don't know."

"Well, guess."

"Well—I . . . really . . ."

"How old, Lili—come, tell us!"

"I don't believe in chronology. Look at you."

"I will tell you frankly, I'm an untampered fifty-six. At fifty, when a woman must choose between her face and her bottom, I chose bottom. What I always say is, nature provides your face when you're twenty, life shapes your face at thirty, but you must earn the face you have at fifty."

The waiter arrived with the first course, a spinach-celery soup, at the same time delivering to Gabrielle a carefully folded note, which she opened and read immediately. "A Baron von Spatz, the textile administrator, is honored to be in the same restaurant with me and begs to make my acquaintance. Have you noted, Philip, that we are surrounded by vons—and they are small vons to connote old aristocracy, not the brassy *nouveau* capital Vons. Well, what say, shall we ask the textillian Baron to join us for a drink?"

"Yes," said Lili, "all of us small vons crave company."

Baron von Spatz was a tall, slender mustached man with handsome features and a deferential air. He brushed his lips on the ladies' hands and in a low voice thanked Mademoiselle Chanel for honoring him with her invitation.

"We are speaking English," Gabrielle said, interrupting his

German. "I do not deal with the Teutonic tongue."

In smooth, Cambridge-educated English, the Baron said that was fine with him. He explained that he had been put in charge of textiles but that there virtually was no textile industry in Paris because of shortages of materials and the absence of transportation.

"So many of the famed couturiers are closed, it would be a boon to my position, Mademoiselle Chanel, if you were to reopen your boutique. I would, of course, assist you in procuring the necessary textiles."

"It is not the material that is important, Baron, it is my dressmakers. My best women have been sent to Germany to work there—God knows what for—and I cannot possibly open my shop until they return and I can again produce garments of the quality expected of me. Until then I shall sell a small quantity of my perfume, severely limited by the availability of the essences I need from Grasse."

The Baron said that he regretted these lapses, but wished to further investigate the matter. Having finished his wine, he rose from his chair, again kissed the ladies' hands and asked whether he could assist them with transportation at the conclusion of the evening.

"Very kind of you," Gabrielle said. They had come by *vélo* bicycle-taxi, and even if one could be located when they left the restaurant, she did not relish going back to the Ritz that way, nor subjecting herself to the erratic vicissitudes of the Métro, whose last scheduled run was ten-thirty. "But I wouldn't want to take you out of your way."

"Not at all. I live at the Ritz also. And the Countess?"

"She too."

"I have my own conveyance," Philip said.

"Dine at your leisure," the Baron said to Gabrielle, "since it won't be necessary for you to observe the curfew."

During the course of the meal, which caused exclamations of pleasure, Philip tried to draw Lili out about what she did, where she lived, how long she would be in Paris, if she was married, but although she gave him answers she did not give him any information.

"Oh, you are so slick, Lili," Gabrielle laughed, "a dainty little *danseuse* on the high wire, twirling your parasol."

Lili was much more successful finding out about Philip. "And what do you paint?" she asked.

"I'm afraid nothing original."

"He has talent with colors," Gabrielle said.

"I don't have the painter's eye," Philip said.

"Would you paint me?" Lili asked with a put-on coquettish smile.

"I don't think I could do you justice."

"Just give me four eyes and three breasts like Picasso."

A little after ten-thirty, Philip prepared to leave in order to be back at the Ritz before the dreaded curfew.

"I'll go with you," Lili announced impetuously.

"But I go by bicycle."

"Yes, Coco told me. That should be fun."

"It isn't, really. I can't see where I'm going, and half the time I don't know where I am."

"Why, that's the story of my life! I'll sit on the crossbar—you're not using a woman's bike, are you?"

"But, Lili, the Baron will take us by car . . ."

"I have a feeling the Baron would like to be alone with you."

"For God's sake, Lili—I'm much older than he is. The Germans like plump, young chickens."

"Oh, there goes your chronology again—what nonsense! He's attractive and you're of a delectable ripeness."

"Oh, Lili, you're incorrigible! Well, all right, go ahead and ruin your behind on Philip's crossbar. You're all set at the Ritz—your baggage is in your room. Just give the concierge your passport."

"Which one? What do you suggest, Philip?" She took four passports from her handbag. "Shall I be Italian, Polish, Spanish or American?"

"For God's sake, Lili, put those away!"

"It's all right, Coco, I have quadruple citizenship."

"Be Italian," Philip said.

"That's what I like—a man who makes decisions. I shall be Italian."

"Under what name?"

"My own, of course! I am Lili von Jorosjc on all my passports."

"That isn't an Italian name."

"Neither is Titian." She put away the passports. Philip was about to say that Titian's true Italian name was Tiziano, but he didn't want to contradict her.

Gabrielle joined Baron von Spatz at his table, where he was dining with another German officer. Philip led Lili to his bicycle. The night had grown blacker and a misty rain was falling from the starless sky. Philip felt his way to the curb with his feet, and then, following the curb, his arms outstretched, he located his bicycle. Lili followed him by holding on to the back of his coat, and even that remote a touch aroused him. He placed his bike in the gutter to make it easier for Lili to mount it from the elevation of the sidewalk. She gathered her coat tightly around her to keep it from interfering with the sprocket and pedals, laughing delightedly, a child's delight, as Philip pushed off and started to pedal down the Rue du Bac, then across the Pont-Royal toward the Place de la Concorde. Twice he got confused and had to stop to reconnoiter, which only added to Lili's enjoyment of the adventure. It was difficult for Philip to concentrate on navigation with the distraction of Lili's faintly perfumed hair in his face and the feel of her small body against the front of him. At one point, as he came off the bridge, he bumped the curb and she almost fell off, but he grabbed her with his left arm and pulled her back against him.

He made two wrong turns until he finally found the Rue Cambon. Twice they passed German curfew patrol cars, their headlights blackened to slits, but they were not stopped. It was ten-fifty-five when Philip pulled up in front of the Cambon entrance. Lili slipped off, gave him a hug and, briskly rubbing her numbed behind, entered the Ritz. Philip wheeled his bike to the service entrance, chained it to a water pipe inside the door, and went to find Lili.

She was at the concierge desk surrendering her Italian passport. The concierge had a sheaf of messages for her. A groom waited, with her key, to escort her to her room. As Philip walked toward the desk, she turned and followed the groom into the elevator without saying a word to him. It was as if they had never met. The elevator doors closed and Philip was left alone, looking after her.

"Have you ever seen a more beautiful woman?" the concierge asked. His name was Pierre Duvay and he had worked the Cambon desk for twenty years. He liked Philip, who patiently answered his endless questions about life in the United States which was, for him, an inaccessible dreamland. "She's a friend of Mademoiselle Chanel. You should ask to be introduced. Such a dainty one—she belongs on a cameo brooch."

Philip nodded agreement and walked away, headed toward the alley of glamorous showcases that connected the Cambon side to the Vendôme. He was bitterly disappointed. Of course, Gabrielle had warned him, but why would Lili behave like this, arousing and rejecting him almost as if there was a purpose in her behavior?

Henri Bretonne, the concierge at the Vendôme desk, had an inborn hatred of the Germans. His father had been wounded in the First World War, and as a boy Henri suffered from watching his father's losing battle against the ravages of shell-shock and mustard gas. Once Henri had worked his way up from groom to concierge, he discovered he could inflict little retributions on German tourists by not providing them with the precise services they requested. He experienced a feeling of satisfaction from informing some arrogant German guest that a particular restaurant or nightclub which he had requested was *complet* when Bretonne knew full well that the magic name of the Ritz could probably get a table if he really wanted one.

When Bretonne was approached by the Underground, it was this innate hatred of the Germans that goaded him into joining the dangerous movement. All that the Underground asked of him was that he file a daily report listing all the Nazi notables who were staying in the hotel. Bretonne was given a list of political and military figures, each name preceded by a number which was the code for that name. Bretonne was to write out a daily wine order that would incorporate the numbers of those on the master list who were staying at the hotel, and pass the wine order to Louis Delor, who was in charge of the cellar and had joined the Underground about the same time as Bretonne.

Delor's motive for joining was his Communist leanings, and he was attracted to the name of the Underground group which contacted him, Francs-Tireurs et Partisans Français. Delor was rather naive about political matters, and his Communist affiliation was based more upon his negative feelings about the French government than on a desire to overthrow it for Russian-style Communism.

Delor's function in the Ritz Underground was to receive the concierge's list each day and give the order to a wine merchant whose establishment was in the suburb of Ivry-sur-Seine. The wine merchant, who had a permit to place calls outside the Occupied Zone, would, in turn, telephone his supplier who was located in the Unoccupied Zone. Telephone calls in the Unoccupied Zone could be placed without restriction, so the supplier had no problem putting through a daily call to a certain railway man in an office near the Swiss border. The railway man, whose job it was to relay information about train traffic approaching the border, would telephone an office in Switzerland to which he relayed the list of Ritz numbers, this time associating the numbers with fictitious trains. The Swiss contact then relayed the numbers by short wave to London, where they were immediately taken to Army Intelligence.

When information other than the daily guest identification had to be dispatched from the Ritz, the procedure was for Bretonne to put a note in his empty half-bottle of Beaujolais after lunch and pass it in that manner to Delor, who collected the empties in the employees' dining quarters.

The other member of the Underground operating in the Ritz was in the kitchen, a *sous-chef* named Yves Cressier. He was a rather simple-minded fellow who had no convictions about the Germans one way or another, but who had intense carnal convictions about a chambermaid who worked at the Crillon. The chambermaid, a star recruiter for Francs-Tireurs, had made it very clear to Yves that she put out only for fellow members of the Underground.

5

Hermann Goering wore his white Luftwaffe uniform with four rows of decorations on his left breast and a ribboned Medal of Merit around his throat when he received Joseph Goebbels in his suite. In contrast to Goering's resplendent, imposing presence, Goebbels was a short, thin, emaciated-looking man with the sharp, pinched face of a weasel, who was dressed in nondescript officers' green and who limped heavily on his club foot. He had invited Goering to his suite for their meeting, but Goering's slightly superior rank gave him the privilege of facing Goebbels on his own turf.

They exchanged "Heil Hitlers" but did not give the salute or shake hands. Goering motioned Goebbels to a chair which was faced toward the fireplace. There was a good fire in the grate, and on the wall above the mantelpiece, where Goebbels couldn't miss it, was Rembrandt's *Man with a Turban*. While the impact of the Rembrandt was setting in, Goering summoned Robert Kropp to serve drinks from a silver service wagon which he wheeled to Goebbels' chair. Goebbels indicated the Courvoisier bottle, and Kropp poured him a generous helping in a Baccarat snifter. Goering chose champagne. Neither spoke. Goebbels rolled the snifter between his palms, warming it. Goering agitated his champagne with a twenty-four-carat swizzle stick. They did not look at each other. Nor did Goebbels, after the initial shock, look at the painting again.

"What was it you wished to discuss, Dr. Goebbels?" Goering finally asked. They had known each other since the early days of the Nazi Party, but they addressed each other formally.

"Property of the Fatherland which appears, by some error, to have passed to the Ritz Hotel."

"And what property is that?"

"The Rembrandt which faces us now."

"The august Minister of Enlightenment and Propaganda is under a mistaken impression. This Rembrandt is hung here only temporarily. It will eventually be shipped to my Karinhall collection, which will be open to the public after the war. What I acquire I acquire as a trustee for the Fatherland. I will build a special gallery there. The Hermann Goering National Art Collection. Cut-rate tourist trains will come from Berlin."

"Karinhall? Which of your six establishments is that? I lose track." Of course Goebbels was very familiar with Karinhall, and Goering knew it.

"That's my country place outside Berlin, the one that honors my status as Reich Master of the Hunt and Master of the German Forests. One hundred thousand acres—you must come hunt with me—I have stocked it with deer, bison, elk, moose and wild boar."

"Have you given a thought to one of the museums *inside* Berlin?"

"You mean for the Rembrandt?"

"Yes."

"Is that where you're sending Rubens' *Diana at the Bath?*"

"Oh, yes, that's another thing I wanted to discuss with you. There was an attempt last night to remove it from the loading area at the railroad station."

"You don't say!"

"I wondered if you had any information about that."

"Well, I'm surprised to hear that you appropriated the painting."

"On behalf of the Fatherland."

"Really? I understand it was loaded onto your private train and the crate is addressed to your residence."

"You certainly spend a great deal of your time in the world of art, don't you, Reichsmarschall? You seem to be in Paris more than in Germany these days."

"It is easier for me to direct the Luftwaffe from here." Goering poured more champagne for himself and took two of the white tablets from the bowl. Then he said sarcastically, "We are attacking England, or didn't you know?"

"The way we hear it in Berlin, it is England which is attacking you. I have heard it said that if you cared as much about the Luftwaffe as you do about your stolen art, there would be fewer wrecked Messerschmitts in the English countryside. I cover up your inadequacies with my propaganda as best I can, but when the real air war comes, and they start to fly their planes at us, will you be able to fly my typewriters?"

"I am going to my headquarters on the Normandy coast

tomorrow morning—the air command post for Air Fleet Two near Cap Blanc-Nez. Would you like to come and see our operation for yourself? I don't think you have yet been in the vicinity of actual fire, and it might purify your soul."

"No, you are wrong, Reichsmarschall, I have been in actual fire—"

"I don't mean the sound of a few pop-guns. There is something about a squadron of attacking Spitfires that might work wonders for you."

"The point I make, Reichsmarschall, is that I spend most of my time working long hours at my offices in Berlin, while most of your hours are spent here at the Ritz, gobbling up the art treasures of the Jews."

"Is it your impression, Dr. Goebbels, that I am accountable to you for where I go and what I do? Perhaps I should discuss with the Führer precisely what your duties are—it is my impression that I am second in command, the Deputy Führer, but it seems you have a different idea."

Mention of the Führer's name had the desired effect upon Goebbels, who drank off his cognac and changed his position in his chair. "We should not be at loggerheads. But Bormann makes serious trouble for me. And for you. His mouth is all over Berlin. I was at a dinner party last week given by that ass Rosenberg, and Bormann was regaling everyone with how you connived to get hold of the *Victory of Samothrace,* the pride of the Louvre. Those huge stone wings, and you stole them right out from under everyone's nose."

"What a lie! The *Winged Victory* I have is only a copy made for me by the Minister of Education, Abel Bonnard."

"There, you see? Also, Bormann has attacked me for allowing you to acquire Jewish art. As Minister of Enlightenment, it is my responsibility to purge the Reich of tainted art, so he holds me responsible for all the Rothschilds and Seligmanns you have acquired. Behind your back he calls you 'the Keeper of the Jews.'"

Kropp refilled Goebbels' snifter.

"Bormann is the malignant tumor of Germany," Goering said. "He's an ignoramus. I don't have one painting, tapestry or statue signed by a Jew. I don't think there's ever been a Jewish artist who amounted to anything. What's more, every painting, every stick of antique furniture, everything I have I confiscated, not one pfennig was paid to any of the Jews in Poland or Holland or France who owned the art I took. The next time Bormann opens his big mouth, you tell him that. Rembrandt was not a Jew."

He took a couple of the tablets and washed them down with the champagne. "You and I should have no quarrel, Goebbels. We should cooperate one with the other. Bormann is allied with Himmler, and we should be as one against them. The other we can count on is Speer. Not Himmler—he tried to muscle in on the E.R.R. allotments by having his SS police seize the Jewish documents on the grounds that the Jews were enemies of the State. But I fizzled that by cutting off funds for the SS to operate with in France. And we must watch that nitwit Rosenberg. He has the power to take everything, but he's too dumb to know how to use it. He knows as much about art as my pet lion."

"Don't worry about Rosenberg," Goebbels said. "He has to spend all his time behind his desk in Berlin in his Office of World Outlook."

"That's what they call it? Really?" Goering laughed deeply and his belly shook. "What an outlook he must have!"

Ordinarily a spartan drinker, Goebbels, feeling the cognac, was staring dreamily at the Rembrandt. "It is a marvelous painting," he said with a sigh.

"I will give you an even better one," Goering said. "It will be put aboard your private train tonight. Rubens' *Venus and Adonis*. It is one of the finest naked Venuses in all Europe. I would like it for my own collection—I have seven naked Venuses, the Führer has nine, but I'm giving it to you."

Goering was perspiring heavily now. He had finished the bottle of champagne and had started on another. "Listen to me, Joseph, we have always worked well together. The beautiful way we duped the American, Lindbergh. He still believes we have a tremendous air fleet. He convinced that idiot Chamberlain, and now he's making speeches for us in the United States. Joseph, you and I together, we can rule the skies of the world without dropping another bomb."

Goering sat forward in his chair, leaning closer to Goebbels, his nostrils spread with excitement, his eyes penetratingly alive. "I will tell you my dream, Joseph, in strictest confidence—just between you and me. My passion."

Kropp again refilled Goebbels' glass. Goering took a couple of tablets from the bowl, and chewed them like gum as he spoke. "I care more about preserved beauty than any man alive. The great paintings, the immortal tapestries and sculptures, the master-piece furniture. Just imagine this, *imagine* it! All the great art of Europe that has been scattered all over in museums and private homes, I will have it under one roof at Karinhall. All of it!

"Oh, Joseph, I tell you it is an exquisite joy to walk along the halls and in the rooms at Karinhall and behold these wondrous objects! I am the Medici of the Third Reich, and my collection will be my monument. The world will forever remember Hermann Goering for the glory of his collection. My Gobelin tapestries, Oriental weapons, alabaster vases, Renaissance sundials! Did you know that the desk at which I write once belonged to the great Cardinal Mazarin?"

Goering took from his pocket a spectacular emerald, an inch in diameter, and handed it to Goebbels. "Have you ever laid eyes on such a stone? I adore jewels. There is nothing finer to the touch than emeralds or blue diamonds. In this bowl here I keep my favorite gems, and what could be more exhilarating than to fondle them with my fingers as a Greek fondles his beads? I am the last Renaissance man, Joseph, and the world will profit from me. I have a special art office on the Quai d'Orsay run by a knowledgeable woman, Fräulein Gisela Linberger, but I'll tell you, what I need is someone impartial to keep an eye on all of them. Someone outside the intrigue, the secret deals with Rosenberg and Bormann—I suspect that some of my spies are double agents, and I am losing many of the best canvases that way. But, no matter, I am doing very well. By the end of the week my private train will again be filled and ready for another run to Germany."

His eyes glistened, the pupils constricted by the morphine. A thin line of perspiration mustached his upper lip. He took Goebbels by the wrist and held him in a firm painful grip. His face was inches away from Goebbels'. "And you will get your share, my friend," he said, intently. "I will see to that. From now on, I will send you a monthly list and you can take your pick. There are thousands of pictures still to be inventoried. Hundreds of Rothschild canvases, and say what you will they had the best collections in Europe. So don't get upset over a single Rembrandt. There may be an even better one in the next Jewish batch."

Goering stood up, maintaining his grip on Goebbels' wrist. Goebbels was unsteady on his feet and held on to his chair back for support.

"Hermann, this is the first good talk we ever had," Goebbels said. "You can certainly count on me. I have admired you ever since the early days in Berlin, and seeing as how you confide in me, now I can confide in you: I have just come from Rome, where I had an audience with Pope Pius. I wanted his cooperation about the Jews . . ."

"That he condemn the Jews? Oh, I doubt—"

"No, just his silence. It has been arranged. We will be sending the Vatican a certain amount of art and money. The Pope will keep his eyes on the heavens and not on what we are doing with the Jews." Goebbels' speech was a bit slurred.

Goering walked him to the door, an enormous figure beside the skinny, gimpy Goebbels. "I am showing a film tonight," Goering said, "Marlene Dietrich in *The Blue Angel.* Here in my suite. Ten o'clock."

Goebbels frowned and swayed slightly. "I believe *The Blue Angel* is *verboten.*"

Goering laughed. "Then we will look at it as censors to determine if it is decadent."

After closing the door, Goering went directly to the telephone and put in a call to Baron von Behr at the E.R.R. "Baron, if you will look on today's inventory you will see that there's a Rubens *Venus and Adonis* marked for the Führer. I've just received word from Berlin that he's changed his mind and doesn't want it. So switch the destination to Dr. Goebbels' address in Berlin and put it on his private train right away. Do it yourself. I don't want any mixups. Go over to the Gare Saint-Lazare and don't leave it out of your sight until it's locked aboard."

After he hung up, he went into the bedroom, where Kropp undressed and bathed him and anointed him with 4711 cologne. Then Kropp completely covered his huge body with cold towels to bring down his body temperature.

6

Philip always rode his bicycle through the Jardin des Tuileries when he went to paint in Man Ray's studio. He would go down the Rue Cambon, enter the park by the Place de la Concorde entrance, and then pedal along the paths toward the juncture of the Louvre with the Seine. Before the Occupation, bicycles were strictly prohibited, but the Germans imposed no such restriction.

As Philip turned into the park from the Place de la Concorde, he became aware of a commotion a short distance inside the gates. A group of French workmen, blue denims, berets, yellow cigarettes stuck to their lower lips, who had been working with picks and shovels at the entrance, were running toward a *pissoir* which was located a hundred yards or so inside the Tuileries Garden. A ten-year-old boy, who had just run out from the *pissoir,* was howling incoherently and running toward them. The fly of his pants was open and his penis was partially visible. Philip stopped his bicycle and dismounted.

The first workman to reach the boy lowered his ear to hear what the boy was trying to say between his sobs. Other people in the park were quickly gathering. Suddenly, two of the workmen went charging into the *pissoir* and emerged with a German soldier, a sergeant, whose face was white with fear. His cap had been knocked off and the two workmen held him roughly to face the boy. Emboldened by the protection of the workmen, the boy shouted at the sergeant, "That's him! He grabbed me in there while I was peeing, he grabbed my penis and he put his mouth on me and I tried to push him away but he was sucking on me, that's him, he . . . ."

There was a collective roar from the workmen and the crowd. Pig! Fag! Animal! Then the foreman, who was the workman who had first heard the boy's gasped words, picked up his flat shovel and swung it violently at the sergeant's head. He swung too low, however, and the staggering blow fell on top of the sergeant's shoulders. Another workman swung his shovel, knocking the sergeant to the ground. Now in a frenzy of outrage and anger the workmen attacked the fallen soldier. Meanwhile, the crowd roared its approval as they kicked and spit at the corpse.

Finally realizing that their work was finished, the men rested on their shovels, and the crowd's shouting gradually subsided to a murmur of approval. During all of it, Philip had stayed resolutely at the rear of the crowd, his face rigidly tense. He felt neither outrage nor revulsion, nor compassion for the boy. It was an event too mesmerizing to reject, but too dangerous to become involved in.

Two German MPs on motorcycles, closely followed by a staff car, came careening through the gates in a billow of dust. The MPs drew their pistols and pointed them at the crowd. The doors of the staff car were flung open. A colonel and several aides quickly emerged. Two of the aides were armed with automatic weapons. Another aide carried a motion picture camera, and a still camera hung from a leather strap around his neck. The crowd parted to make a path for the colonel as he walked toward the corpse.

He studied the mutilated sergeant, walking slowly around the body to observe it from all sides. Then he turned his attention to the workmen; he took one of their shovels and held it up to inspect the blood on it.

"If the colonel please," the workman from whom he had taken the shovel said, "the boy will explain what happened—"

The colonel held up his hand to stop him. The photographer, who was also the interpreter, came forward and repeated to the colonel, in German, what the workman had just said. The colonel turned to look at the boy, who was trembling.

"Go on, tell the colonel what you told us," the workman said.

Hesitatingly, his throat dry with fear, the boy repeated the details of the sergeant's behavior in the *pissoir*. The colonel never took his eyes off the boy as he listened to the translator.

"You are the six men who committed this murder?" the colonel asked. The workmen received his question from the translator and then admitted that they were.

"You will line up in front of me," the colonel said in a matter-of-fact voice. "If, as the boy alleges, an improper act was committed by this noncommissioned officer, then the proper course of action would have been to file a complaint with the local police, who would have then brought the matter to the attention of the German military. As it is, you six men have taken the law into your own hands. What you do not seem to comprehend is that the Germans are now the law and no Frenchman can put himself above the law."

"What if this were your son?" asked the foreman. "What would you have done, Colonel?"

"This is not a matter of sentiment. How do we know the boy is telling the truth? How many boys are liars and hysterics?"

"But look at him! Just look!"

"Are you a judge? Are these other laborers the jury?"

"And how much judge and jury do you give us? My son was grabbed off the street and sent to a work camp in Düsseldorf. Where was the judge and jury for him?"

"Your son is doing honorable service in an honorable cause. At my feet is a dead soldier of the Fatherland whom you have cold-bloodedly killed and mutilated. There is no more to be said."

The colonel looked in the direction of his two aides with the automatic weapons. They moved forward. "The *Kommandantur* of Paris," the colonel said, "has decreed that for the taking of the life of a member of the German military establishment, the retribution shall be the lives of ten Frenchmen." The colonel pointed to four men standing in the forefront of the crowd. "These four," he said.

The MPs took the four men by the arms and jostled them over to the group of workmen. Nothing further was said. The photographer readied his movie camera.

"Shit on the Boche!" the foreman shouted. The two aides raised their automatic weapons and fired several rounds at the ten men while the photographer recorded the event. It would be shown in movie houses in all the occupied countries, accompanied by a suitable narration of warning.

The executioners walked over to the fallen men and fired short bursts at each of their heads as the photographer snapped still pictures of them. The colonel turned his back on all of it and returned to his staff car.

Philip pedaled his bike away from the scene as fast as he could.

7

The killing of the ten Frenchmen had a curious effect upon Philip: some anger and revulsion, of course, but a predominant awe of the omnipotence of the Germans, which was rooted in Philip's admiration of his St. Louis hero, Charles Lindbergh. Lindbergh had been living in Paris, and before that London, to escape the publicity after the murder of his baby son. He often dropped by the hotel to see his friend Charley Ritz, and it was Charley who had introduced Philip to Colonel Lindbergh in the Little Bar. Lindbergh was a teetotaler who drank only Vichy water, but he did not mind the drinking of others.

"Philip is a great fan of yours," Charles had said. "He's from St. Louis."

Philip was so in awe of Lindbergh that he blushed and at first could not get any words out. After an awkward pause, he finally said, hesitatingly, "I was with the crowd on the St. Louis levee that day you came back and flew *The Spirit of St. Louis* along the Mississippi and under the Eads Bridge. I think I know your book, *We,* by heart."

Lindbergh had just returned from still another of his many trips to Germany. His first visit had been in 1936 as the guest of Hitler and Goering at the Olympic Games. For all his skill and courage at flying an airplane, Lindbergh was at heart just a naive Midwest country boy with limited education and a relatively uninformed, restricted view of the world. He was made to order for the German propaganda machine.

All of Lindbergh's statements were extensively and seriously covered in the press, and Philip, following his hero's pronouncements closely in *Le Temps,* accepted everything he said as readily and fully as Lindbergh had accepted the German propaganda.

On that evening in 1938 when Charley Ritz had introduced Philip to Lindbergh, Lindbergh took a red plush box from his pocket, opened it, and showed Charley the Cross of the German Eagle. Goering had personally decorated the American flyer with one of the highest honors that could be bestowed on a civilian.

"I think you should not have taken it, Lindy," Charley said.

"I am proud of it," Lindbergh said feistily, jamming the box back into his pocket. "I admire the Germans and I'm flattered that they've honored me with a medal."

"If you like them so much, why don't you live there?" Charley asked in a rancorless voice. He was a tall, spare man with a trim mustache, trustworthy eyes, and the bearing of a Coldstream Guard. He spoke faultless, Etonian English which had been acquired during his school days when his father, César Ritz, had been establishing the London Ritz.

"That's just what Anne and I have been thinking," Lindbergh said. "A few days ago we saw a house just outside Berlin, in Wannsee, which we wanted to buy—a little overfurnished, but a beautiful garden and a river and swans. A perfect place for our two boys, but unfortunately we discovered that the owners were Jews. I think it best to steer clear of Jews."

Charley frowned. "Did you know, Lindy, that the Jews in Germany are being rounded up and put in compounds behind barbed wire?"

"I've heard that, but why not? I guess the German government will process them and put them into other kinds of work, like farming and coal mining and such."

Charley shook his head. "No, I don't think the Nazis want them in any line of work. I think they just want to eliminate them."

"The Nazis are doing what they think is best for their country," Lindbergh said, with a trace of annoyance in his voice. "They have purpose and vision—unlike the British."

"Then you don't think Roosevelt should be siding with the British?" Philip asked.

"Of course not. You don't know the Germans, do you? They are so like our own people. We should be working with them, for we have a lot in common."

"Well, I'm impressed with what you've got to say about the German war machine," Philip said, "but all this Jewish business—the ones I know are pleasant, efficient people with a good sense of humor. Still, I guess you're right that we shouldn't be interfering—what's happening here is none of our business. We did it in 1917 in the big war and what did we achieve? Don't you think, Charley?"

"No, I think the Germans are everyone's concern. Have you

read *Mein Kampf?* I think you are on the wrong track, Lindy."

After that initial meeting, Philip often spent time with Lindbergh whenever he came to the Ritz. By the time Lindbergh returned to live in the States in 1940, he had convinced Philip that America had no business getting involved in a matter that was strictly European.

8

Philip let himself into the cold studio and looked around at the paintings on the easels as if they were strangers. The incident in the Jardin des Tuileries had alienated him from his bearings. There was a smell of cat piss in the room. Philip took an old newspaper from a pile in the corner and unfolded it. He took off his jacket and his sweater and carefully wrapped the newspaper around his chest and held it in place with his chin while he put the sweater and jacket back over it. He had learned that from Man Ray as an antidote against the nagging cold.

The scream of the boy reverberated in his head and he couldn't shake it, like a noxious smell that persists long after the offending object is gone. It wasn't really a scream, it was the howl of a terribly wounded animal, an incoherent wail of horror. If that were your son, Colonel?, the workman's voice on the sound track of his mind. Well, Philip? He was no good at taking moral positions.

He went to look at the painting on which he had been working on the previous day. The colors had dried disappointingly. It was—well, he didn't know exactly what was missing, but as he looked at it in the light of a new day it seemed inconsequential. When he had finished yesterday, he had felt very good about it; when he walked into the studio this morning he had hoped for the best—but it just wasn't there. Flat, no vitality or emotion, the work of a stranger.

He crossed the studio to where the last painting of Man Ray rested on an easel, face in. He turned it around and stepped back. It was a wide, short canvas that was overwhelmed by a pair of huge red lips floating in a bluish-gray sky over a twilit landscape with an observatory on it, its two domes like breasts dimly indicated on the far horizon. The lips had an erotic effect on Philip. Their size and their sensuous contour suggested two closely joined bodies. Man Ray had written across the bottom of the canvas, *"À l'Heure de l'Observatoire—Les Amoureux."*

Shaking his head sadly, Philip went back to his own canvas and jabbed a palette knife through it, ripping it up, down and across.

Philip missed Man Ray. He painted better when Man was in the studio. Philip never asked him for advice, nor did Man behave like a mentor, but Man's physical presence seemed to give off a certain communicable spark. Philip had originally met Man because of his access to Lindbergh. Man, who was as adept with a camera as he was with a paint brush, had an assignment to photograph Lindy for *Vanity Fair,* but Lindbergh would not even speak to him on the telephone. It was at that point that Man one day had sought out Philip, introduced himself, and asked for his help (a barman had told Man of Philip's friendship with Lindbergh). Philip had succeeded in arranging the rare photographic sitting, with the understanding that Lindbergh would have approval of the print to be used and custody of all the negatives.

Philip felt isolated and pierced by the damp cold of the studio. He put some water into a little saucepan, lit a small can of Sterno, and put the pan over the flame. There was a small amount of half-congealed powdered coffee in the bottom of the Nescafé jar. He held his hands near the tiny flame to warm them while he waited for the water to boil. He thought about Wally MacHugh and Hercules Bolquist, English friends with whom he had often lunched, and he wondered what branch of military service they were serving in.

He poured the boiling water over a spoonful of the stale but priceless Nescafé, and stirred in a spoonful of beet sugar. He sat back on the couch and sipped the hot coffee, letting his thoughts drift to Lili as she leaned against him on the bicycle, feeling the soft strands of her hair caressing his face. He could feel her skin, the fullness of her breasts, the way her lips parted when she smiled, and he got an erection. He couldn't stop thinking about her. He went into the bathroom to masturbate, but after a few minutes he stopped, dissatisfied.

He was too discouraged with his painting even to try to work. There was no one to lunch with, no plans for the evening. The morning sun had become swiftly obliterated by turbulent clouds, and a cold relentless rain was now pelting the skylight.

Philip took an old, paint-stained quilt from the cupboard and stretched out on the cot. His lids closed involuntarily. His erection had receded, leaving a trace of cold wetness. He resisted falling asleep, so that when sleep did come the dream about his aunt had a heightened reality. He couldn't understand why he always dreamed about his aunt, and never about his uncle. The only dream about his aunt which he had enjoyed was one in which he drowned her in a bathtub filled with red wine—or perhaps it was blood. But even that dream had a disturbing element in it: the fact that they were naked, having a bath together in the blood-red water when Philip drowned her.

Philip had never been beyond the confines of his native St. Louis, not even to Springfield or Jefferson City, when he was taken to Paris in July 1928 by his Uncle Gerard. Philip was twenty-seven years old at the time, and the trip was Uncle Gerard's present to him on his graduation from Washington University. Gerard's brother, Henry, Philip's father, had died in 1920, Philip's mother was confined to the Fee-Fee Sanitarium with a lung disorder called consumption, and despite the vociferous objections of Gerard's wife, Adele, who had always looked down upon his brother's family, Gerard felt that he owed this graduation trip to his brother's only child.

Gerard had no children of his own, and this was one of the rare occasions when he imposed his will on that of his wife. This confrontation did not make for a very pleasant voyage on the *Île-de-France,* despite the fact that, as a sop to his wife's contempt for Philip, Gerard had put Philip in cabin class while he and his wife traveled first, as always. On two occasions during the crossing, Gerard invited his nephew to dine with them in the sumptuous first-class dining room, but on those occasions Adele spoke not one word to Philip, nor to Gerard, for that matter, and both times she left the table before her *café filtre* without so much as an "Excuse me."

Philip, however, was so dazzled by the adventure of being aboard one of the world's great ships that he was not fazed by the contemptuous behavior of his aunt. He knew very little about the niceties of life. When he had graduated from Soldan High School in 1920, just turned eighteen, there was no money for him to go to college. His father had recently died, his mother was in frail health, and Philip had to go to work to earn enough money to support his mother and himself, while putting aside a little each week toward college.

To accomplish this, he held two jobs: day work at Famous-Barr, evenings at Garavelli's. Philip's first job at Famous, St. Louis' biggest department store, was in the stock room, where he earned $27.50 a week. He considered himself lucky to get the job, since there were still a lot of World War veterans out of work, and luckier yet to land the job at Garavelli's, a busy, popular Italian restaurant.

Philip worked six evenings a week, got a free meal, and was able to put something into his college account every week except when his mother had medical expenses not covered by the free clinic at Barnes Hospital. Those days when she felt up to it, his mother went door to door selling lingerie which she got on consignment from the Milady Lingerie Company in Chicago. Her best customers were the women who worked in the whorehouses on Market Street and on the other side of the Eads Bridge in East St. Louis.

Philip's father had started life on an equal footing with Gerard, who was a few years older, but he had dealt poorly with himself. Their father, an immigrant from Belgium, had left them equal amounts of a modest inheritance, but conservative Gerard slowly prospered, while Henry, more audacious, had consumed his inheritance with small, impetuous failures. With each loss, Henry moved his family a step downward, until they wound up in a three-room cold-water flat over Sorkin's delicatessen, next to a firehouse on Page Boulevard.

At about the same time, Gerard moved into a Normandy-style mansion which he had bought on Lindell Boulevard opposite Forest Park, often referred to as Millionaire's Row. Gerard was not yet a millionaire, but he was well on his way. He had married his bookkeeper, an ambitious woman who had a masterful knack with account ledgers, audits, billings, postings and other such skills of her calling.

For several years, Henry had been hitting Gerard for small loans to bridge his fiascos. As bookkeeper, Adele knew about these loans, which she rightly called handouts since there was little or no prospect of repayment. She stridently objected to these importunings, and to keep peace Gerard limited family contact with his brother to Thanksgiving, Christmas and their respective birthdays.

As Adele felt about Henry, so Philip's mother felt about Adele—"that stuck-up, money-hungry bookkeeper who grabbed him"—and the eventual cancellation of the four shared events pleased both women. It was a disappointment to Philip, however, for this was the only family he had, and after his father died of a heart attack—the victim of Lucky Strikes and hypertension—Philip eagerly accepted Gerard's occasional invitations to play tennis or lunch at his club.

*   *   *

The first two of the six weeks they were scheduled to stay in Paris were pure joy for Philip. He had been half afraid that the Paris of his dreams would fall short of the Paris of reality, but in fact reality exceeded fantasy. From the time he was a boy, Philip had had a great curiosity about France, doubtlessly engendered by Gerard's stories about his annual Francophilian odysseys. In his reading, Philip had a marked preference for French literature: Stendhal, Jules Verne, De Maupassant, Victor Hugo (particularly *Les Misérables*), Balzac, Proust, and a book by George Orwell called *Down and Out in Paris and London*. Those first two weeks, Adele devoted all her time to the fashion collections and to the ministrations of the Elizabeth Arden and Helena Rubinstein beauty salons, so that Gerard was entirely free to show Philip traditional sights and his favorite haunts.

One noonday while they were having an *apéritif* in the Ritz bar, Scott Fitzgerald, whom Gerard knew from his previous visits, came in and sat at their table.

"Philip," Uncle Gerard had said, "this is the great American writer Mr. F. Scott Fitzgerald."

"Did you know, Philip," Fitzgerald had said, "there are three kinds of greats? The real greats, the near-greats, and the ingrates."

"But they're spelled differently," Philip had pointed out.

"Ah," Fitzgerald had said with a sigh, "there's truly nothing more fascinating than the literal mind."

On another occasion, it was Fitzgerald who introduced Gerard and Philip to Hemingway, who was joining him for a drink before going to lunch. But while they were having drinks, Fitzgerald and Hemingway began to quarrel, at first about something Hemingway had said the night before about Fitzgerald's wife, Zelda, and then they began to insult each other about their respective writing. But they didn't raise their voices or shout at each other. They said awful things to each other, but in calm, quiet voices. At one point, Scott turned to Gerard and said, by way of explanation, "The trouble is, Gerard, that Hem and I love each other so much that there are times we can't stand each other."

"Your trouble, Scott," Hemingway said, his voice a deadly whisper, "is that as a success you were a failure, but even worse, now as a failure you're a failure." That said, Hemingway took his drink and poured it on Fitzgerald's lap and left.

Scott didn't react. "It'll just look like I peed in my pants," he said calmly, and ordered another drink.

On another occasion, Gerard took Philip along with him when he visited his old friend Leo Stein, who had the best private collection of Postimpressionist paintings in Paris. Leo's sister, Gertrude, was there, and later on it was through his friendship with the Steins that Philip began to develop his interest in and knowledge of art.

During the third week of their stay, Philip was awakened by the phone at six in the morning. His uncle had had a severe heart attack. He was to come to his suite at once. When he got there, he found two doctors and a nurse in attendance. The older doctor, who was in charge, said that the attack had been so severe, and Gerard's heart was in such a precarious state, that he could not be moved, for the time being, to the American Hospital in Neuilly. Adele sat on a chair in the corner of the living room, weeping.

Gerard's lawyer, Harrison Myles, was ushered in, and, in a failing voice, Gerard dictated several codicils to his will, which he signed. Then he sent for Philip. He breathed with great difficulty, sucking in each breath as if through a collapsed straw. "I'm sorry to leave you, Philip. We were having such a good time. I've tried to provide . . ." He couldn't catch his breath to say any more.

"Where the hell are they with that oxygen?" the older doctor asked. "Nurse, go get his wife."

The nurse went into the living room of their suite to fetch Adele, but Gerard died before she could get from the living room to the bed.

In one of the codicils, Gerard had provided a stipend for Philip, "for however long he wishes to stay in Paris." The stipend was for a set sum which covered the rent at the Ritz and for ordinary living expenses. Philip was also provided with the return half of a cabin-class ticket to New York on the *Normandie.*

Adele tried every which way to break this codicil, but Harrison Myles, who disliked her, assured Philip that as long as he continued to live in Paris at the Ritz the provisions of the codicil would remain in effect. Of course, it was not contemplated by Gerard that Philip would choose to stay on indefinitely, but the codicil had specified no time limit.

Less than a year after Gerard's death, Philip's mother succumbed to her long bout with consumption. The Webers had no family at all, not a single living relative, and Philip simply could not face returning for a funeral which he would have to attend by himself. Also, if he left Paris, Adele could probably have succeeded in cutting off his support as provided in Gerard's will. So Philip arranged for the funeral parlor to inter his mother's body in a plot near his father's. His mother had been in the tuberculosis sanitarium on and off for so many of the past years, and Philip had seen her so infrequently, that he had little emotional connection with her death.

Not too long after his mother's death, Adele married a dance instructor from Argentina and they went to live on her money in Buenos Aires; she never again bothered Philip after that.

The knock on the door was at first involved with his dream, but then his consciousness intervened and he opened his eyes, unsure of where he was.

A woman's voice on the other side of the door called out, "Philip, are you there?"

He hurried to open it, smoothing his hair as he crossed the studio. It was Lili.

"I was about to leave," she said as she entered inquisitively. She wore a bright-red coat and a white knit hat which she pulled off her head and tossed on the couch. She shook her head vigorously to release her hair, which fell in golden folds to her shoulder. It seemed to Philip she was even more beautiful than the night before.

"What a darling studio!" she exclaimed. Her eyes fell on the lips painted by Man Ray. She looked at the painting for several minutes, her face sober. "Is this what you paint?" she asked.

"No, that's the work of Man Ray, who owns this studio."

"Man Ray—what kind of a name is that?"

"He's an American."

She read the inscription on the painting. "'Observatory Time—The Lovers'—well, it looks more like a billboard ad for Benson and Hedges cigarettes, if you get my drift. Is he a Dadaist, this Man Ray?"

"Well, somewhat. He's a Surrealist, really."

"And you? How does Philip Weber paint?" She looked around and saw the slashed canvas on the other side of the room. She let out a little cry of dismay. "Is this yours? Why did you cut it up? Why, it's lovely! You seem so steady, but is this your disposition—slash, slash? Well, anyway, I came to pose for you. I said I would, didn't I?"

She took off her coat and flung it on top of the couch. She was wearing a white, yellow-yoked peasant blouse with puffed sleeves, and a tight black skirt. Her arms and neck were bare.

She shivered and rubbed her arms. "Why do you keep it so cold in here?"

"There's no central heating, and no wood for the stove."

"What about that electric heater?" She picked up the cord and plugged it in.

Philip laughed. "Don't you know the Germans only provide electricity from five to seven in the evening?" To his amazement, the coils of the heater began to turn bright red.

Lili seated herself on a stool in front of the heater. "Ah, that's better," she said. She put her head back, a wisp of hair across her eyes, and put her arms on the back of the stool for support as she leaned back. "I'm ready," she said. She opened her lips slightly and moistened them with her tongue.

Philip set up a freshly stretched canvas on his easel. He picked up a piece of charcoal to sketch in an outline for the painting; his hand shook slightly from the effect she had on him.

"Is this a good pose?" she asked.

"Well, it's rather stagey," Philip said. "A little too Hollywood."

Lili straightened up and quickly and deftly pulled off her blouse. "How's this?" she asked. She wore no brassiere or undergarment, and her breasts, larger than Philip had imagined, were very firm, with upward pink nipples. The sight of her bare breasts, her lovely sloping shoulders, the arch of her thin, graceful neck, aroused him.

Lili laughed. "Have you turned to stone?"

Philip had difficulty finding his voice. "I am always paralyzed by a work of art. The first time I laid eyes on Botticelli's *Venus Rising* at the Louvre, I could neither speak nor move. I just stood there paralyzed, until the guards made me go when the museum closed. That's the effect you have on me."

Lili laughed, the notes of her laughter again affecting Philip as they had the night before. "And I'm a work of art? Maybe I'll be your Venus."

"I'd have to have a full pose for that." He was trying to sketch her, but he couldn't concentrate.

"No, full-length is impossible. I have no pubic hair, and I am self-conscious about that. I have tried everything, special pomades and hormones, but nothing works. I am destined to go through life with a Venus mound bereft of vegetation."

"But that's all to the good. Many models shave themselves. Botticelli's Venus has no pubic hair."

"Perhaps I could get a toupee," she said, and began to laugh.

"It's called a merkin," Philip said.

"What is?"

"That kind of toupee."

"You mean there's a word for it?"

"Yes, false hair for a lady's private parts."

"Merkin! Oh, that's too rich for words! I must go to my beauty parlor first thing in the morning. 'And what will Madame have today?' 'Why, a merkin—a nice blond one with a few curls in it.'" She was laughing uncontrollably.

Philip could no longer restrain himself. He walked over to her.

"You are simply too beautiful," he said. "I can't keep my distance." He put his hand on the side of her face and looked into her eyes.

"Oh, my God!" she exclaimed. "I almost forgot about my appointment!" She jumped off the stool and dressed quickly.

"You're not leaving!"

"I must—it's . . . business. We will resume another time. I'm sorry—really and truly I am."

Swiftly she moved to the door, carrying her hat, and let herself out. Philip was stunned. His entire body ached. The electric heater continued to hum. He threw the piece of charcoal at the door with all his might, and it shattered to bits.

9

Fortunately for Philip, that evening he had his weekly rendezvous with Camille at 122 Rue Provence. It was his Uncle Gerard who had initially brought Philip to Rue Provence and introduced him to Madame Rounpé, who was unlike any other madam in the world. She was in her thirties, slim, dressed by Jacques Fath, intelligent, well read, and as particular about her clientele as the exclusive Travelers' Club on the Champs-Élysées.

"What you've got to understand, Phil," Gerard had warned his nephew, "is that sex is different in Paris than it is anywhere else. It is open and aboveboard, an appetite to be fulfilled just like other appetites. I myself have never trafficked with a streetwalker. I think one's much better off in an established house. Like 32 Rue Blondel in Montmartre, or the House of All Nations, or 122 Rue Provence. Now, I know you're not very experienced in sex, Philip, but I can tell you're *very* interested. Ah, the joy of a beautiful woman, delicately perfumed, devoted one hundred percent to the gratification of your body, anything you'd like, the way you'd like it. Sound good?"

"I'll say!"

"You betcha!" Gerard laughed and patted Philip's back. "Now, like I said, there's these three places. Rue Blondel is really just for laughs and drinks, and I think you'll prefer 122 to the House of All Nations. But I'll take you to all three—a Cook's Tour of the Cat Houses. But first, a bite of lunch at Fouquet's. I'm going to introduce you to my prickly friends the *oursins*."

In the taxi on the way to 122 Rue Provence, Gerard explained that it was run like an exclusive gentlemen's club—White's of London, say, or the Travelers' on the Champs-Élysées. No one was allowed patronage who did not come highly recommended. Many members of Parliament and ministers of this and that, French nobility, top industrialists, members of the Académie, stars of the Comédie Française, titled English, Belgians and Italians. The chef was formerly with the Tour d'Argent, and an evening with one's lady of choice usually encompassed formal dining and dancing as well as extraordinary sex.

On his initial visit to 122 Provence in the company of his uncle, Philip had not "indulged" with one of the women. On that particular evening, all of the resident ladies were with gentlemen who had previously booked them, as his Uncle Gerard had a week in advance engaged Blanche, his regular woman during his past three visits to Paris. Madame Rounpé offered to try to contact someone for Philip, but he said he preferred simply to dine with his uncle and Blanche and sit this one out.

Later that night, on their way back to the Ritz, Gerard further expanded on the felicitous joy of being a regular at 122. "At my age," he said, "my infrequent visits there suit me fine, but at your age you want to establish one of the girls as your regular, once a week—I always liked Wednesdays—it's something to anticipate all week long, dressing up in your smoking jacket and having an evening devoted solely to the libidinous pursuit of gratification of all your senses. You have only to present yourself—no complications, no moodiness, no untoward emotions, tap on the door and there is this well-mannered, delicately perfumed, beautifully gowned beauty who wants nothing more than to please you."

After his uncle's death, Philip occasionally thought about the entree arranged for him at 122, but he didn't have the impetus or, to put it more precisely, the courage to pursue it. It was Charley Ritz of all people who reintroduced Philip to 122. They had arranged to have dinner together in a new small fish bistro near the Place de la République, but Charley had knocked on Philip's door and explained, with some hesitation and embarrassment, that his regular Thursday evening rendezvous at, ah . . . ummmm, his club had been pushed up a day and he wondered if Philip would . . . ah . . . well, have any interest in joining him there. It was in this dribs-and-drabs manner that Charley finally revealed the true nature of his "club."

"I just spoke to Madame Rounpé, the, ah, directress," Charley said, "and she says she has a very fine girl, recently arrived, who she's sure would be pleasing."

It was a perfect match for Philip. Camille had been on the premises for only three days. She was shy, blond, peach-skinned and possessed of even teeth of dazzling canescence. She came from the little town of Mayenne, where her father had been a small-time mushroom grower who spent all of his non-mushroomed hours in the playing of *boule,* a bowling game which is to the Frenchman what cricket is to the English, baseball to the Americans. He was a member of the Mayenne *boule* team, eventually captain of it, and when he became a widower he immediately inscribed his four young daughters with the sisters of the Seminary of the Sacred Heart, thereafter being free to devote all his time to his mushrooms and his *boule.* The seminary was an order devoted to silence, obedience and dogmatic conformity, with severe punishments liberally administered for infinitesimal flutters from grace. The only exception to the rigors of this numbing repression was the program of religious music. The Sacred Heart was traditionally famous for its secular music, and every Easter the large chorus of girls performed at sunrise in the cathedral at Rouen. It was at one of these Easter performances that Camille, with careful planning, made her escape.

Camille was eventually brought to Madame Rounpé via the mysterious scouting system which Madame Rounpé never divulged, and after a period of indoctrination she had just made her debut as one of the ladies of the house. She was the perfect choice for Philip. When, after a dinner of *langoustines, gigot* and *frais de bois,* they withdrew to the seaside room, the unhurried, gentle, natural quality that Camille brought to Philip's body made his rite of passage serene and satisfying. After that initial meeting, he saw her every Wednesday evening, his uncle's will having envisioned this expense, although not by itemization.

Philip had something with Camille that transcended his sex with her. She had a liberating effect on him: he was more open, looser, when he was with her, more caustic, funnier, and her sharp sense of humor appreciated him. In a short time, they grew to like each other very much.

In the beginning at 122, he had tried making love in the steam room and the hayloft, but he found he did not like the feel of Camille's perspiring body, nor was he enchanted with the odors of the hayloft. He much preferred the railroad stateroom or the seashell. There were some rooms he never even tried, like the Marquis de Sade room, the mud bath, the hospital room and the boat cabin. He had decided that the sex he had with Camille in his two favorite rooms was just what he wanted, and although he often had to scrimp for days to accumulate his fee for the evening, even skip some meals, he never regretted it for a moment.

* * *

But on this particular evening, when Philip needed to be cheered up after his aggravating experience with Lili, he found Camille in a thoughtful, subdued mood. She was wearing a peach-colored silk evening gown, with a spike of zircons in the knot of her blond hair. There was an elegance about her, and as she crossed the dining room to greet him she could easily have been a young duchess. She wore long white silk gloves with mother-of-pearl buttons at the wrists, and her perfume was as delicate as spring mimosa.

"You're *triste*," Philip said as the waiter poured champagne. "I don't want you *triste* tonight."

"I must tell you some things, Philip. Because . . . well, I must tell you . . . we always talk gay and inconsequential, but I want you to know that of all my clients, year in and year out, the only one I respond to is you. I mean, I feel everything, you complete me. The last time you were here, we had such a grand time that evening, and I was tempted . . . well, after you left, I really considered that I wouldn't wash. Hélène has a child, and she gets along very well, and I really considered that I would skip the bidet and have your child. You are the most constant man in my life, all these years, and, well, it was just an impulse. I came to my senses, and Philip the Second is not to be."

"I have often wondered how it would be to see you away from here. To dine somewhere or go to a concert or whatever."

"No, that might unsettle us. What we have every week here, our evening together, how could it be better? But listen, dear Philip, I tell you all this because I must give you bleak news. The *Kommandantur de Gros Paris* has requisitioned all our evenings for the high-ranking members of its staff. Madame Rounpé has protested, and many of our influential clients have intervened, but there is nothing we can do. The fact is, I am desolate to say, that you and I are obliged to give up our Wednesday evenings. After all these years . . ." Tears came to her eyes when she saw the effect of her announcement on Philip.

"But the afternoons, Philip, I can still have the afternoons for my civilian clients."

"It isn't the same."

"We can have a nice lunch, and the afternoon . . ."

"It won't be the same," Philip said sadly. "There is something about the evening, and dressing up, and dancing here on the marble floor—oh, Christ, must they take everything away from us!'' His voice had suddenly risen, and he was embarrassed when a number of gentlemen at other tables turned toward him.

Camille took his hand in hers and leaned forward, smiling up into his face. "We are powerless to protest, of course, but my Wednesday evenings have been assigned to a General Meissinghaus who is head of the Paris Gestapo. Perhaps in a moment of simulated passion I could put him out of commission."

She laughed, and so did Philip, and although it was tinged with sadness they thoroughly enjoyed their last evening together.

10————————

Mademoiselle Chanel was surprised and more than a little apprehensive when she opened the envelope handed her by the Ritz groom to find a request from Reichsmarschall Hermann Goering that she come to his suite at six o'clock that evening. She immediately phoned Philip. "You must come with me, Philip. Whatever can he want?"

"But you can't bring me if I'm not invited."

"As my interpreter. Otherwise, how will I communicate?"

"He probably has his own—"

"Philip, you *must* come, that's all there is to it. I can't face that monster alone."

"He's not as bad as you may think. I met him in the elevator—"

"He's fat, suety fat, and I'm told he's boundlessly in love with himself. You are coming, that's all there is to it. If it makes you feel better, when I acknowledge the invitation I'll mention you. Why do you think he wants to see me? Since I closed the shop I've been quiet as a church mouse."

"He probably wants some Chanel No. 5 for his mistress."

"Very droll. Well, even Hermann Goering won't get a bottle of No. 5 unless he allows the essences from Grasse to get to Paris. No, it's probably Chanel suits for Frau Goering, the little woman back in Berlin—or, perhaps, for der Führer's sexy Eva."

Gabrielle and Philip were received by Goering's military aide, the one Philip had encountered in the elevator, but the aide gave no sign of recognition; he simply bowed to Gabrielle stiffly from the waist and wordlessly led them into the salon, indicating where they were to sit by gesturing with his hand. Philip was fascinated by the Rembrandt picture, as Goebbels had been, and studied it intently. Gabrielle's attention, however, was riveted on the large cut-crystal bowl in the center of the coffee table, which, if she was not mistaken, was laden with unset precious stones; it was difficult for her to believe that all those diamonds, emeralds, rubies, pearls, garnets, moonstones and the rest were real, and yet she had a practiced eye which told her that they were.

"Do you think they're real?" she whispered to Philip, but he was so absorbed in the painting that he did not hear her. She studied the gems more closely. "I do believe they are real," she whispered. "Philip, you've got to look." But Philip could not take his eyes off *The Man with a Turban*. Something peculiar . . . something . . .

There was a stirring in the doorway, then the military aide reappeared and announced, "His Excellency, Reichsmarschall Hermann Goering."

Philip got to his feet, and Gabrielle, uncharacteristically nervous, sat on the edge of her chair. Goering entered and Gabrielle could not restrain her gasp at his appearance. He was wearing a commodious free-flowing green velvet togalike garment with an enormous ruby brooch at the throat. He wore gold sandals and carried the marshall's baton which was a symbol of his illustrious office. There was artificial color on his face, and he was steeped in a musky perfume.

He went directly to Gabrielle. "Mademoiselle Chanel, it is an honor to meet you," he said. He took her hand and touched his lips to it. "You are a revered name in Germany."

Philip translated Goering's German into French for Gabrielle, and she nodded graciously.

"You are the American from the elevator," Goering said to Philip. "The Lanvin dresser."

"Yes, Your Excellency."

Goering's valet, Kropp, came in with glasses and champagne. "May I offer you champagne?" Goering asked.

"Yes, of course," Gabrielle said. Now that the initial shock of his appearance had subsided, Gabrielle was able to assess him overall. What struck her most forcefully were his eyes: clear, cold, mercilessly hard, and restless to the point of what the French call *oblique*, which inadequately translates as "devious."

Goering held up his glass in a toast. "To your genius, Mademoiselle Chanel." He drained his glass and took two white tablets from a bowl near his chair and began to chew on them. "My passion in life is art," Goering said as Kropp refilled his glass, "but for me it doesn't exist just in great paintings like this Rembrandt but can be found in clothes, especially those of certain silks and leathers and velvets, in the genius of a perfume, in a restaurant's kitchen, in the jewelry of the Italian masters. In my country house outside Berlin, Karinhall, named after my first wife—perhaps you've heard of it? no matter—I have these collections of Oriental weaponry, alabaster vases, porcelain, Renaissance sundials . . ." Goering reached into the crystal bowl and lightly worked his fingers over the jewels, caressing them while waiting for Philip to translate.

"I love clothes, Mademoiselle Chanel, the right clothes for my body. I like free-flowing garments, like the one I'm wearing. A man must have vanity, don't you think, Mademoiselle? The Old Testament says, 'Every man at his best state is altogether vanity.' And I, be assured, am at my best possible state. And my vanity would be even more enhanced by beautiful lounging gowns— gowns of your creation. The fact is, Mademoiselle Chanel, that I was hoping I could prevail upon you to create such gowns for me, of the fine silks and velvets which I favor."

"It would be an honor, Reichsmarschall, but please tell His Excellency," she said to Philip, "that my shop has no fabric and is not functioning."

"Why, that is no problem, Mademoiselle," Goering said. "The Chief of Textiles for Paris, Baron von Spatz, is right here in the Ritz and he can procure for you any fabric you desire."

"Ah, but it is more than that," Gabrielle opined. "My dressmakers are also gone, the artistic ones on whom I rely— they were all conscripted and shipped to Berlin. I myself cannot even thread a needle, so there is no one to execute my designs, and thus no Chanel clothes for the shop. And soon there will not even be Chanel No. 5 because your army will not allow the essences to be shipped from Grasse to Paris."

"Well, I must rectify that at once. If you will just give to my orderly the name of your supplier in Grasse . . . Is there any other inconvenience, Mademoiselle?"

"The curfew, Your Excellency. I am a night person, and it inhibits me to scamper back here so early."

Goering pointed his finger at his orderly. "See that Mademoiselle Chanel is immediately issued a *laissez-passer* without limits—I shall sign it myself. And one for Mr. Weber. You seem very interested in my Rembrandt, Mr. Weber."

"Philip knows a great deal about the art world," Gabrielle said, grasping the opportunity to boost Philip. "He is an artist himself and he has studied at the Sorbonne and at the Louvre for many years. He is also a positively super tennis player. He and I have won the mixed doubles at the Racing Club."

"How interesting! I adore tennis," Goering said, "as long as I play with players who have control."

"Control? In what way?" Philip asked.

"I love the tennis stroke," Goering answered. "I have really good form, but I don't like to play with anyone who doesn't have the ability to hit balls within my reach."

Gabrielle was fascinated by this requirement. "Perhaps you'd like to hit some with us?"

"Oh, yes, indeed I would. I don't get enough exercise. We will arrange it. And I will look into the matter of your missing dressmakers, although if they have been assigned to attend to the needs of various wives in Berlin—well, we will see, we will see."

"You are most kind," Gabrielle said. "We should be going, Philip."

But Philip had now moved close to the Rembrandt and was moving his head this way and that, studying the canvas.

"Is there something about the painting?" Goering asked.

"Well, sir," said Philip, stepping back, "there is, yes, there is something . . . Mind you, I am not an expert on Rembrandts, and I'm very probably wrong as I can be, but it bothers me that the free brushwork that is so characteristic of Rembrandt is not in evidence here. This has been painted with a very controlled brush, methodical, and the colors—there is a certain glow to Rembrandt's strong colors, a patina, but here . . ."

Philip broke off as he moved his eyes along the canvas. Goering was looking at him with an expression of frozen disbelief, but behind his impassive mask there was already mounting suspicion, tinged with rage.

"At any rate," Philip said, backing away, "it's probably just my own limitations. There is a curator at the Louvre, Professor Chavelle, who is a great expert on Rembrandts—I studied under him, and he would be better able . . ."

Goering was gone; so swiftly did he leave the room that Gabrielle, who had been looking at Philip, was surprised to discover his absence. The military aide was also gone, a swift shadow. Gabrielle and Philip looked at each other, feeling awkward in the deserted room. Gabrielle shrugged. Neither spoke.

Eventually, Kropp came into the room and asked them please to follow him to the door, where he let them out without comment.

11

When Philip got out of the elevator, he could hear the phone ringing in his room at the end of the corridor.

"Philip, it's Janet. Something rather important. Meet me at the Café de la Paix in half an hour. We mustn't talk on the phone." She hung up before he could answer.

Totally out of character for Janet to be so dramatic, Philip thought. She is usually low-key, unflappable. He hoped she wasn't in some kind of trouble. "We mustn't talk on the phone" certainly sounded like trouble. He slumped back on his bed, feeling dispirited. Every day brought more erosions, defections, disappointments. It was as if life in Paris had been attacked by hostile sandpaper that had scraped it down, but smoothly. The people he had enjoyed in the carefree days of Paris were now changing under the rigors of German stress. He closed his eyes, trying not to see the massacre in the Tuileries Garden, but there it was again, playing itself out for the hundredth time.

Janet Flanner was one of the first people whom Philip had met when he started to live in Paris on his own. She was a slender, handsome woman who wore her hair brushed back, no makeup, Oxford-style shoes, and kept her nails cut short. Although she had lived in Paris since the early Twenties, she had no interest in Paris clothes and fashions except to report them, as she occasionally did, in her regular dispatches to *The New Yorker,* which she signed with her *nom de plume,* Genêt. She had a wickedly perceptive eye for the foibles of the French, and Philip was always amused and startled by her acidulous observations. They would often dine together in one of the small, cheap restaurants that Janet had discovered, and Philip learned from her a great deal about cuisine and wine. In fact, their relationship was almost exclusively confined to restaurants and cafés.

Janet was already sitting on one of the wicker banquettes at the rear of the terrace at the Café de la Paix when Philip arrived. She poured him a glass of wine from a bottle that had been resting in a cooler beside her. A waiter hurried over to proffer assistance, but she waved him away.

"You've ordered a *bottle* of wine?" Philip asked.

"Harold Ross just gave me a raise," she explained.

"Well, here's to Harold Ross."

They drank. It was a fruity, zestful Sancerre, and Philip nodded in appreciation. Janet moved closer to him on the banquette and spoke in a low voice.

"Sylvia Beach is in trouble," she said, "and we've got to help." She could feel Philip's body grow tense. "Do you know about the List Otto?"

"No."

"There's a German professor, Otto Something-or-other, who's compiled a list of eleven hundred offensive books that must be seized and destroyed. I've seen the list: Thomas Mann, Zweig, Freud, Werfel, Vicki Baum, Feuchtwanger, de Gaulle's book on the Army, Heinrich Heine, Erich Remarque, André Maurois—that gives you the idea. Of course, Sylvia's shop is loaded with these *verboten* volumes. She's received word from a confidential source of hers at the Gendarmerie that there will be a bookstore sweep tomorrow. If the Germans find so much as a single volume from the Otto List in Sylvia's store, they will close it down and God knows what they'll do to her. I've talked to Sylvia. On principle, she refuses to destroy any of her books. She will confront the Boche, she says, and show them the error of their ways."

"Fat chance," Philip said.

"We have a plan to help Sylvia," Janet continued. "That's why I wanted to see you. We need you tonight. Only for a couple of hours after dark. We are going to empty all the books out of Sylvia's shop, cart them over to Adrienne Monnier's bookstore, which only has books in French, and turn Sylvia's shop into an antique store. Monsieur Ruhé, the *antiquaire* on the Rue Bonaparte, is lending Sylvia a batch of surplus pieces from his basement on consignment. So, *voilà!*, when the SS or the Gestapo or whoever arrives tomorrow, they will find nothing but innocent antiques and Sylvia, the prim, innocent shopkeeper."

"But how will you move the books? There are no trucks—"

"We have rented *vélotaxis* and we'll peddle them over to Adrienne's load by load, picking up antiques on the way back.

What do you say, Philip? We need your strong back. You know
what a good friend Sylvia's been to you—as she's been to all of
us."

"Well, let me think about it." Already, Philip could feel a
wedge of apprehension in the center of his breastbone.

"All right, you think about it all you want, but show up at
eight o'clock. There'll be eight or ten of us, I hope, and it
shouldn't take too long. I must hurry off." She gave him a peck
on each cheek. "The wine is paid for—please stay and finish it."

Philip was not a member of Sylvia's inner circle, the entrenched expatriate writers who drifted into her little shop,
Shakespeare & Company, at 12 Rue de l'Odéon, and treated it
like a literary club. They would thumb through books and sit
around for endless hours discussing literary matters or reading
from works in progress. Gide, Joyce, Jean Schlumberger, Valéry
and Gargue, the poets, the novelists Larbaud and Jules Ro-
mains, Sherwood Anderson, Gertrude Stein with Alice B.
Toklas, Ezra Pound. Hemingway was an habitué, and a couple of
times he had brought Philip along, but Philip always felt like an
awkward outsider. He liked Sylvia, a gentle, soft-spoken proper
woman whose father was a Presbyterian minister in Princeton,
New Jersey, at whose church Woodrow Wilson had worshiped.
Without credentials as a writer, however, Philip had only a loose
relationship with Sylvia, although he did visit Shakespeare &
Company regularly to take out her English books; not only was it
the only book rental shop in Paris, but it had the best stock of
English books, especially recent ones.

Sitting there alone on the banquette on the Café de la Paix
terrace, Philip experienced a distinct rise of resentment toward
Janet. He watched the street lamps blink awake on the boulevard
and thought, What right has she to involve me like this? Either I
cooperate in this ill-advised, risky, dangerous undertaking or I'll
never be able to show my face at Shakespeare & Company again.
And if I don't cooperate—well, how easily the word "coward"
can be passed around until it reaches the ears of people I care
about. He could imagine Hemingway's reaction. The thought
made him shudder.

His mind wandered back to an evening when he had sat with
Janet and Hemingway at a quiet rear table at the Deux Magots in
Saint-Germain-des-Prés, which was one of Hemingway's favorite
late-night hangouts. The evening had started by Ernest reading,
in an overenunciated whisper, a poem he had just written. There
was a line in the poem that led Ernest to talk about his father and

how he had put a gun to his head and killed himself. That prompted Janet to tell about her father's suicide.

"It's easier for me to understand what my father did," she told him, "because I don't believe in God as you do. As an agnostic, I see suicide as an act of freedom. I can accept it both in my mind and in my conscience as an act of liberation from whatever humiliating bondage on earth could no longer be borne with self-respect."

"Well, my father's humiliating bondage," Hemingway said, "was my mother, that bitch, and I guess you could say that that bullet in his temple restored his self-respect . . . but it didn't do much for me."

"There's a theory that it's hereditary, you know."

"What? The tendency to self-destruct? Like father, like son?"

"It's just a theory, and we know what that's worth. But let's make a pact, if suicide-prone we are: if either of us ever kills himself, or herself, the other won't grieve but will remember that liberty can be as important in the act of dying as in the act of living."

"I'll drink to that."

They clinked glasses, and Hemingway then turned a hard look on Philip. "What about it, kid, you going to raise your glass? Someday you may want to become a member of our firm."

An awareness reached Philip, working its way through his reverie, that there was some unusual activity to his left. Two men dressed in civilian clothes were standing at the table next to his, inspecting the papers of the couple who were seated there. Philip now realized that elsewhere on the terrace there were pairs of interrogators going from table to table, inspecting papers. A cold band of fear circled Philip's chest. He touched the outside of his jacket to be sure that his passport and papers were in the leather wallet in his inner pocket. The interrogators at the next table were asking questions, but they spoke in low voices and Philip could not make out what they were asking. He did not look directly at them, but out of the corner of his eye he saw them return the papers they had been inspecting and begin to move toward him. The band circling his chest tightened.

The men stood before him now, and he looked up at them. The taller man held up an identification card which he quickly pocketed. "We are Geheime Staatspolizei," he said. "Whom do you wait for?" He spoke in German-accented French. Philip knew that the contraction for Geheime Staatspolizei was Gestapo.

"No one," he said in English in a constricted voice.

"Do you have papers?" the Gestapo agent asked, switching to English. Philip took his wallet from his inner jacket pocket and handed it to his questioner. Inside the wallet were his United States passport and identification papers issued by the French authorities. The tall man took each item out of the wallet and inspected it carefully. Although, as far as Philip knew, all his papers were in order, he nevertheless had a terrified premonition that something was wrong and he would be arrested. If only he already had the *laissez-passer* signed by Goering.

"Do you know a man who calls himself Pierre Gravet?" the Gestapo agent asked, his eyes still scrutinizing Philip's passport.

"No, sir," Philip answered. Then he said, immaterially, "I live right down there at the Ritz."

"How long have you been sitting here?"

"About half an hour."

"Do you recognize this man?" The agent showed Philip a small glossy photograph of a man's face. Philip was shocked to see that it was a waiter who worked at the Café Flore. The risk in lying dried his throat.

"No," he said, returning the photo.

There was a screech of chair legs as a man darted from the terrace toward the boulevard, but as he reached the sidewalk he was nabbed by three men who had been standing at the curb. They thrust his arms behind him and roughly hurried him into a waiting automobile. Philip did not get a good look at the man's face, but it could have been Richard, the waiter they were referring to as Pierre Gravet.

Philip's interrogators left abruptly, joining the men already in the automobile, which pulled away as soon as they closed the door.

Philip watched them go as one might watch a poised adder that abruptly breaks off its imminent attack. He got to his feet unsteadily and walked back to the Ritz as fast as he could.

Reichsmarschall Hermann Goering's huge white body lay naked and motionless on his bed. Several bath towels had been arranged under him to absorb the sweat running off the fat slopes of his body. A towel that covered his forehead partially deterred the pouring sweat from his eyes, which were open but unblinking. The pupils were severely constricted. During the course of the day he had consumed much more than his usual quota of pills, and he was suffering the consequences of having taken more morphine than his body was accustomed to. Every morning Kropp filled the crystal bowl with one hundred tablets, which was the daily quota, but on this day the stress had been such that the tablets were all gone by late afternoon, and Goering had indiscriminately filled his pocket from the large tin canister that was kept under lock in one of the closets.

It did not matter about the pupils of his eyes being con-stricted—that would affect only his ability to see in darkened places, and he had no plans to leave his bed. He had already taken the strong laxative which Kropp gave him every day to counteract the constipation caused by the morphine. It was the sweat which he hated and about which he could do nothing. It washed away the body lotion, powders and perfume from his pores and gave him a disagreeably musty smell. During these sweat spells, it was Kropp's custom to allay the odor by spraying him with cologne from a rubber-bulbed atomizer, but Goering had been annoyed by Kropp's presence and had ordered him out of the room. Now he wished he were there to change the towels and dab his body with cold compresses.

He despised sweating like this; the rivulets meandering down the inclines of his stomach defiled the sanctity of his flesh. Running into his eyes, his mouth, his scrotum, wet narrow fingers curving around his neck and armpits, itchy streams on his scalp beneath his thick, drenched hair, even between his toes. God, how he hated to sweat! His testicles itched from the converging, dripping sweat, but he was too inert to move his hand to scratch the annoyance.

During the course of a normal day, even when he had not overdosed, he sweated profusely, and when he could he changed his clothes, especially his underclothes and socks, three or four times a day. Kropp always carried a supply of fresh silk underwear and silk socks, even when they were in combat zones. Goering disliked taking off his sweat-soaked underclothing, so Kropp had to undress and dress him. His skin was not like the skin of other men, he believed. It had a translucent quality, he felt, an opaque mother-of-pearl sheen that was exotic to the touch. One paid the price for such a phenomenon, and Goering's price, he believed, was his ultrasensitivity to sweat.

It was time, Goering admitted to himself with a heavy sigh, to summon Professor Hubert Kahle from his sanitarium in Co-logne. Goering resented morphine getting the better of him, as it did two or three times a year, but when it did he never hesitated to call for Professor Kahle. Goering needed the drug, as he had for the past eighteen years, to function, and when he took it in the moderation he had set for himself neither the public nor the Führer nor his enemies were aware of it, but when overdosed he ran the danger of giving himself away. Whenever asked about the little white pills, he simply explained that they were appetite suppressants.

The room was in semidarkness. Beside his bed, arranged on a table top, was a small portable shrine that was flanked by lighted candles. The centerpiece of the shrine, which was in twenty-four-karat gold, was a small oil portrait of a smiling woman, above which were angels hovering over a beatific Jesus with his hands outstretched in blessing. The woman was Goering's first wife, Karin, who had died ten years before, but who still lived in Goering's mind, and his heart, as if she had never died. Seven years after her death, to combat loneliness more than anything else, he had remarried, this time an actress named Emmy Sonnemann, but on the day of the wedding, after a lavish feast at the Kaiserhof attended by Hitler and other notables, the first thing Goering did on returning to Karinhall with the wedding party was to excuse himself and spend an hour in solitude beside Karin's coffin in the ornate mausoleum.

Now in his sweated anguish he felt Karin's presence in the bed beside him. He felt her cool hand on his fevered forehead, comforting him, as she had comforted him countless times in the past. He could feel her body beside him. He closed his eyes and tried to pull his thoughts away from her.

He thought about the day, the worthless infuriating day. First, the visit from Professor Chavelle of the Louvre, who came with two assistants and a machine with which they examined the Rembrandt. The young American had been proven correct—the canvas had not been painted by Rembrandt. Professor Chavelle thought that perhaps it was the work of the brilliant Dutch counterfeiter Hans van Meegeren.

"Could the fake have been in the Rothschild collection?" Goering had asked the professor.

"No, Your Excellency, that canvas had originally been inspected by the Louvre and certified. Someone has switched the paintings on you."

How Goebbels would gloat when the news reached him that he hadn't lost out on the real Rembrandt after all, and thinking of this made Goering groan aloud. He had confronted Baron von Behr and Dr. Lohse, singly and then together, but neither had displayed any sign of complicity. He had always been suspicious of von Behr, but that was an emotional suspicion not really founded on fact, nor even on circumstantial evidence. Yet surely there had been complicity on someone's part. In Goering's mind, every member of his Paris art staff had now become suspect. He worried that among the scores of treasures he had had transported to Karinhall there might be other forgeries. If only there was one person in the art enclave he could completely trust.

And then he had received the report on the most recent night run over England. There was a bomber's moon and he had sent the Luftwaffe in a force of a thousand planes to hit Coventry, but despite the fact that the target was left in ruins he had lost far more Messerschmitts than projected. And even more disturbing was the report that many Messerschmitt pilots resented having to carry bombs and had aimlessly dumped their load as soon as they crossed the Channel. Discipline would have to be tightened. He would immediately instigate court-martials with exaggerated sentences.

He felt nauseated but at the same time ravenous. The craving for food dominated everything else. He reached his hand to his bedside table and pressed the button for Kropp. He resolved to try to overcome his condition by himself and not summon Professor Kahle. At least, not yet. He would walk more, play some tennis, send for that masseur, Müller, who used to come to Karinhall to give him those deep massages. Where the hell was Kropp?

There was a discreet rap on the door, followed by Kropp's entrance. He carried a silver tray on which were sandwiches of cheese and sausage, beer in a capped stein, and a slice of cream-filled Napoleon covered with icing and whipped cream. So ravenous was Goering that he began to gorge himself on the sausages even while Kropp was in the process of struggling to raise him up.

On his way back to the Ritz after his disquieting encounter with Janet Flanner in the Café de la Paix, Philip decided to discuss the matter with Gabrielle Chanel. She always had a good, solid, levelheaded reaction to situations like the one in which Philip now found himself.

At first there was no response when he knocked on Gabrielle's door; in fact, he had started to walk away when he heard the door chain rattle. He turned back as the door opened and Gabrielle, wearing a silk Chinese robe, looked out.

"Oh, it's you, Philip!" Her voice had a strained heartiness

which Philip picked up on immediately. He also picked up on the cigar aroma emanating from the room.

"I'm sorry, Gabrielle, I just had something to discuss . . ." He was ill at ease, and felt badly that he had come to her door without warning, but in the past they had often visited each other in this impromptu manner. Through the open door he caught a glimpse of a man in a dressing gown; it was unmistakably Baron von Spatz.

"I'll phone you later when you're not busy." Philip was already halfway down the corridor, his words retreating quickly.

"Wait, Philip, I want to talk to you . . ."

But he was gone.

12

There was no love lost between Dr. Bruno Lohse and Baron Kurt von Behr. Although von Behr was the titular chief of the E.R.R., Lohse was in many ways directly responsible to Goering, who had deliberately clouded the area of von Behr's authority. Goering knew that this would create a rivalry between them, and that that rivalry would create a certain check and balance on what disposition was being made of the flood of art that was gushing into the Jeu de Paume every day. Lohse and von Behr each knew that with one substantiated revelation of double-dealing he could eliminate the other; two fencers, parrying and thrusting, waiting for the proper moment for the kill.

After Goering had confronted them with the fiasco of losing Rubens' *Diana at the Bath,* von Behr had gone all out to pin the switching of the consignment labels on Lohse, but he was not able to collect the hard evidence that he knew Goering would demand. Part of the difficulty for von Behr lay in the fact that Lohse had Fräulein Gisela Linberger by the tail. As manager of Goering's personal art office on the Quai d'Orsay, she had access to records and inventory sheets that would have been very useful to von Behr, but she kept him at arm's length. On several occasions the Baron had tried to dazzle her with his handsome charm, hoping to lure her into his bed and break Lohse's hold on her, but she never fell for it. That in itself further fueled von Behr's resentment toward Lohse. What von Behr didn't know was that his English wife, Lucille, also found Dr. Lohse most attractive, and that when they danced together at the last reception there had been close and exciting contact between their groins. But von Behr had no fear that Lucille would ever have an affair; despite his own dalliances, he knew that the strict surveillance he kept on his wife would insure her faithfulness.

Now the matter of the fake Rembrandt had intensified von Behr's desire to get Lohse. Von Behr had never seen Goering in an uglier mood than he was when he confronted the two of them.

And the brunt of Goering's anger seemed, to von Behr, to be directed at him.

"How do I know there aren't other forgeries among the paintings which were sent to Karinhall?" Goering had shouted. "You are the expert. Whom am I to rely on? I warn both of you, the next time I am given a fake I will have your heads—both of you! Is that clear? You have any questions? The Reichsmarschall of Germany is not to be made a laughingstock. Understand?"

Von Behr's animosity toward Lohse now reached the point where he urged Ilse Pütz to try to seduce Lohse in order to get the goods on him. Von Behr broached the subject after one of their masked sessions; they were recuperating before returning to the office.

"You mean you want me to go to bed with Dr. Lohse?"

"You don't have to actually fuck with him. Just work on him a little, arouse him, then when you get him to the state where men will promise anything, pump the information out of him. It's worth a try."

"I'm not a whore. I use my body for pleasure and that's all."

She got up and started to dress.

"Ilse, don't be upset. I only meant—"

"I'm not a whore!" She was getting angry. "I have a master's degree in art history. I am more than a hot piece of flesh."

Philip got off at his floor, but he was too upset to go into his room. In all the years he had known Gabrielle, she had never been involved with a man. She had many male friends who adored her and smothered her with presents and affectionate words and kisses, but they were either homosexuals or men who had been decorated with the Legion of Honor. Now that she was a rather old woman of fifty-six, it was simply unbecoming to get involved with a man who looked to be about forty. And a Nazi officer at that. Whether she was in it for passion or for what she could get out of it, either way it was disgusting.

And it suddenly occurred to him that because of this traumatic interlude he had come to no decision about Sylvia Beach. The door to Charley's room was open, and the sound of the trains indicated they were going full tilt. It was difficult to get Charley's attention when he was operating his trains, but Philip thought that it might help him come to a decision by simply hearing himself explain his dilemma to someone else.

Two trains, one a twelve-car passenger train that was a replica of the Orient Express, the other a thirteen-car freight, were running on three levels. There were tunnels and signal lights, automated railroad crossings with gates and warning lights, station stops, viaducts over lakes, factory sidings, light towers, and freight depots where cargo could be loaded and unloaded from the boxcars automatically. There were even miniature waiters in the dining car in the act of serving meals to seated passengers.

Charley Ritz was sitting in an easy chair beside the control panel, eating spaghetti and drinking beer. Despite his grim mood, Philip burst out laughing.

"Hallo, Philip," Charley said in his clipped Oxford English, "why the laughter?"

"Charles Ritz, scion of the House of Ritz, dishes invented by Escoffier at his beck and call, lovely ladies anxious for his company, but here he sits with a plate of spaghetti, a glass of beer and his trains for a dinner companion."

"I like their conversation better than any woman's I know. Clickety-clack, clickety-clack, whoo-woo, clickety-clack, clack, clack . . ."

"Better than Rosemarie's?"

"Ah, that's something else. But this is not my scheduled day at 122, and, besides, it's not the same now that they've taken away the evenings, you agree?"

"Absolutely."

"It's more like a whorehouse when you go in the afternoon."

The freight locomotive caught a wheel on the switching track, and several cars ran off the track before Charley could shut off power at the transformer.

"Bloody damn hell," he said, matter-of-factly. "By the way, I hear that Hermann Goering has a model railway setup that makes mine look sick. Four times the track I have, all the locomotives and cars are handmade, and he even has miniature bombers that circle overhead and drop bombs on the trains."

While Charley reassembled the tangled freight cars, Philip explained his dilemma about helping Sylvia Beach remove all the books from her shop.

"That kind of thing, Philip, is for those who say yes without second thoughts. My rule is, whatever the problem, if you waiver, hesitate, or question, then don't. That's been my yardstick for getting married. And that's why, to my eternal delight, I am still single."

When Philip returned to his room, Coco Chanel was sitting on his bed waiting for him. Philip went over to her as she stretched up her arms, and they held each other tightly while she wept.

"I'm sorry, Gabrielle, really I am, I didn't mean to . . . it's just, you know, so many things happening . . ."

She pulled him down beside her and dried her tears with the handkerchief he offered her. "It's strange, Philip, all the many things we've talked about but never really about affairs of the heart. You see, I had one big love in my life, quite long ago, actually two, I suppose—anyway, both times I came out of it so . . . injured I decided it was better to exist with one's work and good friends and eliminate lovers. There had been a time, when I first came to Paris and didn't yet know who I was or what I wanted, and . . . well, my blood ran very fast and I had several gentlemen friends, and that's when I first lived at the Ritz, but not on my own. I mean, quite honestly, I was a *cocotte,* although certainly of the highest order, but I finally realized that a *cocotte* was a *cocotte* whether she luxuriated at the Ritz or worked a Pigalle sidewalk, and that's when I induced my 'sponsor' to open a little millinery shop for me.

"My hats rescued me. Right away I acquired a clientele of enthusiastic ladies, and from that moment on I've paid my own rent. But my experience with love was not as successful as my venture into the world of fashion. The first man I truly loved, oh, how I adored him!—an Englishman named Boy Capel, but he was killed in a car accident on the Côte d'Azur. For a long while my emotional life was in limbo." She sat motionless for a while, staring at the carpet, thinking of Boy Capel.

"I refused to accept that the man I loved was dead," she continued. "All I was interested in was the occult, because I believed that he was not gone forever and that I could establish contact with him. I often thought, If only I could have had a child with him . . . I tried—I think he would have married me—but, alas, it didn't happen." She got up now and moved to the window and looked out.

"Years passed, and I had a gay, wonderful existence, all the wild parties of the Twenties . . . and then it happened, when I least expected it. One evening at the Hôtel de Paris in Monte Carlo I was introduced to the Duke of Westminster. It was the beginning of the only real love-life I've ever known. Until then, a man was just . . . well . . . someone to romp with. But the Duke was someone I could lean on, depend on. I was his little girl even though I was forty-five when we met.

"But in some ways it was difficult. He was without doubt the richest man in Great Britain. He owned hundreds and hundreds of buildings in the section of London that bears his name. He was related to the royal family. Oh, what a lovely man he was! His wealth was immaterial to me. At first I was overwhelmed by all the gloss and glitter, but soon I was as unaware of the riches as he was. We were inseparable. We lived together for three years." She turned from the window and sat on the edge of the bed.

"You're probably wondering what he saw in me, when he could have had his pick of royal, wealthy young beauties. Well, I was probably the first attractive woman he had met who had amounted to something on her own. Whatever the reason, he adored me. When I had to be in Paris to tend my business, he sent me love letters and gifts every day, but, not trusting the mails, he set up a courier system so that one of his messengers arrived at my portal every morning. By then there was no doubt in my mind we would be married as soon as the Duke's divorce became final. The papers were full of speculation. I was prepared to close down my Paris business and devote myself full time to being the Duchess of Westminster. But I knew that for the Duke marriage was not as important as having a son, an heir to his title. His first marriage had not produced one, and I knew he would be concerned whether in my late forties I could bear a child.

"I became obsessed with getting pregnant. We never mentioned it, of course, but it was an obvious prerequisite to our getting married. I tried, God knows I tried. I went to all kinds of doctors and midwives, anyone I thought could help. Down deep I knew my failure to conceive would be a fatal barrier between us. But . . . well, I was nevertheless unprepared for what actually happened." She turned her head away and paused so long that Philip thought that perhaps she would not continue.

"One day I was in my shop," she finally resumed, "when in walked the Duke with a lovely young woman. He introduced her to me—the Honorable Loelia Ponsonby, daughter of Lord Sisonby. Introduced her as his fiancée. My knees trembled and I could feel my blood draining from my forehead. But I screwed up my backbone."

"'She admires your clothes so much,' the Duke said, 'and would like to become a regular customer. I'm sure you two will get along fine.'

"And that is how it ended—my lovely dream." By now, Gabrielle was sitting on the bed with her back against the wall.

"Now, suddenly, after all those years, I seem to want a man in my life, and Baron von Spatz is good company. I no longer have a business to look after, life is so uncertain, I don't want to be alone just now. He is gentle and considerate. But it must not change anything between us, Philip. You are dear to me. Please accept von Spatz—*please*. I know you have an understanding heart, and I appeal to it now."

"It's all right, Gabrielle. I just wasn't . . . prepared. I don't seem to be prepared for anything that's happening these days."

Gabrielle got up and went over to him. She knelt before him and took one of his hands in hers and held it against her. "Dear, dear Philip. I have sometimes thought that . . . well—I am self-conscious about saying it—you are the son I never had." She kissed his hand lightly, then quickly got to her feet. "Okay, end of Mademoiselle Chanel's tearful saga of her lost loves and ruptured dreams. Did you know that Goering wants to go to the Racing with us tomorrow and play tennis?"

"No!"

"His aide phoned this afternoon. He said to remind you that the Reichsmarschall does not like to have to move to reach the ball."

They laughed as Philip accompanied her to the door. She hesitated, not wanting to leave Philip without making sure that he understood her relationship with von Spatz.

"I just felt the need to have a man in my bed," she said. "To wake up to maleness. All of my life, it seems, except for the interlude with the Duke, I have awakened to the romance of my profession, you might say. But that's over for now. And my mornings are empty—stripped of expectation. So I'm trying to adjust—but I don't want to lose you in the process."

"Lose me? Why, you are my family, Gabrielle, my entire family! You are mother, sister, aunt and the skeleton in my closet. As a matter of fact, beginning tomorrow, I will call myself Philip Chanel, bastard son of the Queen of Haute Couture."

13

Hermann Goering wore the most elegant tennis costume the Racing Club had ever seen, and it had seen quite a few in the hundred years of its existence. It was situated in the heart of the Bois de Boulogne, on the Route of the Lakes, a lob away from the Longchamp Racecourse. It was an austere club, originally founded to espouse bicycle racing, but long since diverted to tennis and snobbish social events for its exclusive membership. For winter play, there were several indoor courts with huge skylights, the surface traditional *en tous cas,* red brick dust packed to a hard consistency.

Goering appeared punctually in a white silk long-sleeved shirt, impeccable white flannels, and a white shantung jacket with his coat of arms in gold—a mailed fist gripping a bludgeon—on its pocket. In the throat of his shirt he wore a white silk foulard with a stickpin in the design of a diamond-encrusted tennis racquet.

To Philip's surprise, Goering had very good strokes, both forehand and backhand, and he could imagine that when the Reichsmarschall was younger and trimmer he was a formidable player. As he had been instructed, Philip hit the ball with precision within a few feet of where Goering had planted himself on the baseline at the center of the court. Despite his two hundred eighty pounds, Goering was light and graceful in his movements. There were two ball boys on his side of the court who ran down errant balls and handed them to him when he indicated his readiness to receive them. Even around the Racing Club, new tennis balls had become as scarce as steak, but Goering's aide had broken out a dozen new Slazengers for the occasion.

In the midst of their rally, a member of the club named de Forrestière, who was an executive with the Citroën automobile company, asked Philip whether he and his guest would like to play a set of doubles. Philip declined, saying they were just going to hit a few, but to his amazement, after he had translated the request for Goering, Goering readily accepted. De Forrestière was a fairly good player, as was his partner, Lapautre, and Philip was puzzled by Goering's acceptance of the challenge. He had been informed that the Reichsmarschall couldn't abide losing, but Goering's disinclination to move from a fixed position made winning against this able, experienced team a virtual impossibility.

Coco, who had been watching them volley, called Philip over and had a whispered conference with him. "Pretend you're playing mixed doubles with me," she advised. "The Reichsmarschall won't appreciate losing in front of these spectators. Who is this cheeky fellow, de Forrestière?"

"He's with Citroën. He's here most every day."

"Well, all I can say is, you better play it as if it were mixed doubles with your grandmother as your partner."

And that's what Philip did, with surprisingly good results. Goering defended his terrain effectively, and Philip covered the rest of the court with determination and agility. Under the pressure of the situation, Philip raised his game, hitting out, scrambling, taking risks on his serve and overhead, backing up Goering to reach balls that had eluded his stationary reach. Philip's tactics confused his opponents, who were used to a more traditional game.

Goering was elated with their 7–5 victory, and he invited everyone into the clubhouse for champagne. Although he had not moved more than three feet in any direction, he was covered with perspiration, but he nevertheless put on his shantung jacket before going into the bar.

With the first glass of champagne, he lifted a toast to Philip. "To your marvelous tennis, Herr Weber, and our victory! Ach, that's very good. Cliquot is a favorite of mine. That was the first exercise I've had in months. We must play more often. It makes the body feel so good. Now I can have a good dinner tonight without feeling guilty. Perhaps you and Mademoiselle Chanel would join me at Maxim's. Are you free, Mademoiselle Chanel? I promise you an exquisite dinner."

"Oh, I would very much like to," Gabrielle said in response to Philip's translation, a note of reluctance in her voice, "but I'm not sure . . ."

"I shall also invite Baron von Spatz to round out the table." He smiled at her and she looked down at her glass in embarrassment. The Reichsmarschall obviously was on top of everything going on around him.

De Forrestière came over to Philip. "Do you and Goering play very often?"

"No, this was the first time."

"But you see him at the Ritz, I suppose?"

"Occasionally."

"You play very well together."

"Thanks, but I wouldn't like to have to face a match like that every day."

"He certainly seems to like you. I would think he doesn't invite many foreigners to sit at his table at Maxim's."

"Well, he's happy about the tennis."

"Maybe we could play another time—I mean singles, just you and me."

"Why, of course."

"How about Thursday, same time as today?"

"All right."

"I'll furnish the balls. I look forward to hearing about your dinner at Maxim's."

Maxim's was the German High Command's favorite restaurant, in fact its personal kitchen. Maxim's owner exerted every effort to please the Nazis, and they, in turn, stocked the Maxim kitchen with delicacies not encountered in other Paris restaurants: caviar, venison, truffles, pheasant, fresh foie gras, Belon oysters, *langoustines,* fresh brook trout. The Germans were not very adventurous about their dining, however, and their favorite dishes continued to be schnitzels, braten, either sauer or hasen, steak, hasenpfeffer, suckling pig, and similar familiar entrees from their domestic menus.

When he dined away from the Ritz, Goering ate only at Maxim's, at a table in one of the alcoves or, on occasion, in one of the small private dining rooms. Upon being seated, he was brought Dom Perignon champagne without having to order it, and slices of fresh Strasbourg foie gras on a bed of its gelatin, but without truffles, which he disliked. Tonight he was in excellent spirits and spoke mostly about his adventures in hunting wild game. In that connection, he made numerous references to his first wife, Karin, who had often gone on shoots with him, but his current wife's name did not once enter his conversation.

The meal was capped by his favorite crêpes, concocted at tableside with apricots and apricot liqueur, and topped with whipped cream. Montecristo cigars and Maxim's choicest cognac, marked "*Âge inconnu,*" completed the meal. Baron von

Spatz drank a great deal of champagne, ate sparingly, spoke not at all, but paid rapt attention to Goering's every word.

At the end of the evening, as they were returning to the Ritz in Goering's limousine, the Reichsmarschall asked Philip whether he could impose upon him for a second time in one day. "The first imposition was the tennis, and now I wonder if you would translate Lindbergh's speech for me. I understand you knew him quite well, and I would like to know precisely what he will be saying in New York City tonight. We will receive it here on the short wave, but because of the time difference it will be one o'clock in the morning, our time."

"That's perfectly all right," Philip said. "I'm a night person. And besides, I believe in Colonel Lindbergh's philosophy and would be very interested to hear what he's got to say."

"Splendid! We can have a few drinks and chat until it's time for the speech."

Two signal-corps officers were manipulating the controls of a massive short-wave radio that had been set up in Goering's salon. Philip noticed that the Rembrandt was gone from the wall and that in its place was a painting of a little girl at play by Chardin, which Philip recognized as having belonged to the collection of Baroness Alexandrine de Rothschild.

"You were quite right about the Rembrandt," Goering said, noting Philip's appraisal of the Chardin painting. "Professor Chavell confirmed your observation."

"I love this Chardin," Philip said. "Doesn't it . . . didn't it belong to the Rothschilds?"

"Did you know the Rothschilds? It's all right—Jewishness doesn't rub off, it isn't catching. Well, as you probably know, the Jews here had a stranglehold on objects of art, as they did on banking and commerce. One of our missions has been to liberate these Jewish collections for the benefit of the French people. Of course Jews have no property rights, so those of us who appreciate fine art have had to take custody of these liberated paintings."

Only with great effort did Philip overcome the inhibition he felt at speaking his mind to Goering. "Herr Goering, I hope you don't mind," he began tentatively, "but I happen not to agree with you about the Jews here. No one has a stranglehold on the genius of spotting great art before it becomes great, when it is nothing but another canvas by an unknown artist. The Roths-

childs weren't only rich, they were people of remarkably good
artistic judgment. There are many richer Frenchmen who inves-
ted great sums of money, but they did not achieve collections
that came anywhere near what the Rothschilds did. I know two
American Jews who lived here, Leo and Gertrude Stein, brother
and sister, who are not what you would call rich, but they have a
genius for picking the great artists of our time—"

"You mean the decadent nonsense of Picasso and Matisse and
those other fellows?"

"I know that they don't rate very highly with the Third
Reich . . ."

"The Führer has banned them."

"But you know their names, don't you, such is their fame, and
they were discovered and sponsored by two American Jews."

"Well, I grant you that the Rothschilds had a good eye."

"A genius, Your Excellency."

"Even that. I don't underestimate the artistic eye. For
example, I was very impressed with your discovery that my
Rembrandt was a forgery."

Kropp uncorked a new bottle of champagne and filled their
glasses. "I have been thinking of means to safeguard myself
against fake pictures in the future. Obviously, someone on my
staff either perpetrated this crime or was aware of it. I have many
good art people working for me, but I need someone to keep a
watch on things. It occurred to me that if you would do that, you
would be the perfect person. I could say that I had commissioned
you to write a book on the Hermann Goering Collection of Fine
Art. That would give you a good, believable cover for asking
questions and poking your nose into everything. What do you
say? I would naturally pay you an adequate amount for your
endeavors."

Kropp offered Havana cigars, which Philip declined, and
placed the inevitable crystal bowl at Goering's elbow.

"Well," Philip said, "may I think it over for a day or two?"

"Of course, of course—take your time." Goering opened a
drawer in the little table beside his chair and took out a file
folder. "Everything I read in this report on you indicates that
you would be ideal for the job. Especially your background in
art."

"You have a dossier on me?"

"I have a dossier on everyone I come in contact with."

"On Mademoiselle Chanel?"

"Naturally. She is some woman—quite a life she's had. I admire her enormously. We do not have women of such accomplishment in Germany."

"She is my best friend."

Goering was looking at a sheet of paper in the file. "What about a painter named Man Ray? Is that really his name?"

"He is also a good friend."

"An opera singer named Helga Friebe?"

"You know about her! How did you . . . ? But I don't see her anymore—she disappeared."

Goering laughed.

"Is she in Germany?" Philip asked.

"I wouldn't know. But I can locate her if it's important."

"No, no—just curiosity."

"Ah, but that is something I find very dangerous with women—curiosity. It is the bait with which they spring their little traps. Now I see here that you also know Ernest Hemingway. That right?"

"Yes."

"I admire him very much. As a man—the bullfighting, soldiering, boxing—and as a writer."

"He was with the Lincoln Brigade in the Spanish Civil War, you know."

"Yes, I even admire him for that, despite the fact that he was on the wrong side. But as a writer, ah, what power he has! The book about the war in Italy, where the nurse who was the lover died at the end in childbirth. And especially the book about Paris—the young Americans and Britishers in the Twenties . . ."

"The Sun Also Rises."

Goering looked puzzled. "No . . ."

"In Europe it was called *Fiesta!*"

"Yes, yes, what a fine book! Tell me something: the hero, whatever he was called, he had lost only his balls in the war, or his whole business? The book doesn't make it clear."

"His penis, I think."

"Hemingway is anti-Semitic, isn't he?"

"What makes you think so?"

"Well, the Jew, Robert Cohn—the way Hemingway portrays him, certainly he makes him out to be a despicable character."

"I'd say more pathetic than despicable."

"Is Hemingway anti-Semitic when he mentions Jews to you in conversation?"

"I'd say demi-Semitic."

"How do you mean?"

"In Ernest's estimation there are good Jews and kikes, nothing in between."

American voices came into focus on the short wave. The sound of the cheering crowd in New York filled the room. A speaker was introducing Charles Lindbergh. Goering and Philip moved closer to the radio as Lindbergh began his speech, Philip translating.

His words were obviously pleasing to the Deputy Führer. Philip cringed as Lindbergh insisted not only that America had no business in the war, but also that England had brought the conflict upon herself.

Philip looked at Goering, who was staring fixedly at the radio, a great wide-eyed smile of satisfaction on his face. Lindbergh was throwing England to the lions, and, from the look on his face, Goering was already anticipating the feast. It is one thing, Philip thought, to warn us about the German war machine, but why push poor England down in the mud?

Philip left Goering's suite with the cheers of his fellow Americans for Lindbergh's pro-Nazi speech ringing in his ears, cheers that disturbed him. Americans shouldn't have cheered like that. He felt rather ashamed of them, fat-cat Americans untouched by the rain of bombs falling on the Britishers; somebody should be cheering for the underdogs.

14

The following morning, with his lawyer's office on the Champs-Élysées as his destination, Philip went far out of his way in order to pass by Sylvia Beach's bookstore on the Rue de l'Odéon. As he pedaled away from the Cambon entrance of the Ritz, a black-bearded man in a black turtleneck sweater and black beret, who had been sitting on his bicycle at the curb, followed him.

Philip bicycled through the Jardin des Tuileries, avoiding the entrance where the massacre had occurred, and then across the Pont-Royal to the Boulevard Saint-Germain, but as he turned onto the Rue de l'Odéon he had such strong feelings of guilt for not having appeared for the book moving that he braked his bike and considered turning back. His curiosity was too great, however, and he eventually hunched down over his handlebars to make himself as inconspicuous as possible, and bicycled past Shakespeare & Company.

It had miraculously disappeared, and in its place was a well-stocked antique shop with the legend "S. BEACH, ANTIQUES" above its door. As his bike went by, Philip could see Sylvia inside the shop, standing near the door, talking to someone. Not a book was to be seen. Obviously there had been no trouble and he could have helped move the books without suffering adverse consequences. But the risk had been there, he reminded himself, to assuage his hindsight guilt.

He bicycled back to the Place de la Concorde, the cyclist in the black sweater following at a discreet distance. Philip turned onto the Champs-Élysées and began the gradual but punishing ascent toward the Arc de Triomphe. At the Rond-Point, however, police barriers stopped him, and his breath caught at the prospect of this being a random search and interrogation; he was relieved to discover that it was simply the changing of the Nazi guard which formed every day at the Rond-Point at noon and marched up the Champs-Élysées to the Étoile to the music of a military band.

While he waited for the stroke of twelve, Philip wheeled his bike over to the public bulletin board which the *Kommandantur* had erected on the side of the building which had formerly housed *Le Figaro*. While Philip read the notices posted there, the man in the black sweater, sitting on his bike seat, smoking a cigarette, watched him from the opposite side of the Champs-Élysées.

On the bulletin board were posters to induce unemployed Parisian workers, whose numbers were steadily mounting, to join the work force in Germany ("Give Your Work to Save Europe from Bolshevism"); yellow posters with black borders containing the names of persons executed as spies; a notice establishing the hours of curfew; another notice forbidding food trucks and civilian automobiles on the streets; a poster extolling Nazi war victories.

There were other notices about the issuance of ration cards (four hundred grams of bread for those with worker cards, two hundred grams for all others), a notice that Jews had to wear a yellow Star of David on their chest with the word *Juif* in its center, and a notice that listed the places that were off limits for Jews: restaurants, cafés, movie houses and theaters, concert halls, public telephone booths, swimming pools, museums and libraries.

At the end of the bulletin board, a notice bordered in red caught Philip's eye:

CAT EATERS, ATTENTION!
In these times of restrictions, certain hungry persons haven't hesitated to capture cats to make a nice "rabbit" stew. These persons don't know the danger that threatens them. Cats, having as their useful mission the killing and eating of rats, which are carriers of the most dangerous bacilli, can be for this reason particularly harmful.

As he read the announcement, Philip could feel his stomach constricting. How many filets of cat had he unsuspectingly eaten, he wondered, in the guise of a rabbit casserole?

At twelve sharp, the air-raid sirens went off for their daily testing, and the German marching band cranked up with a garish flourish of drums and trumpets; then up the Champs-Élysées they moved, with the drum major goose-stepping in his polished boots. Philip began slowly to wheel his bike in their wake, keeping to the sidewalk in order to look in the shop windows along the way. Across the Champs-Élysées, the man in the black sweater kept pace with him. Philip looked up the broad avenue, to its summit at the Étoile, and he was struck by how the color of the green uniforms of the Germans, and their green vehicles, dominated everything: the cafés, the sidewalks, the queues in front of the cinemas, which predominantly played German films, the shops—all German green.

Philip stopped at the window of his favorite charcuterie, where, in place of the delectables he was used to admiring, there were now just the drab offerings permitted by the authorities—tray upon tray of beets done in a dozen different ways; a variety of rabbit dishes, from salads to roast sections; a few trays of soybeans, vinaigrette and in mustard sauce; and a large tray of small fish that looked to be all bones. He shook his head sadly and saw in place of the dismal food in the window the succulent offerings of his memory: salmon in aspic, glazed breast of chicken, eggs in their oval *gelées,* an infinite variety of herring from rollmops to Bismarck, roasted quails and guinea hens, and *langouste* with fresh mayonnaise.

Philip suddenly experienced a keen yearning for an *oeuf en gelée;* he could feel the first touch of the cold aspic on his tongue, then the bursting egg, the yoke yellowing the amber aspic with its egg flavor, then picking up a morsel of the bottom slice of ham to enhance its texture and embolden its flavor. Although the Ritz's pampered menu provided such delicacies, Philip's meager monthly inheritance precluded dining there. And now even that was as insecure as everything else; the current month's allowance was ten days overdue, which was the reason he was making this infrequent visit to the office of the lawyer who handled the trust.

As Philip wheeled his bicycle across the Rue du Colisée, he become conscious of a wave of disruption rolling toward him. The sound of shouting and cascading glass. Bands of Jeunes Gardes in open iron-gray German touring cars were riding down the Champs-Élysées, standing on the seats of their automobiles and in unison screaming, "Down with the Jews!" They wore khaki pants, navy-blue shirts, cross-belts and riding boots, a uniform created by the Germans to lure French youth into the Gardes, which had been established as a counterpart to the youth group that had worked so successfully in Germany. The screaming youths were hurling bricks through any shop window that did not display a sign, "Jewish Patronage Not Accepted."

The military band and the marching soldiers passed the Jeunes Gardes, but neither group paid any attention to the other. And French pedestrians did not acknowledge the presence of either group; looking neither right nor left, they continued at their regular pace as if nothing out of the ordinary was happening. The frenzied hate on the young people's faces, and their brutal behavior, linked Philip again to the massacre in the Jardin des Tuileries. It was with a feeling of great relief that he reached the Rue de Berri, where his lawyer's offices were located.

In the lobby of the office building, Philip passed a tall, ascetic-looking Frenchman on whose expensive lapel was a yellow Star of David with the word "Goy" embroidered within it. It broke the tension in Philip, who was smiling when he entered the elevator. Now, that took balls, Philip thought; probably a French aristocrat, but nevertheless the Germans had no sense of humor about such things and, aristocrat or not, he could be jailed for his insolence. Philip, who knew he was incapable of such defiance, was filled with admiration for the man's protest.

Harrison Myles was a member of the law firm of Burke and Snavely, which had offices in New York, Paris, London and Geneva. He had been a close friend of Philip's Uncle Gerard, and it was he who, after Gerard's death, protected Philip's bequest against Adele's efforts to overturn the will. He had run the Paris branch for twenty-two years and had been a source of counsel and advice for Philip on things nonlegal as well as legal. Myles was usually cheerful and unhurried, but now, as his secretary ushered Philip into his office, his face was grim.

"Bad times, Philip, bad times," he muttered, rubbing his glasses over his gabardine sleeve. "The blockade has shut off our pouch, ergo, no funds."

"But I thought there was an account in the Morgan Guaranty . . ."

"Yes, yes, my boy, was, *was,* but like the waters of Babylon it has to be replenished. Hasn't been a sou come in for months now, and the riverbed is dry. Of course, it's piling up in New York, and *if* the war ever ends, there it will be, but in the meantime, my lad, in the meantime—well, I myself have a few heirlooms and what not to market, but you, poor boy, devoid of capital, devoid of possessions, I'd say you've come to the end of your rope and your Ritz. A sorry state, a truly sorry state but *res ipsa loquitur,* the thing speaks for itself, *n'est-ce pas?"*

"But, Harrison, there must be *something* we can do? Won't a Paris bank give us credit based on our Morgan Guaranty account? Can't they verify that the money's in New York—"

"Ah, yes, of course, of course, we've been through all that, two very nice banker lunches at Fouquet's, but German controllers are now in all the French banks and they have put an absolute clamp on what funds can go anywhere except for the upkeep of the German occupation forces. I'll tell you that I, for one, am pulling up stakes and skedaddling. All these years, I have proclaimed that I would never leave my digs in Neuilly, but, dear boy, the handwriting is all over the damn wall, Uncle Sam will be sucked into this, you can bet on it, and better leave now than later in a panic. Last night I was obligated to eat spaghetti at La Tour d'Argent. Spaghetti! *That's* when you know it's time to leave."

Too dejected to listen to any more, Philip left with the understanding that he would phone Myles the following morning after sleeping on the proposed departure. Too shocked to think, he unlocked the chain on his bicycle and began to pedal down the Rue de Berri in the general direction of the Parc Monceau. Whenever he was troubled, he sought the sanctity of this little park as a refuge.

The man in the black sweater followed him. Directly across from the office building from which Philip had just emerged, there was a telephone booth in front of the Val d'Isère Restaurant. A portly man who had been standing at the bar of the restaurant, which had a clear view of the street, now emerged, entered the phone booth, and dialed a number. Without preliminaries he said, "He is being tailed. Black beard, black sweater, beret. Also on a bicycle. Headed toward the Boulevard Haussmann."

"Do you recognize the tail?" the voice on the other end of the telephone asked.

"Never saw him before," the man answered, hung up and went back to finish his drink.

On his bike, Philip was again hearing Harrison Myles's voice telling him to give up the Paris ghost. He did not share Harrison's prescience about the United States getting into the war, not with Lindbergh there to keep them out of it. But the forbidding cut-off of funds—that was something else again. Of course, there was a solution at hand, but that would mean that Goering was his employer—or the German government, which was even worse. If only he could discuss this with Gabrielle. She was always good at reasoning out these dilemmas, but von Spatz's presence in her life would possibly affect her judgment.

As he turned onto the Boulevard de Courcelles, Philip thought about all the changes that had taken place, how much had been taken away from him; Paris was a mistress who had run away, he thought, and left him only with memories. Although it was a non sequitur, it was then that it suddenly occurred to him that he could have a talk with Charles. Now, why hadn't he thought of that before? Charles was just the person. Philip turned around and headed back toward the Champs-Élysées. The man in the black sweater followed him all the way back to the Ritz.

Charley Ritz was sitting at a table in the room he lived in, which was smaller than his adjoining train room. He was tying exotic flies. It was impossible to get to trout streams now, but Charley liked to tie flies anyway, and sometimes he would practice casting from the shore of one of the little lakes in the Bois de Boulogne.

"It's a solution, no doubt about that," Charley said, "but to be involved with Hermann Goering—hell, Philip, I don't think you realize who he really is. You and I are neutrals. We're not made for involvement. I long ago made up my mind about the Ritz. I could have taken on a lot of the responsibility. I know the hotel business. I was weaned on it. But I don't like to deal with other people's problems. I don't care really about their comfort or their needs or whether their eggs were boiled a minute too long. In that respect, our friend Lindbergh has the right idea: stay to yourself, don't get involved. Once you get involved with Goering . . . Well, listen, all of Paris is involved with the Germans, I know that. But there are those who do what they do because they have to: we have to keep running the Ritz or they'll take it away from us. Then again, there are those who *willingly* do what they do—go out of their way to please: Maxim's, Sacha Guitry, that choreographer at the opera who is *creating* ballets to please the Boche. Get the point?"

"But I have to, don't I, Charley? How will I stay on in Paris?"

"Is it so terrible to go back to the States?"

"Where would I go? Which state? Which city? How would I support myself? It scares the hell out of me, Charley. I don't even have the scratch to get back."

"Well, I could help you there."

"Why would I have to get involved other than to go through the motions with these art types? Goering is so occupied with important things he won't be aware of my existence, and I'll make enough to get by until the war ends. Why not? It isn't as if he's asking me to be the *Kommandant* of Paris."

"Look at that one! Have you ever seen a prettier fly?"

"What do you think, Charley? I mean, looking at it that way?"

"What can I say, Philip? I'm delighted if you stay—you know how few friends I have. But I don't want you to get hurt, and I don't think you have any idea what these people are really like. It will be like walking barefoot through a pit of snakes."

"I'll be careful, Charley."

"Sure."

"I'll watch every step I take."

"You better."

Part Two

TODAY

There is only the immediate;
All else is illusion.

15

There was a note in his box from Lili. "Phone me—I must see you." She invited him up to her room.

She was wearing a white Japanese kimono with her hair drawn back tightly and swept up in a single spiral. She was drinking Chablis and poured Philip a glass without asking.

"I am so happy to see you, Philip," she said. "It has been a hectic time. Distraction, not neglect. Do you forgive me?" She smiled at him and raised her glass, and as they sipped the wine she kept smiling at him over the edge of her glass.

"Have you been working hard at your painting? I *must* come pose for you—I promised, didn't I? I'm curious to see how you think of me."

"In my painting?"

"Yes, of course. I'll bet it will be full of lust and resentment." She gave him a look of mock wickedness. "Are you free this evening?" she asked. "I do hope you are free, Philip."

"Well, yes . . ."

"Lovely. I am dying to go to La Dernière—do you know La Dernière?"

"No."

"Well, it's a little, crowded *boîte* in Montmartre, on the Rue du Chevalier-de-la-Barre, in the back of Sacré-Coeur. There is a little singer there I adore—Piaf, have you heard her, Edith Piaf?"

"No, but Janet Flanner raves about her."

"Oh, how she sings! The voice of a deserted railroad platform, an empty rumpled bed, lovers on the guillotine. It is a voice that destroys me, and a face to go with it. I will meet you there at eleven."

"Eleven? But isn't that rather—"

"That's when she sings. She's a night bird."

"But what do people do about the curfew?"

"Nothing. They stay until five in the morning, when the curfew ends."

"Then how about dinner beforehand?"

"Well, beforehand I have a bit of a favor to ask of you. Something you could do for me and I would be so grateful. There are some things we have to do in life, Philip, that are awkward, and that's what I'm usually able to avoid. I detest being awkward at something I know would be better done if someone else did it for me. I mean, God help us from people who want to be self-sufficient. Especially women. I know it's the new vogue—women who open their own doors, speak directly to the maître d', pay their own rent, and on and on—well, I say heaven forbid! I want to be as un-self-sufficient as I possibly can. I am a shoulder-leaner, and I love it. Do you like these women who want to be as self-reliant as men?"

"No, actually not. But I don't like them utterly helpless either."

"No, of course not. Oh, we do speak the same language! What a civilized man you are, Philip! Do you know what a rare breed that is?"

"What do you mean by 'civilized'?"

"Gentle, well dressed, fluent in languages, and not afraid to spend money."

Philip laughed. "I'm flattered."

Lili poured more wine.

"But shouldn't the gentleman pour?" he asked.

"Not when the lady wants a favor," she said, batting her long eyelashes in playful seduction.

"Which is?"

"Oh, really a very simple thing. This book which I have here—" she picked up a volume from the end table—"it's an illustrated edition of some bawdy short stories by Balzac—I would just like you to go to Lipp's in Saint-Germain-des-Prés around ten o'clock tonight, find a seat on the enclosed terrace, and wait for a friend of mine while you're reading the book. He'll be carrying a book identical to yours. His name is Roland. He'll sit with you and order a beer and when he leaves he'll pick up your book and leave you his—which you'll bring with you to La Dernière. That's all there is to it. That's the favor I ask of you. I will then leave the book at La Dernière for a friend of mine."

"Of course there's a lot more to it than you're telling me."

"No, no—that's it! That's all there is to it. I promise you. It just would be awkward for me to . . . go to Lipp's."

"But what is the purpose of exchanging identical volumes?"

"Part of the favor you're doing for me is in doing this just for the sake of doing me a favor with no questions asked." There was a touch of peevishness in her voice.

"You must admit that exchanging identical volumes of Balzac with an unknown man in a Saint-Germain restaurant does arouse one's curiosity."

"Oh, well, if you must know, the volume you'll be getting is a first edition, very valuable, and this one will replace it."

"And someone, the owner of the first edition, let's say, won't be aware of its absence."

She held out the book to him and smiled. "Well?" she asked.

As he took the book he shook his head in consternation at his helpless involvement in this ill-advised adventure.

"Piaf has a little song," Lili said, "about a fellow from the North who had a very gentle look, dreamy eyes, gold in his hair and an angel's smile. You'll hear it tonight."

The bearded man in the black sweater went directly to Goering's suite and knocked sharply on the door. He carried a large manila envelope. When Kropp opened the door, the man in black handed him the envelope and quietly withdrew, without saying a word. Kropp immediately carried the envelope to the bathroom, where Goering was speaking on the telephone while soaking in the tub.

Kropp opened the envelope and took out a sheaf of papers which he handed to Goering, who was finishing his conversation. He handed the telephone to Kropp and took the file of papers in exchange. Goering settled back in the water, which was dark green and perfumed from a heavy dose of Badedas, and started to read black beard's report on Philip.

The entrance to Lipp's was only a short distance from the sidewalk, so that the terrace, which occupied this space, was, of necessity, small and crowded. Lipp's was one of the oldest and finest brasseries in Paris, and it had become a great favorite of the Germans, who had restricted its military patronage to officers (and provided it with choice German beer and comestibles). The Lipp "regulars" were tolerated, but it was clearly understood that no Parisian would be seated while a German officer was waiting for a table. Those waiting for tables crowded onto the small terrace along with those who were there just to drink Lipp's exemplary beer. The terrace, as a result, was filled with sitting and standing customers who besieged the harried waiters with their drink orders.

Although Philip was intrigued by his mission, he was nevertheless wary of it, and he was grateful for the bustle and noise on the terrace. He placed himself in a rear corner where he had a clear view of the entire sidewalk in front of the restaurant, but considering the circumstances, he kept his book under his arm rather than trying to read it as he had been instructed. He wanted to size up Roland before Roland could identify him.

At twenty minutes past ten, Philip realized, with a shock, that a German artillery captain was standing on the sidewalk outside the entrance, with a book in his hand. The captain was young, rather handsome, with a deep scar that transected the corner of his upper lip, giving him the semblance of a sneer. He was casually looking at the crowd on the terrace.

The captain shifted the book to his other hand, and the name of the author, Balzac, in large gold letters, became clearly visible. At the same time, the captain moved toward the terrace, but as he reached the entrance three men in civilian clothes moved up to him and eased him over to the curb, where one of the men took the book from him and started to riffle through its pages. The two other men turned and peered into the terrace. The captain was talking earnestly to the man who was examining the book.

Philip moved immediately, but not quickly, which would have attracted attention to himself, but in a deliberate way he eased himself through the revolving door and into the interior of the restaurant. He knew the restaurant very well, having dined there many times with Gabrielle, who shared his weakness for the fresh Baltic herring with peppercorns, and the *choucroute garnie.* As he moved through the revolving door, Philip slipped the book under his suit jacket. He walked casually past the crowded tables in the narrow anteroom, turned toward the mirrored back room where the "in" people were eating, and disappeared down the narrow winding staircase that led to the telephones and toilets below. A woman attendant sat at the bottom of the stairs, outside the toilet entrances, next to a table with a saucer on it that contained a cluster of coins. Philip noted that underneath the table was the woman's large cracked-leather handbag, a bag big enough to carry a bread or salami or whatever else the Lipp kitchen might bestow on her when the restaurant closed.

Philip went into the men's room, urinated, washed his hands, and left the water running into the basin. He went out and, after putting a tip on the plate, advised the woman that the basin was stopped up. She went in to investigate. Philip picked up her bag, quickly slipped the book into it, then put it back under the table and mounted the stairs. He deliberately left his jacket open. As he worked his way back to the entrance, he was aware of the three men who had stopped the captain. They were moving from table to table; one of the men held the book in his hand.

Outside, as he left the terrace, Philip saw the captain sitting with two men in the back of a German vehicle that was parked at the curb. Philip walked away, taking care not to appear hurried. He had left his bicycle around the corner on the Rue du Dragon. He moved stiffly, infusions of fear in his knee joints.

If there had not been a full moon, Philip would never have found La Dernière. As it was, it took him twenty minutes of searching up and down the Rue du Chevalier-de-la-Barre before he located the narrow, unmarked door. The subterranean room was smoky, warm, and fetid with the stench, so common on the Métro, of unwashed bodies. Soap and hot water no longer existed in Paris, although soap was available on the black market if one could locate it, at twenty times its regular price.

On a small dais at the far end of the room, away from the bar, there was a piano player playing with one hand while he sipped a drink from a glass in his other hand. The ceiling was low, the walls were bare and in need of paint. The waiters collected each time they brought a drink. All the tables were filled, and the bar was packed solid. After his eyes adjusted, Philip saw Lili sitting alone at a very small table against the wall. As he sat down, her eyes searched for the book.

"You didn't tell me that Roland was *Captain* Roland, if that is really his name. Well, he's in the clink by now—"

"Clink?"

"—or maybe up against a wall with a blindfold on."

"No book?"

"I made a present of mine to a student of literature who tends the Lipp's toilets."

"Your book doesn't matter."

"I could be on the rack in leg irons right now, thanks to you."

"I'm sorry—I didn't think there would be any risk."

"Sure, that's why you ducked out and sent me."

"No, it's Roland's fault—he was supposed to send someone else. But I don't care, I have no stake in it, and this way it's a load off my back. Failure suits me just fine. I was obliged to do it, that's all."

Philip ordered a whiskey, but the waiter said they had only

wine and beer. As the waiter left to get Philip a beer, Janet
Flanner, who had been at a table on the other side of the room,
came up to Philip, who was surprised and glad to see her. He
started to get to his feet, but Janet put her hand on his shoulder,
stopping him.

"Philip," she said in an even voice, "I do not think you and I
should ever speak to each other again."

Before Philip could recover and reply, Janet had disappeared
into the smoky crowd.

"What's that all about?" Lili asked.

"Cowardice," Philip answered.

The lights flickered, and the piano player forsook his drink and
began to play seriously with both hands.

"She'll be coming on now," Lili said. "Oh, how I envy you,
hearing Piaf for the first time."

Throttled by anticipation, conversation stopped and all faces
turned toward the stage. On came a very small woman, well
under five feet, weighing ninety pounds at most; she wore a
nondescript black dress, no jewelry, impromptu hair with hap-
hazard bangs, a slash of lipstick, and there were bloated red
patches around her eyes. She stood with her feet apart, her fists
clenched, staring somberly at the hushed audience. When she
started to sing, her voice seemed to rise slowly, with tremolo,
from deep inside her. There was a remorseless sadness to her
tone, to her expression, to her pathetic size, as she sang about
the woman of the Rue Pigalle who was black with sin, but that
deep in her eyes there was something miraculous that put a little
bit of blue into the dirty sky of Pigalle.

Philip was enthralled, the voice a lasso that had spun out and
trussed him. Piaf went effortlessly from song to song, each word
distinct, poetry of the streets, moving and arousing and tragic.

Lili took his hand under the table and pulled it over to her.
She was sitting back in her chair, her mouth slightly open, her
eyes closed, her breath irregular. Piaf was pouring out her pity
on a little doll of the streets. "Life's been hard on you," she
sang, "don't cry, come back to me, I am near you."

Lili put his hand underneath her skirt and guided it to her
vagina. She was wearing no underclothes. As she had told him in
the studio, she had no pubic hair. Piaf's mournful voice was
commiserating with a woman who waited hopelessly for a train in
the night.

Philip's hand felt Lili's clitoris, wet and erect, and gently his
fingers caressed it as she kept her hand lightly on top of his,

moving in unison with it. "Then his hand took mine, and I was afraid dawn would come . . ." Lili's breath was coming quickly now, accompanied by staccato murmurs, responding to Philip's fingers, her groin moving slightly as Piaf's voice rose in a plaintive cry: "I don't know his name, I know nothing about him," her husky voice reverberated off the walls. "But he made love to me all through the night . . ." Lili came with a fierce shudder, pressing down on Philip's hand, a low wrenching sob accompanying its spent force.

Up on the little stage, Piaf was also breathing hard, her song ended, her eyes closed, applause in her ears, the look on her face not unlike that on Lili's.

The captain, whose name was not Roland, could not describe the person he was supposed to meet. He did not know, he said, if it was a man or a woman. Various kinds of inducers were used on him, including one which slowly removed the fingernails on his right hand, but they did not elicit the identification of the intended recipient of his book.

The volume itself mystified German intelligence. They could detect nothing in it that was out of order. What eluded them was one sentence on page 182 which contained words not written by Balzac. The page had been painstakingly reprinted on matching paper and bound back into the original volume after the authentic page 182 had been removed. For the Germans, it remained an unresolved bafflement, and many futile hours were expended studying the book. The captain, although charged with no offense other than carrying a book of Balzac stories, was nevertheless executed for suspicion of treason.

When the toilet attendant went home that night, she was amazed to discover a handsome book of Balzac stories in her handbag. She had passed his statue on the Boulevard Raspail many times, but she had never read anything he had written. She enjoyed the stories very much.

16

When Philip made the appointment to see Goering, it was to inform the Reichsmarschall that he did not wish to undertake the peculiar art job he had been offered. As determined as he was not to get involved in Goering's art world—Charley Ritz was certainly right—Philip nevertheless felt a certain trepidation at having to face Goering and turn him down. After all, Philip was an alien from the unfriendly United States, living in Paris on German indulgence. But after the terrible sequence of events at Lipp's, he was intent on resisting any involvement with the Germans, especially this kind of in-house espionage proposed by Goering.

Despite the aftershock of the Lipp's incident, however, Philip had experienced a certain unexpected satisfaction. Reliving the sequence of events, he could not believe that he, Philip Weber, was the man who had extricated himself from that very dangerous situation.

As he waited in the salon for Goering that evening, Philip kept rehearsing in his mind what he would say, but the longer he waited, the more his apprehension increased. All of which was immaterial, actually, because when the Reichsmarschall finally did make his entrance, his appearance routed all of Philip's carefully prepared plans.

As a matter of fact, when Goering first entered the room, Philip did not even recognize him, for he was dressed in women's clothes. He wore a deep-purple velvet evening gown with a diamond choker at his throat, his face was powdered and rouged, lipstick adorned his lips, and his nails were lacquered with a red tint. He wore several diamond and emerald rings, jeweled slippers on his feet, and a floral perfume. Goering's small, regular features accentuated his feminine appearance.

But, for all his feminine aspect, Goering walked into the room in his usual forthright manner, and he shook Philip's hand forcefully.

"Sit down, sit down, Herr Weber, I am very glad to see you, Kropp is off, so do you mind pouring the champagne?"

The champagne, already opened, was in a cooler beside Goering's chair, and Philip poured each of them a glassful.

"Herr Weber, I find you very sympathetic. I judge you to be someone I can trust. The way my life is, there are very few people I can be friends with, practically no one. Certainly none of the men of the party, or any of the people who work for me. They are all full of jealousy, hostility. There have already been three unsolved attempts on my life. But you are an outsider, you share my love of great art, you think like our friend Lindbergh. I have had you observed. The reports on your day-to-day habits are excellent." Goering took some tablets from the crystal bowl and put them into his mouth.

"These are morphine tablets. I tell you this as a confidence between us. It goes back to my early days in the party. The Nazis were just a handful of men then. One afternoon, Hitler and I were leading our small group of storm troopers down the Residenzstrasse in Munich when the police opened fire unexpectedly and I was shot in the groin. Somehow I managed to escape, and my dear wife, Karin, my first wife, hid me and tended me as best she could, but my thigh became terribly infected. There were secret operations because we were hiding, and to help the pain they gave me morphine. Even with the drug, I had to chew on my pillow to help bear the pain. My leg took a long time to heal, and by the time it did I was addicted to the morphine. I had to inject myself every day. Heavy doses. That's when I became as large as I am. In my days as a pilot, I was as slender as you are. But . . . well . . . I was once put in the violent ward at the Langbro Asylum as a dangerous drug addict because they said I attacked a nurse who wouldn't give me morphine. But I have no memory of that one way or another."

Talking about the morphine compelled Goering to take two more tablets. He also took a long Cuban cigar from a gold case, snipped its end with a gold cutter, and lit it. It gave a comic look to his feminine masquerade and reminded Philip of a production of *Charley's Aunt* he had once seen.

"That was fifteen years ago," Goering said. "I have now leveled off my habit with these tablets. But morphine is nothing to be concerned about, you know. Your Mr. Edgar Allan Poe took much larger doses and yet he wrote brilliantly. There are famous surgeons I know who take heavy doses every day and yet perform delicate operations. But my enemies in the party,

especially Bormann, would like to convince the Führer that I'm
a dope fiend not to be trusted—but the Führer knows better. I
am certainly not a dope head, but I'll tell you what I truly am—
I am a pure sybarite. Morphine simply pleases my sensuality; my
skin craves silk, furs, the smooth caress of diamonds and
emeralds on my fingertips, I adore the delicacy of perfume, the
feel of makeup on my face. That's why I like to dress like this. Of
course it's feminine, but I'm not involved with *being* feminine,
do you understand? Just in experiencing the sensual silks and
perfumes that are associated with women. But I don't want to
fondle men or bugger them. I abhor the feel of whiskers and
body hair. I detest men who kiss my cheeks, the filthy custom
they have here and in Italy. The first time I visited Rome,
Mussolini tried to embrace me, pushing that scratchy chin of his
on my cheek, but I pushed him away and reminded him that we
were soldiers and that *'Sieg Heil!'* was enough of a greeting.

"Do I make myself clear? You have your hero—Lindbergh.
Mine is Wagner, Richard Wagner. Our greatest composer. You
probably don't know this, but Wagner wore dresses and silk
underclothes as I do, and what he said was, 'I am myself only
when I dress as a woman.' Did you know he composed *Parsifal*
wearing the silks and satins of his wife? Unfortunately, I must
wear uniforms, but I make them as beautiful in look and feel as a
woman's dress. But, like Wagner, I am myself, the true
Hermann Goering, only when I dress in women's clothes. And
intellectually Wagner and I are also alike—he loathed the Jews
as I do."

The telephone rang, and Goering gave orders for repositioning
a Luftwaffe unit in Normandy. Philip listened to the authoritative orders and shook his head in disbelief at the spectacle before
him: the commander of the German Air Force, dressed in
feminine attire, giving military orders of death and destruction
from the most opulent suite in the Ritz Hotel.

"One of the reasons I make the Ritz my headquarters,"
Goering said after he hung up, "is that I have freedom here, I
can breathe. I keep my wardrobe of clothes here so that I don't
have to worry about the gossips in Berlin. Of course, what I do, I
do quietly. The Ritz, Maxim's . . . it all suits me. But there is
one thing—perhaps you can assist me in this: I have heard that
the celebrated barman, Georges, can do wonders for the guests
here. Do you know him very well?"

"Yes, quite well."

"Good. So, tell me, is it possible he would know someone who would visit me on occasions without advertising herself? Someone of . . . how can I say? . . . with a certain amount of class, someone befitting a man of my position?"

"I can certainly ask him."

"What I had in mind . . . would you mind phoning him?"

"You mean, someone now?"

"Yes, if possible."

Philip asked the operator for the bar and got Georges on the phone. Goering left the room.

"Georges, Philip Weber here."

"Good evening, Monsieur Weber."

"A matter has just arisen that requires utmost confidentiality."

"Of course."

"I am with . . . the Reichsmarschall. He would like to establish a continuing liaison with someone special—in other words, a lady you have confidence in, Georges. And, Georges, he would like her now."

"Yes, of course. There is no problem, Monsieur Weber, someone comes immediately to mind—no problem at all."

"One other thing, Georges. I think you should prepare the person, tell her that the Reichsmarschall enjoys feminine clothing."

"He will be dressed that way?"

"Yes."

"Do you think he will require, forgive me, abnormalities?"

"I wouldn't know."

"Are there any physical preferences to be considered—size, hair color, anything?"

"No, not that I know of—but Aryan. And German-speaking, of course."

"Of course."

Toward the end of the conversation, Goering had returned to the room. "It is arranged," Philip told him.

Goering had brought in a platter heaped with sausages, cold meats, cheeses, butter, bread and caviar. "Help yourself," he said as he picked up a *weisswurst* and swallowed it in three quick bites. "Tomorrow I will introduce you to the key people in the art offices here—Dr. Lohse, Baron von Behr, Ilse Pütz, Fräulein Linberger, Walter Hofer, Gustav Rochlitz and the others. I will explain to them that you're writing a book about my art collection and I'd like them to give you all-out cooperation. You will be paid five hundred francs a month and expenses if you have any. Just ask them questions—for the book, of course—

constant questions, and sooner or later someone will start to get nervous and that's the one we're after."

Goering opened the center drawer of the Napoleonic desk and took out a file folder, which he handed to Philip.

"Now, then, here's an inventory of all the art obtained from Paris which I now have in Karinhall. After you get the procurement lists from von Behr, Lohse and the others, you'll be able to determine what I didn't get—and where it went. That's where to ask your questions. In that way we may find out what happened to the authentic Rembrandt, and maybe other Jewish-owned art that I don't even know about. Here's your first pay in advance."

He put a packet of franc notes on the table next to Philip, then went over to a console near the window and put a record on the phonograph. It was a Glenn Miller recording. "I love to dance to American bands," Goering said. "In Berlin, this music is forbidden as decadent, but here in Paris . . ." He shrugged. "My real pleasure is to dance the woman's role; I prefer to follow. Despite my size, I am quite a good dancer. Tennis players are always good dancers. How do you like the *braunschweiger*? It is made especially for me in Stuttgart."

Philip put a slice of the *braunschweiger* on a piece of dark bread and agreed it was delicious.

"Have you ever tried wearing women's clothes, Herr Weber? Every man should—what a relief from the scratchiness and heaviness of tweed and worsted. And the freedom a skirt gives you in the crotch! We've got it all backwards, you know. Women, who have nothing there, should wear trousers, and men should wear skirts and liberate their balls."

"The Scots figured that out long ago."

"Yes, but I'd rather wear tight-fitting pants than have to be tortured by bagpipes."

There was a discreet knock on the door. Philip went to answer it. Georges' lady looked like someone who had just stepped out of a page from *Vanity Fair*. Philip let her in, directed her to the salon, and then departed. He walked up to his floor rather than take the elevator. Only when he went to put his key into the lock of his door did he realize that he had the packet of francs in his hand.

17

Philip awoke feeling a pervasive bleakness, a hangover unrelated to the champagne he had drunk the night before. On the night table beside his bed was the packet of franc notes, but the sight of the money gave him no satisfaction. He knew he had sold his soul. But underneath the layer of bleakness was the counter feeling of relief that his means of existence had been solved, at least for the time being.

On the way to his usual breakfast at the café, Philip stopped at the desk and gave Henri Bretonne, the concierge, a note to put into Lili's box. After their night at La Dernière he had phoned her several times, but had never found her in.

"There is a message in your box, Monsieur Weber," the concierge said, handing it to him. "I put it there last night when Monsieur Man Ray called."

"Man is back? That's wonderful news!"

"He would like you to come to his studio this morning. He said it was important. I rang your room several times during the evening to tell you."

"Well, I didn't get back until late."

"Beyond the curfew? How did you manage?"

"I was . . . visiting in the hotel."

"If I had known the room number . . ."

"Yes, I should . . ."

"Mademoiselle Chanel doesn't mind."

"It wasn't Mademoiselle Chanel."

"Oh, I see. Well, if it was the Reichsmarschall, it's for the best I didn't ring. Phone calls annoy him."

Philip did not reply; he was reading Man Ray's message, but he had heard the concierge's remark. "He likes to talk about art with me," was all that Philip said. He put the note into his pocket and bid the concierge a pleasant goodbye.

The concierge turned his back to the reception desk and wrote something on a pad of paper next to the telephones. He slipped

the piece of notepaper into his pocket, on top of the folded tips
he had received that morning. At lunch, down in the employees'
dining room, when Louis came around to collect his empty half-
bottle that had held a robust Beaujolais from Pontanevaux, he
would slip the note into the bottle as he handed it to Louis. The
note would report, in a code that used no names, that Philip
Weber had spent the evening in Hermann Goering's suite talking
about art. It would also report that Georges' favorite lady of the
night, Monette Lynette, was observed entering the suite at
midnight.

Later that afternoon, Louis Delor would load all the empties
on a horse-drawn cart that would deliver them to a bottle
supplier in Montmartre. Bretonne's note would eventually reach
the chief of that district's Underground cell, whose code name
was Pelican.

Man Ray was busily stuffing clothes into a suitcase when Philip
entered the studio through the open door. Man's mistress,
Clarisse, was in bed, covered up to her eyes, sullenly watching
him. Man was jabbing each item of clothing into the suitcase as if
they were daggers aimed at Clarisse's heart. But at sight of
Philip, his angry face cheered up. "It's Philip the Weber,
himself!" Man exclaimed. They embraced heartily. Clarisse's
dour expression did not alter.

"I see you've been mutilating your works of art." Man
indicated the painting that Philip had lacerated.

"I haven't been here that much since you left," Philip said. "It
was strange working here without you around. I really couldn't
concentrate."

"No wonder. Bloody damn Nazis all over the place. We're
pulling up stakes, Philo, we should get our asses out of here fast
as we can. You should see what the bastards did to my place in
Saint-Germain-en-Laye. Busted it up just for the hell of it. We
went by there on our way back into Paris. The pricks used all my
paintings for target practice. They shit on the Persian carpet.
Stuffed rags in the toilet drains so they would overflow. Dumped
garbage in the beds. Our enlightened conquerors!"

"But we're all right here in Paris, Man. Look, they haven't
touched your studio, have they? Picasso is working his usual
hours on the Rue des Grands-Augustins, and Derain is unmo-
lested in his place."

"You see, you coward!" Clarisse exclaimed. "Turning tail the
minute you see a uniform! And he wants me to run away with

him. Cowards love company! Well, he's got another think
coming! You run off and leave me, that's the last you'll ever see
of me! I went running to the South when the Germans first came
in because you were so scared, but now I don't run, because I
don't like the company of a coward!''

She had lowered the blanket to make her impassioned charge;
now she pulled it back up to her eyes. She was a truly beautiful
woman, a mulatto dancer from the French colony of Guadeloupe
whom Man had met four years earlier on an exclusive little
beach, La Garoupe, in Antibes. At the time, Man had just ended
a long affair with the model Kiki, and he had gone to Antibes to
visit his old friends Pablo Picasso and the poet Paul Éluard. But
one look at the beauteous young Clarisse, her *café-au-lait* skin
glistening in the hot Riviera sun, and Man became instantly
involved. They had had a chaotic but intense four years together,
aggressively passionate and interdependent, but the present
schism over abandoning Paris for New York seemed more
serious than others they had bridged in the past.

"You notice that she's playing the death scene from *La
Bohème,* little Mimi breathing her last. It's a wonder she hasn't
developed Camille's cough.''

"Coward!" Clarisse growled.

Philip felt uncomfortable. He had been trapped in these
violent confrontations all too often.

"Perhaps you should talk to Picasso," Philip suggested,
"before you make up your mind."

"Philip, my poor Philip, Picasso is a Spaniard, and who was
Franco's ally in the civil war? Good ol' Germany, sending good
ol' reliable Messerschmitts to dump on Guernica. So why would
the Boche bother Picasso when Spain is a pal of the Third Reich,
or Derain, the Frenchman? But Man Ray of Brooklyn, U.S.A.,
land of the President they call 'Roosefeld the Jew,' who sends
battleships and food to Britain—how about that? Especially if we
get around to sending a few soldier boys inside those battleships.
Wise up, Philip, we go to the American Embassy and get some
skidoo papers as fast as we can. And even though she doesn't
deserve it, we'll go to the French Embassy and get some papers
for her.''

"No, you won't! He just wants to humiliate me on the streets
of New York. How many restaurants will seat us? How many
nightclubs will let us past the velvet rope? I know how they treat
nigger girls who go with white men in your Land of the Free. He
thinks the world is like Paris, where everyone thinks I'm

beautiful and no one notices my color. Well, there is only one Paris and that's where I'm going to stay—even though he deserts me and leaves me to the mercy of enemy soldiers."

"You cheap bitch, accusing me of deserting you—I want you to go with me, don't I? And what do you know about New York? Have you ever been there? It's not as if I'm taking you to Alabama."

"I am not cheap nor a bitch, but you are an awful stinking weasel!" she screamed, throwing off the covers and coming at him. She was wearing a bra but nothing else. "A weasely coward, a no-good motherless bastard who deserts—"

Man hit her so hard she staggered backward and fell on the bed. He flung himself toward her with intent to strangle her, but she rolled over and eluded him. She dashed over to his work table, picked up a bottle of black India ink and threw it at his head. It hit the white wall and made a splatter that dripped in a symmetry that would have made any contemporary action painter proud.

Man, doubly infuriated now, came hurtling after her, but she broke a pane of glass in the window with her fist, pushed the casement wide open and, screaming at the top of her lungs, threatened to jump if he came any nearer. Man yelled that she was nothing but the dirty cunt of a hog, but he kept his distance, not at all sure that she wouldn't carry out her threat. Her hand was covered with blood.

Man took Philip by the arm and dragged him through the door as neighbors began running up the stairs and assembling in the hall. In all the confusion, Man was able to steer Philip and himself down the stairs and onto the sidewalk. They looked up. Clarisse was sitting on the windowsill, her bare body exposed to the elements, still screaming invectives.

"She really has a beautiful ass, hasn't she?" Man said in soft admiration.

There was plenty of time to get to the American Embassy before it closed for the lunch break. Philip left his bicycle in Man's courtyard, and they took the Métro to the Chamber of Deputies stop. They walked along the Quai Anatole France, and then across the Pont de la Concorde. The sidewalks and the cafés were crowded with German soldiers.

They passed a long queue in front of a tobacco shop, and an even longer queue in front of a bakery. The café at the corner of the Quai Augustin, where it transects the Pont-Royale, had a sign outside its sidewalk terrace which said: "ARYANS ONLY."

Man stopped and glowered at the sign, his dark recessed eyes growing darker. His eyes were the dominant force in his face.

"Let's put 'em to the test," Man said as he entered the café and found a table on the terrace. He and Philip were the only two civilians in the place. An elderly waiter with sore feet came over. "Messieurs?"

"His name is Mordecai Cohen," Man said, pointing to Philip. "Are you Aryan?"

"No," Philip said, falling into step with Man, as he always did.

"You're not Aryan?"

"No." The old waiter was watching them patiently.

"Well, what will you have, Mordecai?" Man asked Philip.

"A kosher beer."

"What?" the old waiter said.

"You heard—the man wants a kosher beer."

"We have only Vatel on draft and Kronenbourg in bottles," the old waiter said.

"Is it kosher?"

"I don't understand."

"Did a rabbi put his blessings on it?"

"I don't know," the old waiter said. "I only came on at twelve o'clock."

"I'll have a Kronenbourg," Philip said, pitying the old man. "Two Kronenbourgs."

The waiter started away.

"The name Cohen is not Aryan," Man persisted, loudly, in a last attempt to bait the waiter.

The waiter shrugged philosophically and continued on his way. None of the soldiers was paying any attention to Man. Philip figured that Man's truculence was spillage from the unresolved fight with Clarisse.

When the beer came, Man took one sip and loudly called it German horse piss. He clinked a few coins into the saucer, and they resumed their journey toward the American Embassy, which was at one corner of the Place de la Concorde, across from the Hotel Crillon. Man didn't know that the Crillon, where he liked to drink at the bar, had been totally taken over by officers attached to the German Chief of Staff. An enormous Nazi flag, emblazoned with a swastika, hung from a balcony in front of the hotel. The terraces and the roof were dotted with manned machine gun emplacements.

Man was further provoked by the sight of a group of French war prisoners, supervised by a couple of armed German soldiers, demolishing balustrades and removing bronze ship prows from the columns in the Place de la Concorde. Bronze was in severely short supply, and the pieces would be melted down and shipped to munitions factories.

There were wooden barricades in front of the Crillon; the gendarmes on duty prevented Man and Philip from crossing the street to enter the American Embassy, requiring them to go all the way around the block to reach the embassy entrance.

After a lengthy wait, Man's name was called and he motioned Philip to accompany him to the cubicle to which he had been directed, one of the many in which clerks were conducting interviews.

"First of all," Man said to the clerk, a small man with spots on his tie, "I want to send a cable to New York."

"Not possible," the clerk said. "Direct communication with the States is no longer permitted. You'll have to send your cable through Berlin for censorship."

"Is the Ambassador in? He's a friend of mine."

"No, sir, the Ambassador has returned to Washington."

"For good?"

"Yes, sir—at the request of the German government."

"I've heard there are American ships at Bordeaux to take United States citizens back to the States. Is that true?"

"That's the first time I've heard of that. The only method of return we can suggest is to take a train to Spain, and from there to Lisbon, Portugal. In Lisbon you will find American boats boarding passengers for New York."

"All right, how do I go about that? I want to make arrangements for myself, my wife and my friend here, who is also an American."

"Well, I don't know if I—" Philip started to say.

"You'll need your passports, your French papers, a United States identity card, and a departure permit from the German headquarters."

"What about booking seats on the train and passage on the boat?"

"I'm afraid it's all on a catch-as-catch-can basis."

"In other words, money talks?"

"Well, yes, it is the universal language, is it not?"

After leaving the embassy, Man and Philip walked leisurely up the Champs-Élysées to the Café Richelieu, where they ordered a *croque-monsieur* and a beer.

"What if Clarisse won't go?" Philip asked.

"Oh, she'll go. I'm giving up the studio, so she won't have a place to stay. Besides, she can't live without me."

"Is it true that mixed couples have a hard time of it in New York?"

"Mixed couples have a hard time of it everywhere."

"Well, as for me, Man, I've made up my mind to hang on here a while longer."

"Mistake, Philip. This thing's going to turn ugly, and you're bound to get the shit knocked out of you. Anyway, what's it all about? I mean, hanging on here? Everyone's gone, or going. All the fun, the good times—what the hell? Now, with my studio gone, you won't even have a place to work."

"Could I ask you something about my work, Man? I mean, be a hundred percent honest with me—do you think I have enough talent to, you know, get somewhere as a painter? Sometimes, *most* times, I feel so . . . so disappointed in what I paint."

"Look, Philip, technically you do all right, you've got good color sense and good brushwork and a strong sense of composition, but you've got one big deficiency—it's not in your nature to take a risk. Your nature is to play it safe. Of course there is safety in imitation, but innovation is what advances armies and one-man shows. And innovation requires risk. Did you ever place a bet using all your rent money? Did you ever have an affair with a friend's wife? Would you ever paint a face green, like Chagall? You see what I mean? Risk."

"I would like to open up—I really would," said Philip. "But it's like—don't laugh— when I was a kid playing baseball, I always wanted to stand in there and not flinch when they threw me a curve, but no matter how hard I tried I always pulled back when the baseball came spinning at me."

Man paid the bill, pushing aside Philip's offer, and they slowly walked down the Champs-Élysées toward the Métro station at the Rond-Point. "I'll leave you all my paints and canvases," Man said. "There must be some place you can work in the hotel. Give it an out-and-out try. Get drunk. Smoke some hash. Rough up a woman now and then. Try to put something on canvas no one's ever seen before. Or felt before. Especially that."

They took the Métro back to Man's studio. Clarisse was gone. She had squeezed the contents of every tube of paint all over the walls and furniture. All the canvases were in shreds, and Man's clothes had been taken from the suitcase and stuffed into a turpentine vat that was used for cleaning brushes. Across the far wall, scrawled in vermilion, was the single word "Adieu."

Man walked slowly to the center of his beloved studio, where he had done such good work and had lived so satisfactorily, and he slowly turned, surveying the ruins around him. "Well, I guess this means she's not coming to America with me."

When Philip returned to the Ritz, he checked his box, hoping for a message from Lili. There was none. He phoned her room, but there was no answer. He decided to go to the Cambon side and have a drink in Bertin's Little Bar.

While he waited for Bertin to make his Bloody Mary (a drink Bertin claimed he invented for Hemingway), Philip looked around to see who was there. That was when he saw her, Countess Lili von Jorosjc, sitting on one of the banquettes with a man on each side of her. She was drinking a Pink Lady and laughing at what one of the men, who were Japanese, was saying. They were speaking Japanese. Philip asked Bertin who the men were.

"Munitions people. We see a lot of them now. From all over. A lot of Japanese, but also from the Middle East. Just last night there was a whole table of Turks here, talking bombs and bullets in terrible French. The Germans buy from all of them, but mostly from the Japs. The Ritz is full of munitions people these days."

Lili looked toward the bar and saw Philip watching her. She did not give him so much as an eyelash of recognition. After a moment, she rejoined the conversation with her escorts. Philip turned his back on her and talked to Bertin, who refilled his glass with the residue in the Bloody Mary shaker.

"What is she up to, Bertin, do you know?"

"Who?"

"The one who calls herself Countess von Jorosjc. What's her game?"

"It is my policy not to discuss clients, as you know, Monsieur Weber, but—do you know the expression 'Leave well enough alone'?"

"Yes."

"I would urge you to be guided by it."

"But what is she all about?"

Bertin's attention was diverted to a gentleman from the Swiss Consulate who had appeared at the bar, and Philip took his drink and moved over to a small table in full view of Lili. If she is going to ignore me, Philip decided, I will make her as uncomfortable as I can. Besides, I want to look at her.

Philip studied the Japanese men, who were well dressed and obviously affluent; their proximity to Lili, their easygoing conversation with her, the way they touched her hand, aroused envy and jealousy in him. Bertin kept a practiced eye on Philip, sensing his upset, topping his Bloody Mary. Philip noted that the tenor of Lili's conversation with the Japanese had changed: their faces were now sober, their voices lowered, their heads conspiratorial. Lili was listening intently to what one of the Japanese was telling her, nodding in understanding, but not looking at him.

Then, abruptly, the men rose, made way for Lili, and all three quickly left the bar, Lili again completely ignoring Philip. He tasted the bitter gall of her rejection and was angry with himself for being stupidly and deliberately vulnerable. It's almost as if I wanted to be humiliated, he thought.

He carried his glass to the bar and surrendered it to Bertin in exchange for "*un* dry." The Swiss colonel had left and Philip began to regain his composure as he sipped the exquisitely cold gin and felt its reassuring fingers course through him. A Frenchman he knew who worked for the Ministry came in and they played poker dice at the bar while consuming several martinis. It was much more than Philip usually drank, and he also played for higher than his usual stakes, but he needed these stronger distractions.

When the Frenchman left for a dinner engagement, Philip signed his check and went up to his room. As he closed the door behind him and took off his jacket he felt a sudden flash of anger at Lili. "No!" he shouted aloud. "No!" He thrust his jacket back on and angrily left his room, took the back stairs to the second floor, and hurried along the corridor. When he located Lili's room he found the door ajar and heard the sounds of a string quartet. Without knocking, he quietly entered, closing the door behind him. He found himself in a small foyer that opened into the room itself, which was dimly lighted by several candles. The music was coming from a phonograph. The room appeared deserted.

"I've been expecting you," Lili said, in a soft voice. Then Philip saw her, lying on a chaise longue of brocaded silk, a silver champagne cooler beside her. Her hair was piled haphazardly on the top of her head, blond wisps straying, and she wore a thin silk kimono of pale gold.

Philip walked over to her, and she made room for him on the chaise beside her.

"Oh, I'm tired, Philip, I'm so tired. Like a wind-up toy that is almost at the end." She leaned her head against his chest and sighed deeply. "I have been drinking all day, and I suppose I am drunk, but I do not feel drunk at all. I feel that I see everything very, very clearly. I see you very clearly, Philip." She put her arms firmly around him, pressing him against her as she raised her lips to his, her small, warm sweet-tasting tongue exploring his mouth. Philip's entire body swelled in response to her, the thin silk of her robe intensifying the appeal of her supple body.

She pulled back her head and looked up at him, still holding him tightly, the front of her robe fallen open. "Oh, Philip, I would like to be involved with you, I *am* involved with you, but I have made some serious mistakes . . . some very serious mistakes . . ." Tears came to her eyes and she bit on her lower lip.

"We all make mistakes, Lili."

"And we pay for them."

"Well, yes, but then after we pay, we're in the clear. I can help you—"

"No, no, Philip, darling man, you cannot, that's the hell of it. It would make it worse . . . worse . . ." She was crying now, a strand of hair fallen across her face. The record had run its course, and the revolving turntable made an endlessly mournful whisper. "What do you want of me, Philip? Do you want anything of me?"

"Only to be with you, Lili."

"Would you like to live with me?"

"More than anything. I think about you all the time." He put his lips on hers, sharing the salty taste of her tears as he kissed her, her firm, bare breasts against his shirt.

She moved her lips to his ear, holding him even more tightly. "Listen, Philip, I am going to try to redeem myself. In the beginning, I thought it was a game, you know how I love excitement, but, God, how was I to know it wasn't a game at all, and now I don't want to play anymore, but that's not the way it works, Philip. That's not in the rules. I only want to back away, just stop playing, that's all, but they say I can't."

"We can run away from them, Lili."

"I can't."

"Why not?"

"They know my every move. We wouldn't have a chance, and they would get you too."

"But you must tell me, Lili, so I can share—"

"Oh, no, Philip, oh, no! You are the only decent—listen, Philip, I am frightened, but I have a plan."

"You must be careful, Lili."

"It's been so long since I've cared about anyone, Philip. Oh, I've been in love a little bit, but to care is more important than all the rest, and I *care* about you, Philip. They won't let me go. It was just some funny business, a game of hopscotch. And now they have me. But you do want me, Philip, don't you? Please, Philip, please want me. But why won't they let me . . . why do they . . ." She was fiercely clinging to Philip, her voice a strident wail, her tears choking her.

Philip stroked her back and murmured soothing words to her until her frantic grip on him began to loosen, and her head lowered to his shoulder, and her tears turned to intermittent sobs.

After a while she fell asleep, protected in the shell of his body.

He awoke in the pitch dark not knowing where he was. The candles had burned out and the acrid smell of their extinction hung in the room. Philip jumped up from the chaise and groped his way across the room to the light switch.

Lili was gone. Her closet was empty and her suitcases weren't there. Again she had disappeared from his life without warning. On the desk there was a piece of Ritz stationery on which Lili had written in large letters: "Philip, darling—believe in me!"

He left and returned to his room, taking Lili's note with him. He was not at all sure he would ever see her again.

Every other Friday, Charley Ritz lunched with his friend Marcel de Forrestière at Prunier. There were only two people in Paris whom Charley saw on a regular friendship basis, and Marcel was one of them. This was the same de Forrestière who had challenged Philip and Goering to the tennis game at the Racing Club.

For several years, Charley and Marcel had lunched at the same table, attended by the same waiter, who, without being told, brought them a lunch invariably consisting of a dozen Belon oysters, Dover sole *amandine,* endive salad, a bottle of Quincy wine, cassis sherbet, *café filtre* and Montecristo cigars. The two men shared a passion for fly-fishing, travel, Proust, Bach, and 122 Provence, where, before the Germans, de Forrestière used to visit on a regular three-times-a-week basis.

But on this particular day, the consistency of their luncheons dissolved. To begin with, the captain came to the table and regretfully informed them that, because of the war, not even Prunier could procure Belons from the North Sea, nor sole from the English Channel. Without enthusiasm, Charley and Marcel settled for a fish bisque and broiled *lotte.* The captain had more bad news: endives had also disappeared from the marketplace; but, on the brighter side, Quincy and cassis sherbet were still in abundance. As for the *café filtre,* Prunier was experimenting with a substitute for the black coffee bean which was no longer obtainable. The captain retreated, mumbling apologies.

"The bloody Krauts are destroying us, Charley," de Forrestière said, with a sad shake of his head. "And it's just the beginning. Citroën can't produce cars. The Ritz is not the Ritz—it's a refuge for German madmen, butchers, and schizophrenics."

The *sommelier* poured a dollop of the cold Quincy for de Forrestière to sample. He nodded appreciatively, and the *sommelier* filled their glasses.

"You should be more careful, Marcel—the Nazis have ears everywhere."

"That old *sommelier?*"

"Why not? People of all ages are selling their souls for a brisket of beef and a scuttle of coal."

"And some people are not selling their souls." De Forrestière took a long swallow of his wine. "Did you hear De Gaulle on the short wave from London? 'France has lost a battle, but it has not lost the—'"

The steaming bisque, giving off a strong fish aroma, was placed before them in a silver tureen, from which the waiter ladled portions into their bowls. This time Marcel suspended his conversation until the waiter had gone.

"Charley, we've got to do something. We can't just sit back and hope that the fog will lift so that we can go back to our fly-fishing and our Belons."

"What are you alluding to, Marcel? This is a very strange lunch we're having. Very strange indeed."

"Yes, it is." Marcel lowered his voice. "Face it, Charley, there simply won't be any trout fishing unless we get involved."

"In what way?"

"Resistance."

Charley sat back and looked at him, dumbfounded.

"I'm in on it, Charley, and I want you to be."

"Doing what? What in God's name could I—"

The busboy removed the soup bowls.

"We need a message center. Somewhere that will baffle the *Funkspiel's* locators."

"I don't understand."

"The *Funkspiel* has direction-finders that are disguised as garbage trucks, ambulances, police vans, all kinds of vehicles. But if a radio transmitter were set up in the Ritz . . ."

"You're talking about a short-wave station?"

"Yes."

"In the Ritz?"

"Yes, right smack in the midst of all those German big shots."

"To do what?"

"Send and receive coded messages to and from London—a very sophisticated transmitter. We had one operating from an apartment near the Eiffel Tower, but the *Funkspiel* located it and destroyed it."

"And the man who ran it?"

"Two women. I may as well tell you that the Nazis consider a transmitter a weapon of war; to use it is considered an act of treason. The two women were put in front of a firing squad. Since then we've been forced to use couriers, but it is a cumbersome method, too slow for our needs."

The waiter served their fish and refilled their wineglasses.

"If we could set up a transmitter in your room, Charley, we could blend it with the transformer you use for your train. One of my Citroën engineers who is part of my Underground cell has invented a little device called a scrambler that would make it very difficult for the *Funkspiel* to locate the transmitter. He assures me that even if a Kraut detector picked up the short-wave beams, it would be almost impossible to locate its source. It would drive the Krauts crazy." De Forrestière chuckled.

"And if they did locate it?"

"What the hell, Charley? What I'm doing—well, it's best not to compromise you by telling you about it, but I can assure you I'm a hell of a lot more vulnerable than you would be."

"I have to stay out of it, Marcel. I'm sorry, but I have to think of my mother—what they might do to her to make me talk if I got caught."

"And what about my wife and children?"

"Listen, Marcel, the point is, I'm not a joiner. You know me. It's against my nature. I don't have the mentality for it. I would have no confidence."

"We must help out, Charley. Those of us at the top, with titles, executive positions—we are much less vulnerable than the ordinary fellows who are doing all the dirty work. The Nazis won't suspect us. I would be your only contact. My Underground name is Pelican. No one else would know your identity, other than I. London would have only your call letters. We must help out, Charley, we simply have to."

"Marcel, I have already made my contribution. The last war, I was a sergeant in the United States Army—did you know that?"

"You were what? How could that be?"

"I had gone to America in 1916 to work at the Ritz-Carlton in New York. When the war broke out, I joined the American Army. I was assigned to a public-relations outfit that processed foreigners who wanted to join the Army. After the war, I stayed in the States and developed some business interests—the Ritz Motion Picture Corporation and the Ritz Import and Export Corporation with an office in Times Square. I loved New York and I felt at home there, but in 1928 my mother forced me to return to Paris."

"Well, Charley, the time has come to serve your own country."

"But now I'm forty-nine, Marcel, not twenty-seven."

"And I'm fifty, Charley. We are both strong and healthy. Our duty is to do whatever we can. What do you say?"

Charley leaned back in his chair and looked away. He watched two chic ladies at a nearby table, their heads bent so low in gossip that their foreheads were almost touching. He envied the simplicity of their lunch. He returned his eyes to the anxious face of his old friend.

"Let me think about it, Marcel. Needless to say, at forty-nine I am not as brave as I was at twenty-seven. Living dangerously no longer appeals to me."

18

Philip suffered through an uncharacteristic sleepless night. He desperately tried not to think about Lili, but could not put her out of his mind. And when finally he did fall into a turbulent sleep, an ominous, threatening word hovered over him, "PRELOON."

He sat up in the dark, clutching the sides of his narrow bed, not knowing where he was. Then he tried desperately to identify the word. He thought of all the people he knew, all the places he had been, but no association brought him a clue. The word would now haunt him, not only the following day, but for months to come. At night it would often perch in his dreams and threaten him, a vulturous, hulking presence, endlessly repeating itself, the "L-O-O-O-N" stretched floating into the darkness, a howl, a wail, a cry of despair.

The message from Goering was to meet him at the Jeu de Paume at five o'clock. The Jeu de Paume was a small museum in the Tuileries Garden which had formerly devoted itself to Impressionist paintings, but which had now become the clearinghouse for confiscated art. It was here that the E.R.R. director, Baron von Behr, staged special displays for Goering from which the Reichsmarschall selected those works he wished to add to his collection. The Baron always made these occasions as festive as possible, filling the display rooms with potted plants and stationing a string quartet in the entrance foyer, where champagne and hors d'oeuvres were served.

Philip arrived punctually, but Goering was an hour late. The Reichsmarschall wore a high-necked white gold-braided uniform with a white, gold-lined cape over his shoulders. He carried his Reichsmarschall's baton, with which he occasionally tapped the palm of his left hand, and he smoked a thin cigar in an ivory holder. He was in a very good frame of mind, for he had just received word that an attacking force he had dispatched to the

Mediterranean had trapped a convoy of British ships and had sunk four cruisers and six destroyers and had severely damaged the aircraft carrier *Formidable*. He beckoned to Philip, wordlessly handed him a glass of champagne, and immediately started his tour of the paintings.

Goering inspected each painting carefully, indicating those he wanted by pointing at them with his baton. The titular head of the Jeu de Paume, Dr. Bruno Lohse, noted these choices on a clipboard. Goering spoke to Philip only once, to ask, in a low voice, his opinion of a large Coypel canvas. "It was one of the finest paintings in Baron de Rothschild's collection," Philip said. Goering pointed his baton at it.

Goering chose sixty-three paintings in all, most of them portraits, and a large "G" sticker was immediately affixed to the frames. In the foyer afterward, while champagne glasses were being refilled, Goering introduced Philip to von Behr, Lohse, Fräuleins Linberger and Pütz, Gustav Rochlitz and Dr. Bunjes, the key people in his art operation. He explained that Philip would be writing a book about his collection, and instructed all of them to give Philip all the information which he might seek. Goering then drained his glass of champagne and left abruptly. Baron von Behr invited Philip into his office.

"My principal office is at the E.R.R. in the Commodore Hotel," he explained. "I think it's best that you come there for your interviews. Of course, it's understood that, as chief of the operation, I will double-check for accuracy any information you receive."

"I will be most careful with my facts, Baron."

"What nationality are you, Herr Weber? Your German is so perfect, it's hard to tell, although I think I detect a very slight accent."

"American."

"Really? I have never known an American to speak German as well as you do, and rarely an Englishman. You have a background in art?"

"Yes."

"I am rather surprised by your selection, since Dr. Bunjes, whom you just met, is director of the German Art Historical Institute here in Paris and has several historians on his staff who certainly would be eminently qualified to write about the Reichsmarschall's collection."

"As he explained it to me," Philip replied, "the Reichsmarschall wanted an outside perspective."

"I see."

"An overview, you might say."

"Yes. But without the background of facts and knowledge of the experts on Dr. Bunjes' staff."

"That will be the object of my interviews, to collect all that information," Philip explained.

The telephone rang. It was the Baron's wife asking if he could spare Fräulein Pütz for a few hours to help with some letters and household accounts. The Baron was extremely jealous of his English wife and demanded close accounting of her every activity. In fact, the guard at the entrance to their commandeered apartment on the Avenue Victor-Hugo was under strict instructions not to let anyone visit the Baroness who did not have the Baron's approval. Although Ilse Pütz went to assist Baroness von Behr every week, the Baron nevertheless required his wife to get his permission each time.

On this occasion, he hesitated a moment, toying with the notion of spending a few hours after work with Fräulein Pütz in his Commodore apartment, but then he recalled that he had a seven-o'clock appointment with the head of Hitler's art office, and gave his permission.

As she did whenever Fräulein Pütz was scheduled to arrive, the Baroness went through a ritual of preparation: she lit sandalwood incense in her bedroom, iced a bottle of champagne, and anointed her body with Shalimar perfume, which was Fräulein Pütz's favorite. Baroness von Behr did not know about her husband's sexual involvement with Fräulein Pütz, any more than he knew about hers. As for Fräulein Pütz, she enjoyed her masked sessions in the black silk bedroom with the Baron, but her real passion was for his wife. In bed with the Baroness, she was the aggressor, extracting uncontrolled ecstasies, the staid Baroness losing control of herself as Fräulein Pütz fed her own aggressive passions. The Baroness had never had any sexual response to the Baron, certainly never an orgasm, although she pretended to in order to satisfy his ego. Her attraction to Fräulein Pütz had come as a shock and a surprise to her, but now she was constantly hungry for Fräulein Pütz's weekly visits. The Baroness daydreamed about her, could feel her mouth caressing her vagina, and during the infrequent occasions when the Baron made love to her the Baroness's thoughts invariably turned to Fräulein Pütz.

After the initial introduction at the Jeu de Paume, Philip went to the E.R.R. offices every day. He was given access to inventories, acquisition records, analyses of the physical state of the acquisitions, but the key people in the offices treated him in a perfunctory manner, especially Baron von Behr.

It did not take Philip long to conclude that the only two people in the E.R.R. with sufficient authority to influence the disposition of confiscated art were the Baron and his assistant, Dr. Lohse. It was also quickly apparent to Philip that the two men were suspicious and jealous of each other. The Baron resented Lohse's superior knowledge and expertise, and Lohse resented the authority of the Baron, who, he felt, was a total ignoramus about art.

Three weeks after Philip began his investigation for Goering, there occurred a confrontation that made him regret having accepted Goering's assignment. Of all places, it occurred at 122 Rue Provence during one of Philip's weekly rendezvous with Camille. They had finished a splendid lunch and had just entered the railway-carriage room to go to bed. It was their ritual, on entering the room, for Camille to undress Philip and give him a *friction* with rose water, but on this occasion Camille said, "Philip, it will just take a few minutes—I want you to meet someone."

She led him to the railway carriage, opened the door, and turned on the motor which activated the sound and motion of the simulated train. After she closed the door of the stateroom, she opened a door in the compartment itself, and a trim, bearded man stepped out. He wore a corduroy coat over a turtleneck sweater, and tinted eyeglasses.

"This is Muskrat," Camille said.

Philip was too disoriented to shake hands.

"We must be quick," Muskrat said.

"Muskrat is with the Underground," Camille said. "The Resistance. He is in charge of this *quartier*."

"We are aware of your involvement with Goering," Muskrat said, speaking rapidly. "Your position makes you invaluable for us, and we need your help."

"But I have no involvement with Goering. I know nothing about the military—"

"We know that. But you do know about his art, don't you?"

"Well, yes, somewhat, but what does that have to do with the Underground?"

"We want to know where it's going. Some of France's greatest art is being shipped off to destinations unknown to us. Thrown to the winds. We may never recover those pictures unless we know where they are being sent. All we ask of you is a list of the art and where it has been sent. We know how much you appreciate great paintings, and we're asking you to help keep them from getting lost."

"Now level with Philip about the risk involved," Camille said.

"Naturally there is risk. I think you know how the Nazis operate and what they do to those who are caught. What we are asking, quite frankly, puts you in the category of spy—and even though you are an American, that wouldn't deter the Germans from torturing you. But what we are asking of you entails low risk. It's information that would be coming to you anyway, and art *per se* doesn't really interest the Gestapo."

"But why should I get involved in all this?" Philip asked. "It's not my country, and it's not my war."

"It's your art, Monsieur Weber. Great art belongs to every citizen of the world. It doesn't have nationality."

"But what good would it do for you to know where the art is taken? You can't get it back."

"Of course we can. When the war ends."

"I don't understand what you mean. You've already lost the war. It's ended for you and for most of Europe."

"Yes, we are momentarily defeated, but the war is not over. And when it is over, we will be in a position to reclaim what they took from us."

"But I'm an American. I'm neutral. I don't see why I should get involved in a French matter," Philip said.

"How long have you lived in Paris, Monsieur Weber?"

"Since 1928."

"You've lived here by choice, haven't you?"

"Yes."

"You've enjoyed all the things Paris has to offer."

"Of course."

"Thanks to the Sorbonne and the Louvre you've become very knowledgeable about art and art history, correct?"

"Why are you asking me these obvious questions?"

"I want to impress upon you the fact that Paris has given you a great deal, and that you owe her something in return. You talk about being a neutral American, but what has nationality to do with your way of life? The very art you love is threatened. The life of Paris is in jeopardy. He who sups at the table helps wash the dishes."

"It's time you go, Muskrat," Camille said.

"Think about it, Monsieur Weber. You will be contacted again."

"I really don't need to think it over—" Philip started to say, but Muskrat stopped him.

"I must go. We try to limit our risk. You are an intelligent, compassionate man, Monsieur Weber, and you will give some thought to our proposition whether you want to or not. Your answer will eventually have to be given to your own conscience, not to me."

Muskrat quickly crossed to the door and disappeared.

"You shouldn't have done that to me, Camille," Philip said. "It's very unfair of you to take advantage of me like this."

"I'm sorry, Philip, but I have decided to do whatever I can. You and I have a long relation—I'm not just your whore—and I thought you might have understanding for what has to be done. If you don't want to get involved, all you have to do is say no."

"I realize that. But it was wrong of you to tell them about my involvement with Goering."

"Not I! I told them nothing. They came to me knowing everything about you. They even knew that you were with me on Wednesdays. All they asked of me was to arrange this meeting."

"You mean they've been checking on me? How would they know . . . ?"

"Philip, on the surface you see nothing, but down below, in the Underground, are quite a few Parisians who are already hard at work for the Resistance."

She started to undress him. "But if you think I've been presumptuous, please forgive me. The evenings here are filled with Nazi officers. They are a breed of men who don't appeal to me, either at the dinner table or in bed. They have no business being here. It is . . . humiliating. Even for someone in my . . . well, way of life. By helping the Underground I feel like . . . something. Please understand." She began to rub some rose water on his chest and across his shoulders. There was a film of tears in her eyes. "This is a most peculiar time," she said. "Even for a woman like me."

Philip was suddenly angry. "What have I got left?" he blurted out. "My friends, my life here in Paris, all the people I loved to see and the things I loved to do—gone! Except for you. You were what I could still look forward to. It will never be the same now. Not knowing when and where your Muskrat fellow might jump up. Maybe next time he'll get into bed with us. You shouldn't have brought him here, Camille—what a hell of a thing to do!"

Philip had started to put his clothes back on. Camille went to him and again unbuttoned his shirt.

"Don't be angry, Philip. I don't blame you, but please understand. I am only trying to help in whatever way I can. It should not affect us. I look forward to you, even more than you do to me. We must not quarrel or be angry with each other."

She had undressed him again, and he did not resist. Camille led Philip onto the bed and folded him in her arms, her full breasts soft and warm against his chest. In no time at all, his anger disappeared.

19

Madame Ritz lived in a suite of rooms under the mansard on the garden side. In order for Charles to go from his rooms to his mother's, it was necessary for him to go down a flight of stairs to the floor below, follow a long corridor that linked the two sections of the hotel, and then go up another flight of stairs that led to his mother's apartment.

Madame Ritz was a small woman with carefully arranged white hair and an air of stern aloofness. Her employees were in fear of her, the Ritz guests in awe of her; her son's attitude was one of both fear and awe, compounded with a streak of resentment. She spoke sparingly, but when she did address someone she invariably smacked her lips a few times before speaking, as if pretasting her words to make sure they were bitter enough. She lived in her neat rooms, white curtains, pots of yellow flowers from the Ritz greenhouse, with two Pekingese of snappish disposition who followed her wherever she went. Along the windows in her sitting room were six separately caged canaries.

Charley saw his mother on a regular basis once a week for Sunday lunch, which was served promptly at two o'clock in her sitting room. The food came up on a dumbwaiter to the serving pantry on the floor below and was carried up the stairs by the two best waiters on the floor. Charles neither looked forward to nor resented these Sunday lunches. It was an event to which he had long ago resigned himself, and he never allowed his mother's carping to upset him.

"Can you imagine," Madame Ritz was saying, "that this Colonel Stuppelmayer came up this morning to complain about the quality of the wines on the *carte des vins*. He had sent for me to come to his suite—oh, the gall of it, summoning *me!*—but I sent a little note saying that I preferred to receive *him*. I already knew what was on his Teutonic brain—Louis Delor had tipped me off (what a clever fellow Louis is, someday I shall promote him)—and as a result I was ready for Colonel Stuppelmayer. As you may know, last summer, when we knew the Germans were on their way into Paris, Louis transferred thirty-one thousand of our best bottles to that deserted wine cellar he found in the old church off the Boulevard Raspail. But Colonel Stuppelmayer is clever. He got hold of one of our wine lists from before the Occupation. He knew what was missing. He stood there all scrubbed and immaculate, showing me the list and demanding an accounting."

"What did you say to him?"

"I said I was amazed that no one had informed him that Hitler's personal representative had shipped the whole lot to Berlin for the Führer's own cellar. Of course, I said, I could send word to Hitler that Colonel Stuppelmayer was demanding the return of the wine which was sent to him."

"Do you think he'll check with Hitler's representative?"

"I should think not. Bullies like Stuppelmayer are scared to death of their superiors. I'm sure our wine is perfectly safe." Madame Ritz fed some tidbits of meat to the two Pekingese, who were sitting expectantly on a chair beside her.

After the waiters had cleared away the dishes and Charley and his mother had taken their coffee to comfortable armchairs at the windows, Charley considered it as good a time as any to get his mother's opinion on the Resistance.

"Do you remember Marcel de Forrestière, Maman? He's the fellow I went fishing with last spring."

"Yes."

"He has approached me. . . . He belongs to a group that is operating against the Germans, sub rosa."

"You mean the Resistance?"

"There are many groups in the Resistance, not just one."

"And?"

"He wants me to . . . well, cooperate. He has a specific thing for me to do that—"

"You mean to operate against the Huns?"

"Yes, Maman. It's rather a simple thing, but since I must perform it here in the hotel, I thought I'd mention it to you."

"Charles, we must not go out of our way, neither to help the Huns nor to hinder them."

"But you haven't heard what it is that—"

"I don't need—I don't want to hear. We must not compromise this house of your father. It is a shrine to his name, and we must do nothing to bring down the roof on our heads."

"But what about that secret cache of wine?"

"That wine belongs to us. At worst, if the Huns find it they will simply drink it. But if we perform a treasonous act, go out of our way to do something deliberate, something hostile . . ."

"But, Maman, if they need me—"

"You know nothing about such things, Charles. You will make a botch of it, believe me, just as you made a botch of the few hotel matters which I have entrusted to you. You know how vicious the Nazis are. If they catch you at whatever it is you intend to do, they will punish all of us, not just you."

"It's just a radio transmitter. I would disguise it as part of the transformer for my trains."

"And you and this de Forrestière think your little transmitter will drive the German Army out of Paris?"

"I would set up communication with London—"

"And what good would that do? Enable us to hear those ponderous speeches of De Gaulle? What do you know about such technical equipment?"

"They would teach me, Maman. It's not all that difficult."

"Charles, listen to me. Our one and only object right now is to try to survive. I don't want to provoke them. I don't want them to throw us out on the street and change the name of our hotel to the Hotel Goering or whatever. That is your obligation to your father, above all else."

"I'm not so sure. I mean, that I don't have a bigger obligation."

"Well, Charles, it is a decision you must make for yourself, but whatever you may decide to do, it cannot be done in my hotel. And that is my final word on the subject. I forbid any Underground activity in the Ritz."

In a curious way, Philip enjoyed his new job, because it gave him something specific to do every day, with a payday at the end of the week. He had not held a paying job since his employment years ago in St. Louis, but the fact that he now had a specific daily activity was as important to him as the money.

He really felt no qualms about his masquerade among Goering's art people. He was engaged in a matter that was harmless to the French, a peculiarly intramural investigation. Without this employment, Philip's days would have been particularly empty, because he had taken Man Ray's critique to heart and given up on his attempt to be a painter.

As he was leaving the Cambon entrance one morning, the

driver of a *vélotaxi* parked at the curb called out to him, "Monsieur! I am not engaged. Take you anywhere."

"Thanks, but I have my bicycle."

The driver, a short, chubby man wearing knickers and a knitted cap with a dangling tassle on the top, came over to him. "But, Monsieur Weber," he said, lowering his voice, "the ride is paid for." He opened the door of the enclosed cab that was attached to his bicycle. He was a cheerful-looking man, a wide smile betraying three missing teeth. The fact that he knew his name induced Philip to get into the cab. The driver pedaled down the Rue Cambon, talking over his shoulder.

"My name is Pierre Monet," the driver said, with a punctuation of high-pitched laughter. "A beautiful name, don't you think, Monsieur Weber?"

"How do you know my name?"

"I am your, what-you-call-it—master of ceremonies. I pass you information, I take you places, I am in the center ring, 'Ladies and gentlemen, here are the jugglers and the high-wire dancers and the lion tamers and the clowns . . .'"

"Where are you taking me, Monsieur Monet?"

"Oh, just for a little spin so we can talk. My *vélotaxi* is one hundred percent safe, have no fear, no hidden microphones. But please don't call me Monsieur Monet. It is simply a romantic name I invented for myself. I was really born Dieter Kalvenbach. Is Philip Weber your true name?"

"Yes."

"Ah, you are lucky. But I tell you, as Pierre Monet they do not bother me. I ride them in my *vélo*-bike and they have no suspicion that a German Jew is pedaling them. I speak French with a Yiddish accent, but what do they know? I am happy-go-lucky and full of jokes, and that is the best disguise in the world. I speak broken German to them, comic-strip German, and I make all kinds of funny mistakes. They laugh and want me to say something else, which I do, and it keeps them laughing. I could speak better German than they do, but I make all these funny mistakes and they die laughing." Pedestrians heard his high-pitched laugh and smiled at him. His strong legs effortlessly propelled the *vélo*-bike.

"I have a message for you," Dieter said as he coasted along the Quai Voltaire. "Tomorrow at four in the afternoon you are to go to the bar at the Hole-in-the-Wall."

"The Hole-in-the-Wall? The name is in English?"

"Yes, of course. You know the Hole-in-the-Wall."

"Never heard of it."

"How can that be? It's directly across from the Café de la Paix."

"What? Impossible. I know that area like my own room."

"I assure you, monsieur, it is there as big as life. One of the oldest bars in Paris—although I grant you, the smallest entrance. They say it got its name from a hole left by a cannonball that struck the wall there during the Revolution of 1848. Where the hole was is now the entrance to the bar."

"And that's the name outside?"

"Yes, in neon. You go there four o'clock tomorrow. If the barman, whose name is Gaspard, puts a glass of red wine in front of you, everything is okay, but if he asks you what you'd like, order something, he'll say he doesn't have it, and leave right away."

"But, just a minute, hold on, I haven't said—"

"Yes, okay, yes, yes," Dieter interjected, switching to German, "please do not become disturbed. It's only that someone would like to talk to you, that's all. You will not be obligated in any way."

"If I go, that's the beginning of obligation."

"It's not so bad, really. Being obligated. I enjoy," he switched back to French, "being a spy. I joke about it, so no one takes me seriously. I go all over Paris spreading red herrings. I go to the stamp market at Matignon and Gabriel when it's open Sundays, and I whisper to certain dealers. The puppet show in the Tuileries, I pass notes to the children I sit beside, at Napoleon's tomb I leave a magazine in an obvious place, with one of the pages earmarked—all red herrings. But no one follows me anyway—they would never suspect a man with no front teeth. I have a very nice bridge made for me by a sexy lady dentist in Arles, but I never wear it when I'm out in public."

That evening, Philip had a drink with Coco Chanel in the Little Bar of the Ritz. When he had phoned her, Coco had invited him to her room, but as discreetly as he could Philip had said he would prefer meeting at the bar. Either von Spatz was there or he might show up, and Philip needed to talk to Gabrielle alone.

For once, she was on time. She ordered a champagne and bitters and looked at Philip lovingly.

"I haven't seen you for ages, Ducky."

"I'm busy with that bizarre job I'm doing for Goering."

"I know, but that's no reason to avoid a woman who loves you."

"I'm sorry, Gabrielle. I do think about you often."

"And about Lili, I suspect."

"Yes, yes, very much about Lili. Do you know what's happened to her? When I phoned her room, they said she had checked out and left no forwarding address. How can that be? Do you know where she may have gone? She can't just disappear like that."

"You might as well ask, where did the summer go?" Coco said.

"You have no idea?"

"No, Lili moves in mysterious ways. And you? How does Sherlock Holmes do among the Krauts?"

"Lots of suspects."

"Watch your step, Philip. I asked Von about . . ."

"Von?"

"My resident German. I asked him about your von Behr. He knows him and he says never turn your back on him. Von had dealings with him before the war in Berlin. One of those fellows who slits your throat while shaking hands."

"I know. I'm *en garde*." Philip glanced at the adjoining tables to be sure no one could overhear. He moved a touch closer to Gabrielle; they were sitting side by side on one of the banquettes.

"Listen, Gabrielle, I need your advice. I am being pressured to help the Underground. I am trying to avoid them, but what they want is reasonable, simply about the art; half of me wants to cooperate, but my other half says no. What do you think? After all, I'm not a Frenchman . . ."

"Ah, the French, all of a sudden patriotic, are they? And why? That's the question—why? If you ask me, the French don't give a damn what happens to England or Poland or whether the world is safe for democracy. They despise the Boche only because their precious comforts are interfered with. They abhor being chilly, and they are particularly furious because of their gastronomic deprivation. But morals, principles—don't make me laugh. Did you ever see such a quick, sickening surrender?"

"But there are the men of the Resistance, Gabrielle . . ."

"Yes, of course, there are exceptions and I generalize, but there too they are looking out for themselves. How much do they help the French Jews who are being rounded up every day for slaughter? The French are worse anti-Semites than the Germans. When the trucks come into the neighborhoods for the roundups, the French all peek through their curtains and watch their Jewish neighbors getting pulled from their houses and packed into the trucks, and you know how it makes them feel? Superior. The Germans propagandize themselves as the master race. The French don't need propaganda—Napoleon, Louis XIV. They take it for granted."

20

When Philip returned to his room (he had tactfully declined Gabrielle's invitation to dine with her and von Spatz) he found a message at his door to please call Helga Friebe at the Plaza Athénée as soon as convenient. Helga. Philip smiled as he unlocked the door. Helga back in Paris.

His first encounter with her had been banal, Philip standing in the Place de l'Opéra, his head thrust backward as he studied the figures adorning the roof. As he backed up, the better to see them, he bumped into a woman hurrying down the stone steps. Philip caught her to keep her from falling.

"Oh, I'm sorry, pardon!"

She had grabbed his arm. "It's all right. No harm." She spoke French with a pronounced German accent.

"I was looking at the roof and didn't see you."

She looked up. "I have never once looked at the roof," she laughed. "And I am here almost every day. Isn't that horse exquisite? Why is it people who live in cities never look up?"

"Are you with the opera?"

"Yes, I'm a singer."

"You don't look like a singer."

"You mean because I don't have a double chin?"

She was a lyric soprano who sang *Thaïs, Tosca,* and she had been with the Opéra company for six years. Her voice was only adequate, but there was a dearth of lyric sopranos and the Paris Opéra paid poorly. She was several years older than Philip and she was not pretty, but she had a pleasant face and a good body. Her appearance in *Thaïs* in a flesh-colored body stocking was quite spectacular.

Now, after a long absence, she was back in Paris, and Philip returned her call.

"Philip, *Liebchen,* I am here! You must come! Right away! I have this incredible suite, you wouldn't believe! Number 304. Do you know the Plaza Athénée? Oh, such a hotel!"

"What brings you back?"

"I have a sponsor. I will sing at the opera again."

"A sponsor?"

"A general of the Tank Corps. He sees me only once a month. I have oceans of free time. Come! I am dying to see you."

It was on Philip's lips to ask her about her abrupt departure, something that had deeply bothered him for a long time, but for some strange reason his interest in finding out suddenly disappeared. "I don't want to be a co-sponsor, Helga."

"Oh, Philip, don't be silly, be grown-up."

"I have someone else."

"You do? Oh, what a pity! What a disappointment! I so looked forward to you."

"Well, you were gone for quite a while."

"Such a waste of this beautiful suite. And I have just soaked and perfumed. Oh, can't you come just for now, Philip? I have someone, too. What's the difference?"

He hesitated. "It just won't work out, Helga. I'm really sorry."

"Ah, *Liebchen,* so am I, so am I." She expelled a sigh and hung up.

He sat in the still dark of his room for a moment, trying to figure out why he had rejected her. The reality about Helga, he thought, with her stodgy, practical mind, was that she liked to talk endlessly about stodgy, practical things. Even when she talked about her singing she never discussed it in interesting, artistic terms, nor did she tell past anecdotes or future dreams. No, she talked about her singing only in relation to the practical matters of her bowels (constipated, her high notes would lack luster; diarrhea, her voice production suffered) or her gastronomy (leafy vegetables and salads bloated her) or her sleep (if she did not have nine hours and wake naturally she would have no roundness to her lower register). Helga was good in bed, very good, but she liked long dinners beforehand at which she slowly sipped her red wine and talked her endless talk, and after making love she would renew her banal chatter.

Philip shook his head. Face it, Weber, it's Lili; it has nothing to do with Helga and you know it. It's crazy, but I have to admit that while I was talking to Helga I had this feeling that I was being unfaithful to Lili. Faithful to a fantasy, can you believe it? But then again, maybe she will become more than a fantasy. If only she'd stop disappearing on me. . . .

The phone rang. It was Kropp. Would it be convenient for

Herr Weber to come to see the Reichsmarschall immediately? Always that word "immediately." Goering will want to know the identity of the culprit. I am working on it, Reichsmarschall, but I mustn't rush things or they will get suspicious of me. How does that sound? Worth a try. Charley Ritz was right, of course. Don't get involved, especially with Goering.

Goering was on the red phone, giving combat orders to the commander of the Messerschmitts based in Normandy. He was wearing a white silk flowing robe, trimmed in ermine, that reached the floor. The pattern of the bombing raids, he was saying, was becoming too predictable. There had to be more night attacks with the Messerschmitts carrying full loads of bombs. Monette Lynette was sitting at a table in the corner of the salon, carefully preparing two pipes of opium.

Kropp brought Philip into the room, and Goering motioned him to a chair and pointed to the champagne.

"Now, Philip," Goering said as he hung up, "I have a very good opportunity for you." Goering's face was flushed, the pupils of his eyes constricted, his voice a little louder than usual. "I am going to the Normandy coast to visit our airfields, and while I'm gone, as a Christmas present, I am letting my art people use my private train to go on a ski vacation in Austria. Do you ski?"

"No, sir."

"No matter. The way you play tennis, you'll learn very quickly. But the point is, you will be isolated with these people of mine, and it will give you a perfect opportunity to ask a lot of questions. It's about time someone gave himself away."

Goering took Philip comradely by the arm and started to walk him toward the door. He had never before been as friendly toward Philip. "I want to thank you for Monette," he said. "She is very pleasant company."

As they passed through the study, Goering opened a drawer in his desk and handed Philip an envelope. "This is a list I procured through Goebbels, which shows the distribution of every piece of art confiscated by the Paris E.R.R. It may be useful to you."

The red phone began to ring. "I must answer. Let yourself out. Good luck on the ski trip."

Philip put the envelope into his inner pocket. He realized that it contained the very list the Underground wanted.

After his phone call, Goering joined Monette in the bedroom. There was a pipe of opium on each side of the bed. For several

nights now, Goering had feasted on Monette's morphine con-
coctions, no longer giving any thought to his own one-hundred-
tablet quota. He was enjoying himself. Monette was an artist in
bed. He had not felt so good for a long time. Even the perversity
of the air war over Britain did not dampen his euphoria.

In going to look for the Hole-in-the-Wall, it was Philip's
intention only to satisfy his curiosity as to whether such a bar
opposite the Café de la Paix actually existed. It was clearly not
his intention to go inside. He walked down the Rue de la Paix to
the Place de l'Opéra, turned left onto the Boulevard des
Capucines, and, sure enough, there it was, a short distance from
the corner, a minuscule entranceway with an unlighted neon sign
on the wall over the door:

GALA CLUB
HOLE-IN-THE-WALL
ENGLISH BAR

There was also a sign that proclaimed the presence of Courvoisier within, and another that promised "The Original Guin-
ness Stout." A ragged accordionist stood at the curb playing for
coins.

While Philip was wondering how he had never noticed this bar,
despite having passed it hundreds of times and having sat
innumerable other times on the terrace of the Café de la Paix
facing it, the accordionist approached him and opened the door.

"If you please, Monsieur Weber," he said, "come in and have
a drink."

Philip hesitated. The accordionist, a tall, gaunt man with holes
in his sleeves, continued to hold the door open and smile at him.

The interior was long and narrow and had an L-shaped
mahogany bar, with a bright brass foot railing, curving all along
the side of the room. There were several high-backed booths
along the wall opposite the bar. All the walls were covered with
mirrors, so that no matter where one sat one could observe
everything in the room; even if one sat in a booth with one's back
to the door, there was a clear view in the mirror of anyone
entering.

There was no one in the barroom when Philip entered. He sat
down on one of the leather stools, and the barman, without
being asked, put a wineglass in front of him and filled it to the
brim with red wine. The barman said nothing. He went to the far

end of the bar, where he reclaimed a smoking cigarette from a Cinzano ashtray. Philip sat looking at himself and at the entrance behind him, sipping his wine, trying to screw up enough courage to get up and leave. When his glass was empty, which was the moment to make his move, the barman silently refilled it.

Eventually the door opened and a girl entered, an attractive girl in her middle twenties. She was wearing a raincoat and a rain hat which she tugged off her auburn hair as she entered.

"Philip!" she exclaimed, rushing over to him. "Am I glad to see you!" She put one arm around his neck and kissed him fervently on both cheeks.

"Cóme, let's sit in a booth," she said.

Philip had never seen her before, but he carried his wineglass over to one of the booths to join her. She had removed her raincoat, and now she sat across from him, beaming. The bartender brought her a glass of red wine.

"Well, here's to what may be," she said to Philip, and they both drank. Philip was struck by how American she looked: a faint sprinkle of freckles on her snub nose, no makeup, an athletic body. Her eyes, the color of her hair, were almonds, with naturally shaped eyebrows. She wore no fingernail polish, no rings, no jewelry of any kind. She was dressed in a plain long-sleeved sweater and a plaid skirt. Her hair was short, with modest bangs across the forehead.

"My name is Gaby Duvier," she said, leaning toward him and lowering her voice. "I speak English, but it is better if we converse in French. If anyone comes in, I will be affectionate, your girl friend, but as long as no one but Gaspard is here we need not pretend."

"I don't want to mislead you," Philip said. "I really came here out of curiosity. I have decided it's not a good idea for me to get mixed up in this."

"But do you think it's a good idea for the Germans to steal all this great art? Some of these old masterpieces may disappear forever, or be badly damaged."

"I don't approve of it, of course, but I'm just no good at this kind of . . . of thing."

"What does that mean? All we want is a copy of a list which you probably already have. You give it to us and that's all there is to it."

"Until the next batch of art gets shipped. Then you'll want the new list. And so on. No, I'm an American, I'm neutral. I don't want to get involved. What I'm doing right now is harmless, just finding out something for Goering that affects no one but him."

"But that's an involvement."

"But it's not for or against the French or the Germans. I wouldn't do anything anti-French. Tell me, why do you care so much about the art?"

"Because that's my profession. I'm a conservator."

"Which means?"

"I work on the restoration of oil paintings. There is a special group in the Underground that has been formed just to deal with the plundering of art. Since you yourself are involved in painting, I should think you would willingly join us."

"I don't feel it would serve any real purpose. Americans are neutral in all this and should be."

"Oh, but I think you're mistaken. The mood in America is changing. Rather soon the United States will join the war, you will see, and everything will change. Already your President Roosevelt is moving in that direction."

"What makes you think you know about the mood in America?"

"My father is an American."

"And he lives here?"

"No."

A man and a woman entered and took seats at the bar. They spoke French.

"Where does he live?"

"In Sheboygan, Wisconsin. He came here with the American Army in 1917." She had switched to English, which she spoke perfectly. "He was a sergeant of artillery. The Rainbow Division."

The barman came to them with a bottle of wine and refilled their glasses. *"Des amis,"* he said to Gaby, inclining his head toward the couple at the bar.

Gaby nodded and reverted to French. "I tell you this about myself so that maybe you understand about involvement. Back when my father was a sergeant on leave in Paris, he met my mother and they became lovers. Then, afterward, when he was wounded he was here in convalescence for quite a while. But in all the confusion after the armistice, they fell out of touch with each other. My father had returned to the States, but my mother didn't know where to reach him to tell him that I had been born. She had moved to her parents' house in Lyon, so none of his letters reached her. By the time she finally located him, he had married his girl friend from before. He came to see us, the first chance he could. He had told his wife about us. He came to see me and he contributed toward my support all through my childhood. He was not lovers anymore with my mother, but he came once a year to see me from when I was five years old, so that I would grow up knowing I had a father who cared about me. That's how I speak English, or I should say American. He's a darling man. Sadly, he could have no children with his American wife. Harold Goodwilly—he's so American and kind. But now because of the war he cannot come any longer. So you see, I do know something of the American side of things. I have an American passport—I could escape to your neutrality if I wanted. But I don't think there is any such thing as neutrality. Life is taking sides."

A couple of laughing Germans dressed in civilian clothes came boisterously into the bar. They asked for drinks, but the barman didn't understand German, so they pointed to a bottle of Benedictine. A German soldier entered with a French hooker. They sat in a booth, and the soldier immediately threw his arms around her and kissed her, with one hand firmly cupping one of her breasts.

"I must go," Gaby said, "but try to give it some thought—I mean, about neutrality and not getting involved."

"I'm really sorry to disappoint you," Philip said. "In a way, I do envy your feelings of commitment, but I'm just not made that way."

"Sure you are. We all are. Well, if you ever want to get in touch with me, just contact Dieter. Duvier is the name he knows."

"That's not your real name?"

"No."

She got up and he helped her on with her coat. She slung her large handbag over her shoulder and set her rain hat firmly on her head. She waved a hand to the barman as they left.

"So long, Gaspard."

She clasped Philip's arm affectionately as they emerged onto the sidewalk, then put her arms around his neck and kissed him. To any passerby they were a pair of typical Parisian lovers. Her lips were very soft and warm, and she smelled of hyacinth soap.

She unchained her bicycle from a lamppost and placed it in the gutter. Philip helped steady the bike as she mounted, and he felt a small stab of regret at her departure.

"Think about yourself, Phil," she said in English, smiling at him. "Think about who you'd like to be," she said. She pulled into the bicycle traffic and pedaled away.

Professor Hubert Kahle sat on a chair beside Goering's bed. The room was in semidarkness, the phones turned off, and both doors were locked. Goering was in a deep sleep which the professor had induced by giving him a large glassful of a preparation the professor had brought with him from Cologne. Goering had been asleep for twenty hours, a deep sleep, far below the level of ordinary consciousness. Sweat poured from his flaccid body in a steady stream that the professor regularly absorbed with large bath towels. Every few hours he would pry open one of Goering's eyelids to examine his pupil. Goering made no sound or movement.

Professor Kahle operated a clinic bearing his name on the outskirts of Cologne. He specialized in the treatment of addicts who wanted abrupt withdrawal from the use of drugs without the torturous reactions of withdrawal. Professor Kahle had founded his sanitarium after the First World War, primarily to treat pilots who had become drug addicts. During the war, military doctors had liberally furnished drugs to airmen, possibly with the approval of the German generals, and as long as their dosages were sustained the pilots performed efficiently with high energy. But on return to civilian life, with their supply cut off, many of them flocked to Professor Kahle's sanitarium to undergo his withdrawal treatment. It was Professor Kahle's successful theory that if a patient was put into a deep sleep for the period of time when he would normally be assaulted by the tortures of withdrawal, the toxic residue of the drug to which he was addicted could be removed from his body, and on his awakening his craving for the drug would be gone.

To this end, Professor Kahle had devised this special liquid formula that induced the comatose condition that was needed. During this period, perspiration washed out the drug's poisonous residue while Professor Kahle induced other positive elements into his patient's system.

The morphine binge with Monette had finally caught up with Goering. His breathing and his pulse had begun to have alarming fluctuations, and he was suffering severe glandular disorders. When Professor Kahle was summoned, as he had been many times in the past, his visit was, as usual, shrouded in complete secrecy. Word must not get out that Goering was a dope addict (his enemies would say "fiend"), so the professor came secretly in the night.

After his first twenty-four hours of sleep, the professor would permit Goering to wake, but only to consume some minerals and vitamins, and then another draft of the Kahle secret formula would put him back to sleep for an additional twenty-four hours. No nourishment was administered during the entire stretch of forty-eight hours.

Goering would awake, finally, weak and dehydrated, but able to depart for his Air Corps business in Normandy. His craving for morphine would be gone. His eyes would be clear and his hand steady.

Unfortunately, within a few weeks of the cure Goering's craving would slowly return, and Kropp would again have to start filling the crystal bowl with tablets.

21

The ski trip to Lech was cut short by tragedy, and Philip returned to Paris within three days of his departure.

What had happened was that the long-running but subtly buried antagonism between Dr. Lohse and Baron von Behr had erupted into a competition between them to see who would win in a downhill race from the top of Lech's highest mountain. A guide had led them to the starting point, a three-hour climb with sealskins affixed to their skis to aid in the grueling ascent.

The guide gave a signal to start them off. During the initial part of the run, each man, intent on mastering the tricky powder, paid no attention to the other. A third of the way down the mountain they were just about even, but the paths of their descents increasingly narrowed the distance between them until they were almost on top of each other. It was at this point that von Behr, coming out of a kick turn, took a sudden, impetuous swipe at Lohse with his pole. Lohse avoided the jab, but then veered toward von Behr and tried to retaliate with a pole thrust of his own. Abruptly now, their downhill race turned into a jousting match, two knights jousting with steel-tipped poles.

They traversed, turned, and ran at each other on a diagonal descent, holding out their poles, using them as lances, trying to land a disabling thrust, whirling by each other at high speed, the shimmer of the exploding snow kicking up from their skis, partially obscuring their vision, a sharp whack of their poles as they made contact, but neither man upended as they wheeled in kick turns and again and again ran at each other, thrusting, cursing, missing, the guide bearing down on them, shouting for them to stop. Von Behr stabbed his pole into Lohse's arm as he whizzed past him, knocking him off balance, somersaulting him into the snow, but somehow, miraculously, Lohse regained his stance, his bindings still holding, a long tear in the arm of his parka, but no wound. His cap and sunglasses gone, he turned to run at von Behr for revenge, murder in his heart. But von Behr gave no ground as they came at each other head on, poles extended, the shouts of the guide very close now as the two men collided in a violent crash, skis flying loose, Lohse's pole skidding off its mark, riding up toward von Behr's face, its lethal tip sticking into von Behr's eye like a dart finding its mark. Von Behr catapulted across the back of Lohse's left leg, crushing it with a sickening snap of bone, the snow stained with red from von Behr's spurting eye as the two of them rolled a considerable distance down the mountain before finally coming to a stop.

The guide was at their side. Lohse's leg was grotesquely doubled under him. He moaned in pain. Von Behr was unconscious; the shaft of the pole had broken off from the tip, which was still lodged in his eye. The guide pulled out the tip and rolled von Behr onto his back. He unstrapped a pair of spare skis which he carried on his backpack, and made an emergency sled out of them. Then he recovered Lohse's broken skis, which he used as splints for his fractured leg. Lohse's face was as white as the snow, his pulse was rapid, a nausea was building up in him from the pain and shock of his broken leg. He vomited.

The guide strapped von Behr to one of the skis, Lohse to the other, trussed them together, using his ski pole as a bridge, and then started down the mountain with his makeshift sled carrying its grim cargo.

Lech did not have a doctor. The closest medical facility was in Innsbruck, which was two and a half hours by train from Langen. An emergency railroad car, especially maintained for the hospital run to Innsbruck, was at the station when they got there. The car was a converted baggage car with wide doors that allowed the stretchers to be hoisted directly into the car without disturbing the injured men. From the time von Behr and Lohse were taken from the mountain until their deliverance to the hospital in Innsbruck over five hours would have elapsed.

Of course, there was nothing the doctors could do about restoring sight to von Behr's mutilated eye; they cleaned and dressed the wound, and they gave him a transfusion to replace the blood he had lost.

The bone in Lohse's leg had been shattered, but a specialist, brought in from Vienna, did a good job of reassembling it and placing the leg in a heavy cast up to the thigh.

Now von Behr and Lohse were in the hospital in Innsbruck, and how Goering would react to what had happened was not pretty to contemplate. It had been agreed, on the way back to

Paris, that Dr. Bunjes would be the spokesman, explaining only that there had been an unfortunate ski accident, but none of them really believed that Goering's shrewdness would let the explanation stop there. Not many skiers lose an eye.

It will surely be the end of my crazy job, Philip thought as the train made its way through the maze of the Gare Saint-Lazare railroad yards. He felt a touch of panic at the thought of being without any income whatsoever, but there was also a tinge of relief in the fact that the Underground would no longer be interested in him. During the night on the train, asleep in his berth, Philip had dreamed of the girl Gaby, not in the Hole-in-the-Wall but on the *Île-de-France,* sitting at a table in the first-class dining room with his Aunt Adele and Clarisse, who was naked; there was a sudden, severe storm that pitched everything and everyone about, but the three women at his table were calm and eating soup while the word "PRELOON" appeared in the air, as words appear above characters' heads in comic strips, yet there was no feeling of comedy, just that terror he felt every time he saw "PRELOON" in his nightmares.

22

There was a message for him in his box: "Please call Countess Lili von Jorosjc as soon as possible." The telephone number had a Neuilly exchange. Philip's spirits lifted. He had feared that he might never see her again.

When he got to his room, he went straight to the phone and gave the operator the number, wiggling out of his coat as he waited for the call to go through. The sound of her answering voice shortened his breath.

"Hello, Lili, it's Philip."

"Philip, my love, are you back? The concierge said you had just left on a ski trip. I was so disappointed."

"It was cut short by . . . ah, circumstances."

"Good. I was impatient to see you. Things have worked out wonderfully! And what do you think—I have an apartment of my own now, finally!"

"Why, that's wonderful, but you said they would never let you—"

"They have allowed me to retire."

"You have retired?"

"Yes, my darling Philip, I have decided to be a homebody and live the life of a happy mouse."

"Retired from what?"

"From my . . . well . . . indiscretions. I will finally be a lady of leisure. Now I am bursting with desire to be with you. How shall we do it? Maybe I will be your *cocotte*. Would you like to keep me? Perfumed and waiting for you at your beck and call?" She laughed.

"No, on second thought," she said, "I have more jewels and money than you, so I shall keep you. Would you like to be my *cocotte*? What's wrong with that? Why should it always be the poor man who has to keep the woman? How do you feel about that proposition, Philip? I will keep you in cigars and cognac and give you a billiard table for your birthday."

Philip laughed.

"You must promise," Lili continued, "always to receive me in a Japanese bridegroom's kimono and bare feet. Also, you must grow a beard. I think you would look very handsome with a beard. It would strengthen your chin. And I will like it when you stimulate my back with your beard, like birch twigs at a sauna. My back happens to be very vulnerable. As my *cocotte,* you must remember that my back needs a lot of attention."

"I promise."

"Then you accept?"

"Absolutely. I will be the first male *cocotte,* but don't you think we need a different word? After all, *cocotte* is feminine."

"No, we just drop the final *te.* Can you come to dinner? Just the two of us. I will cook for you, and you will see my splendid new apartment. No one knows I am here. Not a soul in the world. Not even Coco. Only the Comtesse de Voilly who is the owner, but she lives in Geneva. She loves me and she has given it to me for as long as I want. It is on the Boulevard Maurice-Barrès, 243, third floor—it looks directly upon the Jardin d'Acclimatation, a bridle path and acres of chestnut trees."

"Are you sure you want to cook? I'd be happy to take you to dinner."

"Of course I want to cook. It is part of the joy of my new retirement. I went to the open-air market in Neuilly this morning. Oh, what a sight! All the talk about shortages, but there is still everything on the black market. I have partridges—I could tell from their fresh little eyes that yesterday they were sitting in a tree—and I have coal and a coal stove in which to roast them, so the hell with the Boche's electricity cuts.

"Just come, Philip, we will have a grand reunion! The Countess has left us endless bottles of Mouton Rothschild, but would you believe, no candles, so that is the one thing you can bring. The Ritz has them all over for when the electricity fails, so just pluck a few candles and come around about eight. We will eat roast partridges and I will rehearse being a *cocotte.* You see, I'm already reverting to type. I withdraw my offer. I prefer to keep the *te* on *cocotte.*"

"All right, but just remember this—I never promised you a merkin."

She was overcome with laughter. "Oh, Philip . . . oh . . ." She was laughing so hard when she hung up, she could hardly catch her breath.

*   *   *

It was a long bike ride to Neuilly. Philip could have tried the Métro, but service beyond the Étoile was very erratic and he wanted to be on time. The ride up the Champs-Élysées from the Place de la Concorde to the Arc was a slow, punishing incline, but the prospect of spending a candlelit evening with Lili gave extra strength to Philip's legs. From the Arc to Neuilly the terrain was in his favor, descending all the way to the Pont-Neuilly, where Philip turned toward the Boulevard Maurice-Barrès, which ran alongside the Bois. He found the number Lili had given him, a sedate apartment building with a dry fountain in the courtyard. A Christmas wreath hung on the lobby door, which was slightly ajar. There was no doorman.

Philip took the elevator to three. There were only two apartments on the floor; on one of the doors was a small brass plate: "Comtesse de Voilly." Philip rang the bell, which sounded shrilly. No answer. He rang again. He knew it was a big apartment, since there were only two on the floor, so perhaps she was far away in the kitchen and didn't hear the bell. He tried the door. It was open.

He entered tentatively, calling her name, but there was no response. The apartment was elegantly furnished, in the style of a woman of good taste and wealth who lived alone. There was the faint aroma of good cooking.

Philip continued through the rooms, calling, "Lili? Lili, are you there?" as he went. He passed through the dining room, where the table was set for two, and into the kitchen, which was deserted. There were cooking pots on the stove, and the makings of a salad rested on a large chopping board. Philip opened the door of the oven and inspected the browning partridges. "For God's sake, Lili, where are you?" he shouted. He took four Ritz candles from his pocket and put them on the kitchen table.

Perhaps the bathroom. He continued his search, passing through a library with padded leather walls, a music room that contained a harpsichord, and Gobelin tapestries on the walls. Ah, Philip thought, when the French are rich, they are very, very rich. It's a wonder the Germans haven't grabbed this place.

Just beyond the music room was a small foyer with a large carved door that led to the master bedroom—and Lili. Directly facing the door was a canopied bed of antique woods inlaid with mother-of-pearl, four graceful posters supporting a silk screen canopy, and there in the center of the bed, held upright, spreadeagled from ropes that had been strung taut from the posts and tied to her wrists and ankles, was Lili. Her head was at a forward pitch, her eyes open, her tongue slightly protruded from her lips. She was naked.

The room stank of death. Excrement had run down her leg and dripped onto the pink silk coverlet. A thin black metal spike had been driven through her chest, between her breasts, its dagger point sticking out of her back. Another spike had been rammed upwards into her vagina, with only the handle visible, like a grotesque black penis. Blood slowly dripped from her wounds.

All the contents of an armoire had been dumped onto the carpet, but the rest of the room was undisturbed.

Philip couldn't move. He stood transfixed in the doorway, looking at Lili, whose open death-eyes looked at him. He tried to think, to react, but he was incapable.

A surge of nausea finally pulled him away. Vomit boiled up and out of him as, in desperation, he yanked silk flowers from a large Japanese vase and retched into it. He began choking on his vomit, and only with the greatest of difficulty regained his breath. He started to pass out, he could feel himself going, but the next thing he knew he was on his bicycle pedaling furiously through the Bois de Boulogne as if pursued by mad dogs.

23

Dieter's *vélotaxi* was not at its usual place outside the Cambon entrance. Philip walked to the corner and looked up and down the Rue du Faubourg-Saint-Honoré, but it was nowhere to be seen. Dieter was probably on hire, entertaining a Nazi passenger with his fractured German, but Philip was too impatient to wait for his return.

She had said that Duvier was not her real name, but that could have been a sort of perverse disguise in itself. He telephoned the conservation department of the Louvre, identifying himself as an E.R.R. official, and inquired if a Mademoiselle Duvier was on their staff; they said they had never heard of her. He telephoned two other museums and received the same answer. Impatience notwithstanding, there was no alternative other than to wait for Dieter's reappearance.

It was a long two hours. A fat general and his fat wife emerged from the little *vélo* cab with assistance from Dieter, who laughed his high infectious laugh and thanked them profusely for their generous tip. Dieter had noticed Philip standing in the alcove of the service entrance, but he did not acknowledge his presence until the general and his *gnädige Frau* had disappeared through the revolving doors.

Without saying a word, Philip entered the cab, and Dieter pulled quickly away from the curb. Not until they were in the mainstream of bicycle traffic on the Rue de Rivoli did Philip speak.

"Dieter, I must see Mademoiselle Duvier right away."

Dieter made no answer, but swerved into the Place du Palais-Royal and parked his *vélotaxi* at the curb. While Philip waited in the cab, Dieter went into a *tabac,* bought a *jeton,* and made a phone call.

He returned to his bike and continued down the Rue de Rivoli. "It's arranged," he said, and then, as he pedaled along, he began to sing:

"Ya'kah Doo'der wan to tone,
A-ri-dink ona punee,
Poot a fedder in'ees cahp
Acall eet macramome."

His pronunciation made the song sound Chinese. "I have learned it by phonetics from my U.S. vocabulary book. Not bad, eh?"

"Dieter, I have some sound advice for you: avoid English."

"Monsieur Weber, would you think it possible for a man with no front teeth to whistle? What do you think? No? Well, I am about to astound you." He began to whistle.

Philip interrupted him. "Dieter, I must see Mademoiselle Duvier as soon as possible."

"Yes, of course, but these things must be 'synchromized'—ah, how's that for an English word? I know three words of English which I say very well: 'Watch your step.' How's that?"

A few minutes later, Dieter turned his vehicle left onto the Boulevard de Sébastopol, and then left again onto the Rue Marcel. He had resumed singing his version of "Yankee Doodle." He pulled up with a squeak of brakes in front of the Hole-in-the-Wall and smiled toothlessly at Philip as he hurriedly left the *vélo* cab.

The same ragged accordionist stopped playing to hold open the door. The bar was packed, smoky and noisy. All the booths and barstools were taken, mostly by German soldiers, some of them with French girls who had the unmistakable stamp of Pigalle on them. Gaspard was the only bartender, but a stout, vigorous woman was waiting on the booths, carrying her tray high to avoid the carousing soldiers who stood two and three deep at the bar.

In one of the booths there were two French couples, who formed an oasis of civilian quiet. At the end of the long bar, two tall German civilians stood shoulder to shoulder, facing the barroom, not talking, their eyes busy.

The crowded, noisy metamorphosis of the barroom surprised Philip, who hesitated at the door, but the accordionist, who had followed him in, nudged him forward toward the crowd at the bar. The barman handed him a glass of red wine, which was passed to him by those in front of him. The accordionist began to play a German song which the soldiers picked up on.

Philip watched the mirror anxiously for Gaby's entrance, and when he saw her he turned to greet her with open arms, playing the game she had taught him. They embraced, kissing each other's cheeks three times. She took his arm and moved toward the booths, and as she did, one of the French couples got up to leave. It was apparent to Philip that their departure at that moment was not a coincidence. Gaby settled against the tall-backed booth and pulled Philip snugly against her side. The stout waitress, carrying a glass of red wine, bulled her way through the drinkers, which included a sprinkling of French salespeople and civil servants from the *quartier,* holding one arm straight in front of her for interference. The waitress placed a cardboard Byrhh coaster in front of Gaby, and on it she placed the glass of wine. Gaby picked up the glass and held it toward Philip.

"Bonne chance!" she said. "Or I should say, *Merde!"* She drank half of it and then handed the glass to Philip, who drank the other half. As she put the empty glass back on the coaster, she noticed some words written in pencil on the bottom of the coaster: *"Des yeux au bar."* There was a little residue of wine in the bottom of the glass. She pretended to knock over the glass, so that the wine obliterated the message. She flicked her eyes toward the end of the bar and saw the two civilians with their beer mugs and their busy eyes, their precise haircuts, ersatz tweed suits of bilious brown, and heavy briefcases, and with the permeating odor of Gestapo coming off them. The embraced couple on the seat across from them were totally absorbed in each other.

Gaby put her left arm across Philip's chest and pulled him to her. She kissed him on the lips, holding him tightly, a good performance for the eyes at the bar. She rolled her lips off his and pushed her face against his ear.

"We must be very careful," she whispered in English, her eyes closed, her lips slightly kissing his ear as she whispered. "There is Gestapo here, but the ones across the booth from us are our own people."

Philip turned away from her and waved his arm at the waitress, who brought two more glasses of wine, carefully removing the wine-stained coaster as she substituted a clean one.

"Now it's my turn," Philip said, raising his glass. "May you see your father soon." The unexpected toast puzzled her, but she drank and smiled at him. He put his arms around her, and his body responded to the soft press of her breasts against him. He kissed the side of her neck and whispered to her, "The list you want is in my side pocket. You can take it while I hold you like this."

She turned her face to his and kissed him again, her lips slightly parted. Then she pulled back and smiled at him, the look of a girl in love. "No, that isn't a good idea," she said, as if she were telling him how much she loved him. "If I am stopped and searched and it is found on me—well, it's better if tonight we have a date. I'll meet you for the performance at the Grand Guignol. In the lobby. Have the list in your right-hand pocket. Now we should finish up our wine and leave, but not too hurriedly. Let's kiss once more, and then we go."

He kissed her, but she suddenly pulled away and looked at her watch, saying she had to hurry because her mother was waiting for her.

The two Gestapo agents had left their post at the end of the bar and were now quietly working their way through the crowded barroom, going from one French civilian to another, inspecting their papers. One of the agents noticed that Gaby and Philip were leaving, and he started toward them but was bumped by the stout waitress, who cried out angrily as three steins of beer spilled forward, drenching him. The soldiers laughed as the waitress attempted to dry off the beer-sopped German. Covered by the confusion, Gaby and Philip left the Hole-in-the-Wall.

Gaby unchained her bicycle, and Philip took her in his arms to kiss her goodbye, but she turned her mouth away and put her cheek against his.

"You must understand, Phil," she said, "my affection is like play money—it must look real, but it's not. There is no place in what we do for anything else. See you at the Guignol."

Philip met Coco Chanel in the Little Bar before going to the Grand Guignol. She came in looking radiant, her face pleased at the sight of Philip now standing beside the corner banquette to receive her. He felt sad at the prospect of destroying her pleasant humor.

"You've been drinking cheap red wine," she said as she pecked his cheeks.

Philip laughed. "What year?"

"I thought you were skiing in Austria for Christmas," she said as she seated herself on the banquette.

"There was a bizarre accident. Von Behr lost an eye and Lohse has a fractured leg."

"How dreadful. Well, I've always said only real crazies would risk their necks sliding down a mountain on two slats of wood. What does this do to your funny job? Are you unemployed?"

"No, I am more employed than ever. Herr Goering has asked me to help out in the office until they can go back to work."

"You mean you'll be in charge of all those Jewish paintings they confiscate?"

Philip hesitated for a moment, considering whether to mention his impending cooperation with the Underground, but the specter of Baron von Spatz inhibited him. "No, Dr. Bunjes will be in charge. I will just help with some of the administrative work."

"Oh, Philip, my sweet *chou,* what a crazy life this has become. I'm a retired seamstress and you're distributing Da Vincis." She smiled lovingly at him and drank from the glass of champagne and bitters which Bertin had placed before her.

"Gabrielle, I have very unwelcome news to tell you," Philip said, taking her hand in his. "Do you know about Lili?"

Coco's face immediately turned grave, her eyes prepared for what the dark tone of Philip's voice told her would be bad. "You said she had disappeared with no forwarding address."

"Yes, but she reappeared. She didn't call you? There was a message. I spoke to her and she invited me for dinner. She was in a lavish apartment in Neuilly lent to her, she said, by a dear friend, the Comtesse de Noilly. She sounded cheerful and funny and sexy on the phone. I was so excited and happy to go see her . . ."

"Oh, my God," Gabrielle said softly.

"The door was open. The apartment was deserted—except for Lili, who was in the bedroom, brutally murdered. Brutally . . . brutally . . . brutally . . ."

Tears filled Gabrielle's eyes and ran copiously down her cheeks. Her hand intensified its hold on his, her nails biting in. Neither spoke. Philip too was near tears as he re-experienced the terrible moment of discovering Lili trussed and spiked and hung like some beautiful, rare animal mutilated by a crazed hunter.

"I was in love with her, too, Philip," Gabrielle said.

Philip handed her his handkerchief for her tears. "I know," he said.

"No," she said, her tears unabated, "really in love."

"We never made love," Philip said, "but I feel that we did."

"For me, it was more than that."

Philip turned to look at her, not quite but almost comprehending.

"Yes, we were lovers. She was the most sensuous person I ever knew. No man has been anything to me like Lili was. Sex with her was a total joy, the way she reveled in her body pleasures, her senses, her total fulfillment, but it was more than that. I loved Lili's good mind and her lovely heart and the way she dressed and moved and smelled a flower. When we were lovers, I always had a carnation for her so I could watch her put it to her nose and close her eyes in the ecstasy of inhaling its perfume."

A long reverie consumed her. Philip tried to picture Lili with a carnation in her dainty hand, but all his mind offered him was her tortured corpse staring at him.

"Every time she fell in love with a man, she left me. That was Lili. Always faithful. But then every time her love affair ended, I gladly took her back, and it was with us as before. Until one day she said it couldn't be anymore. We would be good friends, but her life was changing. That's all she said. And that was the end of it."

"What do you think changed?"

"I think she became an *agent secret*—Lili was a romantic, if ever there was one. She probably fancied herself in the grand tradition of Mata Hari. She entrenched herself with the so-called international set. I'd see her at receptions at the Japanese Embassy, dinner with the British Ambassador and his wife, a formal ball thrown by the German Consulate. She couldn't have known what she was really getting into. She was such a child about politics and intrigue and, well, ugliness, really. She never comprehended ugliness."

"Whom did she spy for?"

"Oh, I don't know, Philip. I never discussed any of this with her, of course. For all I know, she had become a double agent."

"Double for whom?"

"I should think at first the Germans, and then the British. Oh, what a damn foul business this war is. I may not leave my hotel room until it is over, one way or another. It is so . . . degrading. Yesterday, at lunch, I was in the ladies' room, in one of the stalls, when two women came in to primp their hair.

"'Isn't that Coco Chanel at that corner table?' one asked.

"'Yes, I think so,' the other said.

"'You know,' the first one said, 'they say she's a horizontal collaborator.'

"'You don't say!'

"'Yes, bedded down with some big-shot German baron.'

"'Well, that should keep her warm and well fed.'

"Can you imagine, Philip—a *horizontal collaborator*. What a loathsome phrase. Me, I take nothing from Spatz but companionship. I just suddenly can't live alone anymore. I can't. But I felt shame, Philip. I did. It was a new emotion for me. I've lived an honorable life and worked hard and achieved a great deal, and I've been honored by governments and titled gentry, yet there, in the women's room, squatted on a toilet seat, I felt like a cheap opportunist, fucking for chocolates and cigarettes."

"Why do you think Lili got into espionage? For the money?"

"Oh, no, not Lili. Oh, my, no, she never did anything for money. No, as I told you, for the glamour, the adventure, the intrigue. Oh, how Lili loved intrigue!"

"I'm going into it myself, Gabrielle."

"Don't do it for her, Philip, out of some sense of misplaced sacrifice."

"No, it's just something I feel now."

"Well, outrage has probably pushed you into it. Outrage is the great recruiter."

"Maybe. Maybe you're right."

"Oh, Philip, my Philip, you are as innocent as Lili was. Go away, my love—go back to the States. You'll find a life there. What's for you here? Lili's fate, probably. I'll happily lend you the money to go. Please, Philip darling, get out while the getting's still good."

"If you had seen Lili . . ."

"Listen, there is no Comtesse de Voilly. No such title exists. It was just part of Lili's fantasy. For a long while she was chauffeured around Paris in a sleek new Hotchkiss which she said the Comtesse had lent her. A new diamond necklace, a fur, a trip here and there, always from the nonexistent Comtesse de Noilly. I once asked her to introduce me to the Comtesse, but she put me off by saying that the Comtesse never talked to tradespeople."

"I have to go," Philip said, consulting his watch.

"I'll stay a while longer. Would you please order me another champagne and bitters?"

"I'm sorry to have to leave you, but I have quite a ways to go."

"Where to?"

"The Grand Guignol."

Gabrielle gave him a quizzical look. "I should think you've seen enough bloodshed for the time being."

"I'm not going for the show."

"Oh, dear, you're already sounding mysterious. Well, take care, Philip. Here's your handkerchief."

"Please keep it. I have another." He didn't, but there is nothing worse, he thought, than somebody else's tears wadded up in your hip pocket.

As arranged, Philip met Gaby in the lobby of the Theater of the Grand Guignol, and, as usual, she greeted him affectionately. The theater was crowded, the play was appropriately gory, with heads rolling and blood spurting; when it was over, and they started to leave, Philip realized that the list had disappeared from his pocket.

"Let's go somewhere to have a drink," Philip suggested. "I have a *laissez-passer* for after curfew."

But Gaby declined. She quickly slipped away through the crowd without even saying good night.

24

The dinner at the Ritz given by Heinrich Himmler was the most important social event since the occupation of Paris. The announced purpose of the dinner was to commemorate the installation of SS General Karl Oberg as the new *Höhere SS und Polizeiführer* (Supreme Chief of the SS and the Police) in Paris, but what the event actually celebrated was Himmler's victory over the Army to gain control of the entire German police apparatus in France. The booty that went to the victor consisted of the immense stock holdings that had belonged to French Jews and other German-designated undesirables who had been shipped off to various concentration camps.

By acquiring these holdings, Himmler was able to acquire control of a number of French companies, and this dinner at the Ritz, ostensibly to install Himmler's man, General Oberg, was in reality a broadside to alert all big business in France that henceforth the Himmler people were the only ones to deal with.

So important was the dinner itself to his plans that Himmler had sent his chief assistant, Reinhard Heydrich, to Paris to supervise details. There had never before been such an assemblage of important German and French dignitaries: Hermann Goering, Dr. Joseph Goebbels, Alfred Rosenberg, Heinrich Himmler, General Erhard Milch, Gestapo Chief Ernst Kaltenbrunner, Pierre Laval, the head of the Vichy government, as well as other Vichy and Nazi officials.

One of Heydrich's first acts on arriving at the Ritz was to summon Colonel Stuppelmayer to impress upon him the necessity of providing absolute security for the dinner.

"In that banquet hall will be the heartbeat of the Third Reich," Heydrich said, indulging in his usual hyperbole.

"I will redouble my usual safeguards, Your Honor," Stuppelmayer assured him. "Nothing will escape our scrutiny."

"No one must enter the banquet room who does not have credentials."

"Your Honor, no one will."

"I want security to begin on the sidewalks around the Ritz."

"I assure you it will."

"Are there any employees—waiters, cooks, bellhops, baggage men—hired after we took over?"

"No, Your Honor, the personnel of the Ritz has not been augmented in any way. These are all old employees whom we've checked on."

"Nothing must happen, I mean, not the slightest disturbance or upset of any kind."

"I understand."

"Reichleader Himmler will not tolerate it."

"Yes, Your Honor."

"It must be a triumphant dinner."

"It will be. You have my word on it."

"If it is not, you will be *personally* accountable to Herr Himmler."

The banquet was held in the spacious Salle de Napoléon. The menu had been carefully prepared, primarily to suit the tastes of Himmler, who was the official host, although the Paris office of the German SS was footing the bill. It was an elaborate mélange of French and German dishes, comprised of twelve courses divided into groups of four, with three intermissions to provide time for the long list of speakers to deliver their tributes to Himmler.

Colonel Stuppelmayer had SS men at both Ritz entrances and at the entrance to the banquet room, carefully checking off the diners as they entered. Also, that afternoon, Stuppelmayer had met with his dining-room informers, the waiter Ferdinand Bouchère and the pastry chef Jean Delocque, to impress upon them the necessity of keeping their eyes and ears open.

"I want the slightest abnormality to be immediately reported to me, anything at all which may seem a little out of the ordinary. I am not at all displeased by false alarms. Better to be safe than sorry."

Although Henri Bretonne knew, of course, that a dinner was to be held in the Salle de Napoléon, there had been no advance indication that it was to be a banquet of such magnitude. As the first of the arriving dignitaries passed by his concierge desk on their way to the banquet hall, however, he immediately sensed that this would be an extraordinary gathering. This was Himmler's first visit to Paris, and Pierre Laval had not been in Paris since he had become head of the Vichy government. Bretonne kept tabs on the arrivals, compiling a list of them by code numbers; he knew that the information that all these men were absent from their various posts at the same time would be of considerable importance to the military command in England, and he intended to get the list to Louis Delor in the wine cellar as soon as possible.

When the doors of the Salle de Napoléon were closed, with two security men posted outside them, Bretonne put the list of coded numbers which he had prepared into his pocket, told the assistant concierge he would be back shortly, and walked briskly to the door which led to the kitchens and on down to the *cave à vin*.

Louis Delor was passing through the kitchen galley, carrying a case of wine. He saw Henri Bretonne walk to the door that led to the wine cellar, passing Jean Delocque, the pastry chef, who had just fetched a bottle of Grand Marnier for a *bavaroise aux liqueurs* which he was preparing.

Delor returned to his office in the *cave* as quickly as he could, knowing that only a matter of urgency would have prompted Henri Bretonne to seek him out at a time like this.

It was not until he was in the midst of gentling the Grand Marnier into a mixture of eggs, sugar, milk and gelatin that it dawned on Delocque that there was something a bit odd in Bretonne's coming down to see Louis Delor while such a big banquet was under way. There might have been a special wine order—and Bretonne was known for his meticulous attention to details—but Colonel Stuppelmayer had said to report anything out of the ordinary. False alarm or not, Delocque concluded, Colonel Stuppelmayer would surely be impressed with his conscientiousness.

At that moment, Delocque caught sight of Ferdinand Bouchère, who was about to leave the serving area with a tray laden with bowls of *crevettes*. Delocque intercepted him as he reached the door and asked him to relay a message to Colonel Stuppelmayer.

Delor's tiny office was located at the rear of the wine cellar. Bretonne, anxious to get back to his desk, smoked a cigarette while he waited for Delor to return. For the first time, he was openly passing information to Delor, increasing the risk for both of them. As Bretonne waited in the cramped office, he was fearfully conscious of the list ticking in his pocket.

"These are all the big shots at the banquet," he said to Delor as the latter quickly entered his office. Bretonne held out the piece of paper with its three neat columns of numbers.

"I'll get it off as soon as I can," Delor said. "But how will they know it's a banquet? You don't identify it."

"Why is that necessary? They just have to know that all these Nazi VIPs are in the hotel, don't they?"

"Yes, I guess you're right. Did you have numbers for people like Laval?"

"Yes, the Vichy people are the ones with a *V* in front of their number."

"They thought of everything, didn't they? That's some collection up there."

"Get it off as quickly as you can, Louis. I feel it's important that they know who's here."

"May I see the list?" Colonel Stuppelmayer asked. He had entered the office noiselessly and overheard some of what they had been saying.

Delor's body jerked in shock at the sound of the colonel's voice, but Bretonne's apprehension about this meeting had somehow helped prepare him. Bretonne immediately turned and held out the list to Stuppelmayer.

"Of course, Colonel," the concierge said. "Here you are."

Colonel Stuppelmayer deliberately took his time inspecting the paper, letting the pressure of apprehension build up. It had been his considerable experience that the longer a suspect waited, the quicker came his confession. Louis Delor, near panic, tried desperately to think of a plausible explanation for the list, but his mind was too disordered to deal with it.

The concierge had long ago prepared the answer he would give if discovered, but as he watched Colonel Stuppelmayer studying the lists on the paper he knew that his explanation would be futile, and that he was as good as dead. His mind had already moved to the ultimate reality that the Nazis would not let him see his wife and three children before executing him. He should never have come down here and made direct contact—it was a stupid breach of procedure and good common sense. He felt responsible for Louis's entrapment; he wanted to turn his head and look at Louis, but he kept his eyes on the colonel.

"Tell me, Monsieur le Concierge," Colonel Stuppelmayer finally said, "what does this list of numbers represent?" He spoke understandable French.

"They are wine orders as passed along to me by the chief wine steward, my Colonel."

"Why would the wine steward deal with you? Why not give the list directly to Monsieur Delor, who, after all, is in charge of this *cave?*"

"Because I am the control. This is a checklist which the hotel manager maintains to keep tab on what bottles have been sold."

"And these numbers?"

"Every wine we have bears a number."

"Really? Well, then, Monsieur Delor, may I please see your master list."

Delor opened the top drawer of his desk and handed the colonel a numbered inventory of all the bottles in the cellar. He acted without hesitancy, but he had no faith in Bretonne's desperate charade.

"Now, Monsieur Delor, on the concierge's list we have V-116. Show me which bottle that is."

Delor took his inventory and pretended to inspect it, but he was beginning to resent this unnecessary baiting. The colonel had them dead to rights and he knew it. "It's probably a mistake," Delor said. "The *sommeliers* often make mistakes."

"Well, let me tell you what it is," the colonel said. "It's a bottle of Vichy water. That's what the *V* stands for. The concierge was ordering more Vichy water because he knew we had several distinguished visitors from Vichy. Number V-116 is probably a bottle of Vichy for Monsieur Laval—is that it, Concierge? Is that the number for Monsieur Laval—116? And who is Number One, Reichsmarschall Goering or Reichleader Himmler? I don't think either would like to be Number Two on your list. And which number am I? I should think unlucky thirteen, unlucky for you, that is. Now, just what were you planning to do with this list, Monsieur Delor?"

Louis Delor did not answer. A feeling of defiance was beginning to replace fear.

"Perhaps *you* would like to tell me, Monsieur le Concierge?"

"I've explained to you, sir, that it is simply a list of wines."

"Yes, that was your fairy tale. Well, if you don't want to tell me, then you'll tell the gentlemen who handle these matters for me. They are not as polite as I am, but much more thorough. Now, if you will please—"

Those were the colonel's final words.

On his hurried passage through the kitchen on his way to the wine cellar, the colonel had bumped Yves Cressier, the *sous-chef,* who had been working at one of the ranges. The colonel had thrust Cressier against the hot stove, causing him to burn his hand. But that didn't concern him—he was always burning a hand or nipping a finger with a carving knife. What concerned him was the colonel's precipitous path toward Louis Delor's office. Taking his time, so as not to attract attention, Cressier had slowly followed the colonel and, stationing himself outside the office door, had listened to the fatal conversation. He knew that once they left the cellar with the colonel, Bretonne and Delor would be taken to the dreaded address on the Avenue Henri-Martin and tortured. He also knew that the torture would very likely lead to his own implication. Obviously the only hope of survival for all of them lay in preventing Colonel Stuppelmayer from ever leaving the cellar.

Cressier removed his *toque* and with both hands pulled the halter of his white apron from around his neck, up over the top of his head. The halter was made of thick cotton cord. He advanced a few steps into the office and approached Colonel Stuppelmayer, whose back was to him. Cressier prayed that neither of his friends would betray his sudden appearance with their eyes. They didn't.

The halter flashed forward and looped around Stuppelmayer's neck, and in the same motion Cressier, a powerful man who had played rugby, jerked the halter toward him, garroting the colonel, who flailed the air against his unseen executioner. Delor and Bretonne quickly pinned down his arms as a few strangled sounds escaped his throat before the halter accomplished its work. The Nazi's body went limp. Cressier gave a final fierce tug with his garrot and then, with Delor's help, removed the halter, and Stuppelmayer's body crumpled to the ground. For a moment all three men stood staring at the colonel's dead body.

"We've got to get a move on," Bretonne said.

"We'll never get him out of here," Delor said. "You know how they inspect everything and everyone who goes in and out of the service entrances."

"What about getting him back to his room and letting them find him there?" Cressier asked.

"Someone must have seen me come in here," Bretonne said. "How else would he have known I was here?"

"Yes," Delor said, "good point. Perhaps we could bury him under the stones here."

"Too risky," Bretonne said. "They have dogs."

"No, we must make him disappear," Cressier said. "I've been a butcher's apprentice—I could dismember him, then perhaps we could get him out of here piece by piece."

"How? They make us open even the smallest packets."

"Could we burn him in the furnace?" Delor suggested. "If Yves can cut him up as he says . . ."

"And do you trust those fellows in the furnace room? Besides, once he is missing they will turn this place upside down, and who knows what will remain in the ashes? We must not only make him disappear, but we must make him *logically* disappear."

"That's asking a hell of a lot," Delor said.

"And we've got to be fast about it, before we are missed," the concierge advised.

"I'm very good with a cleaver and meat saw," Cressier said. "We have a big vat where we toss all the discarded fat and suet, the bones and innards of the carcasses and fowls that we dress. I'd just slough in the colonel with the other animals—it would all be carted off in the morning. So, what do you think? We send the colonel to the soap factory in the morning."

"Let's move on it," Bretonne said. "It's bizarre, but what's our alternative?" He started to undress the colonel.

"But what happens when they find out he's disappeared?" Delor asked.

"I've thought of something," the concierge said. "It may work. We have people who will help us, don't forget. Help me with his shoes."

They undressed the colonel, and Bretonne rolled up his clothes and belongings and hid them behind an empty cask of wine at the back of the cellar. Cressier and Delor put the now naked corpse in a handcart that Delor used for moving cases of wine, covered it with an oilskin and put a couple of cases of wine on top for camouflage. Cressier put his *toque* back on his head and hurried out of the cellar to the passageway which led to the basement cold room where the meat hung until needed for the kitchen. Knowing that the butchers were finished for the day, Delor pulled his cart to the entrance of the cold room.

Cressier had already put a striped butcher's apron over his kitchen whites, and with Delor's help, he put the colonel's body on the slaughtering table. Then Delor cautiously left the cold room and went back to the cellar to return the cart. He was surprised to find that Bretonne was still in his office.

"You should get back to your post, Henri. No sense taking unnecessary chances."

"I had to tell you. Pass the word to Cressier—I remembered something: when I came down to see you, I passed the pastry chef, Jean Delocque, coming out of the cellar with a bottle of Grand Marnier."

"Then you think it's Delocque who tipped off Stuppelmayer?"

"Of course. No one else saw me."

"I'll warn Cressier."

"We must do more than that. When they discover that the colonel is missing, they will set the Gestapo on all of us, and what do you think Delocque will do when they question him?"

"He will tell them about seeing you in the corridor."

"You bet."

"All right. I'll take care of Delocque. You and Cressier take care of the colonel."

Using the large butcher's saw, Cressier deftly cut through all the major joints at the thighs, knees and shoulders. He sliced open the colonel's belly and dug out his insides, which he threw into the slop bin. Then he started in with the cleaver, cracking into the joints of the colonel's wrists, elbows and knees. He split the skull several times and discarded the unrecognizable remains into the slop bin.

With a razor-sharp butcher's carving knife, he quickly and expertly stripped fillets of meat from the bones and from the fleshy parts of the back and midsection. When the bones had been stripped clean, he whacked them up and dumped them into the slop bin. The refrigeration of the cold room was causing him to shiver. He hurried. Using a meat hook, he stirred the contents of the slop bin to bury the colonel's remains in the slimy innards of the calves and hogs that had been butchered earlier that day. On the block in front of him now were fillets of dark-red meat undistinguishable from what one would find in the window of a butcher shop.

Cressier was enjoying this dismemberment. Although he had originally joined the Underground only to please his lady friend, he had by now become an enthusiast.

Cressier hurriedly wiped the table and the instruments he had used and quickly went back to the kitchen, apprehensive that he might have been missed. He was relieved to find that the dinner had not yet started.

Henri Bretonne changed from his concierge uniform into his street clothes, as he did every night, but instead of going toward the employees' departure doors on the Rue Cambon he went down the rear stairs and through the door that led to the *cave à vin.* This time he made sure no one was in the corridor. He went to the back of the wine cellar and retrieved Colonel Stuppelmayer's uniform, undressed quickly, put it on, and then fitted his street clothes over the uniform and his overcoat over that.

As he started to leave, he stepped on a round glassy object which crunched under his shoe. He bent to inspect it—the colonel's monocle. That would have been a fatal clue if the Gestapo had laid hands on it, he thought as he carefully picked up all the little pieces and put them into his pocket.

On the evening of the banquet, after his work was finished, Jean Delocque took the last Métro out of the Concorde station in the direction of Porte de la Chapelle. Delor usually took the Métro toward Mairie d'Issy, which was in the opposite direction, but this time he followed Delocque from the Ritz and boarded Delocque's Métro rather than his own. The station platform was packed solid with passengers who had prolonged their evening on the town until the last possible moment. It was easy for Delor to stand near Delocque and not be seen by him in the dense crowd.

When the Métro pulled in, Delor elbowed his way aboard the same second-class car that Delocque had entered. Delor had previously found out where Delocque lived, and he knew that he would be getting off at the Abbesses station. He stayed in the opposite end of the car from Delocque and kept his back to him. Seven stops to Abbesses; the sixth stop, Pigalle, a large station with connecting Métros. It was there that he planned to start his move.

The Métro was delayed at each stop by the size of the crowds getting off and on. As the horde of departing passengers began to move off the train at Pigalle, Delor started toward Delocque's end of the car. He feared that Delocque might get a seat as the car changed passengers, which would have made his job more difficult, but luckily Delocque remained standing in the same place, holding on to a pole near the doors, a perfect position from Delor's point of view.

Delocque was thinking about Colonel Stuppelmayer. He had seen him go storming through the kitchen on his way to the wine cellar, but he had not seen him afterward. He hoped his tip to the colonel about the concierge being in the wine cellar had paid off. He was in this dirty business for the money, and the colonel had promised substantial bonuses for useful information. Delocque lived with a reformed streetwalker who always threatened to return to her profession if he did not take care of her properly. Only this morning they had had a violent quarrel during which she had yelled dreadful things about hating him and wanting to kill him; now he desperately needed a bonus from the colonel with which to buy her some silk stockings on the black market. She adored silk stockings, which never failed to pacify her.

The Métro was now picking up speed as it moved toward Abbesses. Using his left arm to open a wedge for him, Delor pushed his way through the thicket of passengers, some of whom pushed him and muttered curses, but he persisted in his path toward Delocque. Delor's gloved right hand was inside the front of his overcoat. He knew from the slowing sound of the wheels that the Métro was approaching the station at Abbesses.

"Delocque!" He feigned surprise. "I didn't know this was your train."

"Oh, hello, Delor. Yes, the next stop."

"What do you know!"

"Is this your regular Métro? Funny I haven't—"

"No, I met a bird who lives on the Rue des Abbesses."

"Why, that's my street!"

The Métro was coming into the station. Passengers began to jostle toward the door.

"You don't say!"

"What's her name? Maybe I know her."

The Métro was stopping. Delocque and Delor were moving toward the door in a phalanx of departing passengers.

"Informer," Delor whispered in Delocque's ear.

"What?"

"Her name's Informer. First name is . . . Nazi!"

The doors sprung open and the two men were carried forward by the impetus of those behind them.

"You must know her very well," Delor said, "since you've slept with her." His gloved hand came out from under his coat, holding an ice pick, which he plunged deep to the handle into Delocque's chest, a short, quick-wristed thrust, unobserved by anyone in the hustling, shoving, complaining crowd. Delocque looked surprised, then his face contorted into what looked like a smile. The pick had penetrated directly to his heart; he fell forward, but the density of the passengers held him upright until they all reached the platform and started to disperse. And even after he fell, face down, obscuring the short, stubby ice pick handle, the only attention he got from the departing passengers, who were hurrying home to beat the curfew, was that they called to the station attendant, who was on the opposite side of the platform.

By the time the attendant reached Delocque and discovered he had been murdered, Delor was well along the Rue des Abbesses on his way to spend the night in a small, cheap hotel called the Hôtel des Bons Messieurs, which means "Hotel of the Good Guys."

On the evening of the day after the banquet, a German patrol, crossing the Pont d'Austerlitz, came across the jacket of a German officer, which had been neatly folded and placed on the ground below the balustrade of the bridge. In the pocket of the officer's jacket, which bore the insignia of a colonel, were papers identifying the officer as Colonel Hans Stuppelmayer; also in the pocket was a note, signed by Colonel Stuppelmayer, which explained that he was committing suicide because of his betrayal of the Fatherland. In this note Colonel Stuppelmayer admitted that he had been living at the Ritz with a Frenchwoman named Odette Ange, that he had discovered she was in fact a British spy who had duped him, and that he planned to kill her for this transgression, and then himself; that, standing here on the Pont d'Austerlitz, he intended to shoot her and then, holding her, jump into the Seine. On the ground, beside Colonel Stuppelmayer's jacket, was a small Luger from which one shot had been fired.

The matter was referred to the German Secret Service, whose examination of the papers found in the jacket substantiated their authenticity. The body of Odette Ange, caught on a support of the Pont-Royal, was found two days later, with a bullet hole in the middle of her forehead. Ballistic tests matched the bullet to the Luger found in the colonel's tunic. Gestapo forensic experts authenticated the handwriting of the suicide note, matching it with handwriting found in the colonel's wallet.

The assistant manager of the Ritz, Albert de Chabert, known to the Gestapo as a trusted collaborator, corroborated the fact that Colonel Stuppelmayer had a beautiful Frenchwoman living with him, but he said he knew nothing about her. The Gestapo assigned some of their best men to check on her background, in an effort to identify her and her espionage contacts, but not an iota of identification was ever turned up.

*   *   *

There was one niggling detail that continued to nip at Henri Bretonne's logical mind: Jean Delocque had undoubtedly informed Colonel Stuppelmayer that he had seen Bretonne going into the wine cellar, *but how had he informed him?* Certainly Delocque had not gone up into the banquet room in his chef's outfit. There must have been a go-between. And who, most logically, would have had access to both the kitchen and the dining room? Why, a waiter, of course. But which waiter?

"Ah, there's the rub," Bretonne said to Delor at lunch the following day. "Which waiter?"

"What if this waiter, whoever he was, only took a note to the colonel, not knowing the contents?"

"Perhaps, but if the Gestapo should be told by a waiter that Delocque, now murdered, had sent him with a message to the colonel of such importance that the colonel immediately went to the kitchen—well? Would that turn on the heat or wouldn't it?"

"I think you're too concerned, Henri. I agree that Delocque and Stuppelmayer must have had some kind of signal, but I doubt that it involved a courier."

"But you'll admit it's a possibility, Louis, and—"

A dining-room captain and a baggage handler sat down at a nearby table, thus ending Bretonne's discourse. He left shortly afterward, so contemplative that he left fully half of his rare Gauloise smoking in the ashtray.

25

After the tennis match with Goering, Philip and Marcel de Forrestière played at the Racing Club every Thursday afternoon. They were well matched, and, although Philip invariably won, it was good, competitive tennis that they both enjoyed. Afterward they would have drinks in the club's lounge. Philip looked forward to these Thursdays; considering how few people remained in his life now, de Forrestière's friendship, although limited to weekly tennis, was especially welcome.

On this particular afternoon, sitting in the comfortable lounge sipping beer after three spirited sets, de Forrestière made an offhand remark to Philip that instantly changed their relationship. "I understand, Philip," de Forrestière said, lighting a cigarette, "that you like to drink red wine in the Hole-in-the-Wall. It's one of my favorite places."

Philip was stunned. His initial reaction was to recoil inwardly, as if from a physical danger.

De Forrestière blew out his match and looked Philip straight in the eye. "I too drink red wine at the Hole-in-the-Wall."

All right, Philip thought, he's saying that we're both involved with the Underground. But de Forrestière's role puzzled him, and Philip remained wary.

"I don't want you to think that I have been deceiving you," de Forrestière said. "It's true that in the beginning I cultivated you for your connection with Goering, but in the meantime I have become very fond of you, Philip, and I consider you a friend."

"I'm glad to hear that," Philip said, and he truly was.

"You had a rather abrupt change of heart about cooperating with us, didn't you?"

"Yes."

"Do you mind if I inquire what brought it about?"

Philip did not want to go into details. The telling in itself would still have been painful to him. "I became involved," he said. "What hadn't touched me before suddenly did."

"What's happening here will touch everyone in the world before it's over. Early on I saw hundreds of workers, men long in my employ, like family, seized by the Germans for their work camps. My chief assistant had a grandmother who was Jewish. They came by in a green truck with a swastika on the side and ordered him out of his office and into the back of the truck, which was so packed that everyone had to stand. His secretary phoned me and I ran down to the sergeant in charge and tried to intercede. Vice-president in charge of production, father of six, a doctor of engineering—I told the sergeant all this, but he just smiled at me and said, 'You left out one thing, Herr Director, your vice-president has Jewish blood.'

"My friend is gone, Philip, a hell of a man, destroyed by these Nazi monsters because one of his forebears was a Jew. So I have joined the invisible army of France. I am one of the leaders in Paris. The chain of command is set up in a way to protect my identity, but I am revealing myself to you because . . . well, because of the importance of what we are going to ask of you. Your answer will depend on how deeply you feel. If you were cut as deeply as I was when they carted off my friend, then perhaps you will get involved in this."

"Your friend was alive," Philip observed. "Mine wasn't."

De Forrestière nodded and summoned the waiter for more beer. "Do you know about the command that has been established in London?" he asked after the waiter had departed. "De Gaulle and all other refugee leaders in exile are organizing one overall command against Hitler. Naturally, this group is protected by the tightest of security precautions. But for the past several months there has been a growing awareness that certain important decisions have been betrayed to the Germans, with disastrous results.

"Every effort has been made to track down the informer but so far not a clue. It is known that the person involved must be a member of the inner circle, because a fake decision was deliberately planted in one of the Council meetings, but not implemented, so that no one outside the Command knew about it—and yet, the Germans reacted. The leak had to have come from someone on the Council.

"There is one other factor which has narrowed our search: although decisions are made that affect all military operations, only those relating to the air war are leaked to the Nazis. What's more, military intelligence agents recently discovered a short-wave station in Mayfair that was programmed to transmit directly to Paris. Our conclusion is that someone is sending information directly to Goering. London has tried to identify the person responsible, but without success. Now it is suggested that we may be able to help from our end."

"You mean, for me to play detective with Goering? Why, that's preposterous!"

"It only sounds preposterous, Philip. All they need to know is a name that Goering might mention if you could get him to talk about England or . . . or whatever. Just keep your ears open. We're not asking you to put on a Sherlock Holmes deerstalker hat and sneak around with a magnifying glass."

"But I'm not around Goering all that much. I can't say to him, 'Tell me, Hermann, old boy, have you got a pal on the war council in London?'"

"It's a very serious matter, Philip. We have lost a lot of lives because of this rotten traitor, whoever he is. And now there's a large British force that is trapped in Tobruk. They've been under siege for almost eight months. We're ready to mount a counteroffensive with a contingent of twenty-five thousand men, most of them British and French soldiers who escaped from Dunkirk. But if we're to capitalize on the element of surprise, the Italian-German army that has the Tobruk garrison under siege must not be tipped off about our attack plans. Our initial air attack must be a complete surprise, but we can't go forward with any of this as long as we are vulnerable to this damn informer. We're desperate, Philip. That's why I'm revealing myself to you. Those soldiers in Tobruk cannot hold out much longer. We don't expect the bugger's name, but anything that you might be able to pick up from Goering might help.

"All I ask is that you think about it. If you decide to help us, wonderful; if not, well, I'll still be here for tennis every Thursday."

As they shook hands, Philip knew in his heart that he would do what he could to carry out this mission.

On returning to the Ritz, Philip got into a tub of steaming hot water and pondered his disintegrating fate. He closed his eyes and let his body float in the soothing water. This situation with de Forrestière was a hell of a birthday present, wasn't it? He thought back to Man Ray's warning and wished he had followed Man back to the States. His thoughts drifted, rubbing against the shores of recollections, as he was hypnotized by the caressing water.

A sharp three knocks on the door startled him. "Monsieur Weber! Monsieur Weber!" A voice through the door. "There is a phone call for you. The caller says it's very important."

He left the tub, dried quickly, threw on his wool robe and hurried down the corridor to his room. He would return afterward, he reminded himself, to wipe out the tub. He always liked to leave it clean for the next bather.

He picked up the phone. "Hello."

"Oh, hello, Monsieur Weber! Here you have Pierre Monet!"

The voice sounded familiar, but he didn't know any Pierre Monet. "Who?"

"Pierre Monet! I am here with my *vélo* as you requested it."

Oh, of course, Dieter's *nom de vélo*. "But I didn't—" he started to say, but stopped. "I have to dress," he said, "and then I'll be down."

"Fine, fine, okay, Monsieur Weber," Dieter said. "We will be waiting for you at the Cambon as usual." He hung up.

That puzzled Philip who dressed as fast as he could. "*We* will be waiting." Who was the "we," Philip wondered.

When Philip left the Ritz he was surprised to see snow falling. Snowfall was infrequent in Paris and never failed to create an undercurrent of excitement in the city. A thin film of white had already covered the street and the sidewalk.

Dieter was at the curb, standing beside his *vélotaxi,* holding open the flimsy door. "Good evening, Monsieur Weber!" he called out. "At your service!"

Philip walked over to him, leaving shoe tracks in the thin snow. "What's it all about, Dieter?"

"There is a passenger waiting for you," Dieter said.

Philip put his head inside the cab.

"Hello, Philip," Gaby said. "Come squeeze in."

He eased himself onto the cramped seat beside her as Dieter closed the door behind him. She took some of her lap blanket and covered his legs.

"I'm really glad to see you, Gaby. Especially tonight."

"This will make you doubly glad," she said as she took a bottle and two cups from the seat beside her and poured drinks for them.

"What about Dieter?" Philip asked.

"Nice of you to ask, Monsier Weber, but, no thank you, I have a peptic ulcer and my drinking, I am unhappy to state, is limited to milk. Can you imagine milk? I have been drinking so much milk lately that I'm developing teats."

Gaby tapped her tin cup against Philip's. "Here's mud in your eye," she said. "I learned that from an American movie with Jimmy Cagney."

They drank and Philip enjoyed the fiery trickle of the Calvados as it moved down his throat.

"My grandfather, who lives in Honfleur, gives us a bottle every Christmas. But this is last year's. This Christmas, thanks to our conquerors, our family won't be able to get together."

Dieter had turned onto the Rue Saint-Honoré and was moving them slowly past the elegant shops, invisible in the black, starless night. Philip was surprised and happy that Gaby had unexpectedly appeared on his birthday.

"Phil, I want to talk to you about de Forrestière's proposal," Gaby said in a low voice that did not carry to Dieter. "Have you decided to do it?"

"Not yet."

"Then don't. I know I'm acting against the best interests of my organization, but what they are asking of you—don't do it, Phil. You're not experienced at this kind of thing; they are. I know what can happen. I like you, and I don't want it to happen to you."

"I know how to be careful, Gaby—and prudent."

"Look, what you did for us, getting the art list—that was something that came into your possession as part of your job. But now you would have to ask questions, get into things that are none of your business, and once they become suspicious, you're sunk."

"I may be better at it than you think."

"You sound as if you've made up your mind to do it."

"I may."

"How curious that you and I have switched our positions. And in such a short time. When we first met, I was trying to talk you into this, now I'm trying to talk you out of it. What happened to change you so?"

"They took someone from me. I feel I owe it to her."

"Look, you can't get revenge. Not from them. I became involved in this because the man in my life was one of the organizers. He was clever and very careful, but one of his group was a secret informer, and the Germans trapped my friend and two others at an Underground meeting. They were taken to that terrible place on Avenue Henri-Martin and then shipped to a jail in Cologne where . . ." She stopped abruptly and looked out the small isinglass window on her side of the cab.

"Is he still there?" Philip asked.

"No. They did everything they could to him, but he didn't talk. He didn't tell them a thing. Neither did his two friends. Or else I wouldn't be here now. But they paid a terrible price. The Nazis in Cologne beheaded all of them with an ax, like chickens. They took pictures of it. I saw a photograph in the newspaper of this man I loved, with his head on that chopping block. An example, the caption said, to dissuade others from becoming traitors and obstructionists. I like you, Phil, you're a very appealing man. You're not meant to be a part of all this."

"Yes, I am, Gaby. What de Forrestière wants me to find out is important, isn't it?"

"Well, yes, but what he's asking you to do . . ."

"Perhaps I can't do it. Very likely I can't do it. But if I don't try— I thought that this war had nothing to do with me. That all I had to do was look out for myself. But that's not the case. They killed someone . . . someone I cared about very much. I can't get her corpse out of my mind. I've decided to do what I can. If I fail—well, I fail. It won't be the first time."

A battery of lights suddenly shone in their faces. Dieter skidded to a halt. The patrol car doused its lights; a sergeant got out of the car and approached the *vélotaxi*. He opened the door and snapped on a flashlight, shining it first in Philip's face, then in Gaby's.

"Papers!" he commanded.

Gaby handed him a leather case which contained her passport, but before the sergeant had a chance to inspect it Philip took his *laissez-passer* from his pocket and poked it in front of the flashlight.

"You will please note the signature," Philip said in German.

The sergeant took one look and quickly returned the papers and withdrew, mumbling apologies. Dieter continued his slow progress down the street, which had now become the Faubourg-Saint-Honoré.

Gaby poured them another drink. The Calvados had aged for many years in an oak cask which Gaby's grandfather kept in a deep cellar in his Normandy house.

"It is quite wonderful," Philip said, never having tasted Calvados of such quality. "It's like sipping a Rembrandt."

Gaby laughed.

"I can taste certain great art, can't you?"

"How does a Rembrandt taste?"

"Musky, gentle to the tongue, but with powerful aftereffect. There are colors I can taste, can't you?"

"I've never given it a thought."

"When you stand before a great painting, there's an expression, you 'drink it in,' isn't there?"

"Yes, that's right," said Gaby. "Phil, I can't talk you out of it?"

"I don't think so. That's all I've ever done—talk myself out of things."

"Well, then, perhaps I can help you. I've had experience—it might make it easier."

"Yes, fine. I don't know how, though. I really haven't thought it through. But I'm sure you can help. In fact, we can begin by having dinner."

"No, Phil, let's keep it businesslike. I don't want any more involvement."

"Don't misunderstand, Gaby. No involvement is intended. But if you're going to help me, then I've got to establish you as my girl friend. We should have dinner at the Ritz. Let them see us together. I will make a point of introducing you. Don't you see?"

She looked at him, their faces close in the narrow cab. She felt good about him.

"Dieter!" she called out. "Take us back to the Ritz."

Philip smiled. It would be a pretty nice birthday after all. "We must be careful what we say at the hotel," he cautioned. "I'm sure there are listening devices everywhere."

"All right. I will only whisper sweet nothings."

"Fine."

26

Goering was in a foul mood. He had returned from the Luftwaffe headquarters in Normandy, where the air attacks on Britain were not going the way he wanted, to find that a painting which he had coveted, Cranach's *Fountain Nymph,* had somehow been diverted to Rosenberg, of all people.

"I would perhaps understand if it was the Führer, or even Himmler—but Rosenberg, that idiot! To get a painting like that from under my nose! Explain to me how it happened, von Behr, and it better be good!"

Von Behr and Lohse sat stiffly on chairs facing Goering's Napoleonic desk, both men bearing the scars of their misadventure in Lech, Lohse's leg in a cast from his thigh to his toes, von Behr's left eye covered with a black patch which, curiously enough, enhanced his looks.

"I have no knowledge of how it happened, Excellency. Our office records show that the painting was crated and invoiced for delivery to your train. Dr. Lohse has the records."

Lohse took an inventory sheet out of his briefcase and proferred it to Goering, who refused to take it or even acknowledge it.

"What do I care about paperwork? Can I frame your paper and put it on the wall at Karinhall? Who got hold of my painting and sent it off to Rosenberg? That's what I want to know."

Kropp came into the room carrying a silver tray covered with delicate petits fours which he placed on a table beside Goering. The familiar crystal bowl was not in evidence, which meant that Professor Kahle's cure was still working. Goering devoured each petit four in a single bite, delicately holding the little tarts with his thumb and middle finger as he eased the confections into his mouth. Kropp informed him that Herr Weber had arrived.

"Come in! Come in, Herr Weber!" Goering called out. "You may as well hear this. I have lost a prized Cranach, had it stolen from under my nose by that cretin Rosenberg, and nobody can tell me how it could have happened. Correct, Baron von Behr?"

"Yes, my Reichsmarschall, but I assure you I shall launch an exhaustive investigation as soon as I get back to the office."

"And I will have my painting returned by morning?"

"Well, Excellency, I don't think it would be possible in that—"

"You may withdraw, both of you. Our conversation has no point to it. I am doomed to be victimized by idiots and incompetents."

Von Behr helped Lohse to get up and to fit his crutches under his arms.

"I'd like you to stay, Herr Weber," Goering said. He ate several petits fours in rapid succession, swallowing them like oysters.

"Well, what's the explanation? Do you fail me like everyone else?" he asked Philip after the others had gone. "How I wanted that Cranach! Rosenberg will probably barter it for cheese and sausages."

"I believe I know what happened," Philip said calmly. "When the messenger came for the shipping order, instead of going to von Behr's office where the order was waiting for him he was intercepted by someone in the corridor, and this person gave him an order that directed the painting to Rosenberg."

"And who was that person?"

"Dr. Hermann Bunjes."

"How do you know?"

"When I heard what had happened, I tracked down the messenger."

"But why would Bunjes do such a thing?"

"He's a very ambitious man, a fact I discovered when I was interviewing him about my supposed book. Although he doesn't say so in so many words, he would like to be chief of the E.R.R.—feels he's much better qualified than von Behr, and he resents him."

"So he tries to get rid of von Behr by making him look incompetent."

"Yes, sir, that's the size of it."

Goering pushed himself up from his chair and went over to the window which surveyed the Place de la Concorde. For a long time he said nothing. Then: "I'm very grateful to you, Herr Weber. To have a thing explained finally, something that has caused me such aggravation . . . There is much aggravation, these days."

Goering turned back into the room and sat down heavily in his chair. He pressed a button on a control panel on the end table. "I like talking to you, Herr Weber. You are not after anything, like the others." He shook his head sadly. Kropp appeared with champagne. "Bunjes has been with me for six years. . . . Take away these sweets, Kropp, and bring some cheeses and nibbles."

He sipped his champagne, his eyes at a great distance. "Have you ever been humiliated, Herr Weber?"

"I . . . I can't really think . . ."

"Well, I have, thoroughly, sickeningly humiliated, and now I humiliate them. Only once in my life, but it has rubbed me like a saddle sore all these years. Now I'm having my revenge. The latest reconnaissance photos show that London is nothing but rubble. The Britishers are going to their knees. I won't stop till they crawl, *crawl* on their English bellies and kiss my feet. As far as I am concerned, nothing is more painful than humiliation. And nothing sweeter than revenge."

"How did they humiliate you, Reichsmarschall?" asked Philip, suddenly alert.

"Were you here in Paris when George VI had his coronation?"

"Yes, I was."

"Did you attend?"

"No."

"Well, as you must recall, it was the most important event of the decade. I was named to represent Germany at the coronation. It was an event I eagerly looked forward to. I had spent weeks with my tailor. As you know, I'm sure, I love costumes and pomp, and no one does it better than the English.

"But then, virtually on the eve of my departure, a female member of the House of Commons learned of my role and attacked me in Parliament, a vicious, violent speech, saying that my presence at the coronation would be an insult to Great Britain, and that I should not be allowed to walk on their soil with my blood-stained boots. Our Foreign Minister, von Ribbentrop, got hold of a copy of the speech and sent it to Hitler, asking that he send someone else, since my presence might adversely affect our relations with Britain. This was 1936, when Germany was still emphasizing détente. So Hitler designated General von Blomberg in my place.

"I was never so angry about anything in my life. That my own people would subject me to this terrible embarrassment. I decided that I'd go to the coronation on my own, not as an official representative of the German government. I flew in my own plane, but when I landed at Croydon, Ribbentrop was there to greet me and whisked me off to the German Embassy. A delegation of German officials had been assembled to convince me that I must not make *any* public appearance, let alone go to the coronation. I was not permitted out of the embassy building. I saw only one Englishman, who somehow had found out about my presence and managed to pay me a visit and express his regret at this action of his government. Ribbentrop even managed to keep my visit out of the newspapers.

"The next day, in utter secrecy, I was driven back to the airport, and they made sure I was flown directly to Berlin. No one outside of the British Foreign Office ever learned I had been in London. Can you imagine the humiliation I felt, I, the Vice-Marshall of the Third Reich, treated like some common criminal? But they found out about it in Germany. There were jokes about the coronation outfit that I never got out of my suitcase. Well, now when our planes drop their bombs every night, I regard it as an installment payment on the debt they owe me."

Kropp came to the door of the bedroom. "Excuse me, Reichsmarschall," he said, "but it's time to dress for dinner."

"Ah, yes—I mustn't be late. A job well done, Herr Weber. I will deal with Dr. Bunjes tomorrow. Please let yourself out."

Kropp held the door for Goering as they disappeared into the bedroom. Philip looked around the deserted room. He drank off the last of his champagne, and he had started to leave when his eye fell on Goering's desk. There were a few papers scattered on top of it. Next to the telephone was an old black leather address book. Philip impulsively opened it. A remote possibility, but worth the risk. Obviously, he couldn't go through the entire book, but if, by some chance, there were some entries under . . . J . . . K . . . L . . . London—yes, there were! His eyes skipped along the entries: Fortnum & Mason, Harrods, Snavely of Savile Row, Turnbull & Asser, Yardley. Philip closed the address book and moved silently toward the door. He was sick to his stomach with fear. He closed the door noiselessly and hurried down the corridor. Sweat ran down his face as he ran up the stairs to his room.

27

Henri Bretonne made a special point of quizzing Delor and Cressier as to whether they had seen a waiter who spoke to Colonel Stuppelmayer or did anything at all during the past few weeks to attract their attention.

Delor and Cressier gave it some thought, but came up with nothing.

The day after Colonel Stuppelmayer's "suicide," a new *Kommandant* was appointed for the Ritz, General Erhard Schumacher, a slightly over-the-hill army veteran who had been head of the Military Police in France. The first thing he did was to summon the entire Ritz staff for security interviews. While he waited his turn, Ferdinand Bouchère wrestled with his conscience as to whether to tell the new *Kommandant* about the message he had delivered to the colonel on the night of the banquet.

By spilling these beans, it was entirely possible that the new *Kommandant* would provide Bouchère with the same arrangement he had enjoyed with Stuppelmayer—a monthly bonus, plus special payments for special information, and, most importantly, immunity from arrest for his Italian-Jewish wife. With the bonus, Bouchère could put things from the black market on the table for his three kids that he would otherwise not have been able to afford: rice, potatoes, spaghetti, milk. In the legitimate market, rice was obtainable only on a doctor's order; no potatoes were permitted in the Paris stores, and armed German soldiers guarded the potato fields; spaghetti was also nonexistent in legitimate stores, which was particularly tragic for his Italian wife.

But, waiting his turn to be interviewed, Bouchère knew that the price for his wife's immunity, and the potatoes and the rice and the coal, could send Delor and Bretonne to their graves. Perhaps the Germans would forget about his wife now that

Stuppelmayer was gone. In all the time he had "cooperated" with Stuppelmayer, he had not once informed on any of his colleagues. He had reported on German officers who violated the rules, on pilfering by suppliers, on homosexual activity; but never had he planted a Judas kiss on the cheek of any of his co-workers.

When his turn came to be questioned, he followed his conscience and said nothing about the message he had carried from Cressier to Stuppelmayer.

Besides Bouchère's conscience, there was another factor that worked in favor of Delor and Bretonne: the Gestapo; they regarded the natty French police with their capes and fancy uniforms as effete. This disdain foreclosed any cooperation between the two, which suited the police just fine, since they regarded Gestapo agents as sinister thugs.

As a consequence, a report on the murder of Delocque, a Frenchman, in the Métro never went to Gestapo headquarters. Likewise, the Gestapo's report on Colonel Stuppelmayer's suicide was not seen by the police; thus it was not possible for either of them to link up these two events.

28

Gaby lived with her mother, who was a buyer of handbags and gloves for the Trois Quartiers department store, in a small walkup apartment on the Île Saint-Louis. No one answered Philip's ring, so, as prearranged, he went to the corner café to wait for Gaby. He ordered a draft beer, which, on arrival was already losing its insipid foam; Philip knew it would be undrinkably bitter, just as the Nazi-controlled *Le Soir* was unreadable and the Nazi-controlled radio was impossible to listen to.

Sitting there in the Belles-Artes Café, Philip thought about the one other time in his life when he had thrown aside his usual caution. When he was seventeen, there had been a chance for him to land a job as a counselor at a summer camp for boys in the Ozarks. He desperately needed the money, and, besides, it was his first opportunity to get off the streets of St. Louis. But he couldn't swim a stroke, for he had a fear of the water. At that time he attended a public high school that had a swimming pool in its basement, and every day for weeks he went down to the pool after school and tried to swim, sometimes with instruction, other times determinedly on his own. But his hydrophobia kept him from bringing both his feet off the bottom.

Still Philip persisted in his quest for the job. The camp was run by the YMCA, and Philip's final interview was conducted at the Y by the camp director, who had narrowed down the applicants to three. It was Philip whom he finally chose, but, as he was about to leave, the director remembered that counselors must demonstrate their ability to swim before being hired. They went down to the big Y pool and Philip did not hesitate to undress and put on a pair of trunks. He simply knew, at that moment, that he was going to swim. And he did—the length of the pool.

And now his attitude toward the Underground had come around in much the same way. In retrospect, he saw himself on the terrace at Lipp's at the moment when the Gestapo agents seized the captain Philip had been supposed to meet. That was the beginning, he decided; he had simply jumped into the water and, miraculously, had swum.

"Have you been waiting long?" Gaby stood beside the table.

He struggled to his feet. "No, only a few minutes."

"Do you want to finish your beer?"

"It's the other way around—the beer has finished me."

She was wearing a thick white sweater with a black skirt and boots, and her face, without a trace of makeup, was rosy from her bicycle ride. She smiled at him and brushed her cold cheek against his.

"That's pretty stingy for a girl friend."

"It's enough. This is a friendly café."

Her apartment was crowded with a mixture of comfortable furniture and good antiques. "We once lived in a much larger place," Gaby said, "but when we moved, my mother refused to get rid of anything." The apartment was unheated and her breath showed when she spoke. She led him into a small, closed-off library that had a potbellied wood stove whose metal chimney pipe vented into the fireplace.

"It's the only room we can afford to heat," she said.

She opened the door of the stove and put paper and bits of wood on the grate. Philip put a match to the paper, and the fire sprang to life.

She put on a few larger pieces of wood, which she took from a small stack in the corner. Then she took a wine bottle from the sideboard and filled two glasses. The wine was cloudy, but it had a surprisingly clean, fruity taste.

"Is this also from your Calvados grandfather?"

"No, this is from a Burgundy uncle."

On a sideboard were two photographs in twin frames, one of a young man in uniform, the other of a middle-aged man in a business suit; they bore a resemblance to each other.

"Your father?"

"Yes." She picked up the photos. "Isn't he handsome? He tells me he has a house right on a Lake Michigan." She pronounced it "*Mitch*igan." He corrected her.

"But you say 'rich,' don't you?"

"Yes, but 'Michigan' does not rhyme with 'rich again.'"

"That's what scares me about speaking English in America— you're always changing the rules."

"I had a talk with von Behr this morning," Philip said, getting down to business. "Told him I wanted to include some reference to British art in the book—asked him if Goering had collected any English paintings."

"A way to get him talking about Britain."

"Exactly. Well, he said, yes, the Reichsmarschall had several English favorites—Gainsborough, George Watts, Turner, Sir Joshua Reynolds, Whistler . . ."

"Whistler was an American."

"Yes, but lived most of his life in London. Anyway, von Behr said that Goering had once had splendid canvases by these artists but that quite abruptly, in 1936, he had ordered that all of his paintings by British artists be sold. Had them stripped from the walls at Karinhall and carted off to an auction house."

"Did von Behr find out why?"

"No, but I think I know the answer. That was the year of King George VI's coronation, and Goering was not allowed to attend."

"Who was to blame for that?"

"Hard to say. He mentioned some woman member of Parliament who had it in for him, but I suspect it was more than that."

"Who was the British Ambassador to Germany then? Maybe that has some bearing on it."

"I mentioned that to de Forrestière after we played tennis yesterday. Sir Eric Phipps to 1937, and then Nevile Henderson."

"Is either still around?"

"They both are, but de Forrestière says that neither one is on the Command Council, so that rules them out."

"What about Gisela Linberger—did you talk to her?"

"Yes, she insisted on cooking for me. She's very proud of her garlic soup, God help me. But I did get her to think about Goering and his relations with the British. She came up with one thing: after Edward abdicated and became the Duke of Windsor, Goering became great friends with him and his Duchess. They even went to Karinhall a couple of years ago and stayed there as his guests."

"But the Duke of Windsor has nothing to do with the war."

"Yes, of course, but that may be a clue. I mean, through the Windsors, Goering may have met the Mr. X we're looking for."

"That's possible, I suppose." The room was warming up, so she took off her thick sweater. Underneath she was wearing a much thinner sweater that accentuated her firm breasts. She refilled their glasses.

"So what's your next move, Philip?"

"I don't know. I really don't know."

"What about the fancy lady you told me about—the one you got for Goering from the barman?"

"Monette Lynette? What about her?"

"She may have heard some things. Sex and drugs are supposed to be great tongue looseners, aren't they?"

"Worth a try. We should talk to Georges. Let's go have a drink at the Ritz bar."

"I was going to ask you to stay to dinner. You haven't tasted *my* garlic soup."

"I think we should see Georges."

"All right. Just give me a few minutes to change."

"Don't change—nothing will look better on you than that sweater."

She laughed at him. He reached out and pulled her against him and kissed her tenderly on the lips, a kiss of affection that she would not misunderstand, tentative, gentle, a harbinger of deeper feelings. She leaned back her head and looked at him rather soberly.

"No, Phil—no."

"It's just the sweater. I got carried away."

"Then I'd *better* change!"

Georges was indeed helpful. Monette Lynette had telephoned him that very afternoon with an urgent, in fact desperate, request for some "friendly tobacco." Georges was just about to send a groom with the Ritz envelope which he now took from an inner pocket of his white jacket and handed to Philip.

"You can be the messenger," he said. "Her address is on the envelope." He refilled their glasses from the wine bottle on their table and then moved on to greet a group of Nazi brass who had just entered the bar. Georges never stayed at any one table very long, which was one of the secrets of his success.

Monette Lynette was desperately in need of a smoke, her graceful beauty dissipated by the drain of her body's craving. She had not smoked a pipe for almost two days, and the black horrors of her deprivation were assailing her.

With desperate efficiency, she immediately began to prepare her pipe. She lit the flame of a small burner and with trembling fingers ripped open the envelope which Philip handed to her. Inside the envelope were black treacly cubes of chandoo, which was the inspissated juice of the poppy. She picked up a stylet, thrust its sharp end into one of the cubes and held it over the flame, rotating it, painfully enduring the anxious, interminable wait for it to be roasted. She was oblivious to Philip's presence as she agitatedly watched the small flame licking against the chandoo, changing its color, until at last it was ready for the bowl. As her lips sucked the smoke into her famished lungs, the lines on her face slowly softened, a drowning woman pulled to shore, resuscitated.

"I'm sorry," she said. "I usually take better care of myself. But it has become so difficult . . . to get a pipe . . ."

"Since the Germans?"

"The rotten Boche. There used to be a nice opium parlor on Rue du Dragon in Saint-Germain-des-Prés where one could go comfortably whenever one wanted, but the Boche closed it down. But . . . what difference? There isn't any stuff coming into Paris anymore. It was all right for me while I was seeing . . . a certain German . . ."

"Goering, wasn't it?"

She gave him a look. Philip caught his breath, wondering, for a split second, if perhaps she now recognized him as the one who had opened the door for her on her first visit to Goering's suite. "I work for Georges, don't forget," Philip said. "We know how to keep our secrets."

"Thank God for Georges. I'm going to pay him double his price for this delivery. I could not live without smoking. A couple of pipes and I can have sex with my customers without feeling troubled. Life is pleasant and I can sleep peacefully at night."

"And if you don't have your pipes?"

"You saw how I was. I weep uncontrollably, my hands fail me. Twice I have committed suicide."

"You mean tried to."

"I was over the line. I have no right being here. It's what happens when I don't have my pipe."

"I should think Goering could get you all you want."

"I haven't seen him for a while. I think he took a cure."

"How do you like him?"

"We have a good time. Eight or nine pipes while we eat and drink, and I do whatever he wants. He's fat, but I don't mind. He's a sybarite, a pure sybarite, which, to me, is very, very attractive." She put another cube of chandoo on the stylet for a fresh pipe. There was color in her cheeks now and she had stretched herself full length on her chaise longue. Philip admired the wonderful contours of her body.

"Is he regular?"

"How do you mean?"

"About sex. You know, normal."

"Oh, I guess so. But what the hell's normal? He doesn't go for female goats, if that's what you mean. The longer I'm in my profession, the less I know what's normal. Would you like a pipe? I've got plenty of stuff now."

Philip had never taken any kind of dope, and he had no desire to try the opium, but he felt that Monette would talk more freely if he shared a pipe with her.

"I don't like to smoke alone," Monette said as she prepared a second pipe. "That's what I used to like so much about the parlor in Saint-Germain-des-Prés."

She puffed his pipe to start its draw and then handed it to him. He drew on it, but he didn't inhale.

"It's my first pipe," Philip said.

"Do you like it?"

"Yes, it's nice."

"Goering also smoked his first pipe with me. Of course he had indulged in morphine for years, but he'd never smoked it before. He really liked it. He called me his *rauch Engel.*"

"He fascinates me—Goering. His lifestyle. The way he runs the war from the Ritz."

"He told me he used to stay there before the war. Told me of some of the great dinners, and there was a chef there—I forget his name . . ."

"Escoffier."

"Yes, that's the one."

"Goering used to like the English. Did he mention any of his friends?"

"No, not really. Well, he did talk about a great time he had with a couple of English people he knew, but I don't recall he mentioned their names. One of them who had been nice to him, something like that. They were in Paris together, and he told me about masquerades and fancy-dress balls they went to. What Paris must have been!"

"How long ago was this?"

"I don't know—a few years ago. One night they all went to the Bal Musette, and Goering was costumed as Henry the Eighth— isn't that perfect for Goering? The ball went on all night long with much drinking and dancing and wild carrying on, and afterward Goering said he and the two English fell into bed together. You should have seen his face light up when he told me about that!"

"But he didn't mention any names?"

"No, just that they were a threesome. So I thought he might like me to bring a girl friend of mine, but he wasn't interested. It wasn't that kind of threesome, he said. Besides, they were aristocrats, he said, and that's what made it so enjoyable. 'I love to fuck with the upper classes,' he said."

The phone rang. It was a client. Monette told him to wait a minute; she put her hand over the mouthpiece. "You want a little time with me?" she asked Philip.

"I wish I could, but Georges wants me back by now."

"It's on the house."

"That's nice of you. Another time. I don't want to get in bad with Georges."

She gave him a "too bad" look as she told the client to come right along. Philip felt that she had told him all she had to tell.

That night Philip had another of his "PRELOON" nightmares, dominated by a fat Chagall-like figure who resembled Goering but who was someone else, someone who was desperately trying to tell Philip something.

When Philip awoke, sweating and short of breath, he groped unsuccessfully to recall a particular fragment of his dream that almost, but not quite, reached his consciousness. He poured himself some Perrier from a bottle on his nightstand. He felt pinched by a sharp feeling of loneliness, which puzzled and upset him. That he lived alone was a state that he had always accepted as natural to his being, like the color of his hair and that he was five foot ten. He had thought about marriage, of course, but only in the abstract, as he might think about the existence of Capuchin monks or mountain climbing. He had never really loved anyone, never told anyone he loved her, even insincerely. His obsession with Lili, overwhelming as it had been, nevertheless had not been love.

But now he sat on the edge of his bed with his glass of Perrier and felt a terrible loneliness. He had a vision of Gaby asleep in her bed, wrapped tightly in a cocoon of blankets against the cold of her unheated room. He could feel the soft press of her lips on his, the warmth of her breasts against his chest. My God, he thought, am I in love with her? The admission excited him, but also made him apprehensive. She does not want any involvement, he thought. She's been honest about that. But I can't help it. "Oh Christ," he said aloud, disgusted with himself, "what's the matter with you, Weber, have you lost all your goddamn marbles? It's just middle-of-the-night craziness, that's all. Tomorrow morning there'll be nothing left of it."

He finished the Perrier and got back into bed. He buried his head in his pillow, and, as he did, the dream resurged. Goering was talking, endlessly, and was holding a long opium pipe which he was using as a dildo to have intercourse with Monette, who writhed in ecstasy. While he moved the pipe in and out of Monette, Goering was moaning about his aborted trip to attend the coronation.

Philip got out of bed again. A fragment of what Goering had told him about that humiliating visit to London had come back to him. There had been one person, Goering had said, but what were his exact words? One considerate Englishman who had come to see him in the German Embassy—Philip kicked himself for not having picked up on this—one Englishman who expressed his regret at the action of his government. Wasn't that what Goering had said? But what Englishman? Certainly someone of position. And could that have been the Englishman, perhaps with his wife, the couple that Monette had told him about? Why not? The English are as kinky about their sex as anyone else.

I will discuss this with Gaby tomorrow, he told himself as he shut his eyes. That took his thoughts back to Gaby. I will tell her that I love her. It was a buoyant thought on which to fall asleep.

29

Gaby met him at the little pond in the Tuileries Garden where, year round, the children played with toy sailboats that they prodded with long bamboo sticks as they ran along the perimeter of the pond. Philip paid fifty centimes for the privilege of occupying two metal chairs at the edge of the boat pond.

"Why not, Gaby? Goering goes to London for the coronation, but is rejected and humiliated. Only one Englishman is nice to him, and Goering invites this Englishman to come to Paris as his guest. And to Karinhall. He comes with his wife, or a lady friend, and after a big drunken night at a masquerade ball they all wind up in bed together. Maybe it happens again at Karinhall. We know Goering's morphine has a variety of effects on him, and who knows, maybe he induced the English couple to try some.

"At any rate, three years later Germany is at war with Britain and Goering has a perfect situation for blackmail. Maybe he has some photographs. Whatever, the Englishman is completely vulnerable. If word of his involvement with Goering got out, he would be ruined, so he caves in under Goering's pressure. German espionage people in London arrange to pick up his information and short-wave it to Goering."

"Well, I think it's farfetched but not inconceivable."

"I think it's damned conceivable."

A small towheaded boy in a sailor coat asked Philip to watch his boat for him and plunked it dripping on his lap.

"But even if you're right, Phil, what help is it? We still don't have the identity of this Englishman."

"No, but there must be a way . . ."

They sat pensively watching the children circling the pond. Philip was keenly aware of Gaby's close presence, her arm on the chair parallel to his, touching.

"I must tell you something that you don't want to hear," Philip said. "I discovered something very upsetting last night. I had a nightmare that woke me, and I couldn't go back to sleep. That's when I made this unfortunate discovery. I am in love with you."

"You found it out in a nightmare?"

"For the first time in my life I felt lonely, and I wondered why, and in wondering I found the answer: I love you." He was looking straight ahead, watching the little boats catch the wind gusts in their sails. His throat was suddenly dry. He moved his hand on top of hers, still not looking at her. "What do you think of that?"

She was moved by his sincerity.

He turned to face her. "I know how you feel about . . . alliances. But unfortunately I really do think I am in love with you, and I have never been in love with anyone. Ever. Having made that clear, I will now go sail my boat."

He joined the kiddies at the pond and launched his little boat on the water, imitating the five-year-olds around him, and making her laugh. But beneath her gaiety she felt unwelcome stirrings of response. She would not tell him, but she too had had an unexpected reaction the previous night, when, as she was gingerly sliding her flanneled form between the frigid sheets, she had thought about him, a flash illusion of his warm body against hers, snuggling against the enemy cold. No more of that, she had promised herself. No more thoughts like that. I have suffered all I ever want to suffer.

But she did like him, and it would be hard to put him out of her mind. Other than her father, Philip was the only American she had ever known. Perhaps it is that he touches the American in me, she thought. He speaks of love, which is a word that I don't like to hear anymore, but I do respond to him, I do, and there's no sense kidding myself about that.

"Well, well, Mademoiselle Duvier, I thought I recognized you."

She looked up, disoriented. "Monsieur de Forrestière! What in the world are you doing at the boat pond?" She was the Underground's direct contact with de Forrestière and knew his identity.

"It is my day with my son," he said, indicating a little boy busy with his boat. "I see that our friend Weber has turned into a yachtsman."

She laughed and called to Philip, who came to them smiling sheepishly and offering his hand to de Forrestière.

"So this is what you do when you're not playing tennis," de Forrestière said.

"Here, sit down with us," Philip said. "I have something to discuss with you. We're all right here, aren't we?"

"Perfect," de Forrestière said as he pulled up one of the iron Tuileries chairs.

Philip gave him a full account of his theory about how Goering was obtaining his information from London. "How does it strike you?"

"Farfetched, but feasible."

"But to identify this Englishman—that's something else again."

"We know he's a man of position, probably has a title," Gaby said. "What about searching through back numbers of the newspapers? We know the visit was sometime after the coronation, so we could go through back copies, beginning in 1936, to try to find a news item about Goering and his distinguished English friend."

"That might work," de Forrestière said, "but also it might take a long time, and time is something we're running short of."

"Can you think of anything quicker?" Philip asked.

"Well, while Gaby was talking, it occurred to me that the place to look might be the British Embassy. There could possibly be an entry in their log."

"Oh, yes, of course!" Gaby said. "I worked there for a spell, as an interpreter, and I was impressed with how methodical they were about their records."

"But the embassy is shut," Philip said. "It's been locked up since the war started and the British evacuated."

"But that doesn't mean you can't get in," de Forrestière said.

"Once inside, I'd know my way around," Gaby said.

"Look it over," de Forrestière said. "If you need help, I can get some expert people."

"But do you think it's worth the effort?" Philip asked.

"It's a possible lead, Philip. We're desperate. The whole thing's a needle in the haystack. But we've got to get this son of a bitch. We've simply *got* to! You might be able to pull some weight and get in with your E.R.R. credentials. But be very, very cautious. In the meantime, I'll query London to see if they have a record of anyone who went to the Continent after the coronation, to meet Goering."

The small boy who had deposited his boat with Philip came to reclaim it. "My boat! What have you done with my boat, monsieur?"

Philip took him by the hand and led him to his boat, which had drifted to the far side of the pond.

"Keep an eye on him, Gaby. Don't let him be a foolish hero."

But Gaby did not hear him.

De Forrestière noticed the look in her eye as she watched Philip with the little boy. He knew that she would look after him. He got up, kissed her hand, and went to find his son.

The British Embassy building is an imposing structure on the Rue du Faubourg-Saint-Honoré, a short distance from the Presidential Palace. An outer wall, with an ornate iron gate, protects an inner, cobblestoned courtyard that leads to the entrance of the embassy proper. Philip casually stopped outside the gate, which was partially opened, and saw that there was a single German soldier on duty in the courtyard, his rifle resting against the steps. There were no lights on in the embassy, nor any sign of occupancy. The brass name plates on the gateposts had long ago lost their polish, the windows were glazed with dirt, and the planted areas in the courtyard were unkempt. An accumulation of dried leaves and scraps of paper had gathered around the base of the front door. The soldier was sitting on the top step, his back leaning against the balustrade, his eyes closed.

Philip proceeded along the Rue du Faubourg-Saint-Honoré to the Place Beauvau, where Gaby awaited him in a small bistro.

"I think we're all right," Philip said after ordering a coffee. "There's only one soldier on duty and the place looks deserted."

"But he may have strict orders . . ."

"I'm sure he does, but the Germans can be coerced by a show of authority. We've got to come on strong, which is something this coffee is not."

"Does it frighten you?"

"Sure."

"You don't have to, you know."

"Neither do you."

They sat with their fears for a moment, the bar patrons pushing around their little table.

"But we've got to, haven't we, Gaby?"

She took a clipboard and a pair of horn-rimmed glasses from her large shoulder bag. Her knit cap covered her hair and she pushed the collar of her coat up to her chin. Philip was wearing a broad-brimmed hat, a heavy scarf and a trench coat. De Forrestière had advised them to neutralize their features as best they could. He had also advised them that he would have three good men nearby, watching their operation, with plans to help them if they got into trouble.

Philip strode briskly into the courtyard of the embassy, followed by Gaby with her clipboard under her arm. The soldier on guard quickly got to his feet when he saw them coming. Straightening his cap, he took his gun by the muzzle and pulled it to his side.

"I'm from the E.R.R.," Philip said in clipped no-nonsense German. "We're here to inventory the pictures." He passed a document before the soldier's eyes, but kept moving toward the door. "Please open up," he said.

The soldier had only time to see that the document bore the E.R.R. logo. "My instructions, sir," he said, tentatively, as he trailed after Philip, "are that no one is to enter—"

"That's right, Corporal, except on special occasions. We have to inventory the paintings."

"Well, sir, I should make a call . . ."

"Corporal, I am under direct orders from the Reichsmarschall. Here!" He displayed his *laissez-passer* under the soldier's nose. "Do you see the signature?"

The soldier had never before seen a document signed by the Reichsmarschall himself.

"Open up," Philip repeated in a commanding voice.

The soldier reluctantly moved to the door and unlocked it with a tagged key he took from his tunic pocket.

"What's your name, soldier?"

"Corporal Hans Haus, sir."

"I appreciate your cooperation, Corporal Haus. I will enter your name favorably in my report."

"Oh, thank you, sir."

Philip immediately began a tour of the entrance hall and the main salon, stopping before each picture and dictating its nomenclature to Gaby, who entered the data on a sheet on her clipboard. The soldier observed them through the glass of the front door until they passed out of sight. He had been on guard duty at the embassy for many weeks, and this was the first time anyone had appeared for admission.

Gaby led Philip up the marble staircase to the second floor, where, at the end of the corridor, there was a door bearing a discreet identification: "Appointment Secretary Marjorie Knightcastle."

Before the evacuation, Miss Knightcastle had taken pains to tidy up her office. Gaby first went to the desk and tried to open the middle drawer, but it was locked. Philip took out his penknife and slid the blade into the crack at the top of the drawer beside the lock, managing to depress the latch far enough to slide it open.

The drawer did not contain the log books they were looking for. Gaby went through all the other drawers of the desk, but the books were not in any of them. They then shifted their attention to the file cabinets, and to the multidrawered antique bureau that ran along one entire wall of the office. On the wall above the bureau were several oils depicting various English landscapes, and it was their plan, if anyone appeared, to be inventorying those paintings.

On the steps, Corporal Haus had become increasingly concerned about his dereliction in not reporting this incident, and he decided it would be best to play it safe. He went down the steps to where, sheltered in a wooden box on a stanchion, there was an army field phone that was connected to the guard officer in the *Kommandantur*. The corporal picked up the receiver and turned the handle, but there was no response. He turned the handle again, this time vigorously, but the phone was dead. It was his duty to report in on this phone in the A.M. and P.M. of his tour of duty, and the phone had functioned when he used it for that purpose only an hour before. Corporal Haus had received no instructions to cover this perplexing situation. Guard Officer Oberleutnant Nordmann was an abusive taskmaster who was a stickler for rules, so Corporal Haus decided he had best go to use the telephone in the café at the corner.

Before he could act on this decision, however, a military motorcycle, with a soldier in its sidecar, appeared at the gate. The passenger, who was also a corporal, descended and opened the gate in order for the motorcycle to proceed into the courtyard. The driver dismounted, and he and his passenger approached Corporal Haus, who started to tell them about the malfunctioning field telephone, but he did not get very far. One of the soldiers rammed his forearm against Haus's throat, and the other simultaneously plunged an eight-inch knife into his chest. He died instantly. The two assassins took the corporal's identification papers and the door key from his pocket, then dumped his slumped body into the sidecar, snapping the boot on over the opening. It was all accomplished very swiftly. The driver remounted the motorcycle, which had been left running, and gunned his departure from the courtyard. The newly arrived corporal put Haus's papers into his tunic pocket, picked up his fallen rifle, and stationed himself on the steps. The body of Corporal Haus would never be recovered, thereby precluding retribution by the Germans, who would probably assume he had deserted. Desertion was more of a problem than the authorities liked to admit.

The first drawer that Gaby opened in the bureau contained the appointment books. Each was clearly marked by year, and it was easy to locate the one for 1936.

"Shall we look at it here or take it with us?" she asked Philip.

"Here," Philip answered. "They would find it on us if we were stopped."

They sat side by side at the desk and began to turn the pages; dinners, receptions, galas abounded, each occasion described in detail with a list of the guests, the menu, the cost and other such information appended.

And then, abruptly, there it was, the needle in the haystack: "November 16, 1936. Reception: Lord Ronald Lornsway (Deputy Minister of Defence), Lady Cecilia Lornsway, Hermann Goering (Vice-Chancellor, Germany), Sir Oswald Mosley," and a long list of other dignitaries. Neither Philip nor Gaby had ever heard of Lord Lornsway, but they hoped he was the man they were looking for. It couldn't be Sir Oswald of the Fascist Blackshirts, for he was now in disrepute. They quickly returned the book to its drawer. Philip replaced the chairs at the desk and made sure nothing in the room looked out of place.

Outside the embassy, Philip approached the corporal, who was standing at the bottom of the stairs, facing the street.

"You may lock up, Corporal . . ." he started to say, then noticed that the soldier was not Corporal Haus. He felt a dart of apprehension that quickly dissipated when the new corporal said, in French, "It's all right. We had to take over."

The corporal ran up the steps and locked the door, then, from the top of the steps, looked to the sidewalk beyond the gate where a man stood casually at the curb. The man looked up and nodded.

"The coast is clear," the corporal said to Philip. "Don't be in a hurry when you leave."

By the time Philip and Gaby reached the sidewalk, the man who had given the signal had disappeared. They were only a few steps beyond the embassy when the motorcycle reappeared, roaring into the courtyard. The boot had been removed and the passenger compartment was empty. As the corporal climbed in, taking the gun with him, the motorcycle took off, zooming into the labyrinth of side streets that adjoin the Rue du Faubourg-Saint-Honoré.

Philip had to give de Forrestière credit: he knew how to take care of his people, all right.

Philip and Gaby separated soon after they left the embassy. In a café on the Rue Montalivet, Gaby went to the ladies' room, where she removed her cap and glasses, putting them into her handbag, and left her clipboard behind the toilet.

After carefully determining that he was not being followed, Philip returned to the Ritz. To make the call to de Forrestière appear casual, he phoned him from the Little Bar.

"Hello, Marcel, Philip here."

"Hello, Philip, how are you?"

"Just fine, Marcel. You wanted to know when I'd be free for tennis."

"Oh, yes, do you have the dates?"

"Yes, as of now, this month on the twelfth, fifteenth, and eighteenth, next month the fourteenth, nineteenth, twenty-third, and then on the first and twenty-fifth."

"Hold on while I check my calendar, will you?"

"Sure." Philip's heart pounded in his throat. If Lornsway was not on the Command Council, then the whole risky undertaking would have been in vain and he would have to start all over and find some new way of solving this bastard's identity. The wait seemed interminable, and Philip became irritated with how long it was taking de Forrestière to count the letters in the alphabet. Twelve is L, fifteen is O, eighteen is R—come on, Marcel, what's the goddamn verdict?

De Forrestière had completed translating the numbers into letters, and now he consulted his list of names on the Command. There it was: Lornsway, Lord Ronald.

"Hello, Philip, the dates are perfectly okay with me."

30

The patrol came at three o'clock in the afternoon, hard-pounding boots on the old wooden stairs, two raps on the door, and despite the pleas and cries of her children, Pia Bouchère, the Italian-Jewish wife of the Ritz waiter, was dragged, screaming for help, down the rickety stairs and flung into the back of the truck, already crowded with Jewish women.

A neighbor telephoned the Ritz and told Ferdinand Bouchère what had happened. Frantically, he ran from the kitchen and up the stairs to General Schumacher's office, where he begged the General's aide to allow him a few important minutes with the Ritz *Kommandant*. After a wait of twenty minutes, the General received him.

Wringing his hands, Bouchère entreated the General to spare his wife in exchange for important information. It depended on how important it was, the General said. Bouchère told him about the message he had delivered to Colonel Stuppelmayer the night of the Himmler banquet, eagerly implicating Louis Delor and Henri Bretonne.

The General said he would consider Bouchère's request concerning his wife if, in the future, Bouchère would continue to inform the General of any activities among the Ritz staff that might be regarded as suspicious. Bouchère assured the General that he could be thoroughly depended upon.

Later that same day, the Gestapo quietly arrested Delor and Bretonne and took them to the dreaded flat on the Rue Henri-Martin to be interrogated. They never returned to the Ritz, nor did anyone ever find out what happened to them, although they must have resisted their torture to the extent of not implicating the *sous-chef,* Yves Cressier, who was never questioned or arrested.

The General kept his part of the bargain and arranged for Bouchère's wife to be released from the holding compound at the Vélodrome d'Hiver, where four thousand Jewish women had been herded together for transport to Dachau and Auschwitz.

Unfortunately for Bouchère, the chambermaid, Jocelyn Gaumier, had observed him as he waited to see General Schumacher. She reported this to Cressier, who, after the arrest of his compatriots Bretonne and Delor, took it upon himself to sentence Bouchère to death for having informed on them. Cressier waited for Bouchère in a narrow alleyway, near where Bouchère lived and, as he passed by on his way home from the Métro, dragged him into the alleyway and repeatedly smashed his face against the stone wall of the building until, horribly mutilated, he was dead.

Part Three

TOMORROW

If you truly believe in your destiny,
Then play blind poker.

31————————————————

After his embassy experience, Philip felt an unusual sense of satisfaction, having achieved something that, a short time ago, he would not have even attempted. Now he would have no further involvement with the Underground—he had made that clear to de Forrestière—and he was enjoying the high of a player who has won the finals at Wimbledon and does not have to compete anymore.

His euphoria was tempered, however, by the fact that Gaby had imposed a stay on their relationship, wanting time to think about what she was getting herself into. For Philip, each passing day intensified his desire to see her. His small room, so acceptable to him for so long, had become intolerable. He found himself keeping late hours in the Little Bar, drinking more than he wanted to in order to avoid going up to bed. He had promised Gaby not to call her, but on the fifth day, when he had just about decided to break his word, she called him. She suggested they have dinner on the following evening after she finished work.

"All right, but why not now? Tonight."

"Because it's ten o'clock, darling, and we both ate dinner hours ago."

"We'll eat another. Nothing like two dinners to keep up one's strength."

Gaby laughed. "Tonight we can dream of tomorrow," she said.

At the very moment that Gaby and Philip were talking on the phone, in another *quartier* of Paris an SS raid was taking place that was destined to have a profound effect on their lives. The raid was on a plumber's shop on the Rue de Paradis, where SS agents found an Underground mimeograph machine in the back of the shop. Stacked on the floor beside the machine were copies

of the Resistance newspaper *Humanité,* some pro-De Gaulle
pamphlets, and other *verboten* materials, including this Underground Christmas card, festooned with angels:

> Christmas will not be celebrated this year.
> The Blessed Virgin and the Little Jesus are
> Displaced Persons.
> Saint Joseph is in a concentration camp,
> The stable has been requisitioned,
> The Angels have been brought down by antiaircraft fire,
> The Three Kings are in England,
> The cow is in Berlin and the ass in Rome,
> And the star has been repainted blue by order of the Chief.

Among the stack of materials beside the mimeo machine,
clipped to inky stencils, the SS agents also found the inventory of
confiscated art which Philip had given Gaby. Copies of the
inventory had already been made and distributed; that it had
been left at the mimeo machine with its stencils and not
destroyed was a fatal carelessness. Although most of the inventory was typed, there were certain entries on the sheet that had
been written in by hand. Americans form their letters, particularly the *b, g, k, r* and *s,* in a unique manner; it would not
take an expert to identify the inked handwriting on the inventory
as that of an American.

There had been no one on the premises when the raid
occurred, but at nine o'clock the following morning, when the
plumber arrived, he was taken into custody. He said he knew
only by name the two men who had rented space from him, and
that he had no other information about them. The Gestapo
agents who were interrogating him tried to extract more information, but the failure of their attempts finally convinced them that
the plumber was probably telling the truth.

As soon as word reached the Underground about the raid, an
attempt was made to contact Philip, but he was not at the Ritz.
Fortunately Gaby was located at her job, and she was immediately taken to a safe house in Montmartre. The SS would
certainly want to question Philip's girl friend. Gaby told the
woman who took her into hiding that she was supposed to meet
Philip at the Hole-in-the-Wall at six o'clock that evening, a
rendezvous that would now be dangerous for Philip.

*   *   *

Baron von Behr was pleased to be the one to give Goering the news about Philip. The Reichsmarschall took one look at the inventory, with its handwritten notations, and began to shake with rage.

"Where is he? Bring him to me! I put you personally in charge, von Behr—find him! If he escapes from Paris, follow him. Don't come back here until you have him in custody. General Oberg will give you all the SS men you need. I want that American son of a bitch! I will make an example of him!"

He was striding around the room, his arms flailing. Now he stopped and plucked some tablets from the crystal bowl and popped them into his mouth. He had been back on the morphine for about a week. He wheeled around on von Behr and grabbed him by the arm.

"You find him, von Behr. I want him brought here—right here to this room. Then he will find out what happens to those who try to make a fool out of Hermann Goering. You go find him, von Behr. Now!"

He shoved him toward the door.

Philip had left the Ritz early in the day; he wanted to find a present, something special to give to Gaby when they met that evening. He had taken most of his savings from the hiding place at the bottom of the vase on his bureau, and he had gone in search of something that would reflect his feelings for her. He had first visited Cartier's on the Rue de la Paix, feeling like an impostor among the rich clients who were sitting at the tables inspecting jewels being shown to them on velvet pads. Afterward he had looked at the windows at Van Cleef & Arpels, but was too intimidated to go in.

He had next gone to the Rue Bonaparte and the Rue des Saints-Pères in Saint-Germain-des-Prés, where there were several shops that specialized in antique jewelry. After that, he had visited a jeweler whom he knew who had a little shop across from Saint-Sulpice. Finally, coming out of a bistro on the Rue du Bac, where he had had lunch, he saw just what he wanted in the shop window of an adjoining antique store: a pendant necklace that consisted of a thin gold chain from which a simple black pearl was suspended. The rich, ancient luster of the graceful pearl seemed just right.

He went to the nearby Café des Deux Magots, where he contentedly passed time until his rendezvous with Gaby. It was with a jaunty step that he returned to the Place de l'Opéra by Métro at six o'clock and walked along the boulevard toward the Hole-in-the-Wall. A bearded man in a sheepskin jacket fell in alongside him.

"I'm Muskrat," he said. "Don't stop—keep walking. You will recall, I spoke to you at 122 Provence. There is serious trouble, the Gestapo is looking for you. You must not go to the Hole-in-the-Wall. Or the Ritz. Or any familiar place."

"What about Gaby? She's to meet me—"

"We have taken care of her."

"Is she all right?"

"Yes."

"You're sure?"

"She's all right. There is an address on this piece of paper. Take the Métro here in the Place de l'Opéra in the direction Daumesnil, and get off at the Bastille stop. Now give me your passport, but keep it out of sight."

Philip slipped his passport from his pocket and passed it to Muskrat as unobtrusively as he could.

"Under no circumstances," Muskrat continued, "are you to return to the Ritz or phone there. You are in extreme danger, but we will try to help. If you are stopped, try to swallow this piece of paper. Good luck."

He disappeared in the throng of pedestrians.

Philip was only a short distance from the Métro entrance, but as he crossed the Boulevard des Capucines to reach it he felt nakedly exposed. Directly across from him was a huge garish banner proclaiming "KOMMANDANTUR DER STADT PARIS"; the headquarters occupied most of the building. Philip hunched his shoulders as he passed by it.

The address on the paper was three blocks from the Bastille station. As he covered the distance, Philip kept close to the buildings, watching for anyone who might be following him. When he reached his destination, he did not go into the building right away, waiting for the street to be momentarily clear. There was no name on the paper, only the address and the apartment number. Philip knocked, and Camille immediately opened the door.

Her apartment was small but carefully furnished. She sat beside him on a tapestried couch, held his hands and explained what she had been told about events: the raid, the discovery of the inventory, the need to get him out of Paris quickly. At the moment, she had to go off to work at 122 Provence, but she would be back later that night, thanks to a *laissez-passer* she had obtained from a grateful client who was chief of staff to the *Kommandantur* of Paris. The fridge had food in it, and wine and whiskey were at the bar. He was not to respond to the door or the telephone, and he should try to make as little noise as possible.

The hours dragged for Philip. He opened the jewel box to look at Gaby's necklace, and felt the pain of loss. He drank the Scotch, mourning for what had escaped him, and finally fell asleep on the tapestried sofa.

Camille woke him when she came home, and undressed him, as she always did at 122, and put him into her bed. They both knew that this was farewell, farewell to Paris and farewell to what they had had for so long, and Camille wept as they made love.

Muskrat showed up at Camille's apartment at four o'clock the following afternoon, with a rucksack on his back and carrying a cardboard suitcase tied with a rope.

"We've done the best we could for you on such short notice. You must leave Paris tonight, before the SS makes it impossible for you to get on a train. Already the risk is considerable. Now give me all your identity papers, everything you have on you."

"Are you returning my passport?"

"No, of course not. That's the last thing you want them to find on you. We have a whole new identity for you. You have a long way to go and you're sure to need it." He took an envelope from his coat pocket and began to exhibit its contents.

"Now, here's your new passport—you're a French Canadian from Montreal, named Robert Huard. This is your new identity card, and a full set of seven ration cards in your name, for meat, wine, butter, bread, conserves, textiles and tobacco. In some places, they may be more useful than money to gain favors. This is a special pass for crossing the demarcation line into the Vichy Unoccupied Zone. This paper is your baptismal certificate from a parish in Montreal."

"Why would I need that?"

"You're circumcised, aren't you?"

"Yes."

"Then if you're caught in a strip-to-the-skin search—which is one of the ways the Boche catch Jews—the baptismal certificate is evidence that you're not Jewish. You better memorize your Montreal address, names of your parents, all the stuff you'd be expected to know. Also, here are some francs."

Muskrat slid the rucksack off his back, placed it on the sofa and untied the rope from around the suitcase. He took out a heavy wool jacket, a dark-blue knit cap, a pair of brown corduroy pants and a pair of rugged hiking shoes.

"You'll be better off wearing this clothing. It's warmer to the south, but you've got to be prepared for crossing the Pyrenees, if you can reach them. In this rucksack are underwear, socks, tins of food, some toilet things, a couple of shirts, gloves and a Swiss officer's jackknife that has a three-inch blade, which will be your only weapon."

"Where am I headed?"

"Your ultimate destination is Portugal, where you'll be able to get a boat back to the States, but getting there . . . well, the only way to travel is by train. The crowds in the stations and on the trains are good cover. Stay out of buses and automobiles—you're sure to be nabbed at a checkpoint. Now, the best route is from Paris to Lyon, from Lyon to Marseille, from Marseille to Toulouse, and then to Pau, at the foot of the Pyrenees, where you can get over the mountains into Spain. But the Nazis know that's the best escape route, the one we use most of the time, and they'll be watching for you, so you've got to go round about and throw them off your scent.

"Instead of going directly south to Lyon from the Gare de Lyon or the Gare d'Austerlitz, which they'll have under tight security, we've routed you due east to Nancy. Most escapees don't go that way, because that route leads to Strasbourg and into Germany."

"But if I went to Strasbourg, I'd be near the Swiss border. Why not—"

"You'd never make it across the border. Every foot of it is covered with Nazi patrols—it's the toughest escape route in Europe. Trust us, we have learned what we know from terrible experience. The best thing is for you to go second class to Nancy—here are the tickets—and then wait for the next train that goes south to Dijon. At Dijon, you should stick around the railroad station and wait for the local that runs to Lyon. But you've got to get off that train before it reaches the North–South demarcation line. There's always a tough inspection there, and you can be sure they've been put on the alert to look for you.

You want to leave the train at Villefranche-sur-Saône, which is just a few kilometers before the end of the Occupied Zone, and about thirty kilometers from Lyon. In Villefranche, you're to go to a little bistro, La Colonne, on the Place Carnot, which you can walk to from the railroad station. Order something, and while you are eating, a man named Junot will come in and sit at your table. Be sure that he identifies himself by name. Junot will manage to get you into Lyon without going through a border check. He'll also take you to a safe house in Lyon where you'll get further instructions."

"I've written a note for Gaby, can you give it to her?"

"No, she's already left Paris."

"Where has she gone?"

"She'll be in Lyon. You'll probably see her there."

"At the same place I'll be?"

"I really can't say. Now, here's a list of all the names and places I've told you about. Before you have to leave tonight, I suggest you memorize everything and burn the paper. You don't want to be stopped with anything like that on you."

"I appreciate all your help."

"Your tennis friend wanted to say goodbye, but it's not possible. He said to tell you that we are all deeply indebted to you, and that we will do everything we can to get you through safely." With a quick gesture of farewell, Muskrat turned to the door and let himself out.

Camille, who had been sitting on the opposite side of the room, now came to Philip, who was inspecting his new passport.

"They've copied the photo that was in my U.S. passport—it certainly looks authentic," he said.

"I'm sorry I can't be here to say goodbye when you leave, Philip, but I'm already late. I have made up a little list of my own for you—an emergency list in case you get into a tight spot. In each of those cities, Nancy, Dijon, Lyon, Marseille, Pau, I've written down the name and address of a woman who might be able to help you. They are my friends, and friends of Madame Rounpé. They are good people, if you get into trouble, because the Nazis certainly don't suspect prostitutes of being patriotic."

"These women are madams?"

"No, madams are often too involved with politics to be completely trustworthy. There is a saying, 'Politicians are madams, and madams are politicians.' The names on this list are working girls with their own places."

"Camille, can I say something that I hope you'll understand?

My wish for you is that you will marry—and soon. I think the time has come, don't you?"

"Oh, I don't know, Philip. There are things against it . . ."

"No, the only thing against it is your fear—of yourself, I think. The safety of the Rue Provence. We are quite alike, Camille. You had 122 Provence, I had the Ritz. I promise you, your time has come to go beyond yourself."

"Maybe, Philip—maybe. Oh, I am so late! I will catch hell from Madame Rounpé. Goodbye, sweet Philip. Be very careful. I'm sorry I got you into all this. But you'll make it if you don't take any foolish chances. You must! I want to see you someday at your Coney Island."

"Goodbye, Camille. You've meant a lot to me."

Around eight o'clock that evening, dressed in his new clothes, his rucksack on his back, Philip took the Métro to the République station. He got off there, changed trains, and descended two stops later at the Gare de l'Est. It was a nervous journey for him, watching for any sign that he was being observed. Every passing uniform increased his anxiety. He felt self-conscious in his ill-fitting clothes; it had been a sad moment indeed when he had hung his Lanvin jacket in Camille's closet and closed the door on it.

Now he walked apprehensively through the cavernous expanse of the Gare de l'Est, thinking, Can this really be my farewell to Paris? In this getup, slinking along in this noisy, crowded railroad station, not a word of goodbye to any of the people I have known for so long? How can I leave without saying goodbye to Charley, to Gabrielle, Marcel, Janet and all the people I've known for so long at the Ritz? No last promenade along the Champs-Élysées; farewell meal at Prunier; final stroll around the lakes in the Bois de Boulogne. Hell, a man should be able to say his proper goodbyes. The dense crowd of travelers pushed and shouted and hurried around him, bumping into his rucksack, elbowing by him.

He finally reached the departure board and strained his eyes to see the listings in the dim, smoky light. The 9:10 to Nancy, leaving from Gate B-11, was departing on schedule. He could see the B-11 sign two gates down the line, but he stopped in front of B-9 to bide his time. The trick would be not to board too soon so as to be conspicuous, but not too late to have a seat. He knew that the train would be packed, for all the good trains had been commandeered for Germany along with their crews; now there weren't enough trains to accommodate the heavy flow of passengers, and the few trains that the S.N.C.F. had at its disposal were decrepit.

Philip watched the gate at B-11, but there was no sign of anyone keeping it under surveillance, just the bustle of passengers struggling toward the platform. He began to move forward, walking close behind a phalanx of Strasbourg farmers who had come to Paris to obtain permits to ship their stockpiling foie gras. There were legions of milling, shouting children of all ages being sent to relatives around Nancy, Metz and Strasbourg, where milk, eggs, cheese, fresh meat and vegetables abounded, small towns where life in general was less oppressive. Along the platform were German soldiers in twos and threes with rifles slung over their shoulders, but they were obviously on assignment and not looking for anyone in particular.

There were several refreshment wagons on the platform, but they were pathetically stocked, offering only half-bottles of reject red wine, a sickly sweet soda called Pschitt that came in orange and lemon flavors, sandwiches of gray crumbly bread that contained a thin slice of cheese or ham for which the traveler had to surrender a food coupon, and Nazi-approved newspapers, magazines and books.

Philip's progress was impeded by passengers attempting to hoist their unwieldy luggage and boxes through the open windows to compatriots inside. Philip pushed his way onto a second-class carriage which seemed to him to be in just about the center of the train. He figured that if there were an inspection, the patrols would work from both ends toward the middle, thereby giving him some time to prepare.

The compartments were already full, and the aisle was filling with people perched on their suitcases, but Philip nevertheless went from one compartment to another to determine for himself if there was a seat available. As he opened the last compartment, a man at the window was getting to his feet, having just discovered that the train to Reims, which was his destination, was on the opposite track. As he struggled to get his bag from the overhead rack, cursing his bad luck, Philip slipped around him and took his seat.

The air in the compartment was already fetid. Passengers in the aisle were beginning to pack against the glass door. Philip looked around at his fellow occupants: a priest, two men with laborers' hands, a fat woman and her skinny husband, a grandmother with a young child asleep in her lap, two middle-aged gentlemen with Masonic pins in their lapels, and a girl with nervous eyes who clutched a hatbox in her lap.

Safe company, Philip thought. He unbuttoned his jacket and stretched his legs. Muskrat was right—it didn't look as if the Germans had much interest in this train. The conductor sang out an "All aboard!" and blew his whistle. Shouts of latecomers rang out. Another whistle, and then, with a heavy jerk, the train began to move. Philip looked out the window, watching the seething *quai* dissolve into the expanse of the switching yards. The acrid smell of the locomotive's coal smoke began to seep into the compartment.

32

The train arrived in Nancy two hours behind schedule. Twice they had been shunted onto a spur to allow trains bearing military equipment to overtake them, and in each instance there was a long wait until they were signaled to resume their journey. The German tanks and trucks and artillery on the fast freight were new and awesome in appearance and numbers. It was dark, but the cold moonlight glinting off the passing metal gave the endless parade a threatening glow.

The station at Nancy was not as big or as crowded as the Gare de l'Est, but there was enough activity and confusion to protect Philip as he slipped off the train and made his way to the arrival-and-departure board. There was a three-hour wait for the departure of the local to Dijon. Philip didn't much like the idea of staying in one place for so long, a sitting duck, but then again, where would he go?

He entered the station restaurant, a large, drafty room, noisy with the clang of dishes. Coal smoke had been huffed into the soot-stained restaurant for generations, permeating its pores the way nicotine stains a smoker's fingers. Philip found an empty seat and eased his pack off his back. The waiters were old and crabbily harried, but, with three hours to kill, Philip was glad to waste time waiting for service. Across one entire wall there was a mural glorifying the men who had built the railroad, but it was so obscured by soot that it was impossible to tell just what the men were doing.

Although most of the dishes on the menu had lines drawn through them, Philip was pleasantly surprised to find a few items long absent from Paris restaurants. He ordered ham and eggs, and his spirits lifted when the dish arrived with three perfectly fried eggs symmetrically arranged on a circle of ham. The acorn coffee was better than most, and the gray bread had a crispy crust; there was even a small dab of margarine.

The local for Dijon left right on schedule, but this time Philip boarded the train early and established himself in a window seat. The train, a relic from the First World War, sent uncushioned tremors from the track directly up the spines of its passengers; however, Philip propped himself in his window corner and managed to doze fitfully most of the way.

When the train came to a halt on the platform in Dijon, Philip was shocked to see pairs of police stationed at each door. His first thought was how he could escape this inspection, and he tried to see if he could slip out the opposite window and run across the open tracks. But a man who had been sitting across from him noted his concern and told him not to worry, it was only a routine check to catch Jews.

The police were sending all male passengers to the far end of the platform, where they were lined up by a squad of German soldiers under the command of an SS lieutenant. When all the passengers had debarked, the men in the line were instructed to open their pants and display their penises; those who were circumcised were detained. Philip presented his baptismal certificate with his passport, and after a few anxious moments while the lieutenant looked it over he was dismissed from the group.

This time there was no wait for the connecting train. A local, which stopped in Villefranche, was leaving for Lyon in a few minutes. On boarding, Philip discovered that his luck had run out insofar as seats were concerned. Many of the passengers were farmers carrying little crates containing live rabbits and chickens and pigeons. One man had a net bag slung over his shoulder, containing three heads of cabbage, and another held a canvas tote bag that sprouted carrot tops. A skinny old woman cradled a live rooster under her arm, his nervous cockscomb constantly on the bob.

Philip arranged his rucksack in a corner at the end of the carriage, outside the lavatory, where there was room enough to sit and stretch his legs. The train made many stops, at one of which Philip nabbed the seat of a departing passenger who had the graceful heads of three white geese protruding from a hemp basket.

As the train neared Villefranche, Philip could feel his pulse quickening; this would be the initial test of Muskrat's escape route, the first contact that Philip would make with the Underground. He hoped they would have some word about Gaby.

In the Villefranche railroad station, Philip found a posted map of the city on which he located the Place Carnot; he did not want to call attention to himself by asking for directions. It was only a ten-minute walk and he easily located La Colonne, a little bistro with a few rooms above it. When he walked in, a stubby woman with a towel over her shoulder came from behind the bar and indicated a seat for him at a table with two blue-denimed workingmen, but Philip said he was expecting someone and she reluctantly let him sit in the corner by himself.

There was no menu. The woman put a carafe of dark-red wine on the table, and a thick slice of rough pâté. This was followed by a large bowl of potato soup garnished with chives, and then a main course of *onglet aux échalotes,* shalloted blood sausages with sauerkraut, dishes that Philip had not seen in Paris's Alsatian restaurants for over a year. While he was on his main course, a thin man with a limp entered the restaurant and sat down at his table, immediately identifying himself as Junot. He refused Philip's offer of food, but drank a glass of wine. He knew nothing about a young woman named Gaby, nor had he seen anyone to fit her description. He referred to Philip as Monsieur Huard, which, in a curious way, gave Philip a feeling of confidence.

Junot delivered detailed instructions: when Philip had finished eating, he was to cross the Place Carnot to a photography shop that could be seen from the window of the restaurant. The proprietor, a Monsieur Delacroix, would be expecting him. The Germans had just changed the form of the identity card, which made the one given to Philip in Paris invalid. He needed a photo for a new card which would be ready by the time Philip arrived in Lyon. Afterward, Philip was to go to the church on the corner, where Junot would be waiting for him in his Peugeot.

"Why am I making this risky border crossing?" Philip asked Junot. "My papers are all in order, so why didn't I just stay on the train and go through the regular inspection at the border?"

"Because it is the most severe inspection in Europe—a combined force of Nazi SS and Vichy police who go through everything with a fine-tooth comb. If you are the least bit suspicious, they search you head to foot, and ask a million questions. Can you take the risk that they have not already been alerted to watch for you? You are high priority, with a fat reward on your head."

Philip found Junot's car in the courtyard behind the church. It was a Peugeot that had seen long service on the streets of Villefranche, powered by the burning of charcoal briquets in its piggy-backed gasogene tank. Junot drove Philip to a café near the cemetery, where he introduced him to a man named Bugeaud who wore a black suit, a white shirt and a black necktie. Bugeaud took a long, appraising look at Philip and told him, curtly, to order a beer at the *zinc* while he had a private discussion with Junot.

While Philip waited, a beefy man in knickers and a sheepskin vest came into the café with three people in tow. He left his charges standing in a self-conscious huddle near the door and went to confer with Bugeaud and Junot. After a few minutes of discussion, Junot and the beefy man departed, on their way out telling the three others to sit down at one of the tables. Bugeaud sat down with them and beckoned to Philip to join them. With some misgiving, Philip carried his beer over to their table.

Bugeaud made no introductions. He simply told them that he would try to lead them over the demarcation line into the Unoccupied Zone that night; in about an hour he would take them to the place on the line where they would wait until it was time for the crossing. Then he departed.

Philip and his companions looked uncomfortably at one another. It was obvious to Philip that the three, two men and a woman, had only just met and that no one wanted to identify himself. The woman, tall, middle-aged, competent-looking, excused herself and went to the toilet. The barman called out that there was no table service. One of the men got up and went to the bar, where he ordered a beer that he brought back to the table. The other, a short, bespectacled man with limp hair and obviously false teeth, sat disconsolately staring at the table top. Philip took a paperback from his rucksack and started to read while he sipped his beer. The three newcomers had no luggage.

Bugeaud came to fetch them about two hours later, driving up to the café in an old black hearse with a carved wooden body surmounted at its four corners with recumbent angels. Bugeaud opened the double doors at the rear and told the four of them to occupy the jump seats which were folded against the body of the hearse. In the center of the interior was a closed wooden coffin on which a large metal crucifix had been fastened. Bugeaud told them that if the hearse was stopped he would explain that they were mourners accompanying the casket. The woman asked if there was a body inside the casket, and Bugeaud nodded.

There were two small windows in the rear doors which admitted the only light into the interior. One of the men turned his back to the casket and faced the wall; Philip wondered whether it was the corpse in the casket or the corpse on the cross which offended him.

The hearse stopped, and Philip heard German voices. Bugeaud had been stopped by a patrol which was demanding to see his papers. The man who had turned his back on the casket clutched his hands to his chest and began whispering a prayer in Hebrew. The woman stood up and peeked out the rear window, but of course she could not see what was going on up front at the driver's seat. Philip quickly rehearsed his vital statistics: name, address in Montreal, mother's and father's name, church . . .

But the Nazi patrol was dismissing Bugeaud: *"Heil Hitler und au revoir!"* The hearse went into gear, and they started to move.

They drove for almost an hour to reach their destination. Bugeaud opened the doors and helped them down to the ground. They were in a driveway at the rear of a small building. Bugeaud hurried them across the open courtyard and into an adjoining barn, where he had them mount a ladder to a hayloft. Through the thin walls they could hear the whir of machinery and distinct voices. Some of the upper planking was missing, so that from the loft there was a clear view of a sloping meadow and a wide, rushing stream. Bugeaud told them that the stream marked the demarcation line, and that they would cross it that night. In the meantime they were to make as little noise as possible, because German border patrols frequently passed by. The adjoining building, Bugeaud explained, was occupied by a shoe repair shop whose proprietor, Monsieur Guillebon, would be in charge of their crossing.

The four of them sat quietly on the thick hay, whispering an occasional word, listening to the voices of customers as they came to have their shoes repaired.

The day passed slowly before their eyes. They spoke, but they exchanged little information about themselves, although the two men did acknowledge that they had worked for the Underground and were now being sought by the Nazis; one of them joked that there was a room reserved for him at Auschwitz. As the first pale stars emerged, a three-man German patrol came into view, tramping across the meadow and into the shoe repair shop. The tension that had gripped Philip and his three companions in the hearse returned. In harsh guttural French the soldiers said they had been ordered to make a search of all buildings along the road, but it was obvious that they were not keen on such thoroughness. They asked about the rooms above the shoe shop, and about the barn. Absolutely no one in either, Guillebon answered, and offered them a bottle of schnapps. After another twenty minutes, the soldiers tramped out and went on their way, more noisily than they had come.

Shortly afterward Monsieur Guillebon, who proved to be a florid man with a shock of white hair and the arms of a blacksmith, brought some sandwiches and beer to the loft. He said the crossings would be attempted as soon as his scouts reported on the pattern of the Nazi border patrols; the patterns were deliberately varied from night to night.

While he waited, Philip stretched out on the hay and thought about Gaby, relived their moments together, fantasized about what might have been, worried about where she was and if she was safe.

Guillebon finally appeared, carrying a kerosene lantern which he held above his head as he called to them in a low voice. He explained that they would cross on planks that had been fitted over the rocks at the stream's narrowest point; the river was shallow and there was no danger of drowning. Once on the other side, they were to hurry toward a copse of trees in the distance. Guillebon gave each of them individual instruction as to how to proceed from there.

The crossing went off without a hitch. Philip's orders, once he reached the trees, were to proceed to a distant road where he would find a café called Chez Pierre, where he would be contacted.

Philip was pleasantly surprised to find Junot waiting for him there; at least he wouldn't have to deal with another new face. Junot ordered a *fine* which he drank off in a single swallow. He had been up all night running guns stolen from the German ordinance warehouse. He took from his pocket Philip's new *carte d'identité,* with his new photograph on it, and handed it to him. Junot said he had asked about Gaby Duvier and had been told that she was in Lyon. No, he didn't know where, or anything else about her, but Philip's Lyon contact would probably be able to locate her. The plan now was to drive Philip to the nearby village of Mionnay, where he could board a train bound for Lyon from the unexpected direction of Bourg. In Lyon, his contact would meet him at a café called La Jolie Huître, which was located across from the railroad station on the avenue that ran alongside the Saône River.

In the Peugeot, en route to Mionnay, feeling more talkative after his second *fine,* Junot briefed Philip on what to expect in

Lyon. "The Underground is strong, but so is the counterespionage of the SS and the Vichy Intelligence Service, so you have to watch every step you take. You'll find that reward posters with your picture have been posted."

Junot deposited Philip at the railroad station in Mionnay, which, fortunately, maintained a little restaurant that stayed open all night. The Bourg local to Lyon made long and frequent stops, so that it wasn't scheduled to reach Mionnay until well after midnight.

As it turned out, it took five hours longer than usual, because Resistance saboteurs had blown up a section of the track that had to be replaced by work crews out of Lyon.

The Lyon station was even larger and busier than the Gare de l'Est had been, and Philip felt a growing confidence as he moved down the platform. But as he emerged from the gate he saw on a post directly in front of him the wanted poster with his picture on it, and his confidence quickly turned to fear. "REWARD," it said in large letters, "for any information leading to the capture of this dangerous American spy and traitor . . ." That was all Philip could read without stopping or turning his head. Now he bowed his head and tried to retract it into his jacket collar, turtle fashion. He knew that the posters must be all over Lyon.

La Jolie Huître reminded Philip of the Hole-in-the-Wall—booths and mirrored walls, with a long, busy bar curved along a side wall. Many of the men there wore railroad uniforms of one kind or another—porters, conductors, maintenance workers, engineers, vendors. In the rear, swinging double doors led to a busy kitchen. The booths were all filled, but Philip found a little table with a single chair. He took off his jacket and stowed his rucksack under the table. His back was to the door, but, as in the Hole-in-the-Wall, he could see everything in the mirrored wall in front of him. He had a flash illusion that he was meeting Gaby. Oh, God, if only I were! He wondered how long it would be until his contact showed up. He ordered a beer and a serving of sausages, which he had seen steamy and succulent on their way to another table.

One of the men at the bar, dressed in workingman's blues, picked up an unoccupied chair from another table and carried it over to join Philip.

"Monsieur Huard," the man said, "they really want you. Informers have been offered special bonuses if they spot you. You've seen the posters, no doubt. Well, you're a hot com-

modity and we must handle you quickly before we all get burned.
We can't move you by rail—they've got the SS checking every
departure. And there's a checkpoint on every road and highway
out of Lyon. Not just for you—the Nazis know we funnel a lot of
refugees through here. But we do have a plan, which will take
me about an hour to put in motion. You wait here. Just fill up on
beer and sausages and don't get into any conversations. There's a
cook back there in the kitchen, Arnaud, he owns this place and
he's your contact if something happens."

He reached into an inner pocket and brought forth a document
which he handed to Philip. "This paper is important. It's your
permis de séjour, issued by the Rhône prefecture—well, actually
faked by us, but you'll be stopped for it all the time. When I
come back, I'll bring you some different clothes. And you'll have
to get rid of that rucksack. Our people tell us they've got a pretty
good description of you. Now I've got one other thing to give
you. It's a little grisly, but what the hell, reality is reality, isn't it?
There's a pill in this little box, if you ever need it. You can put it
in your mouth, under your tongue, and it's safe until you bite
down on it and break the crust. Listen, we've all got one, just in
case . . ."

"Do you know anything about my friend Gaby Duvier? Is she
here? Do you know her?"

"Yes, indeed. I took care of her myself. Met her right here, as
I'm meeting you. Damn pretty girl, she is, and first thing she
wanted to know was about you."

"When can I see her? Is it possible for us to leave Lyon
together?"

"She wanted to wait for you, but we wouldn't let her. Such
damn good luck came our way—we had been working on a
connection that was going right through to San Sebastian, and it
just happened to fall together the day your friend arrived.
Sometimes it takes us weeks to crank something up, but here she
arrives in the morning and we have her on her way that
afternoon. And to San Sebastian! Why, you can see Portugal
from there."

"Then she's gone? Gaby's gone?"

"You should be happy as the devil. With any luck, she could
be on her way to the United States by now."

"She's going to America?"

"Not much choice, is there, unless you can get a job as a spy in
Lisbon. We used to have a way to England, but the SS got onto

that. Anyway, she did scribble you a little note on one of the menus."

He fished around in his pockets, going through a mass of pocket debris until he found a rather worn piece of paper. He handed it to Philip, got to his feet, and left. Philip watched him in the mirror, a tall, graceful man who waved to his friends as he left. Gaby's note was burning Philip's fingers, but he continued to watch the mirror and saw the green Mercedes staff car as it pulled up, doors flinging open, von Behr with his unmistakable eye patch, and three of his men grabbing the man who had just left Philip's table. Philip's breath caught in his throat as he remembered the terrace at Lipp's, the seizure of Lili's captain.

Philip's reaction was swift but not hurried. The men at the bar had noticed the disturbance outside, and they were moving toward the front to have a better look. Philip slipped on his jacket, picked up his rucksack and moved toward the kitchen. Please, God, there must be a rear door.

The kitchen was a small, cramped room, with very little space for moving around. Philip's heart fell when he saw that there not only wasn't a door, there wasn't even a window. There were three people at work. "Arnaud," Philip said, and the short tattooed man who was slicing potatoes dropped his knife and, without saying a word, went to the rear of the kitchen where, under several garbage cans, there was a trapdoor which he pulled open. Philip put his arms through the rucksack loops and slung it on his back, freeing his hands, and descended the worn wooden stairs to the basement. Arnaud immediately closed the trapdoor, entombing Philip in darkness.

After a few moments, Philip's eyes began to see forms and contours. There was a faint slant of light coming from the far side of the basement, and Philip cautiously felt his way toward it, bumping into crates and old kitchen equipment along the way. There was a lot of activity on the floor above his head. Philip discovered that the light was coming through a small barred windowpane at the top of a locked door. There was no key, and he exclaimed "No!" in his frustration. The sounds from above seemed to intensify, and Philip was beginning to panic as he pulled at the door and heaved his shoulder against it. Nothing doing.

He stood back to reconnoiter, and as he did he saw the key hanging on an old loop of rope beside the door. The lock turned easily, and he relocked it from the other side. He found himself at the bottom of a steep flight of concrete steps, which he mounted two at a time, emerging into a busy alley. A few yards away from him, a delivery boy had leaned his bicycle against the wall, a package in the wire basket on the handlebars. Without hesitating, Philip walked directly to the bike and rode away.

He turned from the alley onto a wide street, then turned again, going from street to street. When he felt he had gone far enough from the Jolie Huître he stopped and hid the bicycle in a clump of bushes. He then walked for several blocks until he found a neighborhood café that looked safe. He needed time to take stock, cut off as he now was from the people who were supposed to help him. His hands still trembled from the close encounter with von Behr. He did not notice that on the telephone pole in front of the café door there was one of the posters offering a reward for his capture.

33

Philip opened his passport and took out Camille's list, which he had put there for safekeeping. Opposite "Lyon" was the name Rosemonde Navarre, and a telephone number. Philip purchased a *jeton* from the cashier and called the number. It rang a long time before it was answered. Rosemonde said that the earliest she could see him was seven o'clock, which meant that Philip had to spend the rest of the day on the streets of a city that was hunting for him.

He realized that the contact man in the Jolie Huître had given him good advice—they had his description, so he must change his clothes and get rid of the rucksack. But he hated to give up its contents. He removed the map, the Swiss officer's knife and the little box with Gaby's present, and fitted them into his pockets. It was then that he realized that in his haste to leave La Jolie Huître, he had left Gaby's note on the table. He felt as if he had betrayed her.

On his way out of the café, he saw a gnarled old man walking the gutter, looking for cigarette butts. He carried a battered shopping bag and wore four hats, one fitted on top of the other. As Philip passed him, he slipped one of the loops of the rucksack around the old man's neck and kept on going. There was a bus at the corner just pulling away from its stop. Philip ran a few steps and swung aboard before the old man had a chance to react to his good fortune.

Philip rode for a few blocks and got off in front of a department store. He bought himself a workman's blue denim outfit, large enough to fit over the clothes he was wearing, and found an oysterman's cap to replace his knit hat, which he rolled up and kept in his pocket. Going out on the street in his new costume, he felt less of a target.

He passed a movie house that was showing Gary Cooper and Marlene Dietrich in *Morocco*. No American films had been permitted in Occupied Paris, so it would be a treat to see Cooper again, despite the fact that he and Dietrich would be speaking dubbed French. And passing time in the dark anonymity of the movie house would be a good way to get through the day.

Halfway through the film, however, the house lights came on and the film was cut off. A German search patrol appeared at the back of the theater. "Everyone rise and show your papers!" the sergeant in charge commanded. A typical random sweep. Philip's first thought was to try to ease himself through the audience and escape through the exit door at the front of the house, but several soldiers had moved forward and he saw he was trapped.

He held out his papers, and the sergeant went through them one by one, especially the *séjour*. After what felt like an eternity he handed them back to Philip. When the patrol left, the lights were turned off and the movie resumed, but Philip departed immediately. He spent the rest of the afternoon in the Museum of Natural History and then drank beer at a workingman's bistro until it was seven o'clock.

Rosemonde Navarre was an Algerian with stunning black eyes. She was indebted to Madame Rounpé, for whom she had once worked, for having lent her money when she wanted to go to Lyon to operate on her own. So she was pleased to do her a favor, she said, but when she heard Philip's story she said she was afraid to get mixed up in the matter, since she was already having her own problems with the Aryan-minded Germans. But she thought that perhaps her brother, Hassid, might be of assistance.

She got him on the telephone and spoke to him in Arabic. From her tone Philip thought it was going badly for him, but when Rosemonde hung up she said that her brother, who operated a moving van, had a load of household goods he was taking to Béziers, and he would take Philip along for a price. She wrote her brother's address on a piece of paper and walked Philip to the door, obviously anxious that he leave her flat as soon as possible.

Hassid was a hefty, churlish man with an incredible amount of hair, a thick shock on his head, sprouts from his nostrils and ears, eyebrows that were hedges, and a solid mat on his chest that extended over his shoulders and down his back like wall-to-wall carpeting. His moving van was loaded and ready to roll, he said, but he would go no farther than Béziers which was his destination. The price was a firm one thousand francs whether Philip got there or not.

"What do you mean by that?" Philip asked.

"If they nab you on the way, I don't know anything about you. Just someone I give a ride. Agreed?"

Philip counted out the money. Hassid and a fat man who was his helper took Philip around the back to the van, which was literally held together in places with wire. The fenders were gone from the rear wheels, and the hood, bound with wire, could no longer close. Hassid unloaded some of the furniture, making a passageway to the front of the van big enough for Philip to squeeze through. Hassid handed him a bottle for pissing and told him to stay hidden until they got to Béziers.

After they got under way, Philip located a couple of sofa cushions, which he arranged on the floor. He got out his map to see where he was headed. The route would take him through Nîmes and Montpellier and on to Béziers, which was certainly in the right direction. Béziers, he figured, was about halfway to Spain.

The van stopped along the way a couple of times at checkpoints where Hassid showed his papers, but the Germans had no interest in shabby household effects jammed in the back of an old broken-down van.

34

Philip had no contacts in Béziers, not even a name on Camille's list. He decided he would have to take a chance on the railroad, perhaps taking a train to some place other than to Toulouse, which was directly on the main line from Lyon to Pau and the Spanish border. But when he got near the station and saw the number of German soldiers and Vichy police on patrol, he got cold feet and quickly turned away. He had asked Hassid if he knew anyone in the trucking business in Béziers, hoping to cadge another lift, but Hassid had said sourly that he had transported Philip only as a favor to his sister and he wanted nothing more to do with someone as *brûlé*, hot, as Philip was.

Leaving the railroad station, Philip aimlessly followed the *quai* of the river Orb, which meandered through the city. He hadn't been able to sleep in the cramped van, and he yearned for a hot bath. He passed a small, dilapidated hotel where he thought he might be able to keep his name off the *registre* by slipping a few francs to the desk clerk. He looked in the grimy window and saw, behind the reception desk, a mountain of a woman with the face of a disgruntled mastiff and arms like shanks of beef. He shivered at the thought of having to face her with his proposition.

He continued on his walk along the *quai* until he emerged onto an ancient square that fronted the fine old Cathedral of Saint-Nazaire. In front of the steps a nun sat at a table registering townspeople for a pilgrimage to Lourdes. Parked in the square was an empty bus with a trailer attached. Many of the people waiting to register were on crutches or sat in wheelchairs. Philip walked past them and entered the cathedral; in the spiritual quiet he would try to regroup his thoughts.

One of the people standing on the line for Lourdes was Antoine Rossier, the postmaster. He was there to register his aged mother, who was severely crippled by arthritis. He was an enthusiastic collaborationist who had given the new Vichy officials useful information about the suspicious activities of some of his fellow townspeople and thus had been rewarded with the postmastership, replacing a Béziers patriot who had been lax in imposing Vichy censorship. Just now, as Antoine stood on line to register his mother, he had taken note of the man in the oysterman's cap who approached the church. Antoine had very good recall of faces, and only the day before he had posted on the wall of the *bureau de poste* an *affiche* that had offered a reward for an American traitor. As Philip got nearer, Antoine's suspicion increased. He left the line and hurried to a nearby kiosk where there was a public telephone.

Philip was sitting on a pew in a small side chapel, in front of a jewel-adorned Virgin Mary, when the police came. Two Sisters of Mercy were also there, kneeling with their rosaries, when the three Vichy officers converged on Philip. Two of the men grabbed him by the arms and roughly pulled him to his feet and led him away. Antoine stood at the entrance, exulting in his handiwork, and he joined the expedition to the police station to protect his claim for the reward. The Sisters of Mercy, who were on the staff of Béziers' Catholic hospital, were appalled at this affront to the sanctity of the church.

Philip was taken to the police station, where he was booked under his proper name and made to surrender all his false papers. Before handing over his passport, he succeeded in removing the list which Camille had given to him. Surprisingly, the police did not search him or ask for any other of his possessions. The police chief immediately placed a call to von Behr's office in Paris, the number of which was listed on the reward poster, but the operator informed him that there was an indefinite delay in placing calls to the north.

The cell in which Philip was placed was cold and dirty and wet. A wooden shelf attached to the wall, its outer edge supported by two rusted chains, was the bed; the toilet was an unwashed slop jar in the corner. The walls were damp and moldy, a single, low-wattage bulb was the only illumination, and there was no window. Philip took out his map and spread it on the floor beneath the light bulb. He added up the red kilometer numbers: Béziers to Carcassonne 56, Carcassonne to Toulouse 92, Toulouse to Pau 178, a total of 326, around two hundred miles. He had been caught just a few hours short of freedom.

He wondered if von Behr would come to get him, or if he would be transported to Paris surrounded by guards. Of course there was no United States consulate in Béziers, but perhaps he could get word to the embassy in Paris. That was his only hope—that they would intervene. He went to the door of his cell and asked the guard who was stationed there if he would be permitted a telephone call. The guard said he would be permitted nothing until they heard from Paris. It occurred to Philip that von Behr, having been in Lyon, was very likely not in Paris, but somewhere in the area. However, the police would have to reach Paris to find out von Behr's whereabouts, and that would take time.

Philip paced in a slow circle to ward off the insistent damp. He stopped at the door and listened. Not a sound of any kind, as if all life had suddenly been frozen. Either he was the only wrongdoer in Béziers or he was in a remote section of the jail.

Several hours later, a policeman appeared at Philip's cell door and led him to a small visitor's room, where the two nuns who had been in the church were seated, waiting for him. Philip was puzzled by their presence and walked over to them tentatively. The older nun motioned for him to sit down at the table, opposite them.

"Sister Marie and I were shocked at the way the police entered our church," she said in a low, steady voice. They were alone in the room, but there was a policeman on duty outside the observation window. "They have intruded far enough into our lives, without violating our prayers."

"Thank you, Sister," Philip said. "I appreciate your coming to tell me that."

"We have come to help you," the sister, whose name was Ursule, said. "We will serve God in our reverence of the church's sanctity, by repelling those who would intrude their brutality into our holy place of worship."

"We have brought you medicines," Sister Marie said, "that will afflict you in a beneficial way."

"Sister Marie is our pharmacologist at the hospital," Sister Ursule said.

"We have brought you this little basket of food," Sister Marie said, putting it on the table. "In the piece of Gruyère you will find a pill that you can wash down with the bottle of wine in the basket. The pill is pinatra, which is a hormone we give to obese women for weight reduction. But in a man the hormone creates a very high fever. In the *baguette* you will find some other pills wrapped in a wax paper. They are *grains de vals,* which is a laxative. You must mash up the pills, adding a drop or two of wine to make a paste. Shut your eyes and smear this paste on both your eyelids. The chemicals in the laxative will cause a severe inflammation very like conjunctivitis. With the high fever and infection, they will have to send you to our hospital. We will be on the alert for your arrival."

The nuns stood up. "Maybe the Lord intended us to help you," Sister Ursule said. "But however it turns out, please don't think badly of the Lord for what happened today."

"No, Sister," Philip replied. "I won't. I'm a fan of His." ·

By nightfall, Philip had a fever of a hundred and four and both of his eyes were swollen shut. His pain was not simulated. The chief of police summoned the prison doctor, who immediately ordered Philip removed to the hospital.

Sister Ursule came down to the admitting room, where Philip was placed in a wheelchair, and she accompanied him to the small, four-bed ward that was reserved for prisoners. The beds were all unoccupied. The windows were barred and the door was kept locked at all times. Philip was undressed and put in a hospital gown. Sister Ursule was joined by Sister Marie and the resident doctor, who diagnosed the affliction as severe conjunctivitis and prescribed a course of treatment designed to reduce the fever and the infection.

As soon as he left, Sister Marie began to bathe Philip's eyelids with a solution she had already prepared, that would remove the residue of the laxative from the lids. She then applied wet compresses and gave him an injection to alleviate the pain.

"Sister," Philip said, "I don't have much time. They have sent to Paris for a Nazi who will come to get me."

"But he must leave you here until your eyes are better. We can prolong it as long as you wish."

"You don't know the Nazis, Sister. This one wouldn't care if I were dying. He is very anxious to take me back to Paris, where I'm sure I will be tortured to reveal what I know about the Resistance. He must not get his hands on me, Sister."

"You think he might arrive tonight?"

"He might."

The two nuns walked out of earshot and conferred. When they returned, Sister Marie took a roll of gauze and bandaged the upper portion of Philip's face. Sister Ursule folded his clothes and rolled them into a tight bundle which she secured with Philip's belt. They brought the wheelchair over to the bed and helped Philip get into it, covering him with a blanket.

"We will come back for you later when the hospital is quiet,"

Sister Ursule said, and they left, locking the door behind them.

Philip was asleep when the door opened and Sister Marie appeared. She pushed the chair to a nearby elevator, where Sister Ursule held the door. They descended to the basement and pushed the wheelchair along a long corridor and up a ramp to where an automobile was waiting. They had encountered no one.. They helped Philip into the car, which immediately drove off.

The nuns returned to the ward and waited fifteen minutes before rushing to the admitting office and reporting, with distress, that the prisoner had escaped.

Von Behr arrived in Béziers at six in the morning, a caravan of three cars screeching up to Police Headquarters. He listened to the stuttering apologies of the police chief with growing fury, incredulous that they hadn't kept a round-the-clock guard watching over the prisoner.

"But, Honorable Baron," the chief said, "we immediately surrounded the city—we have had police and German soldiers stationed at every conceivable exit. The prisoner is very ill, the doctor who examined him is here to confirm that. He can't have gone far."

Von Behr contacted Toulouse, requesting a special detachment of military police to aid in the search. "Look for him as you would look for a rat with the plague. But I want him alive—be sure you bring him to me alive. There are important things he must tell us."

The pilgrims left for Lourdes at nine in the morning. Ambulatory patients were helped into the bus, those on stretchers were loaded into the attached trailer. In one of the rear seats of the bus sat a man who wore dark glasses to cover his afflicted eyes, which he prayed would be cured by a miracle at Bernadette's grotto.

35

The Béziers bus rode through the streets of Lourdes on its way to the sacred grotto, rolling past stalls filled with hundreds upon hundreds of plaster Marys with hands clasped; past rack after rack of rosaries and crucifixes engraved with the Lourdes logo; past countless shelves of metal Marys with the inscription *"Je suis L'Immaculée Conception"* in a garland around their heads; past shops filled with special votive candles to light to Bernadette. The sidewalks were packed with pilgrims buying these mementos of their visit in search of a miracle.

The bus pulled into the parking area near the esplanade to the grotto, the passengers stirring hopefully as the driver came to a stop and opened the doors. A corps of *brancardiers* was waiting to help the visitors into wheelchairs, and entered the trailer to attend to the stretcher cases.

Philip took his time getting off the bus. His eyes, although still red and swollen, were feeling better, but he needed sleep badly. He hadn't shaved since he left Paris and he had the ragged beginning of a beard. A vast conglomerate of crippled humanity trudged by him toward the grotto on the wide esplanade that ran alongside the Gave de Pau, in an orderly procession shepherded by nuns and priests and *brancardiers*.

As his group neared the baths, to be immersed in the ice-cold water of the Massabielle well, water to which superstition attributed miraculous healing qualities, Philip eased away from the group and continued by himself down the esplanade to the grotto itself, a cave with an altar thick with burning candles, presided over by a statue of the Virgin Mary. Years of candle smoke had blackened the walls and roof of the cave, which were covered with the discarded crutches and other votive offerings of those who had been cured. I could sure use one of these miracles, Philip thought.

High Mass was about to begin for the hundreds of pilgrims on stretchers arrayed on the ground before the altar. Philip realized that he had not seen a single German soldier anywhere in Lourdes. I guess the Nazis look upon all the sickness and dying collected here, he thought, as God's concentration camp. He looked around at the mass of terribly afflicted people who still managed to hope. This is true bravery, it occurred to him—to fight like this when all is lost. He walked slowly past the dense lines of stretchers and wheelchairs, which extended all the way across the esplanade, almost to the bank of the rushing Gave de Pau.

At the river, he found a stone bench and sat down. A fisherman, his back to the grotto, was casting into the waters. Philip opened his map to determine exactly where he was and how far he had to go. He was pleased to discover that Lourdes was only forty kilometers from Pau; in fact, the Gave de Pau flowed directly from one to the other. The fisherman let out a triumphal cry as he netted a good-sized silver trout. Philip called out his congratulations.

Okay, he reasoned, so I'm almost there—but how do I manage these kilometers? You can bet the train station at Pau is crawling with Nazis. Von Behr sure as hell knows that I have to get into Spain, and he knows that the only trails over the Pyrenees, and the only guides, go out of Pau. Philip studied the map: only one road from Lourdes to Pau, no secondary roads, no way to loop around, just this one highway.

The man unhooked his fish and joined Philip on the bench. He took a half-smoked cigarette from behind his ear and lit it carefully. He was a solid, stocky man with a swarthy complexion.

"How many?" Philip asked.

"Just the one," the fisherman answered. "God reserves His miracles for the grotto. I've never had much luck here."

"But you keep on trying?"

"Only when I have to bring my aunt down. I have much better luck at the other end."

"Oh, then you're from Pau?"

"I live in Lescar, that's just beyond." He took a flask from his pocket and offered Philip a drink, before taking one for himself, a mixture of strong tea and rum that felt good going down.

"I have an aunt who can't hear worth a damn," the fisherman continued, "been deaf for twenty years, and once in a while she gets me to bring her on down here. Claims it makes her hear better. Course it don't, but I don't mind—it's a nice trip down the river, and I fish while she gets dunked in the holy water and hopes for her miracle."

"You come down the river?"

"Yes, that's my boat right over there, not much to look at, but chugs along all right." He pointed to a small boat with a rather battered outboard motor that was tied to a tree trunk.

"And there's just the two of you?"

"My aunt's a pain in the ass, complains the whole way, afraid I'm going to spill her. The river gets a little nasty in places, but I know the Gave like the back of my hand."

Philip couldn't help but smile—perhaps the grotto was about to perform a little miracle for him. "I wonder if it would be feasible—I mean, I would expect to pay you for it, of course, but would it be possible for me to ride with you as far as Pau?"

"Why, sure! I'd welcome not having to listen to Aunt Émilie all the way. And, hell, you don't have to pay me—I'd be going there anyway."

"No, listen, I insist. You can't imagine what a favor you're doing me."

"Well, tell you what. There's a nice little restaurant in town where you can buy me lunch." The man began to pack up his rod.

"Fine. I'm getting hungry myself."

"The restaurant's black market, if you don't mind."

During lunch Philip asked questions about Pau, hoping to work his way around to mentioning the Underground, but instead he discovered that the fisherman was a Pétainist who had strong negative feelings about the saboteurs of the Resistance.

"We must not lose the quality of life," he said. "and what is really the difference who governs as long as we keep out the Communists and eat well? Those Partisans, posing as patriots, blowing up our railroads, they are Communists, that's who they are, and I would rather have the Germans here any day in the week than those Russian devils . . ."

After lunch the fisherman went to visit a relative who lived in Lourdes and arranged to meet Philip at the boat at four o'clock. Philip walked through the town but found himself repelled by the glut of grotto commercialism that assailed him at every corner. His walk had taken him to the Byzantine Church of the Rosary, whose peaceful interior was inviting, but he hesitated, thinking of his disastrous experience in Béziers. Come on, Weber, he decided, you're going in—and stop looking over your shoulder.

The interior reverberated with organ music, chords rolling along the apse in thunderous waves. There was some kind of ceremony taking place at the altar, but Philip found a removed alcove where he put a coin into the poor box, lit a taper and sat with his forehead resting on his hands. He closed his eyes. The soft peacefulness of the church caressed him. I have been watched over and I am grateful—grateful for the whore in Lyon and the nuns in Béziers and now the fisherman whom You have assigned to me. Please, God, watch over Gaby as well. Thinking of Gaby, he felt an ache of loneliness, of hopelessness. I will never reach her. Perhaps I have used up all the luck I had. All the luck . . .

He dozed off.

36

After the bitter disappointment of Philip's escape from custody in Béziers, Baron von Behr had moved his men to Pau, which the Baron knew had to be Philip's next stop in his attempt to reach Portugal. Pau was an ancient village in the foothills of the Pyrenees, with a certain faded importance as the capital of the Basses-Pyrénées and as the point from which most of the routes ran from France into Spain. A rail line followed one of these mountain passes, which were higher than the Alps, and there were several roads that were negotiable until the winter snows shut them down.

The Baron established his headquarters in the Continental Hotel, which, like all the other first-class hotels of Pau, had been taken over by the Gestapo and the *Kommandanturen* of the Army. No city in France was more saturated with Gestapo agents and informers, but Pau also had a high concentration of undercover agents who served as linkage to guides who, for a price, would take small groups over the difficult mountain terrain into Spain. These guides stayed off the regular mountain passes, which were frequently monitored by Nazi alpine patrols, and instead followed nebulous trails which for centuries had been used by smugglers running rum. These trails were over the most dangerous, difficult parts of the Pyrenees, where falling rocks, deep crevasses, avalanches and sudden drop-offs often spelled doom.

The agents for these guides were primarily found in the numerous cafés of Pau, and in fact some of them were waiters and busboys. The Baron sent his men into the cafés to spread the word (with accompanying photographs) that whoever turned in this American fugitive named Philip Weber, alias Robert Huard, would be handsomely rewarded. The Baron also arranged for Gestapo agents who had studied Philip's photograph to scour the streets, restaurants, hotels, cinemas, parks and public buildings, looking for him.

*   *   *

Geneviève Ortiz had been in the Seminary of the Sacred Heart in Mayenne with Camille, and they had run away together. Their life as fugitives had bonded a solid friendship between them, so that even though they had eventually gone separate ways they had continued to write to each other and exchange confidences over the years.

Geneviève had married a Spaniard from the border town of Andorra, and they had lived there with their two children until Geneviève's husband joined the republican side in the civil war and was killed. Destitute, Geneviève had sent her two children to live with their Spanish grandmother in Zaragoza, and she had gone by herself across the border to Pau to look for work. But there was no legitimate work to be found, and out of desperation she had wound up earning enough money to support her children by becoming a prostitute. Her clients were men of local importance who paid a premium price for the discreet way in which she operated.

When Philip telephoned her, he identified himself as a friend of Camille's who was desperately in need of help; she immediately understood from the tone of his voice that he was an Underground escapee. She warned him to stay out of the cafés and off the streets until dark, and only then to come to her place.

Geneviève had made it a point to avoid what she referred to as the politics of war, which she felt had killed her husband. A few men, lusting for power, pretending altruistic beliefs, duping honest and decent men to kill one another—to what end? For all the killing of the civil war, what had been achieved? But since the caller was Camille's friend, she would do what she could.

Philip arrived an hour after nightfall. He pushed the button beside the outer door, and it clicked open loudly. There were no lights in the concierge's room. He felt his way up the stairs in the dark, and on the third floor, his hands guiding him along the wall, he found the third door on the right which Geneviève had identified as hers.

It was a small, one-room apartment, with a large bed and a mirrored armoire. Through the open bathroom door he could see a line with drying underclothes.

"I am an American," he informed her. "I have no papers, no belongings, no contacts, but I have some francs and I would like to find a guide to take me across the mountains tonight. Can you help me?"

Geneviève explained that she herself had nothing to do with the smugglers, but that she had heard how difficult it was to connect with an honest guide. There was much thievery going on, she informed him. Contact men who took large sums and disappeared, guides who were really informers and led their fugitives into Nazi traps, Gestapo men who masqueraded as contact men and as guides. She certainly couldn't locate anyone for him right away. He would have to be patient while she began to make safe, cautious inquiries. She had no idea how long that might take, but in the meantime he must avoid all public places—in fact, it would be unwise for him to try to register in any hotels, for they were all under surveillance.

"But I have to stay somewhere. What do you suggest?"

"All I can think of is that up in the attic of this building there is a tiny storeroom in which I keep some old things. It has a partition with a lock on it. There isn't any heat, but there's a mop sink with a water faucet, and a dormer window. I can give you some bedding, and some tins of food, but I can't be seen going back and forth. This building has a thousand eyes, and the concierge is a paid informer. I suggest you hide up there while I try to work things out."

She started to round up the bedding, and some canned food, when there was a sharp rap on the door. She looked startled, glanced at the clock, recovered.

She quickly carried a stool to the closet and motioned to Philip. The closet was filled with clothes, which she pushed tightly to one side to make room for the stool. She placed Philip on it, urging silence in pantomime, and closed the closet door.

The client was a high-ranking Nazi official in the *Kommissariat*. He said a curt *"Guten Abend"* and started to undress. All the sounds of the room carried clearly to Philip, and he felt terrible at imposing his presence on something that Geneviève undoubtedly detested but performed out of necessity.

As the embarrassing sounds reached Philip from the whining bed, a backwash of memory carried to him one of the Maupassant stories he read long ago: A poor whore lives with her little son in a shabby room. A client raps on the door—was his memory right, a cavalry officer, *that* coincidental? She hurriedly puts the child on a stool in the closet, warning him not to make a sound, and the child sits there obediently, fearfully, afraid to breathe, the sounds mutely reaching him as he grows drowsy, tries desperately to keep his eyes open, dozes, falls off the stool, the noise disturbing the client, who rushes to the closet, is furious at discovering the child, and storms out without paying, slamming the door behind him.

And here sit I, lamented Philip, fearfully, forced to listen to the animal grunts of some Nazi pig. Then there was the sound of water running, a toilet flushing, and the door closing, not in fury, but a satisfied customer who had paid in advance for emptying himself on his way home.

The attic storeroom was packed with pieces of dilapidated furniture, seedy luggage, twine-bound cardboard boxes, a rusted bird cage and other remnants of Geneviève's past existence. By rearranging the contents of the storeroom as quietly as he could, piling up the objects on top of one another, Philip made room to open an old cot, and for a three-legged table and a chair with a broken cane bottom.

The dormer window, which was nailed shut, afforded a view of the rooftops as far as the eye could see, chimney pots and vent pipes, overlapped roof tiles, a sea of tar paper, and, in the distance, incongruously, a rooster-topped weathervane in the valley of a slanted roof where it could not possibly be seen from below.

This was Philip's world for endless days. The door of the storeroom, made of crude planks, had to be padlocked from the outside by Geneviève when she departed, making Philip a prisoner. Using the soap and towel Geneviève furnished him, he bathed himself with cold water from the mop basin, which also had to serve as his toilet. He rationed the tinned food, which he opened with the can opener that unfolded from his Swiss officer's knife. The first night, the rats scurried in to devour the food remnants in the can, and after that Philip used the drawers of an old dresser for his garbage. The rats still came every night, but not voraciously. He had nothing to write with, and only his one paperback, Stendhal's *The Red and the Black,* which Camille had given him.

He passed the days by sitting at the dormer window, which slanted skyward, wrapped in blankets to help ward off the penetrating cold, gazing endlessly at the sky. Curiously, there were no birds, and no one ever appeared on the roofs. When night fell, the room, which was without electricity, turned black, but on clear nights the darkness was slightly alleviated by the moonlight.

Geneviève had made it clear that she would not make nonessential trips to the storeroom, thus avoiding the prying eyes of her untrustworthy neighbors, so Philip was not too concerned when four days passed with no word from her. But on the afternoon of the fifth day there were sudden noises on the stairs leading up to the attic, and Philip secreted himself in a niche he had prepared in back of a pile of boxes.

The concierge, toothless, in carpet slippers and a blue duster, appeared with a Vichy policeman in tow, her voice volubly nasal. They approached Philip's hiding place, and he held his breath. In his mind, he rehearsed a plan: when they unlocked the door, he would precipitously dart from his hiding place, push by them and then try to run past them down the stairs. But as he tensed his body, his mind racing, they went to the storeroom next to his, the concierge loudly complaining about the rent not having been paid, hoping to find something of value to make up for her lost income. But from her expletives Philip could tell that she had discovered that, like his, the storeroom contained nothing but junk.

As the week passed, both Philip's food and his resolve dwindled. What if something had happened to Geneviève? What if she had made her inquiries on his behalf and in the process been arrested? What then? She likely would not betray him, but who would come to his aid? Seven days was much too long, he reflected, for the simple business of finding a contact, if there were as many around as she had intimated. It might be necessary to try to get out of his self-imposed prison, but the planking on the door was thick and the lock couldn't be reached from the inside. Even if he found a crowbar the noise would certainly imperil him. This long, peculiar solitude magnified his fears and deepened his feeling of hopelessness.

But in the middle of the eighth night there was a scratching on the door and a whisper that identified Geneviève. She carried a candle for illumination, and a pillowcase that was filled with food.

"I'm sorry it's taking so long," she whispered, "but it seems that all of Pau is looking for you, and it's hard to know who to trust. I have a line on someone good, though, who is away right now, and I will meet with him when he returns. Are you all right?"

"I guess so. How long do you think it will be until he comes back?"

"I don't know."

"Do you think you could get me some candles?"

"No, that's not a good idea—the light might be seen."

Philip took some francs from his pocket and offered them to her. "This is for the food," he said.

She pushed his hand away. "You'll need all your money to buy your way across the mountains. I'm sorry to be so slow, so cautious. But if I make a wrong move, I could be in as much trouble as you are. I have two children and an aged grandmother who depend on me—I can't afford the luxury of courage."

Five more days of solitude followed, with no word from Geneviève. Philip's beard was quite full by now, and his dimly reflected face in the windowpane was that of a stranger. He thought of Gaby constantly.

He washed his underclothes and socks in the basin and then attached them to a broom handle and waved them back and forth to dry. He mumbled to himself quite a lot, and sometimes spoke to Gaby as if she were there. He devised a game with a kitchen pot and a wad of paper, endlessly pitching the paper wad toward the pot, counting points when he succeeded, deducting points when he missed. By now he could virtually recite *The Red and the Black* by heart. On the twelfth night, standing at the window, looking up at the starry but moonless sky, he started to weep, but he didn't really know why.

Near dawn on the fourteenth day, Geneviève came to get him. She told him to leave everything as it was—she would come back later to clean up. They crept noiselessly down the stairs to her apartment, where a man was waiting. Geneviève introduced him as "Robespierre."

"It is very likely too late to attempt a crossing now until spring," he explained. "There is a snow watch, and I know of only one guide who might even consider making an attempt."

"I must see him," Philip said. "I must."

"My advice to you is to hide out here until spring, when the snow melts and the terrain becomes passable again. Are you familiar with the Pyrenees? No? Well, they are savage, unpredictable mountains, and the snowstorms are killers. There are more Nazi patrols around the smugglers' paths than ever before. Just last week they caught over ninety escapees, brought them back here and shipped them off to concentration camps in Germany. They're really cracking down. If I were you, whatever the hardship, I would wait."

"I can't. It's simply impossible. I want to talk to your guide."

"Geneviève says you have no papers, not even a Spanish visa, that right?"

"They were all taken from me."

"You're doing the wrong thing, my friend. Take your time, get yourself all the papers you need, including a passport, and you'll have a much better chance. Why, without a Spanish visa, even if you do get to Spain, you'll go right to jail—the Spanish are sticklers about visas."

"I'll worry about that when I get there. All I want is to go—*now.*"

Robespierre shook his head sadly, but asked Geneviève if he could use her phone. His conversation was brief and guarded.

"The guide says he will try it," he reported when he hung up, "but his fee will be fifty thousand francs payable in advance. If you want to pay that, I can take you there right away. I get my fee from him."

Philip hesitated. Fifty thousand was all the money he had. What would he do if he did get to Spain but had no money? "Is the price negotiable?" he asked.

"Not with Sandoz. Nothing is negotiable. He is the head of a syndicate of rumrunners, and when he says something, he means it."

Robespierre had a pickup truck parked in front of Geneviève's building; it was filled with empty chicken crates. He opened the door of the truck and removed the seat-back on the passenger's side. A hidden space had been created by means of a false cab wall, with air vents, that provided enough room for a man to stretch out and ride comfortably without being seen. He motioned to Philip, who squeezed through the opening and settled down on a bed of blankets. Robespierre had lost count of the number of escapees whom he had hidden there for the long ride to the base of the mountain. He carefully replaced the seat-back, making sure it was secure, and then they were on their way to deliver a load of chicken crates to the tough-talking guide named Sandoz.

37

Johannes Fischer was the most experienced Gestapo agent assigned to Baron von Behr. Before the war, he had spent two years at Scotland Yard on an exchange program, and subsequently he had attained the rank of sergeant detective in the Berlin police force. The Baron had made him his chief of staff in the hunt for Philip, and, in fact, didn't make a move without Fischer at his side. They rode together in the back of the Baron's staff car, dined together while they plotted strategy, and von Behr looked to Fischer for the daily duty assignments given to the fourteen-man force under the Baron's control.

Now, on the morning when Philip was meeting with Robespierre in Geneviève's apartment, Baron von Behr and Johannes Fischer had risen early to observe the passengers getting off the train from Béziers. They had received word from a usually reliable source that the American might be on this train, but, like all the other hot leads they had pursued, it had proved to be false; as a consequence, von Behr was in a black frame of mind when he left the stationmaster's office. He resented having to get out of bed so early, and he doubly resented this prolonged estrangement from the pleasures of his life in Paris; Goering's furious directive had ordered him not to come back until he had arrested Weber. And, on top of all that his eye, still not fully healed, throbbed with pain as his car bounced over the rough paving of the Rue Castenau. When the driver came to the intersection with the Rue Carnot, he went through the stop sign, which was a prerogative of Nazi vehicles, and collided with a pickup truck carrying chicken crates that was headed toward the Boulevard des Pyrénées. The truck skidded to a halt, a few of the chicken crates spilling onto the pavement.

Robespierre and the Baron's driver got out to inspect the damage, which was only minor—a bruised front fender on the truck, a wrenched bumper on the staff car. The impact of the collision, however, had jolted the Baron's head, intensifying his pain, and he stormed out of the car, advancing on the two drivers, who were inspecting the truck's fender. The impact had also jolted Philip, who now watched apprehensively through one of the air vents. His first fear was that the police might come to investigate the accident, but then, shocked, he saw the Baron come into his limited view, and his stomach dropped in despair. The Baron, who was excoriating both drivers, was only a few feet away. Philip was afraid that in his anger the Baron might arrest Robespierre. And what kind of papers did Robespierre have? Philip wondered. Philip tried to think ahead: if they arrested Robespierre, and the truck was abandoned, what would he, Philip, do? Go back to Geneviève? Try to establish a fresh contact on his own? The long uncertainty of his existence in the storeroom had shaken his confidence in his ability to survive. The Baron, still ranting, had moved even closer to the truck, and Philip drew back for fear he might be noticed.

Unexpectedly, the Baron suddenly turned on his heel, having pumped out all his bile, and ordered his driver back to the car. Within seconds they were gone. Robespierre hurriedly picked up his fallen crates and moved on.

Robespierre's destination was a farmhouse located in the sloping foothills of the Pyrenees, which could be reached only over circuitous dirt roads with abominable surfaces. It took the better part of the day to get there, with only one stop along the way. When, at last, they reached the farmhouse, a ramshackle building with outlying chicken coops around it, Philip saw in the driveway an automobile from which three men were just emerging. Robespierre removed the seat-back and helped Philip squeeze out of his hiding place, stiff from the confinement. The group of five men then proceeded into the farmhouse, where they were received by a giant, full-bellied man with long stringy hair, a small gold earring in his left ear, the tattoo of an eagle on his arm. He had a gray stubble of beard on his face, which slanted downward in a permanent scowl. He shook hands perfunctorily with Robespierre and the driver of the automobile, and Philip noticed that the little fingers were missing from both of his hands. This was Sandoz, chicken farmer, rumrunner, Pyrenees guide, and once the best picador in all Spain. His brother, a banderillero, used to brag that Sandoz was the only picador in the history of the ring who never lost a horse to the bull.

Sandoz and his brother had retired from the ring at the

same time and, after an abortive attempt at bull-breeding, drifted into chickens, which eventually became the cover for the much more lucrative business of rumrunning. Once established, Sandoz leaned on his fellow smugglers as successfully as he had once leaned on the rambunctious Miura bulls, and eventually formed a syndicate, with himself as the leader. It was at this point that Sandoz moved over the mountains and established his headquarters on the French side of the Pyrenees, leaving his brother to run the operation in Spain. Now the war had added a third dimension to their enterprise, the smuggling of refugees. But by this time of the year, with impending snowstorms, not even the greediest of the smugglers would risk another trip—that is, none except Sandoz.

He poured hefty glasses of hard cider for his visitors and addressed them in a thunderous voice. "Let me tell you straight off, this is no time to be trying to cross. You've already been told that, haven't you? It's thirty-six hours of murderous hiking, eight thousand feet straight up and then down, and we can only move at night because of the Nazi patrols, understood? A snow watch has already been announced and we can get caught at the top, which is serious business. I cannot carry anyone. I cannot be responsible for anyone. Where I go, how I go, you got to go—my job is only to show you the way. The last trip, we lost two. One fell off a peak, the other got tired and had to turn back by himself. I guarantee nothing. I tell you not to go, but if you insist, then I got to be paid fifty thousand each. That's a stiff price, all right, but you're a hot threesome."

Sandoz pointed to one of the men. "They want you for killing a Gestapo pig in Cherbourg, correct? And you for throwing a grenade into a Nazi barracks in Amiens. And as for you, Yankee Doodle, the big, fat one wants you. What did you do, bugger Frau Goering? Well, you can see, you three are some sizzling load! Do you want to kick in with the price?"

Without hesitation, Philip took the francs out of his pocket and placed them on the table. The other two men followed suit.

"*Bien!* Then here's the program: I will provide each of you with a rucksack that will contain blankets, food and drink. We will spend three nights on the mountain, sleeping in shepherds' huts that are not used this time of the year. When we get to the Spanish side of the mountain, my brother, Antonio, will take over and lead you the rest of the way. I warn you that at four thousand feet the air will begin to thin out, and by the time you are at the top there won't be much to breathe. Any of you got trouble with your lungs? No? All right. We will leave at midnight and get to the first hut around dawn. It will be cold as hell, I warn you. *Bien!* You will have to spend the next hours in one of the chicken coops—we get Nazi patrols coming through here, but they never search the coops. I'll have some food brought to you out there."

He picked up some francs from the pile before him and handed them to the two drivers, who thanked him and left. Sandoz then led the men out the back door and across a muddy yard to a tar-paper shack that was crowded with brown pullets. The air was redolent with the heavy layers of chicken droppings. At first Philip's stomach reacted to the stench, but after a while he began to adjust to it. And he was rather amused by the curiosity of the chickens.

By the time a big, rawboned servant girl appeared with bread and a bucket that contained chicken stew and ladled it into tin bowls, Philip was able to eat some dinner, although not with much enthusiasm.

38

They walked in single file, at a brisk pace, the foothills steeper than Philip had expected, footing difficult on the
slippery dry grass, the ascent punishing to the calf muscles of
the legs. The night was pitch dark, so they stayed in close file in
order not to lose sight of one another. As the hours passed,
Philip realized how much strength his legs had lost since he left
Paris. Twice the man in front of him slipped and fell, but quickly
regained his feet.

Sandoz allowed four short rest periods during the seven hours
it took them to reach the first level of their passage. As ribbons
of dawn began to unfurl in the black sky, revealing the granite
panorama around them, they came to the small stone shepherd's
hut where they would spend the day. The flimsy door hung on a
single rusted hinge, and the hut was bare.

The men opened the tattered rucksacks that Sandoz had
provided and took out the food and the two old army blankets
which they contained. There was cheese, dried salami, bread,
chocolate, carrots and a bottle of mountain wine. Sandoz had a
bottle opener for the wine, but Philip used the one in his knife.
When Sandoz told them to eat a lot of carrots to improve their
night vision, Philip smiled.

He was too tired to eat. He nibbled at the cheese, took a
couple of gulps of the abrasive red wine, then wrapped himself in
his blankets and immediately fell asleep on the earthen floor. So
did the other two escapees. Sandoz sat with his back against the
wall and smoked a black cigar. As the day fully broke, the sky
was pregnant with gray-bellied clouds. Through the open door,
Sandoz studied the sky. The birth of a snowstorm was imminent,
but Sandoz hoped it would hold off for the forty-eight hours that
was needed to get into Spain.

*   *   *

Philip awoke in the late afternoon, hungry and thirsty. One of his fellow fugitives was sitting up, the other was still asleep. Sandoz was gone. The man said he did not know what had happened to him. Philip's immediate reaction was one of fear that Sandoz had made off with their money and left them to fend for themselves, but he didn't say anything to his fellow escapee, whose name was Jean-Pierre. He was the one who had pitched the grenade into a barracks filled with sleeping German soldiers. He told Philip he had been on the run for seventeen days, managing to keep a step in front of his pursuers by following an unpredictable route. He was a tall, gaunt man in his thirties, with hollow cheeks, thick glasses, and a cigarette cough. He had been a schoolteacher in Amiens, an outspoken pacifist who had not even held a gun prior to his assault on the barracks, and who, in fact, had had no strong feelings, one way or another, about the occupation by the Nazis until the evening, several weeks ago, when they had raped his wife.

He had been speaking in a low steady voice, but now, with his emotions rising, his voice broke. After a long pause, he continued: On this particular day, his young wife had not been at home, as she always was, when he returned from work. As night fell, he had worriedly phoned her parents and all their friends, none of whom had heard from her. He went all through the neighborhood looking for her, querying café owners and trades-people they knew, and finally discovered that she had been at the butcher's around four o'clock that afternoon. But Jean-Pierre could pick up no trace of her after that. He went to the police, and checked the hospitals, but they had no report on her.

There was nothing to do but return to the apartment and wait, which he did, agonizingly, until at midnight there was an insistent buzzing from downstairs; he raced down the four floors, and there, leaning on the button, barely able to stand, was his wife. He tenderly folded her over his shoulder, an empty rag doll, and carried her up to their apartment. Her dress was ripped and dirty, there were scratches on her face and arms, and her body was covered with blue bruises. One corner of her mouth had been ripped open and was caked with dried blood. Her eyes, which seemed to have receded into their sockets, looked at Jean-Pierre but did not see him. There were deep bite marks on one of her breasts.

The family doctor came, gave her an injection for shock, and examined her carefully. Then the old doctor, who had delivered

Jean-Pierre into the world, took him to one side and with great sorrow informed him that in his opinion his wife had been raped and beaten, and that she was in a state of deep shock.

For several weeks his wife lay there, staring up at the ceiling, not responding to his questions, not reacting to sounds or lights or anything else. Jean-Pierre had to carry her to the toilet. He considered going to the police, but he knew they had no authority over the German soldiers, and, besides, he felt a great shame at having to tell them this terrible and intimate thing about his wife.

Then one night the boil burst and she started to scream, a terrifying animal sound. He comforted her while her body convulsed in a paroxysm of remembrance. In hysterical gasps, she told him about the soldiers in the truck grabbing her on the street with her bag of groceries, a gloved hand clamped over her mouth, her groceries spilling everywhere, and then, and then . . . the barracks—her voice fell to a whisper in Jean-Pierre's ear—the barracks, music blaring from the radio, schnapps bottles, soldiers laughing, smoking, undressing, ripping off her dress, throwing her onto the floor. Hands pinned her flat on the floor, a soldier's wool sock was stuffed into her mouth, and then they started to come at her, terrifying forms lowering down on her, squeezing, sucking, biting her breasts, ramming themselves into her, showing off for one another. Finally, mercifully, she had passed out, with no further memory, not even of how she got home, no memory of Jean-Pierre coming down to get her and carrying her up the stairs.

Jean-Pierre turned to face Philip. "I'm a civilized man, Philip. I have never hated or ever acted out of anger or spite—it's not my nature. At first, I think, I was too stunned by what had happened, to react, other than to try to find some way to console my wife, to try to mend some of the rips and tears in the fabric of her beautiful being, but then . . . that too was taken away. For three days I think she tried, and I was gaining a little heart. She had stopped crying, and sometimes she would answer when I spoke to her, but the doctor had prescribed sleeping pills and . . . when I awoke that morning, without having to look at the night table where the empty bottle of Seconal was, I sensed she was dead.

"That's when I knew I had to avenge her, that lovely, peaceable woman who had been the joy of my life. I managed to get inside the compound and went to the door of that barracks, that foul hellhole where they had destroyed her, and I pulled the pins of two grenades and threw them into the sleeping barracks. As I walked away from the explosions, I tell you, the shrieks and cries of the wounded and dying were music to my ears. That is a loathsome admission, Philip, I realize that. I am a sensible, educated man, and I should feel some remorse at my action, I suppose, but, honestly, all I feel is satisfied revenge.''

In the distance Sandoz was approaching the hut, carrying a large jug which he had filled with icy mountain water from a waterfall somewhere below. Philip watched him trudging up the steep path, then he looked at Jean-Pierre, whose head was bowed against his chest, his eyes closed against his memory. Philip wanted to put his arms around his shoulders to reassure him. I guess we all have our Lilis, Philip thought.

Jean-Pierre raised his head suddenly. "What am I running to, Philip? Nothing. Where am I headed? Nowhere. There is no longer anything in my life. We had no children. I am only on the move to elude them, so that they won't get me as they got her. But I'm not running *toward* anything. And if I do give them the slip—what then?''

Sandoz came stomping into the hut, the snow flying off his boots, the sound waking the sleeping man, who was called Bernard. Sandoz explained that they could not risk making a fire because it might attract the attention of a Nazi patrol, although from the looks of the sky it was not likely that any of them were still around.

Philip sat down on the ground outside the door of the hut and ate some cheese and bread as he watched the fat clouds move across the sky.

As soon as the light began to fade, Sandoz had them back on the trail. Philip's legs felt a little stronger than the night before, but his feet were sore. Inside of two hours they had passed from the ribbed ground of the plateau onto the elevating terrain where the gullies, which became the beds of rushing torrents in the spring, deepened and the going became much rougher. Pebbly earth and stones kept giving way under their feet, tipping them off balance. Philip was now first in line behind Sandoz, and he tried to emulate his steady stride, but he was much less sure-footed, slipping and sliding on stretches that Sandoz crossed as securely as if it were sand. They passed the charred remains of smugglers' bonfires, and occasionally the bleached bones of some mountain animal.

In the fifth hour of their climb, a fine rain began to fall, lightly spraying their faces, and as the ascent precipitously steepened, the rain intensified and turned to sleet. The higher they went, the deeper the gullies over which they passed became, and Philip was forced to keep his eyes riveted on the ground immediately in front of him. As they moved along the crest of one of the deep gulches, a false step would mean a tumble and a severe slide to the bottom—not so far down that, with help, you couldn't get back up, but to be avoided nevertheless. The sleet was coarsening now, and the wind's velocity increasing. There was a cry from Bernard, who was at the rear, and they had to stop while Sandoz went back and, reaching down, extricated him from a gulch. Sandoz then moved Bernard to the head of the file, Philip dropping back to the rear.

After ten hours of hiking, they had reached six thousand feet and were still sharply ascending. The air had thinned considerably, and, as Sandoz had warned, it was becoming much more difficult to breathe. The sleet had turned into a thick snowfall, and the constant windblown barrage in Philip's face made it even more difficult to breathe. He was thankful that he had his sunglasses to put on. He was panting and sheathed in white by the time Sandoz led them to a rock overhang for a short rest. Bernard, who had been falling a lot, asked how long it was to the next hut. Another two hours, Sandoz told him. Bernard said he doubted he could make it. Sandoz took his rucksack to carry for him and told him that if he kept close behind him he would be screened from the wind. Bernard ate some chocolate, and at the end of the rest period he seemed determined to make it.

It took closer to three hours to cover the treacherous terrain to where the hut was. The snow had spread a deceptive blanket over the ground, obscuring the pitfalls, and Philip and the other two men, slipping and falling, began to lose their confidence. By the time they reached the hut, which was considerably larger than the first one, they were at seven thousand feet, and the density of the snowfall had all but obliterated the surrounding spires and peaks that towered over the pass.

The three escapees stumbled through the door and dropped to the floor of the hut. Philip's face was frigid, as were his hands and feet. Sandoz was completely covered with a thick layer of snow, beard and all, which made him look like a gargantuan snowman.

"We can forget about Nazi patrols," he said. "Now the only problem is to make it through the snow."

There was a pile of old bracken in the corner, and some twigs, which Sandoz arranged in the doorway and put a match to. The dried ferns flared to life, and the three men moved their wet clothes and frozen hands over the flame as it caught onto the twigs. Sandoz stomped loose some boards from the floor, cracked them over his knee, and fed them to the fire. He also stripped the broken shutters from the windows and added them to the blaze.

As they sat by the fire, they ate hungrily from their meager supplies. Sandoz brought out a flask of Fundador, which he passed around. He said that their only chance of getting through was to cover ground before the snow got much deeper, and since there was no longer any need to be concerned about the Nazis, they could now travel during the day.

"You've got four hours to sleep," he said, "and then we tackle the roughest part of the ascent. I want to reach the top of the pass by noon, then we will try to get to the next hut by nightfall. That's where my brother will pick you up and take you the rest of the way into Spain."

They were back on the trail in less than four hours. The storm had now reached its peak, and the ground was a virginal, innocent-looking expanse that completely hid the dangerous crevasses. The wind also had intensified, blowing viciously in crosscurrents that occasionally swerved them off their path. With all the landmarks obliterated, Sandoz could no longer plunge ahead, and he had to use his feet as a blind man uses his cane, a slow process of exploration, and each of them, in turn, carefully fitted his boots into the large tracks.

The air had thinned even more, and, with the dense snow-flakes clogging his mouth and nostrils, Philip found himself struggling for breath. Bernard was closely behind Sandoz, Philip in the middle, and Jean-Pierre at the rear. Sandoz had hoped that as they entered the top of the pass the towering mountains on each side of them would afford some protection from the storm, but, if anything, when they reached eight thousand feet and the ground became level, the storm seemed even more savage. We may not make it, Philip was thinking. The heavy snow, stretching before him to infinity, was sapping his strength and his will.

There was a piercing cry in back of him, and he wheeled about in time to see Jean-Pierre hurtling down a ravine and landing with force against an outcropping that saved him from going over the side of a precipice below. Philip called out to Sandoz, who hadn't heard Jean-Pierre's cry. Sandoz took a coil of rope from his rucksack, tied one end of it around a boulder, and worked his way down the ravine to where Jean-Pierre had fallen. Philip took off his rucksack and followed him down.

Jean-Pierre was lying on his back against the rock that had stopped him. He had lost his hat and his eyeglasses, and there was a gash on his forehead. When Sandoz tried to help him up, Jean-Pierre yelled in pain and pointed to his right leg, which jutted atrociously from his body, like a snapped match. The pain was already becoming intolerable. Sandoz and Philip bent down and examined him.

"Can we make some kind of sled and drag him with the rope?" Philip asked.

"Not over this rocky surface," Sandoz answered. Then he said to Jean-Pierre, "I wish I could carry you, but in this storm . . . And there's a long way to go."

"Maybe we could make a stretcher," Philip suggested.

"With what?" Sandoz asked gruffly. "We need two poles of some kind, but there are no trees around here, nothing. Besides, you and Bernard can barely carry yourselves."

"Sandoz," Jean-Pierre said, "I'll tell you what you can do. I saw that you have a pistol in your belt. That is what you can do for me."

Sandoz straightened up and looked down at him intently.

"Please, Sandoz. The kindness you would show your horse if he got gored in the ring—that's all I ask. Please! Get it over with and then you can go on. You cannot leave me like this."

Sandoz thought this over intently. Finally he reached his hand inside his jacket and pulled out the gun. He took a bullet from his pocket, put it into the empty chamber, and rotated it into firing position. Then he clicked off the safety and slowly, reluctantly, aimed. With his arm extended, his finger on the trigger, he tried to shoot, but he couldn't bring himself to fire the gun.

"I'm sorry, señor," he said, lowering the gun, "but I am a Catholic. I cannot."

Jean-Pierre turned his face toward Philip and motioned to him to come closer.

"Philip, you must have mercy on me. You do it, Philip— *please!*"

Sandoz offered the gun to Philip, who hesitated, but, looking at Jean-Pierre's suffering face, he knew they simply could not leave him to what would be a slow death. Philip reached up and took the gun by its muzzle and handed it to Jean-Pierre, who grasped it and without hesitation put it against his temple and fired.

Sandoz reached down and retrieved his gun from the crimson snow. Philip used his hands to push a blanket of snow over Jean-Pierre's body, turning it into a white mound, while Sandoz started back up the ravine, using the rope hand over hand.

Philip looked down at the snow-covered body, and felt sympathy and pity and admiration. Jean-Pierre was a decent and brave man, and Philip wanted to give him some kind of burial. He tried to recall the Twenty-third Psalm, but he couldn't. He couldn't remember anything.

"Adieu, Jean-Pierre," he said aloud. "Sleep well."

Then he abruptly turned away from the white grave and pulled himself back up to the top of the ravine.

The direction of the wind changed and came at them head on, seriously slowing their progress. Darkness fell early in the high mountains, and they were still a considerable distance from the next shelter. After so many exhausting hours, it became increasingly difficult for Philip to concentrate on the foot tracks before him; his mind began to wander, to play tricks on him. Several times he caught himself straying from the boot tracks before him, then, in panic, relocating them, as one falls asleep at the wheel momentarily while driving at night, then snaps to, righting the automobile to its course, just in time.

And then it happened with shocking suddenness: the slip, the fall through open space, the jarring impact of landing hard on his right shoulder, then spinning downward, a hard bump, a jarring stop. Lying deep in the snow, stunned, then struggling out of the snow pocket, rubbing his sore shoulder, trying to stand, falling, trying again, unsteady but all in one piece, his hat and rucksack still in place. But no sign of the others. He shouted Sandoz's name, as loud as he could, over and over again, but there was no response. And he could see nothing through the white sheath of snow falling against the blackness of the night.

He had spun and rolled so much he had no idea from which direction he had come. But by using his foot as a divining rod, probing in all directions, he decided on which way he thought sloped upward, and cautiously he began to move in that direction. As he did, he continued to call out Sandoz's name, as loud as he could. He could not stop and wait for dawn; he realized that movement was his only antidote against freezing, but he was very, very tired and he doubted he could go on much longer. He stopped momentarily and ate some chocolate from his rucksack for energy.

Daylight, when it came, was not much help. The snow continued to fall heavily and there was no way for him to tell one direction from another. For all he knew, he was headed back to France.

39

Philip plodded forward as if in a sleepwalking dream; he had no feeling in his hands and feet, which were frozen to numbness, but his ears and nose ached from the cold. Somehow, he had discovered the center of the pass, where it was at its levelest, and even though it was obscured by the deepening snow he was following it pretty well. He had by now forced himself through fatigue and emerged on the other side of it, into a mechanical, zombielike state where his legs seemed to move independently.

When the ground under him began its downward grade, steadily becoming more precipitous, his legs strained against the downward pull. At one point he sighted the hut where Sandoz's brother would be waiting to shepherd the fugitives the rest of the way, and, sighting it, Philip yelped in joy, new energy propelling him. But when he neared the hut it vanished, a cruel mirage of the snow.

But still Philip persisted, hunching himself against the driven snow and continuing his downward course, becoming more cautious about his footing as the earth steepened and the crags and gullies beneath the snow became more precarious. A few signs of life appeared: he was startled by a pair of rabbits suddenly scuttering across his path; an elk on a precipice ledge above him; a wide-winged hawk circling in the snowy sky, inspecting him. And trees and shrubs began to appear again on the landscape.

As the path veered past a stalagmitical outcropping of granite, Philip spotted a crude shanty that had been erected on the side of the rock—two sides made from tree trunks, with a thatched roof, perhaps a shepherd's respite from the summer sun, or a smuggler's haven for the night. It was not high enough to stand in, just wide enough for a man to stretch out. Philip stooped and entered the tiny refuge. There was old, sour straw on the floor, and remnants of a broken jug. Philip slipped off his rucksack and took out the two blankets and what little remained of his food. He ate the last pieces of his cheese and salami ravenously, and finished the wine. All that was left now was a small piece of chocolate which he saved in his jacket pocket.

He got up on his knees and urinated out onto the snow. Then he took one of the old blankets and started tearing it up into strips. He took off his cap and wrapped a blanket strip around his ears, tying it under his chin. Then he wrapped some strips around his shoes and tied them on the top where the laces were. He took off his jacket and wrapped his body with the blanket he hadn't torn, replacing the jacket over it. Finally, he took a piece of the blanket and, with his knife, which he had great trouble opening with his frozen fingers, cut holes for his eyes and nose. He wrapped the mask around his face and secured it with his cap, which he pulled down as far as he could.

The warmth of the blankets, and the cessation of wind and snow, induced a sudden sleepiness, and with his back against the rear wall, his legs stretched out in front of him, he started to doze off. I will just get a little sleep, he told himself, just a few winks, I am so tired, I have to sleep, only for a few minutes . . .

His head fell against his chest as he flirted with unconsciousness, his body slowly slanting to the side, but an inner warning pulled at him, tugging at his awareness as he battled himself, and then, with a start, the danger translated to anger and he yelled out loud, "Weber! Goddammit, Weber! Come on, wake up, wake up, get your ass out of here!"

As the descent steepened, the snow slowly began to abate, but Philip did not notice it. He did not notice the passing hours, nor was he aware of how far he had gone or how far there was to go—or even where he was headed. Just staying in motion was an end in itself. He drifted into a kind of delirium, talking to himself, calling out Sandoz's name, and then, hearing that familiar, feared word (or was it a name?), first from a great distance, but growing steadily louder, "PRELOON," a magnetic cry homing in on him, reverberating in his ears, "PRELO-O-O-N," the monstrous specter from his nightmares, a siren beckoning him, forcing him down the mountain, no Orpheus to rescue him, blinded now, suspended in space, his legs crumbling, finally giving way, his eyes blanked by the blinding snow, his frozen extremities succumbing, his body embraced by the snow, the frigid kiss of death, a final resting place.

40

The boy drove his two-mule cart along the narrow mountain path in search of his traps. He had already collected a white-pelted wolf and a fox, but he was having trouble locating his third trap, which he had measured from the monument, since the snow had obscured his markings. Perhaps it is farther up, the boy thought, and he began to circle higher, probing beneath the snow with the hickory stick he kept in his wagon. He had learned to trap from his father and his grandfather, and he was good at it. In fact, two weeks ago the four traps he had set for rabbits had each had a big fat hare in it.

Now he sighted the trap he was looking for, much higher up the mountain than he remembered placing it. But no matter, he could see from a distance that it was a good-sized catch which could have dragged the trap all the way to the end of its tether. He hurried toward it, hoping it was a mountain goat. Señor García at the tannery paid good prices for the soft, supple skin.

The boy stopped abruptly as he came close enough to see that it wasn't an animal at all, but the body of a man, partially covered with snow. At first he feared the man might have been caught in the trap, but as he came closer he saw that that wasn't the case. The boy pulled away the man's ragged face mask. From the looks of him, the man was dead. The boy, Tomaso by name, was inclined to turn tail and run, but then it occurred to him that he should quickly check the dead man's pockets for money. He pushed the body onto its back, and as he did the man emitted a groan, startling him. He pushed his thumb into the man's throat and felt a dim pulse beat. Tomaso was the kind of pragmatic boy, a Basque, who might rob a corpse, but who would extend himself to try to save that man's life if it was possible. He now placed his palms on each side of Philip's face and began to rub his cheeks vigorously.

"Wake up, señor," he said in Basque Spanish, "wake up! Wake up!"

Philip stirred, groaned, partially opened his eyes. "Help me," he whispered, barely forming the words with his frozen lips.

Tomaso was pleased to hear him speak English, for Tomaso, who was twelve, worked as a busboy in the Luciano Restaurant in Bilbao, where he practiced his English with foreigners whenever he could.

"Are you a British gentleman?" he asked, but Philip had lapsed into unconsciousness again, and Tomaso had to slap his cheeks to rouse him.

"Gentleman, are you British?"

"I'm . . . American . . ."

"You have no papers? You are one of those who escapes from the Nazis?"

"Help me . . . please . . ."

This was a very important moment for Tomaso, whose dream was to go to America. To be presented an opportunity to help a real, bona fide American appealed to him very much. He put his two forefingers into his mouth and whistled shrilly for his mules on the trail below; they immediately began to pull their cart toward him. Tomaso tried to keep Philip awake by pushing at his eyelids and rubbing his face.

"Gentleman, you must not sleep. Here now is my *carro*. You must up upon your feet, here, gentleman, I am helping you."

Tomaso pulled Philip to an upright position, a dead weight that fell away from him. He tried again, this time pushing Philip up by getting in back of him and then thumping his back with the flat of his hand, as hard as he could. Philip finally reacted, and Tomaso got his head and shoulder under Philip's arm as he pushed up and, urging Philip on, got him into the cart. Although the wiry boy was small for his age, he was strong enough to move Philip to the rear of his wagon where it was partially covered with a tattered canvas tarp. Tomaso smoothed out some burlap and rolled Philip onto it. Then he took the carcasses of the wolf and the fox and nestled them for warmth against Philip.

As Tomaso bent over him, Philip whispered, "I must get to Portugal . . ."

"Sure, yes, the problem is known to me."

"No police . . . no hospital . . . not even . . . church . . ."

"You are very sick."

"I will get better."

"Do not have worry—I will help you. I am not in favor of police or hospitals, or even of the church. I am in favor of nobody. Do not have worry. My name is Tomaso."

"Tomaso, listen. All I need . . . is a helper—you understand?
"*Sí*, yes, most certainly—*asistente*. In this respect we are *pajaros de la misma pluma*."

Tomaso's mules ran smartly along the trail which carried them past the monument and down to the bottom of the foothills. The monument was an imposing monolith of Pyrenees granite, with the word FRANCE engraved on its north side and ESPAÑA on its southern face.

Tomaso lived in a basement room off an alleyway in an old quarter of Bilbao. It was a short distance from the slaughterhouse whose stink fouled the neighborhood. Tomaso's landlord ran a poultry store at street level, and he got the room in exchange for plucking the chickens that arrived at six o'clock every morning. Tomaso did not have to be at work at the restaurant until noon, and he was always finished plucking and singeing the chickens by eleven o'clock. His chicken job paid his rent, and his restaurant job provided him with two free meals and enough money to live on. He had been born and raised in Guernica, which was thirty-six kilometers away, but he had been living alone in Bilbao since he was nine.

He parked his wagon in the alleyway outside his door and, with difficulty, finally got Philip off the cart and into his tiny room. Philip was groggy but able to go through the motions of undressing himself, although Tomaso had to do most of the work. The bed was a thin, lumpy mattress on the floor in one corner; Tomaso installed him there and piled on all the covers. Philip was nevertheless racked by deep chills.

In the potbellied stove at the window Tomaso made a fire with coal which he regularly pilfered from the dealer at the corner. He then placed a pan of water on top of the stove to heat. When the water was lukewarm, he carried the pan over to the bed and, with pieces of toweling which he dipped into the water, began gently to massage Philip's hands and feet, which was what Tomaso's father had done for him when, as a small boy, he had frostbite. After a while the color started to return to Philip's hands, though his toes did not respond as readily. But Tomaso persisted, patiently applying the warm towels, gently patting them on the sensitive flesh.

It was Sunday, so Tomaso did not have to leave Philip to go to work. Tea and bouillon, smuggled from the restaurant, were in his cupboard, and he forced Philip to drink a cup of each. Tomaso was encouraged at the improvement in Philip's pulse, and by the time the boy went to sleep on a makeshift bed he felt relieved about the American's condition.

But sometime in the middle of the night Tomaso was awakened by Philip's restlessness and, going over to him, discovered that the American was burning with fever. Tomaso had never seen anyone in delirium before, and it frightened him. He put cold water on towels which he placed on Philip's forehead and on his chest, changing them frequently, sitting on the floor beside Philip and worriedly watching the increasing difficulty with which the American was breathing; there seemed to be a hitch in his breath, it would catch halfway, causing him to gasp and choke as he tried to get more air into his lungs. His breathing was getting steadily worse, and the towels seemed to have no effect on his temperature. Tomaso felt Philip's pulse, which was now racing faster than he could count the beats. For the first time, it occurred to him that the American might be dying.

In the near dawn, he put on his jacket and his Basque beret and ran as fast as he could to where his friend Dr. Miguel Castillo lived in a flat above an *abacería*. Dr. Castillo had once been a respected physician in Tomaso's home town, but after his wife and four children were killed, and the town was destroyed, Dr. Castillo had moved to Bilbao, where he drank too much to maintain a regular practice, eventually supporting himself by performing illegal operations on pregnant women. He was fond of little Tomaso, having been his family's doctor, and when he was in condition to—which was not often—he would take him to Sunday dinner.

Now Tomaso rapped again and again and again on the doctor's door, trying to rouse him from his drunken sleep. Finally he succeeded. The doctor, who had once been a handsome semipro pelota player, had now become fat and dissolute. But his head began to clear as he listened to Tomaso's graphic description of Philip's symptoms. The boy was so specific that Dr. Castillo was able to prepare treatment before seeing the patient.

"I'll tell you what I think, Tomaso, I think your friend has serious pneumonia. When he struggles to breathe, does he cough?"

"Yes, from deep down, and then he brings up some stuff."

"Yes, no doubt, pneumonia."

"Will he die?"

"It depends. We must bleed him to relieve the passage of blood through his lungs. I will get ready."

*   *   *

By the time the doctor and Tomaso arrived, Philip's condition had perceptibly worsened. Dr. Castillo examined him, his stethoscope magnifying the ominous rhoncus that confirmed his diagnosis. He turned Philip onto his stomach and made a dozen pricks on the back of his chest wall, drawing a bubble of blood in each place. Castillo then opened a small box that he had put into his medical bag, and extracted a number of mottled horse leeches, placing them carefully on the little pools of blood, upon which they immediately fastened their serrated teeth and began to suck blood in a flow from the open vents. The doctor covered Philip's back with twelve of these large leeches, and while they glutted themselves he carefully examined Philip's hands and feet, paying special attention to his toes.

When the leeches could drink no more they rolled off Philip's back. Dr. Castillo applied hot fomentations to the blood points to continue the flow. When he felt he had bled Philip sufficiently to relieve the constriction in his lungs, Castillo withdrew the compresses and used powdered alum to stop the bleeding. Then he gave Philip an injection, and several aspirins which he induced Philip to swallow.

"I will come by later today," the doctor said, "to check on him. Here are aspirins to give him every two hours."

"Will he be all right? He's the first American I have ever met, not counting the ones that come into the restaurant."

"We may have to do something about his toes—we'll see." Dr. Castillo took a silver flask from his bag and drank from it. "Did you know that Father Boaz passed away?"

"No," Tomaso said as he crossed himself.

"Poor man, he lived too long, especially this past year," Castillo said as he put the flask back into his old leather bag and moved toward the door. *"Hasta luego,"* he said.

"Doctor, you won't . . . forget about the American, will you? Shall I come to remind you?"

Castillo smiled at the boy and patted his concerned face. "Don't worry, Tomate, my mind still remembers what it has to."

After the doctor left, Tomaso sat in the dark, listening to the American's painful breathing and thinking about Father Boaz, who had baptized him, as he had baptized all his brothers and sisters. He had always been very nice to Tomaso, and one Christmas when the onion crop had failed and there were no presents nor Christmas dinner Father Boaz had invited all of them to the parish house, where there was a tree and dinner and toys under the tree.

When the bombs had fallen on the church, Father Boaz had been praying at the altar, asking for the protection of the Lord Jesus, but despite his plea the bombs had come crashing through the ancient roof, killing most of the worshipers and blowing off both of Father Boaz's legs, and that was why Tomaso no longer believed in the Lord Jesus Christ.

Dr. Castillo returned late that evening. Tomaso had performed his chicken-plucking duties, but he had telephoned the restaurant from the corner café to inform them that he was too ill to work. The aspirin had slightly reduced Philip's fever, which nevertheless was still at a dangerous level. He remained in his semicoma, swallowing some liquids, shouting delirious phrases, but unaware of his surroundings. His breathing seemed no better.

"We need oxygen," the doctor said after examining Philip, "but that is not possible."

"Tell me where it is and I will try to get it," Tomaso said.

Castillo laughed. "It comes in a big, heavy tank, and not even you, Tomate, could pull off a *truco* like that."

The doctor gave Philip another injection, this time a more potent serum that he had been able to get from a surgeon at the hospital.

"What do you think?" Tomaso asked.

"I'd say he's holding his own."

"Will he die? Do you think he will die?"

"There is a chance that he will. His pneumonia is very bad. I had hoped the bloodletting would do more."

"Please, Dr. Castillo, do not let me lose this one."

Dr. Castillo was examining Philip's feet. "There is another problem for your new friend, Tomate—his toes did not recover from their freezing, especially the little ones, which always give the most trouble. You see the color, how dead they look, and gangrene is already beginning. If the poison gets into his system, in his condition it will surely finish him off—so we must take off the toes immediately. Can you get water to boil on your stove? And I will need some towels, clean ones."

"Will you put him to sleep?"

"In his condition, ether would be fatal. I will inject some morphine into the feet to deaden the pain."

Before he set out the things he needed for the amputations, Castillo fortified himself with a deep swallow from his flask. His hands were unsteady, and the light from Tomaso's kerosene lamp was inadequate, but, after boiling his instruments and injecting the morphine, Castillo made neat, quick cuts and clamped off the veins with slight blood loss. Philip cried out in pain as the scalpel cut into him, but even that did not bring him to full consciousness.

Afterward, Castillo put his stethoscope to Philip's chest. "I am sorry to tell you this, Tomaso, but he is definitely more precarious than this morning. I don't know what else I can do."

"He will die?" The pathos in the boy's voice moved the doctor very much.

"I'm afraid so, Tomate."

Tomaso began to weep. It came as a shock to Castillo, who did not suspect that this street-wise boy was still capable of tears. He reached out and put his arm around Tomaso.

"The only thing that might save him is a new drug called sulfa. Have you heard of it?"

Tomaso shook his head.

"Sulfanilamide is the full name. It is reputed to be very effective against this kind of bacteria, but only the Army has it, I asked today—not a hospital in Spain, they tell me."

The boy stopped crying, suddenly alert. "What do you mean, the Army?"

"The army hospitals and the medics in the field. The Army is always first in everything, especially since we now have our great patriot, Franco, in charge of our lives. Tell you what I'll do—I will go see a man I once knew who is a doctor for the Guardia Civil. I will ask him, but I find that doctors are not very obliging to me here in Bilbao."

Before he left, Tomaso asked him to write down the name of the new drug. The boy was familiar with the army hospital near the Plaza de Toros, which often aided matadors who were gored in the ring and rushed to the infirmary. Tomaso knew the chief groundskeeper of the bullring, who passed him into all the *corridas* and let him watch from the *callejón*. Whenever the groundskeeper came to eat at the Luciano, Tomaso always slipped special dishes on his table and a couple of the best cigars.

On his way to the bullring, Tomaso went into the cathedral to pray for the American. He had not been in a church since the death of his family.

41

Sandoz had spent the better part of an hour searching for Philip, but, finding no sign of him in the snow, he had reluctantly given him up for dead. He did succeed, however, in leading Bernard through the snowstorm into Spain.

But Bernard had made his way only as far as Pamplona, where, in attempting to board a train for Madrid, he attracted the attention of the station's Guardia Civil, who did not like the look of his papers and took him to the local jail. After questioning by special agents who were under orders from Franco to stop the flight of escapees from France, Bernard was sent to the Campo de Miranda de Ebro, a concentration camp in the mountains that was filled with escapees who had been intercepted by the pro-Nazi Spanish police. At the camp it was discovered that Bernard was wanted by the Nazis for murder, and, under guard, along with ten others, he was transported to Gestapo headquarters in Paris.

Rather than submit to torture, Bernard readily gave his interrogators the details of his flight, telling them about the guide, Sandoz, and how Jean-Pierre had committed suicide because of a broken leg, and how the American, Philip, had perished in a fall off the mountain.

His confession did no damage to Sandoz, who was a Spanish citizen and, because of the snow, had remained with his brother in Spain.

As for Philip, Bernard's confession did him a world of good, for the official report of his death was sent directly to von Behr, who happily relayed it to Goering. As a result, Goering closed the book on Philip and, perversely, sent von Behr back to Berlin.

In von Behr's place he appointed Fräulein Gisela Linberger, who became the first woman to hold such an important position in the Third Reich.

42

The groundskeeper had found a supply of army sulfa in the bullring's infirmary, illegally consigned there by a colonel-doctor who was a homosexual admirer of matadors. The groundskeeper gave Tomaso a liberal amount, which the boy rushed to Dr. Castillo, and after three injections Philip's condition took a dramatic turn for the better. His fever started to go down, his breathing became less difficult, and he emerged from his semicomatose state. Tomaso took care of him as best he could, in between his jobs. He smuggled food for him from the restaurant and tended to him like a brother.

After discovering that Philip was an accomplished chess player, Dr. Castillo often came in the afternoon with his chessboard, although his boozy head was no match for Philip's command of the pieces. But Philip deliberately prolonged the games, making Castillo feel that he had come close to winning.

The doctor kept a close watch on Philip's condition, frequently changing his foot dressings to keep the incisions clean, monitoring his chest, respiration and circulation, taking blood samples, intent not to lose his own personal Lazarus.

Philip, for his part, had become fond of the old medic, and he looked forward to his visits; the doctor and the boy gave Philip a sense of family. Then, one evening when Philip was well along in his recuperation, Tomaso came home, much later than usual, with the sad news that the police had broken in on Dr. Castillo while he was in the process of performing an abortion. Tomaso had been at the jail, trying to visit him, but the doctor was being held incommunicado.

"This is a great crime here in Bilbao, which is very Catholic," Tomaso said. "I am so afraid for him. He was our doctor, you know; he took me from out my mother."

"You've never told me about your family, Tomaso."

"It is not easy for me to talk about them."

"Then don't. I don't want—"

"No, I want you should know. You are my brother, Philip, and I must tell you everything. My family lived in Guernica, which is a few kilometers from here. My father, mother, grandfather, two brothers both bigger than me, and one sister, less old than me. We had a farm for onions, and all the family worked there, me included. Now I talk to you about this Monday of *abril,* four years ago. I was eight. My family had a stall in the marketplace where every Monday we sell our onions. One brother and me, we have one other little stall at the plaza of the railroad station. We are selling onions in the two stalls that afternoon when there is one clang of the church bell, and the bombers are suddenly there, the bombs falling, the big exploding ones and also the kind with fire . . ."

"Incendiaries."

"Little children playing on the sidewalk, all smashed to death. Then, I happen to look and there is my brother on the ground, dead from the fall of something from the roof upon his head. The head all crushed, all . . . bones and *sangre* . . . my big brother.

"Everywhere in the plaza there are people who die, people on fire, more bombs falling from many planes. I am very much *espantado*—the noise is terrible, the stink terrible. I run very fast to the marketplace, but there are mounds of broken buildings all over, and people crying out for the doctor and priest, and others who are dead, in pieces, pieces of bodies all over, and some all black from the firebombs.

"The bombs are falling everywhere, then come the little planes, the Heinkels with machine guns, and they come so low I can see the faces of the Nazi demons as they shoot at everyone. But I run to find my family in the marketplace, and as I am running, I pass the candy factory which is burning and some girls who work there are running out the door on fire, their hair and dresses, like torches. I pass the pelota *estadio* which is all bombed into a heap, and also the Bank of Vizcaya, nothing but pieces, and then some persons all crowded in protections from the bombs . . ."

"Air raid shelters?"

"Yes, that's it! Air raid shelters, but they are not so good, and when the bombs fall on them, all persons inside the shelters are killed, but yet I run, and it is a *milagro* but I am not shot or bombed, and I passed the hospital, all bombed, and full of dead, more than thirty children and many dead doctors and nurses,

German airplanes killing our Spanish people for more than three hours, machine guns and firebombs, why, why do they do so terrible a thing? Now, finally, I am at the marketplace. The Taberna Vasca where the farmers eat is only a pile of rocks and broken plaster and timbers, with all the customers dead inside.

"I run to our stall, but it is not there, just mounds of wood, stone and dust. I push with my hands and I find my father, and then my mother, and afterward my brother and sister, all dead, all dead! My sister I *reconoce* only from her pigtail because she has no face, and my brother is broken in pieces. My father and my mother do not have wounds, no signs of anything wrong, but I moved all the dirt and rocks away from them and there's no doubt. They are dead. Still I search to find my grandfather, but I cannot. Finally, I go to the Carmelite convent which is now the hospital to look if I can find him. But I do not find my grandfather there, nor anywheres else, not that day or ever."

Tomaso paused for a long time, again seeing the horrors of that sunny April day, feeling the pain and longing for his dead family. Philip was deeply moved and felt a strong impulse to pull the boy tight against his chest and comfort him and let him know that someone still cared about him.

"So now I pray not to be more in Spain," Tomaso said finally, "that is my wish. That is why I practice so hard, finally, for my English. There is an ancient English lady who eats lunch in the restaurant, and I go to her every afternoon and she gives to me a speaking lesson so that someday I can go live where they speak English. That is my dream."

"Where would you like to go?"

"Chicago in the United States of America."

Philip laughed. "Why Chicago?"

"Because my hero in the cinema is Mr. Edward G. Robinson, who I go to see very often, and he is always in Chicago, so that is where I would like to go. At which place do you live, Philip?"

"Well, long ago I lived in St. Louis, but now *if* I get back, I don't know."

"Maybe you will live in Chicago."

"You never know."

"Maybe you will live in Chicago and someday I am going to visit you. I could work in Chicago."

"You could also go to school, Tomaso. Don't you want to be educated?"

"I am educated, Philip. But I have no hard feelings against school."

"Can you read and write?"

"Oh, yes, *seguro.*"

"How much?"

"I can read the menu and write my name on the pay cards."

"That's it?"

"Oh, listen, I read many things. I am educated, Philip. But I will go to school in Chicago to be more educated if ever you send for me."

"Fine, Tomaso, I'm glad to hear that. But first I have to find a way to get back. I think the time has come to start moving again—you must be sick and tired of your uninvited guest."

"Oh, no, Philip, to have you here is *maravilloso!* I told you— you are my brother. I am to miss you very much when you go and I live alone again."

"And I will miss you, Tomaso. But I must move on. It's not good for me to be in one place for too long—those who hunt for me are very clever. What I need is a passport and a Portuguese visa."

"Listen, Philip, I was thinking a lot about you getting to Lisboa. You do not speak Spanish and they are sure to discover you. What I think is this: I will drive you in my wagon. I will fill it up with sacks of onions to sell in Portugal. I know my way very well—how to make little . . . *sobornos* . . . you know, little moneys to policemen . . ."

"Bribes?"

"Yes, okay, bribes—it is not a word my English lady, who is very correct, teaches me. My father used to take me sometimes to Portugal for the better prices, driving all along the coast and sleeping in our tent at nighttime. Look here, Philip . . ."

Tomaso opened a cardboard box and took out some clothing. "These are my father's best suit, his vest of fine *cuero,* his *camisa,* his hat, all very Basque. He was in size as you, also with a beard, and here I have his *pasaporte,* and a special *permiso* into Portugal. I can drive the wagon full up with onions and we will grease all the palms—I learned to say that, 'grease the palms,' from Mr. Edward G. Robinson of Chicago—and I will get you to Lisboa without worry."

"It's an appealing offer, Tomaso, but I can't let you risk it. If I am caught, you would be in a lot of trouble."

"How can you say risk for me? I am only a boy of twelve years who drives a wagon. The worst that will happen is they kick me in the ass and let me go."

"No, Tomaso, I can't let you take the chance."

"How will you get there by yourself, Philip? Do you consider that? By the train? There is strict control, very strict. You do not talk Spanish, so how will you get there? I am the only way to Portugal, Philip, *comprende?*"

Philip realized that what the boy was saying was certainly true. It looked as if he wouldn't have a prayer without him. "So you want to save my life a second time? You will make me drown in gratitude, Tomaso." Philip put his hands on the boy's shoulders and looked at him with frank affection. "You are quite a boy, Tomaso."

"I am more than a boy."

"Yes, I agree—you are certainly more than a boy."

"So it's agreed? We must go to Guernica for the onions. There is a man now who took over the rent for our farm, and he will load us up."

"There is one more favor I must ask of you, Tomaso."

"Anything, of course."

"Do you know some place where they buy jewelry without questions?"

"Oh, yes, *seguro,* I know such a fine gentleman who buys many kinds of things for his store and asks you nothing about them. He is a *cliente* of the restaurant. I myself have had some commerce with him."

Philip got up and went over to where his jacket was and took the little box from his pocket that contained the necklace for Gaby. It was a painful decision for him, for the present was a strong symbol, especially since it had survived all the hell he had been through. But it could get him into and out of Lisbon. He was sorry he had gone this far with the boy. He hadn't meant to involve him. And yet he had to admit that he felt good at having him along, not yet having to say goodbye to him. Perhaps the boy was right, this was his only chance to get to Portugal, disguised in Basque clothes, his beard full, twenty-five pounds lost in his ordeal, perhaps they wouldn't pay any attention to a couple of Basques with their load of onions. And the proceeds from Gaby's necklace would pay his way to Lisbon and buy ship's passage to the States. It was unfortunate that the return ticket on the *Normandie* which his uncle had given him had been left in his room at the Ritz.

*   *   *

That night, while Tomaso was at work at the restaurant, Philip removed the bandages from his feet and, using his knife, took out the stitches. The incisions had almost healed, but the sight of his feet without the little toes upset him. He thought about the doctor and what might be happening to him, and that upset him all the more. He could feel the doctor's presence in the room, sitting on the bed with the chessboard between them, drawing on his unlit pipe, a kind, defeated man headed toward the end of his road.

Philip got out of bed and dressed in the clothes of Tomaso's father, which were somewhat too large for him. He looked at himself in the mottled mirror on the wall and thought that he looked like an Amish farmer. He then tried walking around the room, a strange, unbalanced feeling without his toes, but he had no pain. He was very weak, however, and after a short while he gratefully got back into bed. He thought about Gaby, about where she might be, what she might be doing, wondering if she was thinking about him, and wondering, too, if he would ever see her again.

They left town in the mule-drawn wagon which had belonged to Tomaso's father. They passed through peaceful hills and into the valley where Guernica lies at the apex of the ría. The streets had been partially cleared of rubble, but the charred, pulverized remains of what had been the Basques' Holy City had not been touched. They passed the blackened shell of the Church of San Juan, the ruined pelota stadium, the ghostly remains of the railroad station where Tomaso's brother had been killed, the burned-out candy factory and the gutted hospital. Tomaso carefully avoided the marketplace.

The Basque who had taken over Tomaso's old home was happy to see the boy and loaded his wagon with sacks of onions which he took from the loft of the big barn. Tomaso also found his father's old tent and he took that too. The farmer asked Tomaso again if he would like to live there with his family; Tomaso thanked him but said he could not ever again live in Guernica.

On the way back, Tomaso took Philip through the one part of Guernica that had miraculously escaped the bombing. The Parliament House still stood proudly facing its plaza, where, protected by an iron railing, there was the ancient, venerated oak tree under which, Tomaso explained, Spanish monarchs used to confirm the rights of the Basques. Tomaso took Philip inside the Parliament building, and Philip noted the pride with which the boy walked down the beautiful old corridors. Even though Guernica was in ruins, the Parliament still functioned for the region.

A distinguished, white-haired gentleman emerged from one of the chambers and, seeing Tomaso, greeted him with open arms.

"This is Judge Fernando Gómez," Tomaso introduced him to Philip in English. "This is my good friend, Señor Weber of the United States of America."

The judge said, in English, that Tomaso's grandfather had been his closest friend. As he spoke to Tomaso, in Spanish, Philip began to think about what lay in store for the boy: the fate of a hustling street urchin, this fine boy with his brave heart, not afraid of risk or authority or injustice. And if he succeeds in leading me to Lisbon and freedom, what then, what is his reward—to stand on the pier and wave goodbye? Deserted again, retracing the long lonely route back to Bilbao, to his miserable life in the chicken cellar—is that his reward for saving my life, for watching over me, for caring for me like a little brother? Can't I share my hopes with him? Is that too much to ask of gratitude?

"Your Honor," Philip said, "will you please excuse me for interrupting, but may I have a few words with you? I'm sorry, Tomaso, but it's important that I speak privately to the judge for a few minutes."

"Sure, okay, Philip."

Philip walked the judge a short distance down the corridor. "What will become of the boy, Your Honor?"

"I don't know, Señor Weber. He is fiercely independent, or, rather, I should say defiant. And very wounded by what happened here, as you can imagine. But without doubt he will survive, if that's what concerns you."

"Yes, I agree that he'll survive, but he deserves better than that. An education. A chance to be a boy. He will have no childhood at all."

"Well, here in Spain now, the way things are, many boys must look out for themselves."

"I want to help him, Judge. Not only out of gratitude, but because he is such a fine boy. I like him enormously. He has become like family to me."

"That is good to hear, Señor Weber. I'm sure he could use whatever you could send him."

"I was thinking of more than that, Your Honor. I am headed to Portugal, which, as you know, is a free port. There is a United States consulate there, and I hope to get my papers in order and leave for America. It occurred to me that I could take Tomaso with me—that is, if he wanted to go."

"But it is very difficult, if not impossible, for Spanish people to go to the United States."

"Yes, I know, but what if I adopted Tomaso? That would make him a United States citizen, wouldn't it?"

"Why, yes, I suppose so . . ."

"Would it be difficult—I mean, adopting him?"

"Not at all. I could arrange it very easily."

"My main concern is how I will take care of us. I have been away a long time and I have no roots . . ."

"I can tell you love the boy, and that would be all the roots he needs. Perhaps you should talk to him."

Philip took Tomaso outside and sat with him on a stone bench beside the sacred oak tree. "What I was discussing with the judge," Philip told him, "was whether there was a way to take you to America with me. You would have to leave now, and that might be too soon for you, and, besides, I don't have much to offer you, since I don't even know where I'll be living or what I'll be doing. I don't have a job or any money or any family, but, listen, Tomaso . . ." He took the boy's hands in his and looked lovingly into his eyes. "I will try to care for you, and put you in school and do the best I can. What do you say?"

Tomaso looked at Philip in disbelief. These last few years, he had been disappointed so often that he could not trust what Philip was saying.

"How . . . could you do such a thing, Philip?"

"I would adopt you, Tomaso. Judge Gómez says he can arrange it. Then as my legal son you would be entitled to an American passport."

"You would . . . make me your . . . son? Give me your name?"

"Yes."

"I would really be an American?"

"Yes."

"Oh, my God."

"That way you could get an American passport."

"Oh, my God."

"We would have to leave the mules and wagon in Lisbon and get on a boat together."

Tomaso slowly lowered his head and rested his cheek on Philip's hand. It was not necessary to say any more.

In Judge Gómez's chambers, the necessary papers were prepared, certain oaths were taken with the judge's two clerks as witnesses, and Tomaso was given a certificate, with the ancient seal of Guernica on it, which legally changed his name to Tomaso Weber.

There was one last stop before leaving Guernica for good: a small cemetery on the outskirts of town. Tomaso stood at his family's plot and looked down at the mounds that were his mother and his father, his two brothers and his sister. He clutched his certificate of adoption in his right hand. Philip looked across the graves at him, a small brave boy trying to cope with all that had happened to him. Regarding the boy with love and admiration, Philip thought about something Hemingway had once said: Man can be destroyed but not defeated. And, looking across the graves at his new little son, Philip thought, They tried to destroy him, God knows, but look at him—is he not undefeated? But what about Dr. Castillo, and Jean-Pierre, and the wife of Jean-Pierre, and Lili—what about them?

Tomaso raised his head and looked at Philip facing him from across the graves. Tears were running down Tomaso's cheeks. "Philip," he said, "is it really true that I am to be an American?"

"You are now."

"No, *really.*"

"Yes, really. Look at your certificate."

"Really and truly? I am an American? I am really and truly your son?" He was crying.

"Yes, Tomaso. I have your father's name, and now you have mine."

Tomaso laughed through his tears. "Yes, that's a fine joke, isn't it?" Then he bent his head and said, in Spanish, looking at his father's grave, "My dear father, God has put you back on earth to take care of me again. I thank Him with all my heart. And I kiss all of you, my dear family, *adiós.*"

He walked away from the graves toward the wagon. Philip put his arm around the boy's shoulders and held him tightly as they walked together, the boy still sobbing. I love this boy, Philip told himself, and I love Gaby, and for someone who never loved before, that is pretty good. I just hope I can find her. I'm sure I will. After all, in a town the size of Sheboygan, how many Howard Goodwillys can there be?

They mounted the wagon, and, with a light flick of the reins, the mules started forward, the wheels crunching on the pebbly road. A rabbit scurried from the brush and darted in front of them. Tomaso wiped his tears with his sleeve and spoke gently to the mules. They were on their way.